TO STEAL AN IMMORTAL HEART

IMMORTALS OF THE VEIL
BOOK 1

H.L. HINES

This is for the baddies who know how to chose themselves and love, and never apologized for either. To those who never needed saving—only the space to be themselves. May you kiss the chaos that shaped you, knowing just how much you shape the world in return. You were never too much—only ever exactly enough. Your fire is a beacon. You light the way to the future.

You are so much more important than you know.

INTRODUCTION

I realize that this book may contain some sensitive themes for some. While I strive to write only what is necessary for my story to shine, there are some dark and disturbing topics.

- Graphic violence and combat
- Implied and open-door sexual content and rough intimacy
- Parental trauma
- Body horror and monstrous transformation
- Death and decomposition
- Psychological manipulation
- Demonic possession and spiritual awakenings
- Explicit language

Reader discretion is advised. This book is intended for those 18+ due to its dark and sexual themes.

PROLOGUE
MOTHER KNOWS BEST

"Fool!"

Like a punch, her tail whipped out. The scorpionic stinger struck with the force of a jackhammer, embedding itself into the center of my cracked chest. My Queen's swollen venom sac pulsed—hot and red—barely squeezing through the eight-by-eleven-inch portal that separated our dimensions.

The portal would only grow larger as the planetary alignment drew near. Soon, my Dark Mother would step through.

And she would not come alone.

"I live only to serve," I gasp and hate myself for the part of me that means it.

"Yesss, you do. I would have killed you long ago if I hadn't put ssso much work into you, pissant."

By the strength of her clutch, she dragged me across what had once been my throne room—my Dark Mother's throne room soon. I stumbled, my foot catching on the eight-foot scar gouged into the polished marble floor. A chasm in the stone. The last remnant of her previous attempt nearly a thousand years ago.

She was a nightmare of evolution with the face of a hornet, a spider's body, and an armored scorpion's tail. But her voice unsettled me the most: serpentine and wet, punctuated by guttural, alien pops Earth had never heard before.

"Everything will be ready," I say. "I only lack the key."

The portal would be wide enough for her to enter and ruin our world in two weeks. Her chitinous exoskeleton, fused with plated metal, made her all but indestructible. Her blade-like legs cut through air and flesh alike. She was strong, swift, and cruel—a Queen bred for domination. And soon Earth would kneel before her, before us.

"Ssstupid pisssant. Without key, I cannot breach firssst veil. Get the key. Now."

The croaking resonance from deep within her chest echoed across the chamber as she paced, each step dragging me across the floor. The alien Queen showed her displeasure, but I needed no reminder of her wrath.

That was why I followed her.

It had been nearly a thousand years since her hive last swept through these halls. No one remembered. Everyone who'd seen it was long gone or dead.

Everyone but me.

I had made sure of it.

I remained bowed, eyes downcast, her curved stinger still hooked into my chest. I was hers body and soul. A creature shaped by her will. A tool sharpened by her rage. After all, she had remade me.

"You ruin everything. Your failure hasss nearly unravelled my plan."

"Yes, my Queen." The taste of blood both metallic and slick coated my tongue as it spilled from the wound, speckling her tail with my life force.

"If I didn't know better, I would doubt my choice of champion. I sssaved you. Molded you. I gave you meaning. That'ss what a mother'ss love doesss."

The words cut deeper than the stinger. The disappointment in her voice hollowed my ribs. I never expected to please her. That was not my role. But still, I had hoped.

I had always hoped.

"Yes, my Queen." I keep my head down.

I thought I understood love. But it wasn't kindness and resilience. It was obedience. It was pain you didn't run from.

A wet, cracking hiss curled through the air. Then her stinger withdrew only to slam back into me with bone-crushing force. Pain radiated across my sternum, and I felt the spines of her tail shred through my robe and cut deep. I dared not cry out. Instead, I pressed my forehead to the cold marble floor and waited.

She remade me. Owned me. That's what love meant: to belong so deeply it hurt.

And I stayed because she chose me. My Dark Mother saw something I couldn't see in myself. What better kind of love is there than that?

"I jusst want a family. Iss that ssso bad, pisssant?"

"No, my Queen."

"You know what you must do?"

"Yes, my Queen."

"Then do it. Be ready for the next event. No more excussess. No more missstakes. I will not wait another thousand years. I will have my mate. My children will thrive in your abundant world as they should have long ago."

"It will be done," I promised.

I felt the vacuum of her departure before she completely left, slipping back into her dimension.

Three... two... one.

A sharp, irritated pop cracked through the room and faded—swallowed by the static hum of the closing portal, leaving behind only the stink of venom and blood.

I remained on my knees, letting the pain settle deep as my chest began to stitch itself together.

The Dark Mother was coming to Earth.

To spawn. To consume. To unleash her alien spawn upon the thirteen realms until nothing remained.

Nothing mattered to her but fulfilling her ambition.

She wanted a family. And I would help her get one. I owed her.

She owned me.

That was a truth I could never escape.

1

POKER, PINTS, AND POOR LIFE CHOICES

05.13.2006

It's not even 10:30 when the boogeyman walks into the bar.

The bass rattles our grimy, empty glasses. Music pulses through the sticky floor like a heartbeat. Sweat, smoke, and stale beer thicken the air. A low murmur of conversation drifts—until it doesn't.

My stomach drops. Hell. We've done it now.

My heart slams against my ribs. I open my mouth, but nothing comes out. All I can do is watch the man approach.

I've seen him before. When I was a little girl dressed in tulle and still young enough to believe in frilly dresses and empty promises. Levi Federov stood at my father's boss's side. I think he's just another employee until Dad hands him an envelope, lips tight. I understand that look now. Fear.

"Oh fuck," Milo mutters.

No shit.

Levi moves through the crowd like a shadow with

weight. Not the biggest man in the room—just the most dangerous. Power clings to him. With every step closer, I count my mistakes:

Followed Sammy.

"Borrowed" Dad's car.

I drank too much, too fast.

Let Ivok drag us here into enemy territory. Now, we're caught red-handed. And Levi has every reason to gut us.

The bar falls quiet.

Levi is the Fedorovs' enforcer, the one who ends problems permanently. I hear the stories: bloodbaths, no survivors. Next to him, my father looks like a priest.

"Don't stop now," Levi says, his smooth voice remaining even. "You were just saying what you'd do to a Fedorov if one were in front of you."

Ivok spits. "You think I'm scared of you? What you got shit for brains?"

Levi's second-in-command shifts—just enough to flash a .45. Ivok pales but doesn't move.

I press a thumb to a hangnail. Pain helps. I can't afford to lose focus.

"Leave him alone," Sammy says, stepping up.

At that, Levi's men chuckle. He doesn't even look at my brother. Instead, his focus turns to me.

Everyone else steps back. Just me, Sammy, and Ivok stand against them now.

"What are you going to do about it?" Levi asks, head tilted, with a smile that's all teeth, like a shark.

"Fedorovs are late. You missed your last payment, and the one before was short."

Oh God. Sammy's not shaking them down, is he?

"That's not my department," Levi says. "And it's not yours, either."

Levi steps closer. Every inch feels heavier.

Our father intentionally kept us out of the business. Even though I was the eldest, the responsibility fell to the son. Sammy still being excluded spoke volumes. Levi knows that and pokes the bruise.

Stay calm. Don't make this worse.

"Natalia," Levi says.

Ice slides down my spine. How the hell does he know my name?

Before I can speak, Sammy squares up. "You don't talk to her. Or we settle this like men."

Levi laughs, short and sharp. "You'd have to be a man to settle anything like one. We settle this how I decide."

I grab Sammy's arm and yank him back. *Think. There has to be a way out.*

The music dulls. The only sound comes from the back poker table. Then it hits me.

"You could beat us bloody," I say. "But that would get our father upset. It would cause tension within the company, and I don't think you want that—not when there's a better way."

I nod to the table. "We play for my father's Escalade. If we win, no harm, no foul. If not, you keep the car."

Levi's gaze slides over me—slow, slick and awful.

"I don't want your daddy's car," he says.

My stomach turns.

"Then what do you want?" Sammy asks. It was a stupid question since Levi's eyes hadn't left mine.

Levi doesn't smile. He keeps watching me. "Guess we'll find out. Clear the table."

About a half dozen of his men spread out, taking their seats around the bar. The poker table clears with only a single muted grumble. Levi sits with his back to the wall. Casual, but I can't forget how dangerous he is.

"You don't have to do this," Sammy whispers.

"What else can we do? Call Dad? Apologize?"

His silence says it all. I nod.

"Just trust me. I've played poker with Uncle Aleksander since before I could count."

"He never taught me."

You were too busy with your bugs. I don't say it. I squeeze my brother's hand. "Wish me luck."

"This is why no one takes me seriously. You always fight my battles."

"People don't take you seriously because you say crap like that. Now, wish me luck."

He turns away, jaw clenched. I step to the table.

"You sure you wanna do this?" Levi asks.

"What, you're scared of losing to a girl?"

He half-smiles. "Deal."

Two rounds in. My palms are slick. The dealer flips the River.

Jack of Spades. Straight.

I don't breathe.

Levi leans back, unreadable, with a smirk that sticks.

"I'll call," he says, sliding in his last stack.

A shiver crawls up my spine. A bluff? Maybe. But, I've gotta risk it. I smirk and flip my hand. "Not your night, Levi."

His grin doesn't move. "Damn shame," he murmurs, then turns his cards.

King of Diamonds. King of Hearts.

On the board: Jack of Spades. Jack of Clubs. Jack of Diamonds.

Full house.

My body locks up. That hand shouldn't be possible.

I scan the board. Then, the mucked cards. Then, back to Levi's King of Diamonds.

My King of Diamonds. I folded that card earlier.

No. Freaking. Way.

With my heart racing, I lunge for the discards. Levi reaches to stop me but he's too late.

There it is—the real King of Diamonds.

I shove it in his face. "You son of a—"

Levi only grins. "Now, now. Don't be a sore loser."

"Loser?" I flick the card at him. "You cheated. Palmed a King, you slimy—"

"What are you going to do about it?"

My body locks unmoving.

Because the truth is nothing. What can I do surrounded by his people, in his territory?

"Well, Natalia," says a gravelly voice behind me, one that freezes my blood. "The man asked you a question."

Of course. As if things can't get worse. Father is here.

Now we're truly screwed.

"Thank you for calling me, Mr. Fedorov."

That voice—cold, calm, deadly. I'd hoped to get home before Father found out. Stupid of me.

With my mask fully in place, I step toward Sammy, face blank. No weakness. Not here. Father will focus his wrath on Levi or Sammy if I'm lucky.

"Father, we were just—" Sammy starts, then wilts under his stare. "Natalia stole your car."

Snitch. I shoot him a glare. He won't meet my eyes.

The bar is empty now. Civilians cleared out. It was just us and the fallout.

"I would've won if he hadn't cheated," I mutter. "He palmed the card. You saw it."

Father steps forward. Immaculate suit. Blank expression. He doesn't need volume. He owns the room with silence.

Viktor Vasiliev always said that power comes from making them wait.

Father waits now.

And in that pause, something in me builds: hope.

Then he speaks.

"Only losers play by the rules. You don't belong at the table if you haven't figured that out."

The words hit like a slap. Especially since I know I walked into the trap smiling. I swallow hard.

Don't cry. Don't throw up. Stay strong. Over and over, I fight for control.

Levi chuckles. "Guess that's a game, then."

My fingers curl into fists, but I say nothing because my father is right. And that? That's the worst part.

Father moves past me then, turns to Levi with a

serene bow, and says, "I hope they haven't been a bother."

"They were lambs," Levi mocks.

A muscle in my father's jaw ticks. My stomach twists. Father's disappointment makes me want to hide. The room shrinks until there's nowhere to go.

"Though the boy did mention money," Levi adds. "You're not going around claiming the Federov family doesn't pay its dues, are you?"

My father flinches. Flinches! I can't count how often I heard him lecture us about never showing our real emotions. Is Levi really that scary?

"Of course not," he says quickly, twisting the pinky ring that never leaves his finger. "I don't know where he got such nonsense."

"Good. Since you've always been a man of your word, the matter will go no further." Levi's tone is light, but his eyes never leave me.

Father's mask holds, but the tremor in his fingers betrays him. "I'd like to repay your graciousness; you've already met my daughter, Natalia; why don't I let you two get more acquainted."

The air leaves my lungs.

I blink at my father, but I still can't breathe.

Surely, he doesn't mean to leave me here!

"Father, no!" Sammy starts.

I know Viktor Vasiliev is cruel, but now I realize he's heartless.

"Mr. Vasiliev, you honor me. I accept."

Viktor nods smoothly, extending his hand. Ready to seal the deal.

My stomach twists. I turn to my father, desperate for something that shows hesitation. That shows a father's regret. But his stare is cold, calculated.

He's not just letting this happen.

My father is offering me up like a bargaining chip.

This isn't just a punishment. It's a lesson.

"But Father?" I whisper.

"You wanted to prove something, didn't you? Unless you think someone else should pay?"

My gaze flicks to Sammy. I catch myself—but not before Father sees. He wants me to beg. To betray my brother. I clench my teeth to swallow the urge.

"No, Father. I don't know what to do."

He sighs, already done with me. "Just do as you're told. Why is that so hard for you to understand?"

Levi hums, bringing our attention back to him. "To avoid confusion between our families, will you bring her to me?"

Iron fingers clamp around the back of my neck. My heart is pounding so hard I don't doubt my father can feel it around the vice-like grip. When Father yanks me forward, I don't resist. I know better. But when he shoves me, I stumble and land in Levi's lap.

His arms lock around me. The sharp scent of gunpowder and black pepper hits my nose. My cheeks turn to ice.

Then he grins.

He grips my chin, possessive. Then kisses me—wet and disgusting.

I gag on whiskey and smoke. No matter how hard I

thrash and slap, nothing works until I yank Levi's earlobe.

He shoves me to the floor.

"Don't do that again," Levi hisses.

I hit hard, biting my tongue. My sticky hands meet the floor as I retch, trying to scrub the taste of him away.

"Then don't tongue-punch my tonsils," I croak.

Silence.

I look up. Everyone's gone.

The ache in my chest flares sharply. I dig my nails into my palms. But even this pain is not enough. Stupid. For hoping my father might care.

My tacky hands tremble. I barely notice the black leather shoes in front of me.

Levi.

"I won't hurt you if you cooperate," he says. "You have three choices: You can walk away right now with nothing, obey your father and allow him to whore you out. Or..."

I clench my fists. "And the third?"

"Give me what only your family has."

"What's that?"

"Your family's been untouchable too long. I want in."

"I don't understand."

"Marry me."

"What?" My voice cracks. "I'm fifteen."

He shrugs. "You think anyone will care?" He looms. "I see what you could be. With me, no one would cross you."

"Even you?" I edge away.

He chuckles. "I could give you everything you dream of."

"You don't know what I want."

"You want power. Your father is right; you did come to prove something."

I swallow. "My cousins promised me a party."

"Bullshit." His smirk deepens. "Promise yourself to me, and I'll make them all kneel."

His words slither—revolting, tempting. My stomach turns.

"I don't need your help."

"You think so?" Levi crouches next to me, breath hot. "Your father gives you away over a minor dispute. Next time? Could be worse."

The truth lands.

"You want Sammy's place. You're the third son. But if you marry me—"

"You're quick," he says. "Your father's desperate for an heir strong enough to take over."

My nails bite deep into my tacky palms. The ground shifts beneath me.

"The families won't allow it. And my father hates me." The words burn.

"Rules bend for rule-breakers."

Wasn't that the lesson I just learned?

Tick. Tock.

He watches. Waiting.

My pulse pounds. Is this my way out?

"You'll keep my mother and brother safe?" I whisper.

"Of course."

"And we wait until I graduate?"

"Whenever your 18th birthday is."

I exhale.

"What if I'm not good at it?"

He smiles, sharp as glass. "I won't stop until you are."

Something cold coils in my stomach. If I make a deal with the boogeyman to take control of my life—there's no going back.

2

MY BIG FAT FELONY WEDDING

10.20.2008

Few things are as satisfying as cashing in on revenge.

Blue and red lights flash against the white and silver Chargers surrounding my parents' sprawling brick estate. FBI, ATF, and three counties' worth of local law enforcement move in careful, tactical waves.

"Come on, come on, come on..." I whisper.

In the safety of my rental, I watch it all, waiting, holding my breath.

I barely make it out before the sirens wail.

I told them I needed a minute. Some fresh air. Some space. A panicked bridezilla is the perfect excuse.

They were happy to see me go.

My mother even presses a champagne flute into my hand before I leave. "Don't worry, darling, take your time. I'll handle everything," she said with a wink that didn't reach her eyes.

I slipped through the laundry chute, heart jackhammering against bone, white satin catching on rusted metal edges. I don't look back—not at the family I betray, the man I escape, or the girl in the mirror who seems too much like prey.

Let them wonder why the bride disappears right before the feds come knocking.

My index finger traces a raw hangnail in shaky pulses. I'm not sure if I'm ready. If we're prepared.

All I know is my mom promised me a clean exit. And I got it. I don't know how, but she pulled it off.

Then it happened.

A boom cracks through the air like a whip. The ground jumps beneath my feet. My chest seizes. I duck instinctively, covering my ears as a second explosion thuds, deeper, heavier.

Orange light blooms against the estate's stone walls, fire curling through a shattered window like a serpent tasting blood.

"Holy shit!" I squeak and duck.

A scream carries across the distance—too shrill to be male and too fast to identify.

Smoke pours into the gray sky in heavy black curtains.

The scent is unmistakable: burnt tulle, melting plastic, and something thicker, darker, like stress sweat.

My breath comes short and quick. That isn't part of the plan.

The agents take cover, startled by the fire, before regaining momentum and descending on the house.

Clark, Ivok, Milo, and Simmons are the first to race out and into the waiting cuffs of the agents. My stone-faced father is next. Then Sammy.

He doesn't look too worse for wear, just a little scratched up. I watch Sammy avoid looking at anyone as he passes. He walks with the agent, smoke still clinging to his cuffs like a trail.

Uncles Aleksander and Davis follow.

I watch them all from my car, trembling, the lace sleeve of my wedding dress dirty and half-ripped, still clinging to a life that isn't mine anymore.

At least they'll look dapper in their three-piece suits for their mug shots. The thought makes me smile.

But the flames keep burning higher, and my smile slips. Then, someone rolls out a stretcher with a white sheet, hiding a body.

"This is not a part of the plan."

My stomach sinks, but I can't afford to get out to throw up. Swallowing down the thick bile, I take a deep breath for a minute. This isn't my fault. Is this my fault?

Their lawyers are already on their phones, scrambling for damage control. With charges that range from extortion and money laundering up to assault and homicide, with all kinds of trafficking on top, these men are about to have a challenging year. Hell, probably a hard twenty-five to life. I made sure of it.

But where's Levi? Did he get out? Did someone tip him off?

My finger taps on the loud taffeta of my dress in a frantic staccato.

I try to tell myself this is enough. That it will still work. But I know the truth. I can lie to everyone else but not to myself.

If Levi suspects I betray him, the company—he'll track me to the ends of the earth.

"You're mine forever."

Once upon a time, those words sounded so romantic. Levi spoiled me with luxury and promises; to my sixteen-year-old self, it was heaven. It was love. But now, I know what it means to shackle yourself to a monster.

Unfortunately, I realized that too late.

Now, it's all I know.

I sit in my borrowed car as the lead agent storms past the line of handcuffed men, barking orders as he crosses the manicured lawn. I tear the flesh from my thumb until it bleeds, the tremor spreading from fingertip to wrist.

My wet palms clench the steering wheel until my knuckles turn white and my nails bite into my flesh. Then, my foot starts to bounce. The need to flee fills me, but I wait a little longer.

I squeeze my eyes closed, refusing to give in to the tears that threaten to spill.

My ribs feel bruised, each shallow breath tore at my lungs. I won't be able to breathe fully until I am far, far away from the police, my family, and the horror chasing me.

The Nissan's engine hums to life, but my heartbeat pounds louder in my ears. I make the first right, forcing myself not to look back. Not at the flashing lights. Not at the mansion where my life was just blown apart. Not at the eyes, I feel are always watching.

California is no longer an option.

The truth that Levi has escaped bounces around my skull like an Atari Pong ball.

The feds should have known better than to get the locals involved.

I shake my head, my dark-red-haired wig slipping out the open window. I pull it back in and roll up the glass. I'll have to lie low until I reach the East Coast.

I'll be dead if anyone knows about my involvement in the sting. Blood means nothing. Loyalty means everything to these people. Instead of nibbling on my nails like I want to, I press my lips together, barely able to control the nasty habit. As I drive, my mind wanders.

Would they suspect me?

I have been careful.

Sitting back, I sigh. The cranked AC swallows the sound under the comfortable background noise of alternative rock.

"What the fuck am I going to do now?"

My shout echoes in my ears, bouncing off the tight confines of the car. I slap my palm against the center console.

I framed my family and burned my bridges, and now my life is nothing but ashes in the wind.

The reality settles in. I played my hand, laid it all on the table. It still wasn't enough. Again. When will I learn? Now I am alone.

No one betrays the company. It is worse than a death sentence. Some connections, you just don't quit.

A pair of dark eyes stare back at me from the rearview mirror.

Eyes that shouldn't be there.

"Gah!"

My scream punches through three octaves as I jerk the wheel, veering onto the highway's berm.

A car and a semi-truck blare their horns as my tires screech to a stop.

Every joint in my body locks up.

My fingers grip the steering wheel, my foot frozen on the pedal, and my breath catches in my throat.

There is someone in the car with me.

My eyes break free of paralysis, darting back to the rearview mirror.

Empty.

I slap at the door handle, scrambling to get out, but when I look again, nothing.

No one.

Leaning backward, I peer into the backseat, half-expecting to find someone tucked into the footwell.

Again, nothing.

I checked the back seat before getting in. I locked the doors. No one could have gotten inside. I shake my head and roll my eyes at my dramatics.

I take a deep breath. Then another. It takes four more inhales before I can shake some sense back. Damn my nerves.

A high-pitched, desperate chuckle escapes. There is no one here. No one knows what I do.

I am safe.

For now.

But even as I try to reassure myself, I know it is a lie.

Tearing into the blemish on my other thumb, my

eyes linger on the envelope beside me, the only thing I took from home.

I want to touch it. To feel its weight, to draw comfort from it.

But instead, I force my attention back to the road. Traffic is about to get heavy, and I have places to be.

I'll go wherever life takes me as long as it's anywhere but here.

3

I CAME, I SAW, I PILFERED

10.19.2024

My fingers tremble as the all-too-familiar buzzing in my head threatens to take over. Swallowing hard, I make a beeline for my apartment, trying to ignore the itchy, crawling sensation spreading over my skin. Lifting my gaze, I scan my surroundings and nearly groan at the sight of the pristine gray stone Victorian with its perfectly manicured lawn.

I run a hand through my wavy, flaming-red hair. Anxiety coils inside me, laced with a strange sense of anticipation. My teeth find the edge of my nail, an old, nasty habit. The sharp snap of it breaking off gives me no relief.

I pause, worrying at another nail as I try to stop myself, even as my feet carry me toward the house. My heart sinks the second I realize the course I'm on. Lifting my shoulders from their slump, I roll them back and stride forward with purpose.

If I do this, I will not get caught.

As I close in on the old house, I lift my bag in front of me, just in case they have a camera. Stepping past the bushes, I pull my hood over my head, obscuring my face. Only then did I notice that the Victorian had been converted into an elegant duplex.

Choosing quickly, I veer left, toying with my hair, and ring the doorbell. After a minute without an answer, I swiftly manipulate my hairpiece, which doubles as a lockpick. A blue Amazon van slowly trails down the cul-de-sac, headed straight for me.

I give the lock one quick jimmy; it resists for just a second. My pulse ticks up. The van pulls to a stop in the driveway. I turn and smile over my shoulder. There's nothing to see here; I'm just a girl messing with her keys.

Then—click. Smirking, I slide the door open and slip inside.

The queasiness vanishes the second I cross the threshold. Imagine that.

Under my hood, I glance at either side of the door, quickly assessing the electrical security system. Without hesitation, I press a localized EMP pulsator onto the panel, confident it will block any alarms from transmitting for a time. Setting my watch for twenty minutes, I step inside and head straight for the bedroom.

I grab a backpack in the closet and empty it onto the floor. Skipping around the room, I rummage through everything, stuffing the bag with anything that catches my attention. The 18K gold TAG Heuer men's watch instantly draws my eye, along with a 10K white gold amethyst bracelet.

Mine.

After a firm bite on my lip, I continue my search, snatching up a charming gold and silver arm cuff. I check my watch and pick up the pace—I only have ten minutes left. I stuff the bag with couture clothes and one of the sexiest pairs of stilettos I have seen before, making my way to the office.

One quick jimmy—the lock resists, then clicks open. I rifle through the drawers, carefully putting everything back in place. I'm a considerate thief, after all.

I find the safe and press my ear to the door. With one last look at my watch, I start cracking into the small black box.

With two minutes left, I sort through the contents: an old-looking pistol, an ancient dagger embedded with enough gemstones to make my mouth water, and an equally old-looking diary. Wiggling in place, I squeal in giddy excitement.

With this loot, I can retire for the season! If I get away clean, I'll finally have some breathing room.

Biting my lip to control my grin, I carefully fold the weapons and book between the clothes, leaving the passports and other business-looking documents behind. Just as I'm about to close the safe, one file catches my eye. It looks like something straight out of a spy movie.

I open the folder and find multiple pictures of a beautiful, scarred man. Each photo is the same: intense, distant, blurry. The hairs on my arms rise. These papers aren't a casual dossier.

Someone is tracking him.

Nibbling my lower lip, I debate my next move, only to be interrupted when my watch begins to vibrate. I put the file back and sling my backpack over my shoulders.

Grinning, I walk out the back door, carefree. My body feels more relaxed than it has been in a while.

No alarms. No sirens. Just silence.

The quiet is the sound of a job well done. I did it. Satisfaction washes through me the closer I get to home.

Adrenaline thrums in my veins as I stroll through my front door, my backpack heavier and my conscience light as a feather. Each step through my home carries me with winged feet like I've just chugged a Red Bull. I could dance with the joy pulsing through me. But I no longer have to contain my giddy laugh when the door closes and locks behind me.

Success never tastes so sweet.

After I clean up, I spread my new possessions across my coffee table. Exhaling slowly, I lean back into the couch.

Spinning the dagger, I watch the gemstones catch the light, sparkling across my dimly lit living room. My thoughts drift to the scarred man in the photos. Setting the knife down, I inspect the clothes and jewelry, giddy again.

"With this haul, I'll be able to replace my savings and stop Levi for good."

I'm only one step ahead of the boogeyman, which isn't much when he has limitless resources. And after Miami, I am all out of hideouts. My meager savings are gone, meaning my plans are back to square one.

Abruptly, my phone rings with an unknown number.

Deny.

They call again.

A panicked jolt makes my stomach cramp. My thumb hovers over the block button, but a text pops up before I tap the screen.

> You've been a very naughty girl, Nadia. Or do you prefer Natalia?
>
> If you don't want this evidence getting to the wrong people, meet me at 697 Lockwood, San Lotuas, Queens City. Tomorrow. 10 p.m.

Then, there's an image, a still shot from a video of me stuffing the backpack with a pair of shoes in my hand and a grin on my face.

Undeniable.

> Who is this?

> Someone who likes your work. Don't be late.

I reread the message three times, my throat tightening with each pass.

Was it him? Has Levi found me already?

4

BLACKMAIL AND BOURBON

10.20.2024

After sixteen hours on the road, even a stiff motel bed feels like heaven. Because of that mysterious text, I have no choice but to leave fast. Miami is my last refuge, and now, I have to put as much distance as possible between me and my past.

Since someone torched my flat and everything I owned in it, a warning has been ringing in my head. *Survive*, it says; *do whatever it takes*. It is an instinct I always obey. And somehow, despite that obnoxious alarm, I drive here: 697 Lockwood, or if the half-lit sign is correct, it's called Infernal Embrace.

I have a bad feeling. But I also have a plan. Get in, find out who's trying to blackmail me, and then find a way to get them off my back. Simple.

From the outside, the wood-paneled bar looks like a dive, overgrown weeds and flaking paint. But as I step inside, it pulses with electric purple light. Black leather and studded seats gleam under shifting neon, brass fixtures catching every flicker of color.

I cross my arms over my chest and run my fingers over the delicate, handcrafted gold arm cuffs I "borrowed." My dress is sleeveless, but the cuffs fortify me, a reminder of who I am: a thief, a winner, a survivor. My hair hangs wild down my back, the sides pinned with gold floral clips that stand out against my wig's blonde waves.

Suppressing a yawn, I head for the bar. Mellow, bluesy jazz plays in the background, and as I scan the crowd, my gaze snags on a man sitting in the back. Black slacks, a black dress shirt unbuttoned just enough to look relaxed, with sleeves rolled up to reveal muscular forearms.

The only thing out of place on him is the vintage pinstripe fedora. A shiver of excitement races through my spine. He radiates danger, the kind of red-flag warning that screams: More than you can handle.

Challenge accepted.

I try to look away, but our eyes remain locked. Heat creeps up my neck, and I turn sharply toward the bar, pretending to search for whoever sent that text.

"I need something strong. Manhattan, heavy on the bourbon," I say, flashing the bartender a tired but teasing smile.

The bartender, who looks fresh off the bleachers—wholesome in a way that doesn't belong in a place like this—blinks as if he has a joke to make, then shakes his head instead. I nod and watch as he makes my drink. He over-pours the bourbon, but I let it slide. When he sets the glass before me, I over-tip for his generosity. It must be the long drive affecting me, I reason.

As I move toward an empty table, I glance back at the man in black—but he's gone.

I make my way across the room, my legs heavy with exhaustion. My heart stutters when he slides into the seat beside me.

After such a long day, I don't want to talk, flirt, or pretend to be interested in anything other than the person behind those texts. But the second our eyes meet, my resolve crumbles.

Everything inside me stills: the nerves, the jittery urge to grab the wallet of the guy sitting at the bar.

"Nice cuff."

His deep voice strikes something familiar, and I pray, Please, don't let me have scammed, stolen from, or used him as a scapegoat in the past. I have no energy to get tangled in a revenge plot tonight.

"Thanks. I'm glad you like it," I say smoothly.

"I'm glad you came. I almost thought you wouldn't."

Him? Is he my blackmailer?

Those calm words hit like an ice-water bath and a red-eye injection combined. My body jolts wide awake, nerves on high alert. I wrap both hands around my glass to hide their tremble.

I lean forward, and his smirk deepens in early victory.

I need to focus. What does he want, aside from the obvious?

"I'm Darius," he says, extending his hand.

When my red-tipped fingers meet his tanned ones, he lifts my wrist and kisses my pulse slowly. My heart slams against my ribs. Damn nerves. He must feel the racing beat.

"What brought you to my safe house?" he asks, still holding my hand.

"Excuse me?"

I pull back, and he lets me go without resistance, but the spark in his smirk tells me this is about to get bad.

In a casual move, I lift my drink to my lips, taking a slow sip as I reassess.

"The Victorian you pilfered."

"I don't know what you're talking about. I was passing through. Whatever you think you know, you're wrong."

He doesn't look surprised at my denial. Leaning back, he rolls his shoulders, effortlessly confident.

Darius is strong, but his hands are smooth—no calluses, no signs of labor. He doesn't work with his hands. Salesman, I guess. But judging by what was in his "safe house," he is either very well off or deep in something bad.

Judging by the easy way he carries himself, I'd bet on the latter.

As my father always says, "I know a drowning man when I see one."

"So, Natalia, are you going to give it back?"

Unease coats my spine in a fine sweat.

"Excuse me?" I say again. "My name is Nadia. And I... I don't know what you're talking about."

This goes beyond simple breaking and entering. Beyond burglary.

Every instinct screams at me to run.

I start to rise, but before I can lift from my seat, his hand wraps around my elbow, anchoring me to the table.

"I didn't travel halfway across North America to argue over your name. You have something that belongs to me."

"Let go of me, or I'll scream."

I stand just enough that my arm pulls between us, brushing against the single daisy in the center of the table.

His eyes flicker with amusement, and another smooth smile pulls at his dimples, but eventually, he lets go. I wipe the press of his touch from my skin.

After releasing me, he scrubs a hand over his face, pausing for a second as if catching my scent.

"That dagger you took isn't just an antique, darling. It's part of a key. And my buyer would kill for it."

The charming man in front of me shifts. The cocksure flirt vanishes, replaced by something much colder.

Shit.

"I don't know what you're talking about. I didn't see any dagger."

"You expect me to believe you missed a twelve-inch, jewel-encrusted blade?"

I exhale slowly. "If you're going to blackmail me, at least show me what you've got. That way, we can skip to the good part. Let me guess—you want it all back. That's how this works, right?"

"You can keep everything. But I need the dagger."

That gives me pause. Even without the dagger, I scored big. But still...

The fact that he is willing to part with everything else tells me one thing: he is terrified of his buyer.

"Why bring me here? Why not a simple drop-off?" I ask.

He smiles like the answer is obvious, then he reaches down and drops a file on the table between us. The manila envelope is the same one I had in my hands the day before.

So I really have been caught.

I study him and it, weighing my options. Behind my sweet, frozen smile, my gears turn, working out the fastest way to escape this mess.

"You see, Nadia, I have a certain gift. What is that gift, you may ask?" He pauses, his eyes going flat. "It's the ability to spot potential. To see golden opportunities. And with you, I see a lot of gold."

"What are you suggesting, exactly?" I ask with renewed curiosity.

"The man in the photo—he's a whale, some old disavowed Prince or something. I've been trying to get into his vault for months. If you can get me that amulet, you can have your fill of everything else. Gold, jewelry, and ancient artifacts that would make the Pope weep. Take as much as you can."

"Oh? And I suppose that's so you can disguise the importance of what you want?"

"Just get me that amulet by the end of the week. This job is no easy take; if you can pull it off, I'll clear the slate, no harm, no foul. You managed to steal from me and might be able to get me this amulet."

His loot was easy to pull. But I can't tell him that.

With a weary sigh, my hand hovers over the file. Debating. But do I have a choice?

I pull the file into my lap and flip through the pitiful collection of notes.

Name: Slasher
Height: 6'6"
Weight: 320 lbs
Hair: N/A
Eyes: Brown
Current location: Boston, United States of America
Outstanding features: Scar diagonally across right cheek
WOC: Bastard sword
History: Contestant of the Agarthan Trials, second place
Current Status: Active
DOB: Unknown, Triassic Period.

This must be someone's idea of a joke. Okay, so he's a Father Time type? Got it.

I flip to the next photo—a thick-banded crystal amulet. Strips of gold wrap the smooth, palm-sized diamond, with three more jewels laid out like flower petals. It isn't particularly ornate. The cut is basic compared to today's precision standards. But without a doubt, it's old.

The following picture is of the big man in a trench. The photos are long-distance shots from a vintage camera. The quality of the film is so poor that the image that looks like cracked clay.

"You couldn't get a newer photo?"

"No one has seen him since that photo."

The photographer must not have wanted to risk getting caught because the man in the photo is distorted and blurry, almost like his image was smeared to nearly twice his size. I pull my phone out.

A quick search of the address makes me whistle low.

The three-level house is made of wide, luxurious stone and stretches about 17,000 square feet. Manicured lawns, pristine gardens, and elegantly placed stone décor surround it.

Biting my lip, I nibble on a nail as the all-too-familiar itch starts small, then spreads between my shoulder blades. I snap my phone down on the table-top, but the image of the house—and the jewels—lingers.

My eyes drag back to the file. One more haul could be possible. Enough to cover new papers. Enough to get this guy off my back, disappear, and have plenty left to live the good life.

I don't need much, just adequate plumbing, hot water, AC, and ample freedom. I lean back, crossing my legs. My mind is already working out the angles.

It may be time to make a deal.

Or make my move.

Either way, my itch for mischief is back.

5

THE MONSTERS BENEATH OUR FEET

I stuck out like a sore thumb on Boston's T. Even with the forced guise, my Stoneborn build was hard to miss, standing a foot taller than most. Despite the late hour, people packed the subway. My fists clenched at my sides in an empty threat. I craved the familiar weight of my bastard sword. It had been an extension of me for so many centuries.

Without it, I felt naked.

Instead of resting at my side, as it had for most of my eternal life, I strapped my sword to my back, concealed beneath my leather cloak. Close, but not close enough to ease my anxiety.

No one else noticed. These mortals had no idea how protected they were from the veil. Human minds always seemed to ignore anything that didn't directly help or harm them.

Little did they know, danger slept all around them beneath their feet.

Finally slipping out of the rush, unnoticed through a back entrance, I followed the rotten scent of my prey. I had been protecting these mortals longer than I cared to count. For just as long, a few others and I had been hunting these abominations. It was our duty. Our responsibility.

After all, it was a Stoneborn who had let them in.

The alien larvae burrowed deep into the earth, festering like an infection. When the time was right, they rose, rupturing like a diseased pustule, spewing necrotic flesh that contaminated the living.

My lips curled in an unusual twist of emotion. I could only hope this batch wasn't as creative as the last. Dark spawn and senior centers were a grotesque horror I never wished to see again.

Their colony had holed up in the abandoned subway tunnels, claiming the eastern labyrinth as their nest. The farther I walked from the human world, the more the scent of earth thinned, shifting into a metallic stench.

It was a full moon tonight. That meant they'd be huddled in their caves, praying for word from their dark mother. The doorways between our worlds were strongest under certain celestial events, like the full moon. My best chance to wipe out as many as possible in a single strike.

When the putrid smell of rotting meat overpowered the comforting scent of soil, I pounded my arm guards together, testing their fit, then checked the hidden blade's release. I stopped at the tunnel's mouth, pulled out my phone, and silenced the ringer.

I gave a sharp whistle, two high notes, then four low ones.

The call had the desired effect. Two pale mantids stiffened in preparation, rocking rhythmically. Behind them, a dark outline spread as another spawn waited. The spawn's caretakers had sheared their lanky forelegs into razor-edged armor that clanked against chunks of loose stone.

My blade sang as it cut through the stale air. It wasn't a challenge; spawn wasn't intelligent enough for that. It was a blink. A feigned weakness to draw them in. And that's precisely what happened.

The first mantid rushed forward, crawling along the walls to close the distance; the second had taken the opposite wall, trying to blend into the darkness. The third, a beetle constructed like a tank, stormed directly toward me. At the same time, another spawn scuttled on as many as eight mismatched legs: each creature was a different brand of twisted and unnatural.

The beetle charged, already halfway down the tunnel. Its mouth gaped, jaw unhinged. Mandible bared. Its heavy stomps echoed through the corridor.

These soulless, sexless beasts were an amalgam of human trash and monstrous insects—flies, centipedes, and any other unlucky creature their dark servants took inspiration from.

Their armored hides gleamed in the dim light, fashioned from glass, steel, and rebar shards. If they stood upright, they'd have towered over seven feet tall, but hunched as they were, the rotting flesh curled like over-stretched rubber bands hanging off the exoskeleton.

All dark servants enhanced their spawn, but these creatures showed no shoddy work.

Which meant only one thing: I was dealing with a master.

The spider spawn lunged from the ceiling. I kicked it back and took three hits as it fell. And that's when I noticed the stitches along its legs—woven through with slivers of glass. My lips curled in disgust.

Another spawn, the beetle, reared, pulling back to stomp. I gripped the beetle by the mandible before it could slam down on me. Then the rest swarmed. Single-handedly, I raised my sword and delivered a heavy strike to the first mantid's chest, slicing diagonally through the chinois armor. It split open in a yawning crevice deep enough to see its pulpy, white insides, yet it kept coming.

It wasn't blood that dripped from the creature's wound but a dull yellow mucus, like snot, that lined the edges of the gash. The more I hacked the creature apart, the more pungent the smell of bile and rot became.

I swung harder until its rebar support caved in. The thing finally dropped into three pieces. But there was no time to admire my work.

Two more tried to pin me. The spider spawn and remaining mantid flanked me from the right and left. With the disjointed gait of impatient predators, they closed in.

With a bitter curse, I stab the beetle under the jaw until my blade bursts from the top of its head. It isn't enough to kill it, but with the twist of my blade, I severed its head, batting it at the mantid with the broad side of my blade. The bear-sized beetle collapsed in a heap.

At once, raptor-like claws tore into my exposed flesh. I elbowed the one on my right. It staggered back but quickly shifted its footing to lean on one of its many legs.

I grit my teeth and spin my blade in a wide arc, cutting the remaining spawn. Despite their spindly appearance, these creatures were heavy.

It reared back five feet away, licked the nails spiked into its jaw, and charged again. Its eyes burned with a vengeance. I had to make it quick.

The last mantid struck to my left, preying on my distraction. It punched and swiped in a one-two-combo that pushed it closer to the spider—but not far enough away to avoid the clean cut of my sword to its long neck.

Hit after hit, the spider struck, piercing me with its sharpened legs. When I put down the last mantid, I could finally turn my attention to the spider. Cutting one leg from underneath it at a time, I work until its belly scrapes the floor. The kill is quick after that.

I whistled again.

A red mold-covered ant crawled from the dark, mucus dripping from its mouth. Nearly hip-height, it moved with eerie patience, its human host's face grotesquely fused to its back. It circled, waiting.

I struck the moment the red-covered spawn lowered its guard to attack. The spawn lunged. I feigned left. In one fluid motion, my sword sliced through its thorax. It clattered against the tunnel wall, mewling, dragging itself away.

I checked my phone as I followed the hobbled creature—6:32:27.

I frowned. If I wrapped this up in half an hour, I might make it home in time to watch *Chopped*—a tempting thought.

But unlikely.

So far, things had been too easy.

Something was amiss.

Before I left, I torched the bodies just as I had done at my last hunt, not even a mile from this den. For some reason, they had been practically living peacefully side by side. That kind of cooperation was unheard of in the thousand years I'd hunted them.

Even within their nests, these things were aggressive. A spawn cut my reflection short with the scrape of exoskeletons against the brick. A streak of red antennas rushed me with a hard knock to my side.

Then, more swarmed.

Three black ants. All led by that damned red ant.

They hit me from all angles.

The four became eight.

Had I just walked into an ambush?

Impossible. Spawn were mindless. Instinct-driven. They weren't smart enough to set traps.

Or so I had thought.

All of them were just as tall as I, at least six feet tall and unstitched. That could have meant only one thing: these spawns were from a fresh brood. Somewhere nearby were four dead human shells, all that remained of the cocoon they had split from.

This night had proven one thing beyond a shadow of a doubt. Something had changed. The dark servants and their spawn were changing their patterns and behaviors. And it didn't bode well for anyone.

After I put them down, I destroyed the spawn's bodies. Fiery destruction was the only measure to ensure their caretakers, the dark servants, couldn't repurpose the spawn. When I left the underground tunnels, my body was exhausted. I closed my trench, feeling oddly heavy at the new development.

Then, I readied myself to do what I'd promised never to do again: return home.

It was time I saw my family.

6

———————

STONE-COLD REUNIONS

"**B**rother, if you'd walked any slower, the stones would've left you in the dust."

My seventeenth brother, Tharnak, lifted a brow and met me halfway. That was the closest either of us had come to a smile in centuries.

Like all Stoneborn, he was hairless, with a craggy surface layered in sandy beige, streaked with vibrant copper veins. But unlike most, Tharnak's terracotta eyes could still hold warmth. Not today. Whether from our time apart or something worse, his gaze stayed dim.

"It's difficult to be back," I said, forcing down the irritation. Not at Tharnak (he had always been steadfast), but at being here. The Whispering Stone Steppes reopened wounds I'd long tried to bury.

Twice, I had to wrestle my thoughts back from the past.

"How is it being topside?" Tharnak asked, his tone hollow as he fell in step beside me.

Crystal vents spewed mineral-rich mist along the

path, sharp with ozone and flecked with metallic shine. I turned my face into the spray, letting the sting of longing anchor me to the present.

"Busy," I said. "Unlike here."

I nodded toward two guards playing Flick the Bean near a corner post. After years in the mortal realm, that name didn't sound quite as innocent.

Tharnak's jaw tightened, irritation or suspicion. I didn't ask. I had too much on my mind. It had been ages since I walked the Whispering Way, where sentient crystal pulsed underfoot and whispers coiled through the jagged stone.

"Much has changed," he warned. "Worse than it looks."

Tharnak never exaggerated. His tense shoulders confirmed what I hadn't let myself see. I might have noticed sooner.

We neared the towering columns of the throne room. The crystals glowed brownish-orange around us. Even the Steppes seemed uneasy.

I said nothing. The Sacred Wall of the Veil loomed ahead. The council had already gathered. The throne sat raised high above the crowd.

To outsiders, the realm might've appeared unchanged. But the red-tinged overcast and the scar gouged into the throne room floor told another violent story. I hadn't expected the memory to hit so hard at the sight.

"Congratulations, my brother. I don't know how you did it, but you've won."

"Thank you." My younger brother looked properly stunned by his accomplishment. "And it displeases me that this must be my first edict, but as your new King, I must send you topside to hunt the Dark Mother's spawn who escaped tonight."

"The Dark Mother? Topside? That's exile. It might as well be a death sentence. Why, brother?"

"A necessary sacrifice. I trust no one else. Also... Clara-bell, my new wife, finds your presence uncomfortable."

"You've made her your queen?"

"What, you didn't think she'd follow you, did you?" He'd chuckled then, pitying my ignorance. "I think it's best if you stayed away. Not forever, just for now."

The memory made me shudder, but I didn't let it halt my entrance. That was a wound I'd learned not to pick. Not here. Not now. Not ever.

"Brother Malriksan, you honor us with an unexpected visit. Tell us, how fares the human realm?"

The room murmured as Gorvoss addressed me. The boy who once followed at my heels now sat on the throne, his features carved into a marble mask. But behind that polished exterior, his jasper eyes still flickered with uncertainty.

He didn't rise to greet me. None of them did. I remained standing, feet wide and battle-ready. It was all I knew.

"The Dark Servants are growing more tactical. They're up to something. I need more warriors."

"Lost your edge?" Gorvoss sighed as though the thought exhausted him.

My jaw tightened. "Something's changed. I can't guarantee containment."

Whispers rippled through the chamber.

"For a millennium, you've hunted them. How have you not eradicated them already?"

"Their regeneration is unnatural; they've learned to patch themselves with rubble and refuse. They've become more organized. If I can't find the source, they'll overrun us."

Gorvoss smirked. Whether he was blind or simply pleased to see me fail, I didn't know.

I forced my voice flat. "I need warriors to hold the line while I track the cause."

"I've heard nothing of this from the other guardians."

"I speak only of what I've seen."

"I think I know the cause," Gorvoss said, pausing for effect.

"What is it?" I heard the demand in my voice, but it was too late to take it back.

"You're starting to crack. You need a break. That's why you've come home."

Another wave of murmurs chipped away at my control. I had long abandoned excitement and passion. But with all eyes on me—especially hers—his words struck like a blade to a phantom organ I'd long since removed.

"Nonsense. Station the guardians near me. We'll strike the source directly."

"The Dark Servants are a bygone fear!" someone shouted.

"Then join me topside," I challenged. My voice rang through the chamber, shaking the stone beneath us. "See for yourselves."

Silence. Gorvoss's glance flicked across the room in a brief panic. I masked my surprise. I'd grown stronger in the mortal realm, more connected to my Stoneborn gifts than ever.

"It seems you have things handled," Drynus, the King's right hand, stood. "But the Infernals are organizing. Riots are growing more violent. They are coalescing. We must act."

"Where's the champion? Why aren't they handling it?"

Silence again.

"We don't participate in such barbaric trials anymore," Clarabell said smoothly. Her posture remained calm, expression unreadable. She didn't meet my eyes. Even her skin, once vibrant blue, looked washed out and sickly. Her fingers tapped a rhythm too measured to be natural.

"The Trials maintain order between the first three realms," I reminded them.

"A convenient lie our forebears told to maintain the bloody status quo," Gorvoss muttered. "Order will come through strength. The Trials are banned. And you will drop this."

Around us, the half-circle of gathered Stoneborn—Igne, Sedi, Morphic—remained still. But I saw it. Fear.

"Please," Gorvoss said, addressing the crowd, "I have not failed you in a thousand years. I only ask for your patience. Now, wife, show our Brother Malriksan a proper welcome. He has been gone so long, alone and away from his people. Let your gentle hands mold his granite heart."

Clarabell hesitated. Resentment flared in her before vanishing behind a practiced smile. She stood and bowed to him.

"Tell him to take an extended vacation," Gorvoss said.

I ground my teeth hard enough to hear the crack. Clarabell's cheeks flushed, not with affection but with humiliation.

"But he is our greatest warrior," she said to the council, not to him. Not to me. "Without him, who will protect us?"

"I will protect us!" Gorvoss surged forward. Clarabell shrank back. "Have you forgotten, wife?"

"Of course not."

No one seemed surprised. That disturbed me the most.

"You've been at it for a millennium," she said. "Take a break, Malriksan." Her hand reached toward mine instinctively. Without thought, I recoiled. I couldn't help it. In response, she folded both hands tightly in front of her.

"That's not necessary," I said. "I'm happy to serve my function."

My muscles tensed before I could stop them. I hoped no one noticed the flinch.

"Malriksan, I insist." Gorvoss nodded to her, the greatest betrayer I'd ever known.

"I came to request reinforcements, and you want me

to retreat?" My voice sharpened.

"Listen to you. You even sound like a mortal. Tell him, wife that he looks tired. Explain how a vacation is in his best interest."

He took only three steps before she stepped toward me.

"Malriksan, you've been going strong for a long time," she said, her voice going as smoothly as a land-slide. It's too gentle for me to stomach. That voice had once undone me. Gorvoss knew it.

"My Queen, what am I if not Rorurik? Some-times, a man only has his work. Would you take that too?"

Her amethyst eyes shimmered. Almost pained. For a heartbeat, she looked torn. Then she turned from me, hiding whatever truth remained.

As a Crystalborn, her aquamarine glow had once responded to every passing thought. I remembered how brightly she lit up in a crowd. She must have mastered remarkable control in my absence or suffered enough to dim it permanently.

"Don't be so dramatic. You will stop hunting imme-diately and resume in, let's say... a decade," Gorvoss said, ending with a hollow smile.

"Ten years?" I echoed, brushing Clarabell's hands aside and turning to my brother.

"It's not forever, it's just for now."

I'd heard that lie before. It rang just as false now as it had a thousand years ago.

"Again, with the dramatics. You've spent too much time among humans. They're making you soft. Spend some time on the sixth or seven planes that will get your head on right."

A hushed murmur swept the crowd. There were no words, but I knew how fast the King's insults would spread.

Nearly the worst insult one Stoneborn could offer another—aside from *She deserves better*, which he'd already used.

"Perhaps, husband, go easy on him," Clarabell said, quiet as a crack forming beneath the ice. "Too much idle time might cause... other issues."

"Oh, very well. You're lucky my wife still pities you."

Beside me, she tensed. The room chilled with her displeasure.

"Rorurik Malriksan, second son of Stenjor, head of the Allurssi order, brother to the King—this isn't a punishment. Your... what's the word? Vacation shall last..." He looked upward, pretending to think. "Until the new year. Though I doubt anyone could unwind in such a short time. But if it pleases my wife..."

She gave one sharp nod and dismissed the court without another glance.

"There it is," Gorvoss said. "Rest easy, brother. Enjoy the break. Visit a demon bazaar. Find a harem. Barter through the Nine Realms. Maybe you'll stop being so tedious and quit scaring off your partners."

I recoiled from his shoulder slap.

I loved my family. I was loyal. I was Stoneborn. Granite hearts. Honor. Integrity.

I was loyal to my people.

I would not punch my King.

With no choice, I did what was expected of me. I bowed. But in my heart, the war had already begun.

With acid on my tongue, I thanked the King for his judgment and exited as silently as I had entered.

Stop hunting? Impossible.

Some said Stoneborn strength was just as emotional as it was physical, rooted in our granite hearts.

But even mine groaned under the weight of what I had just heard. If Tharnak was right, my home realm was more dangerous than I'd realized.

7

DRINK FIRST, ROB LATER

I've never planned a heist in only four days. But I've never been blackmailed into taking a job, either, so maybe that's how these things work. Now, all that stands between me and the safe room is one key, a car, and a dim-witted driver.

My recon shows that once the driver leaves, no one else enters. The Prince has never been seen—a true hermit.

The driver leads me to this dive bar, only fifteen minutes from the estate. I'll be in business once I snag the driver's keys. When I have the car, I'll have the gate card hanging from the rearview mirror, which means one less obstacle to the safe room. If I can't get those keys or that card, I'll have to jump the nine-foot gate and travel the grounds on foot. And I do not want to dirty my boots needlessly.

I glance at my reflection in my rearview mirror, dimly lit by the neon glow of *In Absentia*. It's my latest mark's favorite post-work watering hole. Smiling, I adjust a strand of hair, admiring myself.

Now, all I have to do is wait.

Five minutes turn into ten, then fifteen. Doubt creeps in. The driver should be here by now.

The weight of yet another potentially failed mission settles over me, my fingers tapping an anxious rhythm against my clutch. A familiar car pulls into the lot just as I consider leaving: a 1967 Mercury Cougar.

It's not exactly the ride I expect for a high-society employee, but from my surveillance, this old classic is the only vehicle allowed through the secured gates. My target tonight is the driver. The man at the wheel.

When he steps out, he's nothing like I imagined.

Tall, broad, with an effortless, rugged strength that gym-goers can only dream of, he has an alluring and intimidating presence. My lips twitch into a smile. Tonight won't be such a chore after all.

Sliding out of my flashy red '82 Datsun, I adjust my off-the-shoulder black shift dress, letting it fall effortlessly as I smooth out invisible creases. The studded T-strap Prada sandals clink quietly against the pavement as I make my way to the entrance, my steps clicking in time with my heartbeat. I force my hands to stay still, resisting the urge to fidget with my Saint Laurent clutch.

Tonight is going to go exactly as planned.

Inside, the bar is dimly lit with an assortment of neon beer signs filled with the low buzz of muted amusement and the occasional burst of aggression. My eyes land on a leather-clad man at the bar, a beach-blonde woman draped over his lap, laughing too hard to be sincere. Her shoulders shift to reveal a healthy dose of cleavage—a classic move. I roll my eyes and stride past them without a second glance. I don't have time for clumsy amateurs.

Tracking my target—the elusive driver of this so-called Prince—has been impossible. Neither he nor his employer have a digital footprint. After sifting through his trash and swiping his mail, I finally found what I needed: an American Express Centurion card statement. The charges lead me here. With only his home address and a bar tab, I have to resort to baser methods to secure entry to that house.

This is the closest I can get to that beautiful mansion's owner and glorious treasure, so now I have to try Plan B.

Stealing from this rich old bastard will be even more satisfying now that I have to get my hands dirty. I glance up at the glorified historic barn and sigh. It doesn't matter if I scuff my shoes and rip my dress, so be it. If I pull this off, it'll all be worth it.

Casually, I sit down and order a drink, positioning myself near my target—not close enough to crowd him but close enough to eavesdrop. He's hard and strong, with impossibly broad shoulders stretching the fabric of his jacket. I'm more than impressed. A shiver runs up my spine at the thought of him sweaty and worked over.

As I settle in, I feel his gaze lock onto mine. It's intense, as if he can see through every layer of my carefully crafted façade. I meet his eyes for a heartbeat, but something almost knowing makes me turn away first, taking a sip of my drink to hide the flutter of unease.

Nothing prepares me for the sharp calculation in his eyes—or the surprising fullness of his lips. Part of me is relieved I won't have to flirt with a toad for once, but this might be worse. I shiver again, just a slight vibration across my chest, but I stiffen under his stare.

Then, his stare lingers as if he's debating something. My pulse does that annoying little jump again.

The scent hits me first—leather and cheap aftershave. A new presence moves at my back, unwelcome and too close.

The biker.

I force down my irritation and turn toward him, keeping my expression neutral. He isn't unattractive—thick black hair, most likely dyed—but his features are just off. Maybe his nose is too big or his eyes too small. I can't pinpoint it, but something about the man makes me uncomfortable.

"Let me see those teeth, pretty lady," he says, leaning close enough that my nose wrinkles.

I blink. "Excuse me?"

"Come on, give me a smile."

"I'll smile when you leave."

He chuckles, clearly enjoying himself. Before he can press further, a deep voice interrupts from behind me.

"The lady told you to leave." The words are smooth yet edged with quiet authority. "You should listen."

The driver.

How the hell does he get behind me so fast?

The biker hesitates before throwing a glare my way. With a mutter, he backs off, returning to his table without a fuss. Impressive.

True to my word, I toss him a grin over my shoulder when I turn back. Eyes like old copper connect with mine for a long moment, pinning me in place and not just looking. Seeing.

After a hot day, he smells like a cool forest floor, and I inhale deeply.

My pulse kicks up just for a second. Then I force myself to smirk, tilting my glass to my lips.

"Are you alright?" he asks. His accent is faint but undeniably other.

I sigh lightly, meeting his gaze. He's ascetic, austere, like a man carved from stone. From his well-worn shit-kickers to the complete lack of adornment, he's all function, no frills. Tall, though. And cut.

Grandma, what a strong chest you have.

"Do you always go around saving ladies?" I ask, twirling my straw in lazy circles.

"Would you like me to call him back so you can save yourself?" He shrugs, starting to turn away.

"No," I say smoothly. "I typically try not to destroy the helpless males who cross my path."

A lie. The truth is, I'll take any advantage I can get. But he doesn't need to know that. The price on this job is the highest I've ever worked. Tonight, I have to be better than I've ever been—for one last run.

"Destroy, huh?" He tilts his head. "That's a strong word for someone as small and pretty as you."

"You think I'm pretty?" I bat my eyelashes, grinning.

"Pretty helpless," he amends.

I roll my eyes. "I'm far from helpless."

Something sharp flickers in his eyes, looking like a bet.

"And what about you?" I ask, feigning curiosity. "I overheard you and the bartender talking about the big house. You don't work at the mansion on the hill, by any chance, do you?"

He leans back, his glass tilting as he considers me. "Why do you ask?"

I shrug. "Always wondered what goes on in a place like that. It seems so... grand. Must be nice, right?"

Another lie. I know what goes on in places like that. It's not grand and not nice. Maybe that's why I enjoy robbing them blind. Who says you need to pay for good therapy?

A bitter smile flits across his face. "Nice?" he echoes. "That place is as cold and empty as a tomb."

I raise a brow. Empty, you say?

He nods. "Like a body without a soul."

Or a home without a master? Could it be that easy?

I stifle a laugh at his melodrama. "How... poetic. Maybe you could give me a tour."

He studies me for a long moment. "You'd be disappointed," he murmurs. "People usually are."

This guy seems heavy with deliberation. I let my fingers trail over his arm, forcing myself to lighten my touch. I don't need to know if his chest is as solid as his arms. Focus.

"Do you want to know my first impression of you?" I ask.

"Bar wisdom from a stranger; must be my lucky day."

I laugh lightly, swatting his chest. Holy guacamole, a man shouldn't be that solid. "You have no idea; I surprise myself sometimes with how generous I am." *I will bleed your boss's safe so dry he won't be able to afford you. You better start looking for another job now, big guy.* I smile as I stroke my fingers against his chest.

"Now, why do I doubt that?" His stare is sharp, slicing through my moment of inner glee. Does he suspect why I'm here?

"Here's some free advice: whatever's got you down, stop moping and do something about it."

"What makes you think I'm moping?" he asks.

"You mean aside from your face?"

He looks confused, offended, and then back to confused again. It's kind of... adorable. Time to go. I start to rise.

"Wait, what was your first impression?"

"It was that you're a stick in the mud. You look dangerous, but it's all talk and no bite."

That man *is* dangerous. Too sharp. Too controlled and with eyes that see too much.

But those eyes, though...

No. Focus.

I have a job, and it's time to cash in.

8

GOOD ADVICE, BAD COMPANY

One moment, the mortal woman had given me fuck me eyes. The next, she'd called me pathetic. Then, she'd grinned at me like a madwoman as her hand drifted across my chest. It made something flutter deep in my gut, and my palm twitched with the instinct to act. She sparked something in me so long dead I nearly missed it: interest.

Trust me, I bite.

When she'd first walked into the bar, the light had haloed her, making her look almost celestial. Then she'd smiled to herself—but the moment she spotted me, that sweetness sharpened into something sinful. Just one grin, a flicker of laughter in her gaze, and tension rattled through my spine.

Even in the dim light, I had seen the goosebumps rise along her arms as a shiver danced over her skin. For a heartbeat, I watched the cunning gleam in her eyes as they dropped to my lips, then rose again to meet my stare.

Dread had already begun to churn in my stomach when the changeling biker turned his attention to her. Usually, I wouldn't have cared. Hell, I might not have even noticed. But when she didn't so much as bat an eyelash at the burly chump, the tension in my gut turned sharp, coiling around my focus.

What's the harm in talking to her? I thought. Nothing will come of it. I'll have my drink, she'll have hers, and then we'll never see each other again. It sounded like a perfect plan. After all, I was on vacation.

I never should have interrupted.

But there had been something in her voice that pulled at me. It hadn't been high-pitched or overly sweet; nothing whisper-soft. Every word hit like a punch, then melted through me like hot honey.

"Thanks for the advice. I might take it," I'd finally managed. Get it together; she's just a human.

"I hope you do." She'd grinned, her gaze sweeping over the table to my keys, then drifting toward the door. In a hurry to leave, little one?

Her richly sensual perfume trailed around her like a living thing, and suddenly, a new kind of agony settled over my skin. It wasn't pain—no, this was some-thing raw. Her touch left me burning.

My blood hummed. My skin prickled. I've never felt like this before.

Somehow, with nothing but a wicked touch and those dare-me eyes, this mortal lit up every nerve ending I'd forgotten existed. My blood was on fire. When I imagined her hands on me again, I felt my pants begin to tighten.

Impossible. Stoneborn didn't get erections. Reproduction among my kind was a brutal, solitary rite—a carving of the self to produce life. But apparently, my human body hadn't received the memo. It wanted to play pretend in a real way.

What an uncomfortable sensation. This was awful. How did humans endure it?

And yet, when I caught her watching me—when she looked away with that sly smile—I throbbed. Feelings were madness. But they were... invigorating.

At that moment, I'd made my decision. I was going to see what this world had to offer. I'd lived in this realm, yet always apart from it, for so long that I knew almost nothing about it. She would be my introduction to the mortal world, a guide into something I had long denied myself. For one night, at least, I would let myself belong to it.

"What's your name?" I asked. My voice came out low—and dangerously curious. The sound of it sent a chill up my legs.

If the others ever heard I was craving a human, I'd never live it down. But even as I thought it, a truth surfaced—half-formed but certain: They intend to keep me in the mortal realm.

So why should I deny this realm's pleasures if it were to become my home?

"I... should be going," she said casually, though the words quickened my pulse.

"Tell me your name."

She took a moment, nodded, and sighed. "Well, I guess I can break one of my rules today. I'm Kate."

"Kate. Pleasure. I'm Malrik. And what rule did you break, Kate?"

"Giving my name to a random stranger at a dead-end dive bar, no less. But that's all you'll get. If you want a sympathetic ear tonight, you'll have to tip the bartender extra. I'm not interested."

"I don't think that'll be necessary." I shrugged.

"Good." She leaned back, casual but firm. "Rage against whatever has you down tonight. Wallow if you have to. But by morning, have it out of your system. Tomorrow, focus on you. On what you want. Be the guy who goes after it. No apologies."

Be careful of the advice you give strangers, little one. It sounds too much like an invitation. And you might be surprised just who a man chooses to pursue.

"Will you allow me to walk you to your car?" I offered.

"Alright, I suppose." Her eyes flick to the bikers, and I want to strut and slaughter in equal measure. She looked to me for protection—from them. Even now, humans still turn to monsters to keep the worst ones at bay.

"I'll meet you outside, big guy. I gotta freshen up."

With a nod, I rose and slipped out of sight, giving her a clear path. She wouldn't have to deal with them alone. I waited.

But instead of heading to the bathroom, she changed direction. She pulled up a chair beside the pack of leather-bound shifters.

Curious. What are you up to, little mortal?

"You're from the biker group—the Rift Riders, correct?" Her voice stayed light, but the glint in her eyes and the sharp curve of her lips made her expression anything but inviting.

She didn't know that they rode through realms, working as mercenaries for hire across thirteen worlds.

Well, nine. There were some places they couldn't even go to.

I'd fought beside a few of them. Good men, for the most part. Too loud and messy. But skilled.

"If you know about the Rift Riders, you should be very fearful," the leader said, leaning in. His hairy forearm sprawled across the table like a challenge.

"My date was just telling me what a bunch of dried-up pussies you are." Her tone dripped with mock sweetness. "He used a different word, but I don't use that kind of language. Tell you what—I'll give you two grand right now if you beat the hell out of him."

Her smile vanished. Cold calculation took its place. Whiplash-fast.

Interesting.

"You want us to beat up your date?"

"Yes, please. I'm paying you for an hour. Just keep him busy."

"The one guy?"

"One guy. One hour."

My brow rose for the third time that night.

This woman was full of surprises.

"I'm gonna need hazard pay," Junior drawled.

"No." No hesitation. Then came the cash, a stack of

bills slapped among the empty Bud cans. "Now get to work."

Her voice shifted again. This time, it was cold, detached. Not even close to the spiced honey she'd used on me. Still, I enjoyed listening to her tones, even when she was arranging a hit on me.

And just like that, she sweetened the deal with a sugar-coated squeak: "Thank you."

I moved forward, concealing my amusement. She beamed when I stepped out the door as if nothing had happened.

How cute. She still thought she could play me.

I smiled back, calm and composed, as the burly changelings filed out after her, eager for the job.

Humans. So predictable.

Or so I'd thought.

It didn't take long before I was surrounded—seven surly changelings, all grinning.

I spotted her slip around to the driver's side of my car from the corner of my eye.

Using my keys.

I patted my pockets.

Empty.

What the hell?

With a casual shrug of her delicate shoulders, she slid into the seat and started the engine.

All I got was a pinkie wave and a full-bodied laugh. Her head tipped back in a cruel laugh, just enough for the parking lot lights to catch in her hair. Then she peeled out, tires screaming.

Kate had played me.

But her words lingered: Whatever's got you down, stop moping and do something about it.

Clever little thief, I thought. You'll find out soon enough —I bite.

9

———

THE ART OF THE STEAL

drink, a little conversation, and suddenly, his keys are in my hand. Funny how that works. I wiggle in my seat, trying to relieve the pressure of the driver's steady gaze and the night's excitement. Even after I speed out of the parking lot, the intensity in his eyes follows me.

This is about to be the biggest job of my life. After this, I'll be rich! I'll finally be able to make my move. I scan the card at the gate and giggle the entire ride down his drive. Not the driver's steady stare, nor even the creepy crows circling overhead and cawing, can interrupt my good mood.

For all of Darius's warnings, things are starting pretty easy. I can't wait to see his face when I drop the artifact on his counter and say good riddance tomorrow. Pulling off this job will bank enough money to protect me from my past.

I step past the white stone and creeping ivy onto a porch of more carved stone. Even the roof is stone, complete with snarling gargoyle sentries. Walking up to the vicious guard on the stairway pedestal, I scratch under the stone creature's chin for good luck.

"If I could be half as ferocious as you, I might not be in this mess." I wink, letting the pads of my fingers trail across the smooth stone set in waves.

A couple of the crows sit along one of the manicured tree branches. They've stopped making a racket and instead watch me with a curiosity that makes my arm hair stand on end. "Watch all you want as long as you enjoy the show." I blow the blackbirds a kiss before turning back to the door.

As far as breaking and entering goes, the guy's front lock could be picked by a toddler. How did Darius have any problems getting in? This guy is way too comfortable. I gotta show him the harsh reality of living. To my left, a coat rack stands beside a rug runner leading to a viewing room. To my right sits a table with a single lamp.

My smile withers, then deepens into a frown. So much empty. The confident stride I once had falters as I step further inside. A ball of unease sours my stomach as excitement curdles into displeasure. The abrupt shift of fluttering excitement to growing dread leaves a hollow, aching alarm.

The place is nearly spartan. My heels are the most expensive thing in this room, and they click angrily against the floor. As I stride through his 'living room,' I knock over what little he has in petty frustration.

"This cheap bastard better have everything in his safe for my convenience."

I tear through the first floor, frustration mounting. Usually, I'd have a purse full of loot by now. Instead, I've got nothing.

In another fit of anger, I knock over a heavy wooden table. Heading up the ornately decorated stairs—flanked by two grim statues—I lean around one stone form to check the time on the nearest clock. Of course, the bastard doesn't even have one.

As I go through the second story, one room at a time, I feel the heavy hand of pressure weighing down on me. I rummage through some drawers, adrenaline making my fingers tremble. There's a scrape behind me.

I spin around tight. My eyes scan the room. Nothing.

I can't shake the feeling that eyes are on me, but there's nothing here—not even a camera.

Pulling out my phone, I blink twice at the no-service notification. Damn.

Aside from the lack of dust, it doesn't seem like anyone has lived here for a while. And yet, years of experience warn me that I'm pressing my luck. But I know I can't leave without something. Unless my fortune changes quickly, I'll have to return to try again, which is dangerous.

I sigh in relief when I strike gold in a bedroom. Maybe he enjoys the finer things after all. He must not spend much time in the front of the house. A long silk tapestry hangs from the right wall, woven in different shades of green and blue, with a smudge of red patterned into a beautiful abstract work of art. But as lovely as those few possessions are, I can pocket nothing and make quick money on a flip.

Where the hell is his safe?

I check each room, pulling books from the shelves and knocking over any knickknack that could be a secret passageway handle. Nothing. Where is it?

There's no way I'm asking Darius for help finding the safe. Not after he thinks I botched the last job. Not when it's *my* livelihood on the line.

I want to smash everything in my anger, but before my hands can snatch an ancient and probably priceless lamp, I remind myself that I'm not that kind of thief. Taking a deep breath, I finally find a silver pocket watch. It's antique and beautiful, a mix of silver and gold, and when I open it, I'm pleased to discover it still works. Squinting at the polished silver, I catch an odd shadow behind me. My head lifts abruptly, and I see a mirror reflection.

Malrik! He's here! Behind me.

I barely hold back a curse. When I turn, the form is gone—my breath stills.

Have I imagined him?

Or—worse—is he calling the cops?

That makes me race out the door, only to run into his chest. Bouncing back, I land on my butt and scramble away as he steps forward.

"Well, what do we have here? A thief disguised as a lady?" The deep bass, which previously carried dry humor, is now laced with disdain. I spin around, and it takes a few seconds for my situation to sink in: grand theft auto, breaking and entering, at the very least.

Scrambling backward, I desperately look around but take in nothing; panic fogs my vision.

"Or perhaps a lady disguised as a thief since you never invited me over for that tour," I say, trying to figure a way out as I keep the pocket watch in my hand behind my back. "I thought I'd surprise you."

The silence stretches as he blocks the only way out of the room, his broad shoulders and defensive stance making it impossible for me to slip past. I step back, keeping my eyes on him until I'm far enough away to run to the two-story window. A perfectly manicured lawn and a rose bush right underneath greet me. Damn. That'll be a tough fall.

"You stole my keys, my car—and planned an ambush too? Who the hell are you?" he asks.

"Why are you here?" I demand.

"I live here, what's your excuse?"

At that, my head cocks to the side. The information Darius gave me says nothing about any help living with him. "I thought you were done for the night. Why are you here?" I ask again.

"So you've been watching me." His voice drops lower as his gaze sweeps over me, trying to be discreet. "For how long?" The slow draw makes something in my core tighten.

"I haven't. I just thought I'd check the place out. What are you going to do?" I ask, forcing my voice past the lump in my throat.

"Like you suggested, I'm focusing on me and what I want." He pauses, laughs in a short, hard burst, and then looks surprised by the sound. "First things first. Give me back the pocket watch."

"Are you here alone?" How could he have gotten here so fast?

"Hoping someone will be by to help you out? Don't bother. There's no one else here for you to manipulate."

Closing my eyes, I lift my hand and let the watch dangle from its chain. It's physically painful to give it up. His hand lowers just beneath, and slowly, I release my grip on the chain, one finger at a time. When the watch is safely back in his hand, I lift my hand to my mouth, stopping just before biting off a nail.

His eyes watch my every movement, catching my eyes darting from him to the door and even to the window. By lifting his brow and tightening his eyes, I can see that he's starting to get insulted. Good.

"How did you get past the bikers?" I ask.

He doesn't answer; he only shakes his head and sighs.

"Please..."

"Save the begging for later. You've been caught; the least you can do is own up and accept your just rewards."

Shifting from one foot to another, I keep my knees bent. I have to be ready for anything. But I've never been caught before, not red-handed. This is not my week.

"Are you going to—"

"You're a thief. Who says you deserve answers?"

My heart pounds as he advances until my back meets

the cold wall. His chin dips, the space between us vanishing, and his eyes lock onto mine—not with anger, but with something worse. Something even more dangerous.

Amusement.

His eyes sparkle with mirth, starkly contrasting with the rest of his imposing figure that remains cloaked in shadows. My breath catches between desire and disbelief as I stay secure in his stare. With each step, he closes in on me until his gaze lowers to my lips, then back up to make eye contact.

Is he going to kiss me?

Could I use that to my advantage?

He doesn't. Instead, Malrik takes me by the arm and leads me downstairs. His grip isn't harsh, but his body grows more rigid as he takes stock of the displays of my anger. Every time I try to resist, his grip tightens, and he crowds me just for a few seconds. Those few seconds are all it takes to remind me of his strength, and every flex of his arms sends a spark of awareness through me that I haven't experienced before.

He leads me into the center of the 'living room' and slowly turns me around, making me confront the damage I've created. Even though he cut me off whenever I spoke previously, I need to explain myself. "Normally, I don't make a mess; I'm not that kind of thief. Honest."

"Do you even know how to be honest?" His deep voice drops an octave, making my stomach and knees tighten.

I don't respond right away because, up until now, almost everything I've said has been a lie. Knowing

Malrik has a justified reason not to trust my word doesn't make swallowing his question any easier. Knowing he's right makes the pill even more bitter. Shaking out my hair again, I twist my conscience and admit, "If I tell you it's the truth, it is. It's only when I don't specify that you should question it."

By now, he looks down at me; I can see that my honesty, while perhaps not impressive, hits some chord with him. If only being honest were something I could do all the time. Throughout my past, honesty has only brought resentment and anger. 'If it doesn't get you paid, then no way.' That's my family's motto, and I've learned my lesson well. There's rarely any money in honesty.

"That table has seen worse disasters than you. Clean up what you messed up, and perhaps I won't be inclined to escalate."

I know again that he's justified in his order, but if the truth hurts, I'm stung. My pride burns inside me as I quickly walk over and, bending down, move the furniture back upright. At least he hasn't seen his office yet. The entire act of "cleaning" takes perhaps ten minutes. Longer to fix than to flip.

Standing tall, I walk in front of Malrik, outside of arm's reach, and instead of risking a negative response, I lick my lips and cock my head to the side, sizing him up for the third time. This guy is nothing like I expected.

"I thought this house would be an easy mark; it was wrong. I was wrong. I'll be leaving now." After a moment of silence that I take as confirmation, I turn and head for the open door. The wind catches the door and swings it closed in a slam to block my exit.

"Oh no, little thief." His voice deepened more than I thought possible, heavy with layers that felt unnatural, laden with controlled tension, and thick with disapproval. I continue forward. "It won't be that easy. You broke into the wrong house."

The doors and windows swing shut with a swoosh, thud, and a sharp click. It was the telltale sound of automatic locks, with none of the mechanisms' muted buzzing. I stumble to a halt, tension stringing my body tight like a bow. The military-grade lockdown was a surprise, and I felt foolish for not anticipating it.

Because Darius had been right. Getting in was a breeze. Getting out might be a problem.

10

A STAB AT FREEDOM

I didn't know why I trapped her in the house with me. The reasonable thing would have been to let her go. Stoneborn law demanded it. But there were no regrets when I closed the shutters, shutting out the natural light with a series of resounding clanks.

The regrets might come later. For the girl's sake, I hoped they would. Perhaps reason would follow. Because it didn't seem like honor, logic, or tradition would be enough to fuel my self-control.

The little thief had stolen my car, tried to have me beaten, and then broken into and trashed my home. And then she'd had the nerve to look up at me with wide eyes and a shameless smirk, avoiding all responsibility. Did she really think she'd get out of here so easily?

As the dim lights in the tall ceilings flicked on, illuminating the hallway and her silhouette, I had an unobstructed view of her calm facade, cracking into a panic. Her eyes darted, her body crouched, and her hands lifted defensively. When I started forward, she scrambled back.

She'd scream and run. When I found her again, I'd have to figure out how to stop her inevitable crying.

Instead, she pivoted quickly, whipping the lamp off the table at me. I jerked to catch the antique before the explosion of glass and oil could rain down on us, and my shoulder slammed into the reinforced door jamb as a reward. She was already darting through the kitchen before I could stop her.

Huh.

Her sharp steps grew louder as she gained speed, but I intercepted her at the kitchen entrance. A single clothesline could've flattened her and ended this chase instantly. But despite everything, I didn't want to hurt her.

I hooked my foot around her ankle and lifted. She stumbled forward, fighting to keep her balance as she reached for the railing. Her momentum carried her, and I watched as she desperately tried to keep her feet under her without stopping her run toward the stairs. The effect was knock-kneed, almost laughable, until she used the wall to control her fall and regain her equilibrium.

It wasn't coordinated. It wasn't graceful. But my cheeks strained with a grin, a rare expression buried beneath lifetimes of cold and gray.

In all my years, I had never known such a bold woman. What made her think she could steal from me? Or escape me in my own home? What a silly little human.

She had to know I'd catch her. There was nowhere to run. But the way she eyed my wide-shouldered stance like an easy challenge made me hesitate from the immediate takedown I'd planned.

If I let her run, she might surprise me again. Something fluttered in my stomach, effervescent and unwelcome. I didn't have time to contemplate that bizarre sensation. From the reflection in the stainless steel fridge, I saw her expression shift from desperation to determination. The flutter in my stomach settled. My lips curled into another smile, making it the fifth in my life.

Changing tactics again, she turned to face me, her neck craning to look up. Feeling unusually indulgent, I lifted my phone just over her head. Our eyes locked, and my heart stuttered excitedly at the connection.

Dangerous. I was playing a perilous game. I should have kicked this thief out for the unwelcome feelings she invoked.

A mortal had almost gotten the jump on me. It was evidence of the failing character Gorvoss had accused. Maybe I had cracked.

"Aren't you going to call the police?" she probed.

Who was this woman who made deals with a gang of changelings and now wanted to bring in the cops? Who was she working with?

"You think I'd get them involved? No. This is between you and me."

She hadn't expected to see me again. If she hadn't stolen my car, I would've been gone for at least ten more hours. During that time, she might have robbed me blind.

"Just call the cops." She stomped her foot in demand.

"I don't think I will." I locked my phone and pocketed it.

She shook her head in disbelief, her silky curls bouncing in her ponytail. I'd caught her red-handed. Now, only one question remained: what would I do with her?

Not for the first time, her eyes dart as if debating whether to hide or jump through a window. But then her gaze settled on the butcher's block knife on the kitchen's far side. That's when my grin turned sharper —and my cheeks felt tight, probably because I'd been working muscles I hadn't used in forever.

The kitchen island stood between her and the knives. She could loop through the family room past the breakfast nook. Given her size and strength, her best bet would be to run around the island.

"Don't do it. Don't make this worse on yourself," I warned.

"You're the one making it worse. I'm just doing what I have to do to survive. So call the cops or, better yet, just let me go."

I was so sure of her next move. When she shifted, I moved to counter. But instead of circling the nook, she jumped over the island in one graceful leap, immediately grabbing the knives.

The heavy block clattered, but she'd already seized a blade. She held it awkwardly, clearly untraining, guided by raw instinct as she inched along the wall. The knife shook between us.

I lifted my hands as if worried, though very few mortal weapons could kill me. Slowly, the thief withdrew toward the front door, and I followed, keeping my hands up where she could see them. It seemed to comfort her, thinking she had me on the edge.

"Look," she started. "I don't want to hurt you. Just unlock the doors, and I'll be on my way."

"Or what? You'll stab me and break your way out?"

"I don't want to," she said, voice strained. "I'm really not that kind of thief, but I will do what I have to."

"Is that why you're here in the first place?" I closed the distance, letting myself sink deeper into the warm musk of her body heat.

I could smell her sweat: sweet and spicy, like cayenne-coated fruit. Not sickly sweet, but with a bite, like fire in honey. For the first time, maybe ever, my stomach ached with hunger. Was this hunger just another uncomfortable consequence of being topside for too long? Or was it her?

My amusement dropped, darkening, as the truth hit me. Stoneborn didn't feel hunger. We didn't feel desire or excitement. I had cracked.

For a moment, my world tipped on its axis. All that was good and right seemed long out of reach. The human realm had broken me. My brother was right. I didn't deserve to return home.

That made me a warrior without an enemy, a man without a people, a person without a home. Where did that leave me?

Alone.

And that left me with one option. Why not indulge for a little while? Give in to the curiosity that gnawed at me for centuries.

"You wanna play therapist with me?" she said, her tone shifting. She moved into a less aggressive stance. "Okay, the real reason I'm here is because I had a tragic upbringing and a terrible relationship with my father. I know, it's what every guy wants to hear: daddy issues." She added a wrist flourish and a wink.

She was quick, more mutable than I'd thought possible. From coy, brutal, sexy, and scared to violent, faux contrite, and back again. What could this woman possibly want?

The unnerving sensation tugged at my granite heart again.

"And you see," she continued, "ever since I started taking care of myself, I realized my true problem is: I desperately need to fill the hole in my heart." She paused for breath. "With a reasonable amount of gold. Like, I'm not asking for much, just a nice life and a little security. I can be fair. Now, do you know where your prince keeps his safe or not? If you help me, I'll cut you in. 70/30. I want the first pick."

Did she really think she could bargain with me? At the end of a cleaver? My cleaver, in my own home? With my own treasure? Whoever sent this poor mortal might as well have sent her in clueless.

"Wait, did you say prince?" I asked, genuinely confused now.

"Isn't that who lives here? Some stodgy old bastard who never leaves the tower?"

Is that what they say about me nowadays? Hm. Actually... that was accurate.

"Who hired you?" I asked, cornering her.

Her knife slid across my stomach. The blade met flesh but didn't sink in. The laws of the mortal realm forced every interdimensional creature into a mortal mask, but the earthly form wasn't enough to bring nerves to a stone shell.

The realization that she'd tried to stab me—and failed—hit her all at once. I had a front-row seat as the terrifying truth sank in: her attack hadn't even slowed me down.

By the time horror spread through her stiffening shoulders, I grabbed her and spun her around. I gripped her delicate wrist, increasing the pressure slowly until she had no choice but to drop the knife. A pained mewl escaped her as she instinctively recoiled into me, her back curling against the long line of my body.

As if she didn't know how to quit, she twisted and turned, futilely trying to break my hold. My other arm held her in place, my grip unyielding. I gradually tightened it, watching as she squirmed, her movements growing more desperate. Then, with a slight flail and grunt, I thought she'd finally given up.

I was wrong.

Instead, she stepped to the side, her heels digging into my shin with a powerful kick. Before I could grab her slippery form again, she twisted and lashed out with a hidden steak knife. The sound of the blade slapping against marble rang as she fell forward.

But as soon as she struck, she was gone.

The knife snagged against my skin before it snapped. She'd tried to cut me. Again! It wasn't a fatal blow—far from it—but it left a bitter taste in my mouth. A strange, unfamiliar feeling twisted in my chest, blending ire with a darkened amusement.

She hadn't spared me a second thought. If she had, she might've wondered why the knife she'd tried to stab me with shattered on contact. The blade barely grazed me, yet a new pain lingered.

Then, a disturbing thought stirred in the back of my mind.

Why could I feel at all?

11

SLIPPERY WHEN SEARCHED

I scramble forward, not sparing Malrik a second look, and run for the front door. But as I get close, I see no signs of a locking mechanism I can pick or a system I can hack. What the hell? Where are the locks? How did he shut the building down?

Time weighs heavily on my shaking hands, leaving me no chance to look around. I can already feel the press of his pursuit creeping closer. He moves through the kitchen's second entrance, only fifteen yards away.

How is he still after me? How could I miss twice? I gasp, trying to control the fear surging through my muscles and calm my thrumming heart.

As soon as he steps into the entryway, my bravery breaks. I race to the stairs, trying to slide past the living room entrance.

Only it doesn't work.

As soon as my heels pound the steps, they shift. Under my feet, the edges turn inward, becoming a ramp. My brain short-circuits the moment the stairs melt into a slick slope. No matter how much I scramble and slap the floor, the only way I'm going is down.

What the actual fuck?

He grabs my ankle from behind. I hold on to the handrails and pillars, gripping them tight.

His grip is iron. I twist, kicking into his ribs, his face, anywhere I can reach. His arms wrap around me and lift me off the ground. I kick the scarred wood table, chipping it further and knocking us into the hallway wall. My gaze darts around the room, trying to see any way out of here.

"Struggle all you want. It won't change anything. You only risk hurting yourself."

I shiver as his bored timbre rolls along my nerves. When I eventually relax, he lowers me but keeps his hold tight until both my feet are on the ground. When I don't immediately fight, he loosens his grip.

He keeps my wrists shackled loosely in his massive paws. He leads me into the kitchen to the island's marble countertop, kicking my feet apart until I'm off balance. I try to shake myself out of my stupor, but my head is still spinning from the stair incident.

What kind of mechanism is that? Doors and windows that lock themselves. Stairs that turn into a wheelchair ramp? What other types of traps does this old house have?

Until now, I had a plan, but that all falls apart once I'm well and truly caught. Against my better instincts, I don't lean away from him but follow his insistent hold, pressing me into the cabinet. I keep still and remain silent as he pats me down.

There's no way he can't feel my tremble. His hand brushes over my left hip and then my right, pausing to pull out my cell phone. My phone hits the countertop with a hard clatter, and then his hands continue to search. His touch is firm but cautious, as if he's afraid to touch too hard.

I pray he won't find the lock picks I keep stashed as his hands wrap around my most obvious tools.

I barely feel him behind me. Though I know we'd be touching if I lean back not even an inch. He deftly pulls and releases the belt, allowing it to drop to the ground. I feel him shift as he kicks it away.

"I didn't mean to stab you," I say.

"The first time or the second time?"

Ouch. "I didn't grab it to hurt you but to keep you away. You practically ran into it that first time. That's not my fault, not that you seem to be hurt that bad."

"And breaking and entering wasn't your fault either, right?" He continues without pause.

I keep my hands pinned to the outer edge of the pristine countertop. Nothing binds me but the controlled guide of Malrik's hands.

A thick thumb traces my jaw, pulling my attention back to him. His gaze pins me in six feet of cold discipline like he dares me to resist.

His touch is undemanding but firm. The big guy moves like he knows what he's looking for, and it's not to cop a feel. With the way my skin tingles, I'm almost disappointed.

"What's your name, thief?"

"Kate, but you can call me Kitty. What's yours?" I lie automatically.

"Who sent you?"

"No one." I lie again.

"How long have you been watching me?"

"Since yesterday, when I saw you pulling out of here," I insist.

"What faction do you serve?" he demands.

"I don't..."

"Who sent you?" His voice sharpens, slicing through the dark. He shifts, muscles coiling. What is he going to do? My pulse slams against my ribs as I brace for impact.

For the first time in a decade, I pray—really pray. Words tumble from my lips, old devotions buried deep in memory, the kind that would make my mother proud.

I toss my head back for a headbutt, pushing myself backward. He grabs me by my ponytail and bends me over the kitchen island. His fist is in my hair, and he presses my face against the marble.

"Alright, alright, I'll stop," I say.

"What's your name?"

"I told you it's Kitty."

The tisking sound and the puff of his breath in my hair are my only hint that things are about to escalate. He wraps his arm around my throat and covers my mouth. I struggle, throwing elbows to his ribs and his groin and stomping all over his foot.

Again, it does nothing.

My strikes aren't wild or frantic but controlled and

methodically well-placed. The steel I've added to my heels alone should break bone, but nothing elicits a grunt. He doesn't even move to try to avoid any of the blows.

"You just made this harder for yourself, little thief. You won't be leaving any time soon." He holds me pressed against his arm, hugs me against his chest, and waits for me to tap out.

With no weapons, exits, or way to win a fair fight, I need a tactic sharper than a blade.

I find my answer in his thick arms. There's something about the way he holds me. It should repulse me. But it doesn't.

"Wait, I think I know what you want."

The squeak isn't about giving in—it's about getting out.

"You do?" he asks.

Instead of answering, I roll my hips back, slow and steady, pushing into his touch to see what he'll do.

He freezes. Hands twitch, unsure whether to cling tighter or let go. I don't give him the chance to decide. I squeeze to face him until we stand nose to nose.

His breath stalls. I'm pretty sure he's not breathing. No, he's definitely not breathing.

No words. No commands. Just wide, dilated eyes staring down at me, pupils swallowing gold. Heat spirals off him like steam from a cracked furnace.

If he wants to play dirty, I'll play to win. I've been cornered before. Last time, I foolishly used my body—this time, I'll use his.

Smile like you mean it. Breathe like you're not

afraid. Pretend you're the one in control. I have to keep him off-balance just long enough to escape.

I smile, a long pull of promised sin, and reach for the one weapon he can't defend against, the one between his legs.

He sucks in a breath and holds it like a lifeline.

"What are you—"

The rest of the sentence vanishes, swallowed by the zzzzzip of his pants. The sound is deafening in the silence.

It's too dark to see anything. But I don't need to. It hasn't been so long that I forget where all the parts go. Muscle memory, rebellion, and something darker guide my hand. The chilled fabric slides under my fingertips as I ghost up his thigh.

He jerks sharply, like my touch burns.

Good.

He hardens in my hand, his body locking in place and trembling under the surface like a live wire waiting to snap. I lean in, slow and sure, and slip him into my hand.

I remain still, trapped in his tight embrace, looking him dead in the eyes while my wrist twists.

His fists clench around the counter. Knuckles white. Arms straining with tension. The only thing that moves is his hips, small involuntary pulses that betray everything he's not saying.

My fear has faded. There is only adrenaline now.

And beneath it, heat.

Arousal, masquerading as defiance.

I want to see who will break first.

He doesn't stop me.

His muscles lock until every inch of him winds tight like he's both afraid of hurting me and terrified of what'll happen if I let go.

Then I start to roll my thumb over the head of him, and his knees tremble. A full-body shudder climbs his body and leaves his shoulders tight with restraint. A grunt escapes him as he braces both hands on the counter, gripping it like it was his only tether to reality. Then, something velvety and rich like molasses warms my palm, spreading a lingering heat and tingle.

And then—his voice a sweet, cracked mutter. "Oh, gods. Don't... stop."

It comes out like a plea. Weak. Breathless. Raw with craving. This time, when I smile, it's not forced. I have him.

His hips flex into me again, hands finally finding me, tugging, guiding, surrendering to instinct over uncertainty. When he fists my hair, his hips surge, but I don't let him take control of the pace of his submission.

Then he groans as every muscle in his body tightens. He thickens in my hand, his movements frantic until more of his sweet and smoky ichor coats the back of my hand, and he slumps, spent.

I lift my head, smug and flushed in a job well done, only for the world to tip slightly beneath me. At first, I thought it was the adrenaline. Or exhaustion. But then I feel it.

Heat pulses against my skin and sinks in my gut like molten stone. Malrik leans in, his lips moving—but I can't hear him. There is only the ringing in my ears, like a cave screaming from the inside out.

My nails bite into his forearm.

Too late. The air feels thick, tarred. My lungs refuse to draw in air.

Panic flares. I open my mouth to cry out, but no sound comes.

Malrik's grip isn't cruel. His face is etched with concern and confusion. Before I could fall, Malrik's rock-hard hold keeps me in place.

And then, darkness.

Not sleep.

But a shutdown.

12

THE PRICE OF BREAKING RULES

Well, shit.

After what was the most surprising and erotic act, the little temptress passed out. Was that normal? Not that I was complaining. I needed a moment to gather myself. From the first instant her fingers curled around my length, I'd known I was in over my head. I needed the time to regain my composure.

Jahziel and Hazariah watched outside the window. They didn't say anything and somehow that made it worse. But I wouldn't let the judgement of the cursed warriors distract me from my bounty. My delicate mortal treasure.

"What do I do now with my little mortal thief?"

She lay in a graceful, crumpled heap in the middle of my kitchen. Her auburn hair fanned across the dark marble like the remnants of waves retreating from a brackish shore. When the light caught the brass inlay beneath her, it shimmered like distant fireworks, a fleeting burst of beauty in her stillness.

It seemed oddly fitting. She'd been a bottle rocket that exploded inside my home. Or, more likely, a Molotov cocktail. I crouched down and lifted a lock of her hair, finding it smoother than raw cotton.

So pretty. So delicate. I would have to do everything required to care for her, which meant learning what kept humans alive. As it was, her fainting so fast had caught me by surprise.

Stop looking at her like that and call the cleaning crew. As always, Hazariah voiced the appropriate solution. Hazariah, the most reserved of the three gargoyles guarding my territory, and I usually agreed on all things.

Not on this.

He can't call the cleaners in; they'd scramble her brains. She's just a human—he'll have to keep her. Jahziel offered, with an unusual amount of consideration.

They were nothing more than quiet voices whispering in my head, bound by their curse and loneliness. The mortal, however, was here, in my hands, knocked out cold. And she was the only thing that truly held my focus.

It's obvious he's rebelling after being discharged, Hazariah said, as if I couldn't hear every word or send him to a dark corner for the next couple of years.

"I'm not rebelling, and I didn't get dismissed."

Yes, forced to take a vacation, because you, and by you, I mean we, and by we I think we all know I mean me, as in I haven't had a break in so many centuries I've lost count.

Jahziel's normally cheerful tone turned bitter with his grumbling.

You don't deserve a break, and since when can you count past three? Hazariah quipped.

After all this time, you finally decided to grow a sense of humor, Heziki? Maybe the mortal world is infecting you, too, Jahziel poked.

Not as much as it was affecting me, I thought.

Do you dare challenge the vigor of my integrity? And I told you not to call me that! My name is Hazariah; it's a noble name. And I'll ask you again not to slander it with your shorthand.

"Silence," I hissed, unable to take another second. "Your constant bickering is making me regret saving you."

It's not like we have anything better to do, Jahziel complained.

Especially now that you've been laid off—I mean, assigned to a vacation, Hazariah added.

"At least I didn't get cursed for doing such a poor job," I snapped.

At that, both sulked off into the corners of my mind. With them quiet, I turned back to the mortal. Reaching down, I touched her lip. The skin was red and puffy, rubbed raw. Still, her upper lip was a little fuller and bow-shaped as my thumb dragged across the pillowy swell, a red stain transferred to my skin.

Immediately, I imagined what it would take to smear all her perfectly applied paint. What would she look like stripped bare? I leaned forward, ready to appease my curiosity, but she stirred. She almost looked delicate, passed out.

Almost.

That fleeting stir of exhilaration and wonder told me everything had changed. The cut on my lip had already begun to seal, as had my dislocated kneecap. The pain, though, was a sweet reminder of the temporary rush she brought.

How had she gotten in? Hell, how had she found out about me? How wrong would it be to keep her?

Just long enough to get some answers, I told myself. But I already suspected it was a lie.

Usually, I wouldn't have even considered it. I would have called the cleaners and reported everything, as expected. By the time they finished, the mortal would be gone without a trace or memory. If they survived the mind wipe, they got to live. Other species might be lax in their containment measures, but not the Stoneborn —certainly not the Allurssi order. Too much was at stake.

But when I rolled her on her back, a silent alarm rang in my head. I patted her down, and instead of being repelled, I lingered. Searching for more weapons should've been routine, but the more my hands brushed her body, the harder it became to pull away. I leaned back against the refrigerator, watching the pulse on her neck thrum its steady beat. It might have been my imagination, but my pulse slowed to match hers. I sighed and scratched at my jaw.

There were light bruises on her shins—probably from her fall down the stairs. Was it unfair to shift the structure of the steps while she fled? Undoubtedly. But her frazzled reaction had been worth it.

A smile tugged at my lips. I remembered how the mortal's brow tightened as she tried to rationalize the shift. Now that everything had settled, one thing became clear: I wanted her. It was against all the rules I'd sworn to uphold. But playing by the rules had done nothing for me. I didn't know what to do.

I pulled out my phone, but my thumb caught on something sharp before I could dial. A few dozen hairline fractures marked the screen, fragile as the mortals who made them. I shrugged and tossed the broken thing on the counter.

I'd made up my mind.

It was easy to rationalize. I wanted her. I wanted to touch and explore her body, strip her bare of all her lies. I wanted her, and it had nothing to do with the way she'd touched me.

Well... maybe a little.

I undressed her down to nothing but black lace—bra and panties—and my chest vibrated again. My control nearly crumbled when magnolia and mahogany gripped me by the nose. My knees shook with the urge to kneel and bite the panties off her.

Do it. Wake the girl up by nuzzling her panties to the side and burying your face and tongue between her legs. They love that, Jahziel encouraged.

The want coursing through me shook my hands.

Send her away now, before it's too late, Hezariah admonished.

I ignored them both.

Whispers of spiced honey beckoned, coaxing out feelings, desires, and an appetite I hadn't expected. The pull was nearly overwhelming.

I inhaled her and breathed her into me. Decadent. Nothing sugar-coated or sickly sweet, just a bit of fire in the honey.

The core of my determination pulsed and frayed. My fists gripped the quartz counter on either side of her. Creamy skin, delicate curves, and warmth called to me. Beneath my hand, the counter cracked, then crumbled.

That I could fix.

But I couldn't fix *her* if I lost control.

As a mortal, I doubted the magnets that healed me would do anything for her.

The longer I stayed near her, the more demanding the lure of her skin became. She was yielding. Warm. Inviting. I had to move her. For her sake, somewhere she couldn't tempt me..

The basement.

Leaning forward, I scooped her into my arms, savoring the feel of her against me. I didn't know how long I stood there, staring down at that squishy bundle of mortality in my arms. I had to be diligent.

Even among other immortals, a Stoneborn's strength was legendary. I carried her downstairs with sure and steady steps, careful not to jar her brittle mortal bones. It had been so long since I'd interacted with a mortal woman, but tales of their fragility lingered in my memory.

I couldn't explain it—her arrogant bravado was

addicting. The little thief was unlike any of my people. Gorvoss had been right; maybe I *had* been spending too much time among humans.

Another smile tugged at my lips. The flex felt unfamiliar. Rusty. My hands tingled. My body stirred back to life. This little mortal with a mouth full of lies and a body strapped with surprises had picked the wrong home to break into and thank the thirteen realms she had.

Since Gorvoss's edict, I'd wondered what I would do with myself.

Now I knew.

When I pulled her closer, she shifted in my arms. Her head rested against my chest. My heart jumped, but I shook myself at the dramatics. "Well, little imp, it seems you've offered yourself up as my little... what do they call it? My staycation distraction." My brow twitched. It's odd to feel grateful for Gorvoss's orders.

Once downstairs, I tied her hands—careful not to pull too tight. Testing the straps, a task I'd done in countless interrogations, should have steadied my focus. But all I could think about was how ridiculously breakable she was.

And how selfish it made me to keep her.

Abruptly, I pulled back. This wasn't just a frail human woman. She was a surly, meddlesome thief. She had to have been sent by someone to steal from me.

"What am I going to do with you?" I asked again, this time pinching her chin to study her face.

I would keep her here until I discovered who was after me and what they wanted. Let her test my patience and my restraint—I would not break. I would unearth every hidden part of her until she stood before me, stripped of pretense.

Even if it meant showing her the depth of her mistake. Even if I had to break every rule.

The little thief's secrets were mine now.

I wouldn't let her go so easily.

13

UNCONVENTIONAL METHODS

A throbbing pain yanks me from unconsciousness. It's not lethal, but sinister. My eyes flutter open, and I see only blurry shapes at first. The dim light at the far end of the room casts enough glow to show me just how screwed I am.

Cold, dry air prickles over my skin. My arms are shackled, legs spread-eagled on a tall table. I'm wearing only my bra, panties, and high heels.

Even in the cold air, I feel my face warm. What happened while I was out? I can't even check—that bastard strapped me down tight.

Panic surges. I yank at the bindings. They don't budge, and my struggles rub my wrists raw. A grotesque stone gargoyle stands nearby, its toothy grin mocking me.

Great. A creepy lawn ornament for company. Just what I need.

"What are you lookin' at?" I glare.

Time crawls. I tug until my wrist slips free, sweat

and blood helping lubricate my escape. A sob of relief nearly breaks through, but I'm not safe yet. My other hand and both feet are still tied.

Footsteps echo above. Slow. Purposeful.

My heart pounds. I fumble for the lockpick in my tangled hair. Just as I tug it loose, it slips.

Clink.

The footsteps stop.

So does my heart.

The door to the basement creaks open. A huge shape descends the stairs, each step winding dread tighter in my chest. The man from earlier steps into the light, his movements smooth, but with his edges still cloaked in shadows, he can't be anything other than dangerous.

"So, you're awake."

"And naked," I shot back, struggling harder against my restraints.

"Not entirely," he murmurs as his gaze sweeps over my body. I feel it like a chill.

"Why kidnap me? What's with the wardrobe change?" I snap, trying to mask my unease. Claustrophobic fear swarms me from all sides. I'm trapped, and he can do anything. He might already have.

He ignores me, stepping closer. "Feeling exposed, little thief?"

"Why did you do this? What did you do to me?" I growl, yanking hard until the skin of my remaining wrist tears against the binding.

"You're the one who prompted this, not me," he replies, his expression unreadable.

"You know, I never would've given you a hand job if I thought you'd lock me in your dungeon."

At that, he pauses. Something shifts in his eyes. Curiosity? Regret?

Good.

"You've hurt yourself."

His hand clamps around my free wrist, surprisingly gentle. He stops my struggles and, with infinite gentleness, examines the gash. Heat spreads down my arm.

"Is that what that was? It and you are not what I expected," he murmurs.

"Yeah, well, same."

"You thought I was a servant. Why?"

"Your shoes, your car, you drink whiskey in a dive bar. Don't act like it's not a stretch."

"And now?"

"You're the mark, aren't you?" I ask.

He nods. I drop my head to the table to muffle my groan.

"You've got to be kidding me. This wasn't part of the deal."

He chuckles low, the sound vibrating over my skin.

"I guess we're both full of surprises."

His thumb brushes over my knuckles. My eyes pull to the light sweep, then up to him. He doesn't seem to realize the touch.

When his eyes darken in a subtle but unmistakable interest, I meet his gaze with as much defiance as I can muster. I refuse to let him see anything but my disdain. But it's hard to be intimidating when you're naked and strapped over a table.

"Who sent you?" he asks.

"Said his name was Santa Claus," I smirk. "Should've known the bastard was lying."

"Don't make this worse."

"What are you gonna do, spank me?"

The sarcasm slips out before I can stop it.

But I don't expect the calm in his voice when he says, "If that's how you want this to go, I accept your suggestion."

Wait, what?

He steps backward, breaking the touch. The air between us tightens, sharp and electric. I twist sideways, bracing for a hit.

Smack. The sting booms across my rear end before I even register he's moved.

"Ow! Are you insane?"

He tilts his head. "I prefer the term unconventional. But if this is how your people conduct interrogations, who am I to challenge tradition? Let's try again. Who sent you?" He steps back slightly, his voice smooth and way too calm.

Before I can react, his fist is in my hair, pinning me back to the table. I huff, the sound sharp and startled before it dissolves into his growl. It only fills my ears briefly before his hand paddles down on my other cheek. He delivers another sharp smack, this time to the opposite cheek, and I can't stop my groan.

A laugh bubbles out of my throat, edged with hysteria. "Is this the part where I'm supposed to beg for mercy? Well, I won't do it! You'll have to do better than that. I might like this. Harder, big guy—I can take it."

He doesn't take the bait.

"Let's start with you telling me your real name."

Instead of answering, I look away and lower my forehead to the table.

"If that's how you want to do this, *lil mani*."

"Whatever, you hit like an accountant."

His hand comes down again and has a real bite. A retort dances on the tip of my tongue, but that last hit has me seeing stars, and I decide to swallow it.

I have only a couple of breaths before his hand lands again. With my skin already tender, the sting takes off, spreading deeper into my tissue. Then he strikes again, each time pounding the pain deeper, inflaming my ass until my head spins.

How many swats was that? It feels like dozens.

I wobble, dazed, trying to ride the edge of the pain, so when the warmth of his hands replaces the sting, I can't seem to help but push into him.

"Tell me your name."

Tears fill the corners of my eyes, not from the pain, but his tenderness. I croak out one word: "Nadia."

"Who was the buyer?" he asks again.

"You're pretty terrible at torturing. Don't you know people respond better to rewards for good behavior than punishments for bad?"

I roll my shoulders back as far as his grip allows.

"It's called positive reinforcement. Look it up."

"If I'm so terrible, why are you so wet?" He responds with a tilt of his head.

Without shifting my panties, he traces the edge of

the lace, gathering the slick moisture from between my legs.

"What do you want, applause?" Damn.

His gaze doesn't flinch. He leans in, his breath stirring my hair, warm and maddening.

"I might not have shared intimacies with anyone, but even I know what that means."

"Wait. What? You've never..."

Then my brain does a hard reset. My mouth parts as the big guy licks his finger clean. Slowly. Intentionally, like he's savoring his proof.

I turn my head, but not fast enough to hide my blush.

"Excellent, Nadia. What kind of rewards would you find suitable?" he asks, voice a velvety promise.

I hesitate, my mind finally catching up to the moment. "Freedom."

"What else?" he asks.

"Access to your safe."

"What else?" he asks again, rolling his eyes.

"I'm starting to think your 'what else' isn't an à la carte option but your way of saying 'not going to happen.'"

"That's not true. You'll have your freedom."

"But the safe is a no."

"Depends." He shrugs and steps back, distancing himself.

I want to cry for him to come back. What I wouldn't give for those gentle hands to keep playing with my skin.

"That doesn't sound like a hard no. Can we negotiate?" I squeeze my eyes closed, trying to keep my focus and control.

"That depends. Are you still criticizing my methods?"

"Okay. So maybe your technique isn't total garbage."

A beat.

"You want a review? Four stars. Would misbehave again."

"Who was the buyer?"

I exhale, shaky, the edges of truth and lies bleeding into each other.

"I don't know," I whisper.

He pulls back. His absence left my body chilled.

For a breath, I wonder if his touch leaving my body makes him feel as cold and aching as its absence does to me.

"Lying will only make this harder for you."

"What's harder than this?" I snap. Frustration sharpens my voice, though it can't hide the tremors wracking me.

His answering smile is slow, dark, and utterly predatory.

"You're about to find out."

14

A PRICE TO PAY

"**N**o, wait," she said quickly. "This isn't how we interrogate people. That's... not a thing here. Haven't you ever heard of Truth or Dare?" Her voice was dry, hoarse.

She hadn't stopped looking at my mouth since I'd tasted her spicy honey. Like iron drawn to a magnet, my hands found their way back to her lifted ass, craving the smooth flesh beneath them. The warmth of her plump cheeks helped battle the madness, clawing its way through me. I wanted to rush. I wanted to take. I wanted everything I'd spent years denying myself.

But I held the reins tight and kept my restraint firm, kneading her reddened skin instead. Every moment spent chasing answers stole time from what I truly desired: her. And yet, when her back arched, lifting her higher into my hands, time slowed. I could've lost myself in her reactions all night.

I narrowed my eyes. "Truth or what?"

Interrogation had always been a necessary evil, one

I felt ill-suited for. But *this*? This game? Dangerous. So, even with mischief gleaming in her stare, I chose to play along.

"It's a sacred American tradition," she said deadpan. "Used in high-stake interrogations."

She tugged against me, stubborn as ever, though her breath came in unsteady waves. Her body trembled with tension, yet it yielded all the same. She might've wanted to challenge me, but her body whispered other truths. And I listened.

I studied her like she'd invoked divine law or declared a parlay. "What purpose does it serve?" I ask.

She was right. I needed to change methods.

I couldn't keep touching her.

"It's a contest of will," Nadia explained. "The offended party—you—gets to ask 'Truth or Dare.' I picked one. If I say 'Truth,' you get to ask anything. As specific as you want. And I have to answer honestly. Then we switch."

Willpower was something I found myself sorely lacking lately.

At the first strike, her thighs clenched. Her ass lifted, begging for more. I'd started to enjoy her punishment far too much. Gasp. Clench. Lift. Again. Even on my most brutal blow, she never cowered. Naked and defenseless, she'd shown more fight than many armed warriors I'd faced.

After her challenge, I found myself less bothered by the gargoyle's presence and more bothered by my own dysfunction.

"And if you choose 'Dare'?"

"Then you tell me something to do, and I'll do it. We draw the line at death, dismemberment, and permanent damage," she added quickly. "It's all very civilized."

I narrowed my eyes. "And if you lie?"

She hesitated. "Then... I suppose I'd forfeit, but it's never happened because it's so sacred."

"If you lie," I said, voice low, "we return to the spanking."

After a brief pause, she nodded. "That's... fair, I guess."

She held out her pinkie. I eyed it warily.

"It seals the deal," she added. "Only monsters break a pinkie promise."

I hesitated, then lifted my hand and hooked my smallest finger around hers. Calculated. Controlled.

"Truth or Dare?" I asked.

"Dare," she replied.

"As I expected."

"What?" Her brow furrowed.

"You know I want the truth from you, so you avoid it."

"Dare's my middle name," she said, blinking up at me, feigning innocence. I didn't buy it for a moment.

"Unlikely."

"You'll never know unless I pick Truth."

"Jump on one foot," I commanded.

"That's not how it works."

"Are you refusing?"

"No. But you have to say: I *dare* you..."

"Nadia, I dare you to jump on one foot."

She jumped. Once.

"I didn't say stop."

"You didn't specify how long. Don't worry, you'll get the hang of it. My turn. Truth or Dare?"

"Truth."

"As I expected. Lame. Are you a prince or something?"

"I was. I lost my right when my brother won the Trials."

"You speak of losing your crown with less emotion than I'd talk about missing a cabbage sale. And I *hate* cabbage."

"My people aren't known for emotional displays," I said with a shrug. "Besides, being King was expected. I'm glad I lost. Truth or Dare?"

"Riiight. Dare."

"I dare you to stop picking Dare."

"You'd waste a dare on *that*? Fine! Truth or Dare?"

"Truth."

"How'd you escape those bikers so fast?"

"We run in the same circles."

"That's not a truth. That's a side-step. You forfeit if you don't answer."

"Hm. Then the truth is, we both frequent *In Absentia*. It's a sanctuary for my kind and theirs. They wouldn't dare challenge me."

"So, they didn't jump you?"

"Not even a hop. Truth or Dare?" I lifted a brow.

"Truth."

"How did you wind up here?" I caught the mischief in her eyes and pressed again. "How did you know about me?"

"I stumbled on the intel. Heard about a rich old recluse in a mansion, did a Google search, and the second I saw the place, I knew I wanted it."

Something flickered inside me. Pride, maybe. I shifted from holding her down to simply looking at her.

"Dare," I said before she could ask.

"Dare?"

"That's what I said."

Would she go easy—or go for blood?

"I dare you to let me go."

There it was. "Right now?"

"No time like the present."

I looked away, pretending to consider it.

Then she frowned at me stern and impatient.

"You don't want to break the rules," she tutted.

I let the moment linger, then released her wrist.

Triumph lit her face. That warmth, unearned as it was, chipped away at the jaded edges inside me.

"Hey! I said—"

"To let you go. And I did. In part. Your wrist is free."

"That's not what I meant."

"You'll learn. Specificity matters."

"Funny. Truth or Dare?" she snapped.

Her brief victory faded. I regretted its loss.

"Truth."

"What did you do to me while I was passed out?"

I hesitated. Slowly, she turned to face me. My gaze drifted from her legs to her eyes. My body tightened, and she shivered.

"You're scared of my answer. Why?"

"Because you took my clothes off and tied me down like a fucking weirdo!"

"I stripped you to check for injuries. To make sure you didn't have any more surprises. Then I had to hide you because you smelled like honey and spice. I was worried I'd lose control. I tied you down to keep you safe."

"Yeah, that doesn't inspire confidence in your intentions. What are you doing?" Her voice lifted as my forearm brushed her leg.

"I'm letting you go. Out of your bindings, at least."

"Why?"

"Because I want your compliance. Not your fear."

And maybe, just maybe, it was better if she wasn't so easy to touch.

Nadia swallowed hard and sank back down. I reached for the strap around her ankle. I tried to be gentle, but it felt reverent. The look in her eyes, all cloudy with suspicion, stopped me cold.

I couldn't face it. So, I didn't.

"You're not very sexually experienced, are you?" she asked. The barb landed. And after everything I'd done, I didn't blame her.

"I've had a lifetime of experience, but none of it's been sexual." I reached for her other ankle. My fingers wrapped around it gently. "Now, my turn. Truth or Dare?"

"Dare."

"I dare you to tell nothing but the truth for the rest of the day."

"I don't think you can do that." She shook her head.

"No, *you* don't think you can do that," I said, rising to my feet.

"Oof. Shots fired. That hurts, big guy. And here I thought you'd dare me to kiss you."

"A dare for a kiss?" My lips twitched. "Careful what you ask for, little thief."

The way she moved forward with intention lit a fuse in my mind.

"Well?" I asked.

"Well, what? You asked for the truth." She smiled over her shoulder. Free now, she walked toward the gargoyle. "Truth or Dare?"

My brow furrowed. I took a breath.

"Truth."

"Do you always fall apart that fast, or was that just a special moment between us?"

I blinked. "What do you mean?"

She tilted her head. Calculating.

"The hand job in the kitchen. Was that typical, or should I be calling the Guinness Book?"

My brow furrowed, not in anger but in confusion.

"You're muddying the question. Say it plainly."

Nadia shrugged. "Fine. When I touched your dick, you came in, what, eight seconds? Is that your usual? Because, honestly, it sorta messes with the whole 'stoic and dangerous' thing you've got going."

"Was I supposed to pace myself? I wasn't aware there were rules. You should've told me if you wanted it to last longer."

Her mouth opened, then shut again.

My reply must not have been what she'd expected.

"Your turn. Truth or Dare?" I asked, refusing to be diverted.

"Truth."

I nodded, pleased. "Tell me exactly how you imagined this heist, from the bar to the big score."

"Easy. Get your attention. Steal your card. Break in, find the safe, and clean you out in thirty minutes or less. Then make the drop-off."

"I want the name." It is a demand, plain and simple.

"Don't cheat," she said.

"I'm not. I said tell me exactly. You're avoiding. You're not even following your own sacred rules." I frown faintly. "I suppose we'll have to go with your original suggestion."

"My what?"

THE LITTLE THIEF had no idea how far over her head she was. Even after her beating, she challenged me. Again, I reminded myself that she had no idea how threadbare my control was—one wrong move.

But when she looked at me over her shoulder, there was a dangerous glint in her eyes that warned me maybe she did. Silly little mortal, tempting something she couldn't possibly handle. That look—the brave-faced defiance—urged me to meet her recklessness with my own.

Surely, she couldn't withstand the force of my desires. But when those eyes caught mine, I wanted to try.

Nadia. A little minx.

At least now I knew what I could do with her. She was stronger than she looked, and the truth of that tempted me. At first, I'd been so sure she would shatter under my hand, her bones as fragile as a single pane of glass compared to my dense skeleton.

But when her hips swung to meet my smack, my imagination had somersaulted into fantasy. If I thought I'd looked my fill of the naked mortal while she was passed out, I'd been dead wrong.

No matter how much I'd wanted to keep her bent over and shove my tongue between those plump cheeks, I could never forget how completely incompatible we were. Still, my fingers refused to forget how silky and firm she felt.

My hand twitched, but I pulled it behind me. I closed the distance between us with each step until I pressed her into the edge of the table. She would yield, eventually. I was sure of it. What human in their right mind wouldn't be scared of me?

But my mind wasn't on all the ways I could scare her or even all the ways I could make her talk. If she'd been any of the creatures I hunted, I wouldn't have a smidge of indecision. All I could think about was picking her up, wrapping those curvaceous legs around my waist, and driving her into the wall. I wanted to pin her there like that's where she belonged.

What would she have done if I dropped to my knees and buried my face between her thighs? She'd tasted just as she smelled—sweet and spicy—and I'd wanted to explore more.

Whatever she saw on my face must have startled her because she jumped into motion. Pushing away, she desperately struggled, trying to break my hold. My eyes dipped back down to her jiggling ass, and I nearly lost control.

She'd said positive reinforcement worked better than spanking. Maybe if I gave her something small that she wanted, she'd behave? But she also suggested spanking, so that could be another trick.

"If you stop struggling, I'll give you what you want."

"Are you going to stop spanking and start stroking? Maybe if you touch me nice, I'll consider being more helpful."

Start stroking?

My hand lowered to the front seam of her lace panties.

Immediately, she stilled. Hmm. Let's see if it really did work better.

"Like this?"

I could have sworn that when her hips shifted, deepening the touch, she whispered, "Fuck, yes."

Very good, little thief. I didn't mind if I did.

Then my thumb brushed against her pussy, but this time she didn't lean away. Her legs shifted apart. She was slick and warm, and I hadn't felt like a conquering hero until my fingers slid under the lace of her panties. I trailed the seam of her until my fingers burrowed into her folds. Her wetness spread along the pads of my fingers, saturating the fabric until it coated my knuckles.

Her hips rolled, guiding me deeper. Her breathy

moan curled in the space between us. Why did it sound like an invitation? I froze. Her flushed face focused in a way I'd only seen in the dark corners of the subways. She looked as surprised by her reaction as I was.

What did I do next?

"Well... maybe you're not bad at this after all."

Slowly, warmth filled my chest. Was this what winning felt like? After all, there couldn't have been a better way to coax information out of her. My thoughts spiraled when Nadia's hands wrapped around my wrist. Would she push away?

Instead, she shifted my hand until my palm rested fully against her cleft. Hot silk clenched around my finger; at that moment, nothing could distract me from her. With a slow push, Nadia arched her back, and it opened her up for more of my penetration. Wet heat turned into folded silk.

She gasped, her hips continuing to swivel when my finger curled to stroke her channel. Her hand flattened around my forearm, holding on, while her other cupped her breast. My mouth watered at the sight of her flushed chest and face, her eyes closed, lost in my touch.

Around me, her inner muscles squeezed, and her nails buried into my arm. Her hips swept back and forth, lost in abandon. Sweet gods, I get it now.

Then my phone chimed at my side.

I frowned down at the cracked device. I almost ignored whoever it was. For a little while, I just wanted to be selfish with my time. I only had so much of it with this mortal before I would need to let her go.

But I didn't ignore the call. Duty came first. Only a few people knew my number, and none would contact me without a reason. But I refused to let go of our connection, so I dug the phone from my pocket with my free hand and held it up to my ear, careful with the fragile thing.

Nadia's sigh was long and weary.

I'd never struggled this hard to fulfill my duty in all my years. But its weight was always there, casting its long shadow over even the most intimate moments.

My face tightened as a new kind of pressure-filled my chest: frustration. My jaw ached from clenching, and the tension in my chest grew so tight it nearly made breathing difficult. I told myself to relax, but that didn't help, not with Nadia's eyes fixed on me.

After a few seconds, Garrett's deep voice filled the earpiece. I strained to make out his words, but the metallic crunching in the background nearly drowned him out. I only heard fragments: *surrounded, trapped, help.*

Since the advent of human technology, I'd ensured my topside warriors had everything they needed to stay safe and connected. Phones weren't the only contraption I used. I scrolled through the small list of apps on my phone until I found the tracking one. The dot blinked briefly, just long enough for me to see what street he was on, then went dark.

Not good.

As much as I wanted to shove into the little thief, spread her across the table, and play with her lustrous skin until she made that keening noise again, I couldn't.

One of my warriors was in trouble. That always came first.

Sighing, I pulled my hand out of her panties.

Nadia immediately scampered back and watched me in silence. Was it in my imagination, or did she already have a calculating glower?

15

LEFT TO FREEZE

When I think I've made some progress, he shoves his phone in his pocket and looks me over like he wants to take a mental picture. *Yeah, eat it up. When I leave here, we'll see who ends up on top.*

Then, without a word, he turns to leave.

What the hell?

"What? You're going to leave me hanging like that?" I square off after straightening myself up. I still feel hot and bothered, but my growing irritation already cools me down.

"If you want more, try saying please." Malrik looks up with a flat brow. Is that a joke?

"You're going to leave me high and dry?"

"You weren't dry a minute ago."

"I mean—is that all I get?"

"It's not my fault you can't beat my record."

"Wait, I played by your rules. I did as you asked. Let me go!"

"I don't think you realize this is not a game, little thief."

"Then just kill me and get it over with!" I challenge, then start to squirm under the renewed intensity in his eyes. It's easier to rally against him when I don't have to contend with his heady stare. Especially with my body still on fire and thrumming from his exploration.

"You're going to help me find whoever sent you after me. Call it a fair trade. When I'm done, you walk free."

"Fair? How long do you suppose that will take?" I ask.

"It's hard to say. We'll start after I return and deal with those who target me."

"What do you mean, start? Wait! What do you mean, return? At least let me take a shower!" I demand.

"It'll have to wait until I get back."

"You... you tricked me."

"No, I didn't. Remember the rules: we never specify a time. You'll get out of the basement and get your shower—later."

After a sharp inhale, I pull away from the table, his hand clamping around my arm in a vise grip as he leads me back toward the edge of the table he initially chained me to. Digging in my heels, I struggle against him.

"Stop. If you hurt yourself further, I'll be vexed."

"You'll be vexed? Who are you?" I ask, ignoring his order. I twist and turn, but neither his arms nor his stance budge. His brows bridge as his fingers stroke the smeared blood on my wrist. It's only my hiss of pain that gentles his hold.

"Don't tie me back down, please."

Malrik's sigh is long and suffering as I look up into the copper flecks of his eyes. He stares down at me, looking so forceful that my stomach fills with butterflies. "Please, I won't do anything bad! Just don't keep me down here. It's cold and wet and bad for my skin. I'll get sick! I swear, I won't take anything!"

A war brews behind his eyes. And I already know it isn't going in my favor. It ends with a firm shake of his head while he walks toward the stairs.

"Nadia, I just don't believe you. You're the kind of woman who can't help herself. You're just a weak-willed girl with a smart mouth. And I must go, so I won't be here to watch you." Even though his words are adamant, his hand hesitates around the doorknob.

"Please, don't," I whisper as the door closes with a loud click. "If you think I'm terrible now, you should see me after you break your word! I swear, you won't get an honest word out of me! Gah!" I pound my fists against the door, which helps to release some of the fear and desperation I've been trying to control.

I swallow hard around my now sore throat. The basement is quiet as I wait to hear Malrik's response. Or maybe the sound of his tires peeling out. Anything.

But there was nothing.

Only my scratchy breath and my pounding heart.

My skin prickles with a chill as I fight my useless instinct to run. I clench my fists in frustration until my fingers grow numb. Taking a deep breath, I lean back and race into the door. I stiffen my shoulder and brace for the impact.

The door jerks securely in its frame, and I sail back in two wide and wobbling steps before I fall on my bare ass. Hard. The lace panties provide no cushion, protection, or barrier to the cold concrete floor.

"Gah! I hate this place!" I slam my fists on my thighs. "This fucking man. Kidnaps me? Wrong move." He doesn't even know how bad I can get. But he's about to find out.

"Mark my words, Malrik. You will regret this!"

I storm back up the stairs, building momentum to kick at the frame around the lock—barely a rumble. I try three more times and stop when the pain radiates down my hip.

As soon as I slow down, I feel the first chill. The temperature in the basement is about twenty degrees shy of comfortable, and there isn't a single blanket. Inhaling sharply, I sigh only to see my breath. Grimacing, I sit beside the gargoyle, hoping no creepy crawlies get me with him at my back. With a protest from my tight muscles, I pull my knees to my chest and sit at the gargoyle's feet.

"I hate this guy. What an asshole, you know? Keeping me here. Naked! If I get sick, I promise I will be wretched." I don't know when I decide the stone guardian is trapped in this basement with me. But we are now buddies. "Like, who does that? I know one thing for certain: I entered this house on my terms and will leave the same way." As I make the vow, a new determination fills me.

With another thump on my thigh, my knees clench.

The cold of the gargoyle's paws blissfully pulls the stinging pain from my paddled ass. Unfortunately, that's the only warmth I have left. After another shiver, I know I have to get up.

Pain flashes like cracked glass spreading over my skin, lighting my entire body up like LED bulbs, a bright show of cold sparks. Out of the small pancake-like window, I see heavy falling snow. Of course. Isn't this the perfect time to be wearing nothing but my undies?

Another full-body shake sends me over the edge. "Ahharrraaaaa!" I screech. Even though my throat feels like a horror slasher prop, my mood is much improved. Clutching my throat, I crawl back to my stone guardian's feet.

It might just be my imagination, or maybe my body temperature has already dropped. Either way, it feels warmer against the guard's thick marble legs. It must be from when I sat down last time. Regardless, I cuddle into the space where the giant wing tucks into the thigh, hoping that if Malrik returns, I'll be hidden.

There's no way I can sleep, but I close my eyes and pretend I'm warm on the beach. And on that beach stands Malrik's rigid form.

"No. How dare that bastard. He strips me down, violates me, and then beats me..." I lie to everyone else, but I don't lie to myself. "Okay, he violates my privacy by taking my clothes off, but he doesn't take advantage, and he doesn't beat me. He spanked me. And it's... sexy. Which is both frustrating and confusing."

The thought of his rough hand touching so lightly down my back brings a tingle to my core. I pull my knees into my chest and squeeze my legs. Then I remember his thumb tracing my wetness and how he licked his digit clean. My world knocks as I thump my forehead against my knees.

"No! I am glad he doesn't touch me and make it sexual. Really. He's just extremely rugged, and I think it's great that he seems to have the self-control of a monk or something. Maybe he's a monk or a weird priest. Am I into that?" I ask out loud, tugging my lower lip between my cold teeth.

It's a ridiculous statement. Of course, I want to defile him. What more could a girl want than to lead a good man into the dark, wicked forbidden? To grab him by his belt and spin him into a world of decadence, of seduction, of forever passion. I want to draw him deeper into corruption—to take what I want and leave him high and dry, moaning for more.

Once I figure out how to crack whatever kind of security system he has, I'll use it to get to his safe. No regrets.

"I'm going to find a way out of here," I mutter into my chest. The shiver shakes my upper body, but it's happened so many times already that I barely notice.

Eventually, I tell myself I won't take advantage of the curiosity burning behind the sheer wall of his control. Then, with a jaw-popping yawn, I tuck back into myself, closing my eyes again.

This time, I'm ready for the towering, muscle-bound, steady-eyed warrior type. In my dream world, his square jaw and a slow-as-molasses smile warm me because he is not Malrik. And when he sweeps me into his arms, I bask in the embrace. He's hard and sun-warmed, and as he turns us in a slow, body-hugging spin with a beautiful sunset backdrop—

My unknown, faceless beach lover finally lays us down on my beach towel. His legs and hips press against me as his thick arms brace over my head. As he looks down at me, the metallic flecks in his eyes catch the last rays of the ruddy sun before his lips lower to mine. They hover before making contact, then pull back in a teasing withdrawal.

The heat of his body cocoons me as we lock eyes. I want him to turn up the heat. I'm ready. Instead, he grazes over my lips in a chaste kiss, turning his attention to my neck rather than giving me the sink-into-me passionate embrace I desire.

I groan but turn to give him access. My body rolls like magnets to his roaming grip.

Take it further. Take me. I want to shout and pull at the hands of my beach lover until he turns from his unhurried exploration to the possessive grip I crave.

His other hand cups my neck, supporting me as I fall deeper into his kiss.

But then, Malrik's gruff admission ricochets: "I might not have shared intimacies with anyone, but even I know what that means."

Then, just as I decide that's how I want this phantasmal daydream to go. My kiss trails to the thick cords of my lover's neck and quickly turns into a claim. The hands that hold me now palm me, pulling me closer and pressing me into the warm sand as his fingers delve under my skimpy bathing suit waistband.

"Do you want this as much as I do?" Malrik asks.

Yes! But instead of answering, I roll my hips forward, forcing his inquisitive fingers to explore further as I slant my lips across his once more.

"Not yet, little thief, not until I get my answers."

"Damn it!" My eyes snap open, and I roll out of the statue, but my legs don't cooperate, and I spill at the gargoyle's feet. The seductive daydream does well to warm up my core, but even in the dream world, Malrik is a frustrating ass. But then steel glitters as the first brush of moonlight trails across the floor.

My hairpin. Sweet nothings and high cholesterol, thank you! I reach down to pick up the delicate pin, but both my hands are stiff. I do the only thing I can: stuff my hands in my bra and cup my ta-tas. But even if they are cold, it takes a while before my fingertips feel right enough to pick up the thin stickpin.

My fingers are still too stiff to pick that lock. "I'm so cold." I start to cry. The first tear becomes a warm welcome as it travels down my cheek. I've never been one to cry over silly things, but a swell of discouragement fills me.

I pace back and forth until the early morning frost starts clinging to the windows. I clutch myself tight. I've been gone for a while. Would anyone notice? Chills run down my back, and I shake my shoulders to chase them away.

I could die here, and the only people who know are the guy who kidnapped me and the others who black-mailed me into going after him. I'm on my own, just like I always have been. I'll do whatever it takes to survive.

But first... I need a nap.

16

———

TORN BETWEEN DUTY AND DESIRE

I shook my head, trying to block out the soft, broken whisper, but Nadia's voice kept playing repeatedly. *"Please don't,"* she whispered. It was a plea tangled with vulnerability and resignation, as if she couldn't afford to let go of hope. My jaw pops as my teeth grind; I clenched my hands into fists, barely holding back from using my stone sense to check in on her.

I turned my attention back to the road. Clouds were rolling in, which meant there was bound to be another snowstorm. I couldn't afford to be distracted.

But my thoughts kept drawing me back to my anxious body and her. I ached to explore her. The promise of it built a heat inside me like a volcano on the verge of eruption. Knowing her devious hands had pilfered through my home sent a shockwave of unexpected pleasure through me.

It was impossible to forget the sight of her in my

kitchen, her eyes flashing with panic but still determinedly holding me like a knife. The memory of that look nearly stopped me from leaving the basement.

Chaotic.

Blissfully unpredictable.

She would exhaust herself. Honestly, the best thing for her was some sleep. Humans needed that, didn't they?

As long as the drive was, finding Garrett's last location was twice as difficult. After another tight storm drain finally opened, I knew I was close when a giant wasp spawn greeted me.

The dark servant rushed around the cavern, burning something behind the creature.

The spawn attacked with a single-minded determination. Its pincers spread wide and cut the stale air with scissor-like chops. Another one of the dark servants' grim inventions.

The dark-robed servant remained in the background. Even covered in shabby, tattered cloth, I could see through the veil enough to recognize that the dark servant was of the fourth realm.

Why it was topside in the fifth realm was beyond me. Maybe it was some kind of mortal oceanic creature desperate for immortality.

The spawns were insignificant compared to their dark servant caretakers. Without the servant to mend them, the spawn wouldn't be able to heal and get their upgrades. Despite the three-hundred-pound arthropod standing in my way, I pushed forward. I turned up my internal resonance, locking my feet into the stone beneath me. Step by step, I moved forward, a stiff arm out, sword arm raised in defense as I approached the fires.

Return now. The mortal needs assistance. An unfamiliar voice punches into my head.

Who is this? I demanded.

Ezekiel, who do you think?

For a long second, I didn't place the name, but the fact that his voice was clear in my head could mean only one thing: a gargoyle.

"Ezekiel?" In all our years, I never heard the third gargoyle speak. If it weren't for the life I sensed in the statue, I would have thought the leader was nothing more than an ornate antique.

You left your mortal naked in the basement. In the winter.

Kinda busy right now, I responded, holding off the three-foot stinger flexing to impale me.

She's suffering. Fix it.

The wasp pressed down on me, and black and yellow streaks no longer filled my vision. Now, all I had was the incessant thwapping of the wasp's wings as they beat at my sides, showering me with broken glass and rust.

A thick cloud of dust burned my eyes. Instinctively, I blinked hard and fast, but it only made the pain spread. I was left battling defensively until my eyes cleared.

Darkness enveloped my vision except for light brown and yellow smears.

Trepidation sobered me. It helped me focus. It forced me to prioritize.

I needed my blade, which was stuck in the creature's neck joint, locking the head from swiveling to bite. Releasing my hold on the stinger, I let the sharp and slender stylets cut into my side; the venom they pumped burned but wouldn't prove lethal in small amounts. As it attacked, instinctively taking advantage, my sword's grip slid closer, almost within reach.

Pain seared through me, hot and fast. But the ticking clock of worry drove me forward. I pulled the creature in, spearing myself in the process. But finally, I could reach past its slaps. I snapped both sets of wings like dried spaghetti noodles.

The glass shattered against me, bursting like sparklers. Some were as fine as dust, leaving a wake of minor cuts on my arms, shoulders, and face. Then, finally, with the constant rain of dust and shimmering debris, I grabbed the handle of my blade.

Once my weapon was back in my hands, the kill went quickly.

When things started to come into focus, the dark servant was gone. Damn it! During the struggle, he'd gotten away. My only lead to finding Garrett and the best way to end this infestation was gone.

A failure like this wouldn't have happened if I wasn't distracted. Weakened. Cracked.

Any evidence of what went on down here was burned to ash. Instead of feeling frustrated, a quiet wash of relief filled my chest. Now I could check on her.

I can only hope that I'm not too late.

Immediately, I separated a part of my consciousness and tuned into my home. Having a split focus in the field was dangerous, but I didn't want to risk hurting the girl, especially on her first night. Nadia was a mortal, one with a stronger will than her body. I didn't know why I thought I could keep her without risking permanent damage to her.

What did I know of humans?

When I connect to the stone in my home, I see Nadia. She lay on the floor at the gargoyle, Ezekiel's feet. The sentry had never left my basement and hadn't spoken in over seven hundred years, chimed in, acting like he knew mortals so well. But he was right—she didn't look good. Blanched of color, the little thief's lips were tinged blue.

Turning from the image of her, I started the furnace. It was a system I hadn't turned on as long as I'd lived here. What use did I have for heat when I felt nothing? But mortals needed to stay warm. I should have remembered that.

There were many things mortals needed to stay alive. I'd taken the human captive, and I would have to ensure my little thief was well cared for. I needed to do better.

I hoped I hadn't done too much to dull her sharp tongue. The thought of her losing that edge made something shift inside me. Thinking back on the glint in her eyes, my stomach dropped. She enjoyed testing me, and I couldn't help but wonder if I only thought I had control. Maybe she was stronger than I'd given her credit for. Maybe it was a trick.

But she didn't move when I lifted the stone underneath her, tucked her into the now grumbling gargoyle's arms, and moved them both by the fiery furnace. She didn't move. The lift and transfer weren't smooth or quiet, as I had to build up the stone underneath her to lift her into the arms of Ezekiel.

I wished I could shout or say anything, but I was transient in this form, connected only to the stone I shaped. I couldn't control some parts of the house, but luckily, this basement was not one of them.

But even with complete control, I was powerless to do more. Pulling back into my body, I had to decide: a fellow warrior or my mortal? I'd never struggled to choose my duty before, and the indecision inside me felt crippling.

I'd already searched the area where his signal shut down with no new leads. I should keep my nose to the ground and find out where they might have taken my brother-in-arms. But Nadia's pale lips wore my patience thin. Taking off, I pinned the location, vowing to return once I knew she was safe.

Never in my life had I turned away from my duty, but as I drew closer and a new anxiety filled my chest, I realized I never cared like this. Or I never cared before this. Another discovery tumbled through me and left me hollow like an over-mined mountain.

A new and different sickness settled over me as I left the subterranean tunnel and returned to my car. It reminded me of what happens when the Earth's magnetic field suddenly weakens—like my Stoneborn body was being pulled apart.

But instead of weightlessness, it was a sinking heaviness. A tether. And it dragged my awareness back to the little thief I'd left unconscious in my basement.

I slammed my foot on the gas, the engine roaring as snow-tipped trees blurred by. The distance between us stretched unbearably, and a sick feeling twisted deep in my gut.

Had my selfishness harmed her?

Nadia might be a thief, but she didn't deserve to die because of my ignorance; I wanted to escape my existence for a little while. It was irrational and reckless.

And if she survived, I knew the smart and right thing to do was let her go.

I'd do anything not to feel like this again. No amount of surprise or amusement was worth this dread.

Damn her for chipping away at the stone I was born from.

My kind was never meant to feel—not truly.

Emotion was a flaw mortals carried in their blood, just beneath the skin, too supple to survive the world they lived in.

But she cracked open something I never knew was buried inside me.

And now that I hear the silence of my world, I can't ignore the hollow ache that's been echoing for centuries.

She only knew how to manipulate. I only knew how to hunt. I should let her go and find someone more manageable. Someone less devious.

Keeping her was a terrible idea.

Even unconscious, she held my control—my focus.

Then the thought struck me: I used to scoff at humans, watching how their emotions ruled them.

How awful it must be—to care, to worry constantly.

It hadn't even been a day. And already, I was a lesser man for it.

"Damnable human," I muttered, tapping my fist on the steering wheel.

Another dent marred the once-perfect circle.

Damn it! I'd had this vehicle for how many years and never so much as scratched it. I forced myself to stay focused and to rule my wayward attention with an iron grip. I couldn't let the human rattle me.

"Who does she think she is, stealing her way into my life? Ruining everything."

But the angry fizz in my gut didn't last long. My life had been broken long before I met her. Perhaps that was why I'd taken her. She was everything my people and I were not. Yes, with her coy smiles and hands hiding knives, Nadia was unpredictable.

Beautifully so.

A part of me had always known. Spanking her wasn't about punishment. It was about the way she fought against it, the way she arched and resisted, no matter how hard the stroke. She'd given me free rein over her body before she knew how dangerous I could be. Nadia responded to my touch like a magnet; whether feathery, hard, punishing, or teasing, she pushed back, all but demanding more.

Glancing down at the bulge in my pants, I looked back to the road, ignoring the telltale sign. Stoneborn didn't lust. Yet, instead of listening to reason, the thing throbbed harder. Damn that woman!

"Be boring. Think boring things, like the maze of subterranean lairs carved out of the abandoned subway system." Not how it felt when I peeled off the little thief's dress only to find a silken body wrapped in lace, with the peek-a-boo detail hinting at the delicate, sensitive skin underneath. Or how desire had warmed her skin at my touch. Think boring things like hunting and tracking, not the swell of honey between her legs that called to me and tasted like heaven and Hell soaking my finger.

Damn it! No! Boring things. Think like a Stoneborn, not a randy human.

But the drive was long, and the mental control my peers once lauded me for was nothing but a fractured web that always led back to one thing: the fragile human passed out in my basement.

Regret hit me like a boulder. If the mortal was alright and I turned her away, I'd never know all the secrets she kept or the pride men got when their woman unraveled for them. The heavy feeling in my stomach hit rock bottom and sank into place with a thud.

Nothing could have stopped me from taking her— except an eon-long lifetime of integrity. Her body, bent over the table, was a vision I would never forget. This little mortal thief nearly brought me to my knees and undone centuries of control.

But she was sore. Tired. Restrained. She couldn't say yes, and I wouldn't take what wasn't freely given.

I might not have had experience, but I was not even that much of a monster.

Not yet, at least.

Though maybe I already was, just for wanting her. For lusting after a mortal.

I needed her, even knowing we wouldn't fit. We were wholly incompatible.

But desire didn't grant me rights. Wanting someone wasn't an excuse to take them.

Still, I wanted my thief to be healthy. Safe. Whole. I wanted a yes she could shout, not whisper.

Then I remembered Clarabelle, how fear had flickered in her eyes, how quickly she shrank from Gorvoss. That was never what I wanted.

And just like that, the fire dimmed.

Of course.

When I finally pulled into my drive, I was still going sixty, and loose debris flew in the air as I skidded to a halt. I climbed these steps a million times, but never three at a time. I'd never been so anxious, so worried, that I used my Stoneborn abilities to open doors and lift the stone underfoot to propel me faster.

"Nadia," I shouted before I reached the basement door. The bass of my voice boomed with shocking percussion, but there was no response.

I walked over to the blanket my sister stitched a year before her death, nearly four thousand years ago. Carefully, I unfolded it and took it with me downstairs.

Now that I was home, it was easier to feel the stone.

All the rooms I had shaped left an imprint in my mind. For a second, I didn't feel Nadia's presence.

Like she wasn't here at all.

"Did I kill her?" I ask.

She lives, Ezekiel said.

Then I remembered that Nadia was still in Ezekiel's stone arms and thus blocked from my stone sense. The stomp of my charge eased as soon as I saw her. The blue had faded from her lips, but she still looked unusually pale and lifeless.

What was left of my heart stuttered in my chest. I felt the arrhythmic pound ripple down to my toes. I opened the blanket and took my delicate human out of the immobile statue's arms. Luckily, moving Ezekiel toward the furnace had warmed her up, but her pallid skin was still raised with bumps.

"Did you find what you were looking for?" she asked through a yawn, stretching away the night's stiffness.

She'd tried to tell me not to leave her in the basement.

I hadn't listened.

"No."

"Are you letting me go now?" she asked.

Say yes. Hazariah led. *After what just happened, you know you can't keep her. It's too dangerous for her. You're too much of a hazard to her health and safety.*

With her in my arms, looking up at me with sleepy eyes, I gave the only answer I could. "No."

It was only after Jahzi exclaimed an emphatic *Yes!* While Hazariah groaned, I realized my mistake.

"I mean, yes. Leave now." I dropped her legs to the ground, but she regained her balance slowly. My grip under her shoulders remained not just to help stabilize her but because even after uttering the right words, I wasn't strong enough to be the one to let her go.

COLD SHOULDERS, HOT SHOWERS

"You're saying I can go?"

Suspicion is one of my better traits, but when I search his face for lies, all I see is conflict.

"I think that would be best," he says through clenched teeth.

Oh, now you want me to leave? Now? After I swore revenge?

My glare sharpens, and my vision narrows. I'm not just getting in your safe—I'm getting under your skin and breaking your composure open from the inside.

You pissed off the wrong thief.

"Oh well," I chirp, voice sweet as honey. "That's good to know. I was just about to tell you everything you wanted to know. Whew. Close call." I turn. "Well, bye now."

"Stop."

Malrik hasn't moved an inch. Not since he let me down.

Now he's stone-still, just like the statue beside him.

I turn but don't step away. Yet. If I can get Malrik to turn his attention to Darius, I'll have time to find his treasure. Darius shouldn't mind taking one for the team, and if Malrik happens to get rid of him, then that's all the better. Win-win. "Now, now, you had your chance."

And just like that, I shrug and start to move away. I don't get my first foot down before Malrik's hand grips my biceps. My immediate surge of victory stutters into fear when he pulls me up the stairs.

"What's going on?" I ask in my best 'I'm just a girl' voice.

"I promised you a shower."

Biting my inner cheek, I freeze my face. It's not that difficult, with my cheeks still numb. He leads me to a large bathroom I hadn't bothered inspecting in my initial self-led tour. Before we breach the entryway, the shower turns on.

Weird. Was that another new addition Malrik made to his home?

Next to me, his arms stiffen. Then slowly, he releases his hold, ever so gently, only this time he's already heading back towards the door.

"Truth or dare?" I all but yell as he makes his exit.

"Dare."

"I dare you to stay and prove you're keeping me around for my information and not because you want me."

He looks like he's considering leaving anyway. *What*

will you do, scaredy cat, run away and pretend you didn't hear me?

My hand reaches into the water to test the temperature. I cut through the steam, and the splatter alone was enough to burn. Pulling back, I jerk away. Malrik's already behind me, his arm wrapped around my shoulder, pulling me away from the steam.

"It's not that hot." He frowned.

"No, I'm just that cold; anything even lukewarm feels scalding," I mutter, crossing my hands over my chest.

A different kind of embarrassment fills his face. His eyes lowered, brows drawn in, pulling his lips into a frown.

"I'm sorry." His deep timber almost doesn't register as words, let alone regret.

Did he apologize to me? I pull back to look at him, his eyes avoiding my direction momentarily before locking me in his gaze.

"For kidnapping me?"

"No. For forgetting that cold can damage you."

Damage? Wait, did he forget that people get cold? How is that possible? Where was this guy from?

"That's like saying you forget that we eat."

Again, he stiffens, looking towards the door. "I really have to go."

"So, you're forfeiting. You admit defeat?" Anyone with a shred of ego would never accept those terms.

"No," he denies.

I beam internally.

"If you want my help, you'll honor your dare. I

dared you to watch and pretend you don't want to join me."

At that, a new hardness darkens his eyes. "I'm a man of honor and won't be manipulated."

"I wouldn't dream of trying to manipulate you." I blink up at him with a smile.

Reaching behind myself, I pinch the hooks of my bra. It takes three tries, but finally, it falls off and drops to my feet. I don't have to look to know my nipples are hard and demanding attention.

"I'm claiming one of the spare bedrooms." I assert.

"Sweet molten iron and brimstone, take whatever room you want." He says as he rubs his jaw. His reaction is everything I want and all that I need to see. Immediate slack jaw and body-tensing wonder. That I can work with.

I watch his Adam's apple bob as he swallows a hard gulp.

Bingo. I mean, aw shucks.

"If I get sick because of that little stunt you pulled, leaving me down in your basement, I will make your life miserable, and not just for as long as you want me around, but after that. Long after that."

You can count on it, I vow.

"Just take a shower."

"I'd love to, once you take a seat."

Reluctantly, Malrik stands at the edge of the door, barely inside the bathroom. I watch his thick arms flex as he reaches for the door. As he turns, our eyes connect and hold. My eyes widen in surprise, but I don't look away. *He's going to bolt!* It's not until the bedroom door shuts that I release the body-quaking shiver.

Without glancing at the bathroom door, I close off the room. It's empty. I snoop thoroughly through his room. Maybe he kept the safe in here, somewhere.

I don't find a safe or unusual seam, but I notice he's an organized creature of habit. None of his belongings are out of place. He has everything organized around a four-day schedule. Fingering through his stack of black undershirts, I pull out the bottom one, messing up each shirt above it. Before trying it on, I hesitantly brought the fabric up to my nose. My eyes rolled back, and I buried my nose deeper before pulling it over my head.

I pull it over my head, again appreciating how big he is. Even with my curves, his shirt hits me mid-thigh. That's how he catches me, crouched down, snooping through his drawers.

18

DONUTS AND DECEIT

I looked down at her and swallowed hard. The edges of her ass peeked out from beneath my shirt, and my mouth went dry. Silently, I shook my head, fighting the urge to retreat again. My stance remained firm, and after a moment, I stepped into my room.

"Looking for something else to steal, lil mani?" My hand wrapped around my side as if it were the only thing holding me back.

"Would you think less of me if I said yes?"

Never.

"I'll always appreciate honesty over a lie."

"Well, in that case, yes."

I gritted my teeth and forced my chin up, locking my gaze with hers instead of letting it drift down the long stretch of bare leg she so casually flaunted. It would've been easier if she didn't bite her lip when she saw me.

I needed to clean my wounds and rest, but I

couldn't do that while she was loose. She'd likely try to kill me in my sleep.

"Tell me, Nadia... did I make you regret targeting me yet?"

Her face paled. For a second, I believed she never regretted anything more than stepping into my house. And I hated that thought.

"I regret that you caught me."

I don't. Not yet, anyway. But I don't think Nadia would appreciate how exciting I found her.

"It doesn't please me to keep you here forcefully." I stand at the side of the doorway and wave her out of my room.

"Doesn't it?" she asked, head tilting.

She blatantly ignored my efforts and instead continued to snoop through my belongings.

"It's the nature of my people to be guards and guardians of the iniquitous."

"I'm not iniquitous. I'm barely in my thirties."

"Iniquitous, not antiquitous. I would never comment on your age."

"Yes, you would never dare do something so rude. Kidnapping, on the other hand..."

"You broke in and attacked me. But that's beside the point. You didn't answer my question."

She rolled her shoulders back and lifted a brow. "Regret is just insight a day too late. You set yourself up as a target; it's a shame you're such a cheap bastard who lives like a damned penny pincher. I'd think you'd have the decency to own something worth stealing."

Then she lifted her nose and walked to the blanket

I'd wrapped her in, picking it up between two fingers with theatrical disappointment. I wasn't sure where her attitude came from, but I welcomed the return of her fire.

"Are you blaming me for your predicament?" I asked, tracking her movements as she neared. I smothered my smile until the muscles in my cheeks began to ache.

Behind me I hear the tell tale scrape of stone that signified one of the gargoyles moving. Probably Jahziel trying to eavesdrop. I don' know how I found myself surrounded by so many shameless snoops.

"Where did you go?" she asked instead.

"I got you donuts," I said.

"Don't be ridiculous. Do I look like I eat donuts?" She slid her hands down her rounded hips, showcasing herself. Then, as if she owned the place, the little thief sauntered into the hall without sparing me a glance.

"Then don't eat. That's a great way to keep your figure." I said, just before kicking my bedroom door shut behind me.

A sigh rips through me. I tilt my head back and crack my neck. I feel old.

I let my trench coat drop to the bed and set my sword on it. I sat to untie my boots, but bone knocked against something dense, stopping my progress almost immediately.

Damn, spawn must've done more damage than I thought. All I wanted was to collapse and sleep for days.

"Damn it," I muttered, frustration breaking loose in a low growl.

I braced myself to try again. Then the door creaked open. Nadia stepped inside, her face unreadable. I straightened as best I could despite the pain. Sweat burned down my temple, stinging the cut along my brow.

I expected a gasp. Maybe a shriek. Clarabelle would've fainted.

"Damn. Where do you get your donuts?" the mortal mocked.

My eyes flared—first in surprise, then something closer to defensiveness.

"I can't reach my boots."

"No, it looks like you have a chunk of metal in your side."

I glanced down. Nothing. But when I lifted my arm, I saw it—a shard the size of a post-it note, a quarter-inch thick, lodged between my ribs.

Nadia placed her hands over mine and gently pried them away.

"Don't. Not yet." She vanished into the bathroom, quiet as a ghost rummaging through my things.

When she returned with scissors and peroxide, my body tensed involuntarily. She smiled at the grimace I failed to hide.

"Oh, a flinch? I think I like that you're scared of me."

"I'm not scared. I'm cautious that you'll strike while I'm weakened."

"Typical man. It's just a flesh wound, and you act like you're dying."

She stepped closer, scissors lowered, and I caught her wrist.

"I wouldn't get any ideas, thief."

Instead of pulling away, she looked down at me. "Too late," she murmured. "I've had plenty of ideas since I first met you."

Her gaze didn't waver. After a pause, I released her.

Lowering the scissors to my shirt, she started cutting. I tensed, but her hazel eyes flicked to mine—silent reassurance. Slowly, she sliced through the fabric. The cold metal shocked against raw and inflamed skin.

Her gentleness caught me off guard.

As she peeled away the shirt, her knuckles grazed my stomach. My fingers curled into the sheets, the anger I'd carried earlier dissipating. The morning light caught the lines of my old scars, but she didn't recoil.

Her hand hovered just above my skin. I tensed, but she let the fabric fall instead of touching me. Her gaze mapped my wounds like a surveyor. I fought a flash of shame.

I'd never given much thought to the scars on this human mask. But now as she studied me, my fingers twitched with the urge to cover myself. The insecurity faded when I saw how her gaze lingered. Even bloody, ripped, and scarred, she licked her lower lip and bit it slowly.

She needed to stop doing that.

"That will be all." I nodded toward the door—a reflex—one I regretted.

"Malrik..."

Her voice whispered so lightly I nearly missed it.

I turned, stiff and slow, meeting her gaze. Heat flickered behind her hazel eyes. A warning. A promise. A trap?

She pressed her hand gently to my chest, guiding me back down. After she pulled away, my fists clenched, empty air at my sides. I held onto the warmth of her touch and said nothing. Then I sat back.

It should've felt like defeat. I told Nadia to leave. And here she stayed.

But why did that make my pulse race with the sweetest high?

She positioned herself at my side and rested one hand on my shoulder. "On three... one—" She yanked the shard out.

I sucked in a breath through my teeth as she poured peroxide over the wound.

"No amount of tender nursing will make me forget who and what you are," I say.

"And no amount of sexual teasing will make me forget the horde loot you have. Well, now that we've established, we're only biding our time so we can each get what we want." She smirked. "Can I get back to cleaning this wound?"

"This isn't necessary, Nadia. I'll heal soon enough."

Say nothing more, Hazariah warned.

She'll think you're out of your mind, Jahziel added.

They were right, and those two never agreed on anything. But I don't want to lie to my little thief.

"Of course you will, big guy," she muttered with a chuckle.

"The metal shards will break down, flush themselves out."

"Yeah, okay," she said, distracted. She didn't realize that now that the shard was gone, my wound would begin knitting itself back together, agonizingly slow but steady. By morning, most of the damage would be gone.

Her hands worked quickly, pulling out what she could. Already, my body was healing. As much as I didn't want to lie, I wasn't ready to explain either.

"How did you know how to do this?" I asked, trying to steer her attention elsewhere.

"I took a class once," she said, though her focus never slipped. "Sorry about this," she muttered, using tweezers to dig into the wound.

"You're lying," I said sharply. I wanted Nadia's eyes on me—not the damage. The sting in her expression stilled my breath. I missed the warmth of her tender nursing already.

"You're right. I'm not sorry."

"I meant about the class."

"Oh. Well, life schools you all the time. I feel like I'm in the middle of one right now."

You and I both, I thought, exhaling hard. "Can you hand me that box?" I pointed to the shelf.

"Sure," she said, narrowing her eyes and dropping the tweezers. "What is it?"

"A device that aids healing."

"Oh!" She opened it. "Malrik, these are just a couple of rocks."

"They're magnets. Give them to me."

"No." She clutched them to her chest. "Show me how to use them."

"No. I'll do it myself."

"You can barely move—how do you expect to stop me?"

"Please don't, lil mani. I'm not in the mood for another round." I swayed slightly, my awareness slipping. I needed to stay alert, especially with her so close.

Telling her the truth was forbidden. But with her in my home, the rules felt... flexible.

"You're not in any condition to give chase. Now might be my best chance to leave. Besides, it looks like you got into a wrestling match with a glitter bomb and lost."

The glass.

I shoved her away, twisting sharply to increase the distance between us. My immunities might nullify the poisonous resins. She didn't have that protection.

"Don't touch me." I walked in a wide arc toward the bathroom. "There's another shower upstairs to the right. It's not glitter. It's glass. You must wash it off. Now."

I shut the door and set the magnets down, stripping as I turned on the faucet.

I told you. Keeping the girl is cruel.

As I stepped into the stream, I groaned. Hazariah was right, but even after this, I wasn't strong enough to let her go so soon.

19

SOAP SUDS AND SINS

Those scars. Holy hell.

They *do* something to me, like a cunt-punch that goes straight to my libido. There's something wicked in me that wants—*needs*—to see those scarred arms wrapped around me.

He's not the weak, privileged prince I once thought.

Maybe it's his pain, how he carries it like an old companion, never flinching, never seeking pity. Or perhaps it's that, despite everything, he still moves carefully, like even now, he's making sure he won't hurt me.

However, it could have something to do with him being the first person ever to apologize to me. And he even seems to mean it.

That alone makes my heart somersault.

Hell, maybe it's because, at every opportunity, he avoids my advances. I know he wants me. I can see it. But something is holding him back.

Well, fuck that.

I had a virgin six-foot-five warrior with battle scars

standing in front of me, and knowing he had an ungodly amount of treasure was a cherry on top. He's a unicorn. And I've always wanted to ride a legend.

Besides, virgins are so easy to impress. And to manipulate. Once I have him hooked, he'll happily lead me to his safe. I had to play this right. It should be too easy, like taking candy from a baby.

With my mind made up, I open the bathroom door and step inside. Malrik's shirt hits the marble floor within seconds.

Malrik's head snaps toward me, his dark eyes bright and wide. "What are you doing?"

"I'm keeping you from forfeiting, for one." I shrug and reach for the glass shower door. The thick fog has already crept halfway up, obscuring everything below his waist.

Shame. I'd like to know what I'm about to get myself into.

Then the door opens.

Sweet goddess of thick thighs and bulging biceps.

He's already shaking his head before I can step into the shower.

"It's not safe."

I raise a brow. "No?" I ask and force my eyes to meet his.

"You don't need to do this."

After seeing him naked, he couldn't pry me away from this shower. I step closer, steam curling around us like a closing hand. "What if *you want* to?" The truth was, I'd wanted him from the first moment I saw him step out of his car.

He finally exhales after a silence, his hand clenching open and closed.

I tilt my head. "How else am I supposed to know if I got all the glass off unless you check for me? For that matter, how can you be sure you didn't miss a spot?"

His mouth opens, then shuts. His eyes never leave my body. Speechless.

Did I do that?

He reaches for the handle, then stops as a muscle ticks his jaw. For a moment, I watch his eyes move from me to the door as if he is considering kicking me out. Then, slowly, he inhales and turns his back to me as if he could easily ignore me.

"I'll tell you what," I continued, closing the door behind me and sealing us in. "You wash me, and I'll wash you. That way, we can be sure we're both thoroughly clean."

His gaze lifts to mine. "Wash each other... thoroughly?"

That man should not look so adorably perplexed with a body like his.

"Exactly. I'll go first."

"No, wait." He raises a hand as if he were fending off an attack. It doesn't stop me. I have no intention of listening to him.

He looks one wrong word away from diving through the glass doors to escape. I force myself not to look down. Don't spook him. Don't scare him off.

I reach for the sea sponge in his hand, but he steps back.

"No. I'll take care of you first."

Oh?

I tilt my head. "Okay, big guy. How do you want me?"

Just keep smiling. Keep it innocent. Let him take the lead.

"You should rinse off first. Warm up."

I bite my lip and look up at him. As if he's wallpaper, he plasters himself to the shower wall to give me the space to step into the jets. If I bend away as well, we won't have to touch. But what would be the fun in that?

Leaning forward, I twist to drag my ass against him. I slide across firm thighs, and a quickly swelling member pushes back. He groans a curse under his breath but doesn't step away.

"What if the glass gets caught in the sponge, and you scratch me? We should probably use our hands..." I say, trying with all my might to keep my voice light and melodious, as harmless as possible.

The sea sponge hits the ground with a wet slap.

I smile, then look down and away to hide the tell of my victory.

He shifts to the side, letting the hot spray hit my skin. I'm not sure if this whole 'checking for glass' excuse has any truth to it, but what man would kick himself out of bed with a practically naked me over a lie?

His hands catch my wrists as I lean forward to wet my hair.

"No, don't."

Before I can protest, he steps behind me, his grip firm yet careful. His hands cover mine, wrapping them around the faucet handle with a slight squeeze, lingering just long enough to make my breath hitch. Another curse from him stirs the fine hairs on my neck, a warm exhale that makes my skin prickle and my senses explode.

Then he lets go.

The absence of his touch is immediate, but he doesn't stay gone for long.

A single hand slides across my throat, his fingers ghosting over my anxious pulse. A hesitant thumb traces the curve of my cheek, light as a whisper, before his grip firms against my jaw. He tilts my head back, bringing my hair under the spray.

Everything in me stills as I wait for his fingers to work through the strands, searching for glass. Dark, thick brows draw together as if he's savoring the moment, tender in a way that makes my chest tighten.

I didn't expect gentle concern.

Then his fingers begin to massage my scalp. He moves slowly and purposefully, pressing into places I haven't even realized hold tension. *Shit.*

Then both hands are in my hair.

Double shit.

If this is what it feels like to have him touch my head, I can't wait to feel what he'll do to the rest of my body. I tilt my chin down, hoping to guide his touch lower, but he doesn't stray from his methodical and infuriatingly patient pace.

The man is thorough. It's too much. Well, technically, it's not enough. I'm ready to get to the good stuff.

He grips my hair into a single, coiled tail when he finishes. He rests it against my shoulder, and his hands sweep down my neck and spine to spread suds down my back. There's subtle insistence in his touch, and I don't realize I'm pushing into his hand until he withdraws, leaving me off balance.

Instead of following the rolling dip at the small of my back to the round of my ass, he stops. At first, his hands rest gently against my hips as if thinking about it. Eventually, his thumb starts tapping into my pelvis before his hands wrap around me, spreading fire across my abdomen.

"Malrik..." In my head, it was meant to be a tease, but it came out as a warning.

"Lean back," he murmurs with his cheek pressed against the shell of my ear.

It's not a request. Malrik pulls me in, guiding me until my shoulders flush against his chest. Warm, solid, inflexible.

The spray cascades down my front. Then, finally his hands are back on me.

His soapy palm lifts to stroke down my neck, across my collarbone.

I barely bite back my groan.

His arms frame me, bracing me, before withdrawing too quickly. My knees quiver when he resumes, dragging his touch down my arm, lingering at my hands.

"Tell me more about the rules of this interrogation tactic called Truth or Dare."

"What do you want to know?" I ask.

"What are the limits of the dares?" He asks as his touch sweeps slowly over my stomach, so close.

"The rules are set between the participants. So far, we've established nothing that leads to death, serious injury, or disfigurement."

"Truth or Dare, little thief?"

"Truth." I try not to grin at the puff of disappointment that hits my shoulder.

"Why did you target me?" He asks as he strokes back up my arms, spreading fire up the delicate flesh of my inner elbow.

"I might have stolen something from someone, and even though I gave it back, they're still holding it over me, so I... I kinda owe them. Hitting up your house is supposed to be my last job for them before we clear the slate."

I don't even realize I'm telling him the truth. His hands make me forget myself. That should be my first warning.

"And if you don't follow through?" He leads.

I shift from one foot to another before I answer. "They have evidence that I can get me in some real hot water. I'm stuck between a rock and a hard place. Truth or Dare?"

At that, he chuckles before saying, "Truth."

"Alright. Why do you keep running away from me?" I ask.

His silence is deafening.

"If you can't take the truth, you shouldn't pick it, Malrik." I reach for the shower door. His hands flex, but he doesn't stop me.

"I don't want to push you any more than I already have. I don't want to hurt or scare you." His entire body tenses behind me, going rigid as steel. The tension hums between us, thickening the air.

I lean forward, breaking contact. The big guy immediately shifts and pulls me back against him. His big hands scoop me by my shoulders and press my back into his chest.

"Stay still," he scolds.

His hands trail down my sides with a reverence that undoes me. Each slow pass feels like he's memorizing the shape of a woman he was never meant to know. A man like him shouldn't feel this tender. And yet, his touch is a betrayal of everything I told myself I came here to do.

I had to outsmart him. Use him. Walk away unbothered.

But every careful stroke, every glance that lingers too long, is unraveling the edges of my resolve. It's becoming dangerously easy to forget why I came, and even worse, what happens if I fail.

Soft and hesitant, his thumbs sweep my jaw, while the other hand thrums along my ribs like a question he's afraid to ask. When his arms close around me, strong and scarred, it should feel like a trap. But instead, there's a flicker of safety I didn't expect.

The silence stretches, broken only by the sounds of the shower and my staggered breath, like a secret neither of us is ready to keep. The big guy hesitates just beneath my breasts—close enough to claim, restrained enough to ruin me with his chivalry. And for a moment, I swear he's trembling, too.

And then—

RING.

A muscle ticks in my jaw. I barely smother my urge to curse and pout.

Malrik's hand doesn't move at first. Behind me, he stiffens. By the second ring, he starts to lift his hand in the water. I watch the suds spread down his wrist and forearm before dripping off his body. By the third ring, I can no longer mask my glare.

The sharp chime shatters the moment. With a curse, the big guy's hand vanishes. The loss of pressure feels like a slap, and before I can even process the withdrawal, he's opening the shower door.

I suck in a breath, my skin still burns as cold air blasts my raw skin. When the big guy shifts away, I turn in time to watch the bunching, layered muscles of his back and sides stretching and dripping with suds.

"You have *got* to be kidding me." I sigh. He really shouldn't look so tempting.

He doesn't let me drift too far. As his fingers curl around his phone, his other hand finds the back of my neck, anchoring me in place: the firm and controlling grip sends tingles across my hairline and shoulders.

"What is it?" His voice is steel. Back in the shower, his hand pulls me closer into his eyes that refuse to let me go.

While the person on the other end speaks, Malrik's fingers keep moving, kneading slow circles at the base of my skull, methodical and knowing. My pulse spikes. His touch isn't just grounding me but holding me in place.

I sway before I can stop myself, my knees betraying

me. Malrik's grip tightens. My hands clench into fists that press against the cold tile.

"Is that necessary?" His voice darkens, that deadly edge creeping in. After a slow exhale. "Fine. I'll be there."

The phone clicks off.

His hand lingers against my neck, thumb tracing the pulse hammering beneath my skin.

I swallow hard. "Let me guess, you have to go."

He doesn't answer right away. He watches me. The silence of his stare rests on top of my sternum.

Then, in one fluid motion, he lets go. The sudden absence exposes me to the cold bite of air. My arms wrap around myself as I fight the sudden feeling of bereft isolation. But then his hands lower to my hips, his fingers digging into my sides.

He still doesn't speak; he holds my gaze. It's intense. His consideration feels like looking into a distorted mirror, almost as if he could see the deepest parts of me that I hide even from myself. Immediately, my body went on high alert. I didn't want to see myself as he saw me.

I can't.

My heel lifts, but Malrik catches me mid-turn, suspended between fear and need; his grip on my hips turns into an uncompromising claim that sears my bones. He's already pulling me back before I can lift my other foot. His breath is hot and ragged, like a man trying to keep a storm under control.

He draws me in, one step at a time until he squeezes us so tight not even steam can slip between us.

"We're not done," he murmurs, his voice low and steady. "Not by a long shot."

Promises, promises. And for the first time in as long as I can remember, I believe it.

He steps in slowly, deliberately, his eyes sweeping over my body with a reverence that feels like worship. He rubs the next batch of soap into my skin, his hands gliding across my chest and my ribs everywhere *but* where I ache for him most.

"Truth or Da—"

"Dare."

The word leaves my mouth on a breath, my hips shifting forward, the need to grind against him barely held in check.

His grip tightens, just once, a stern, grounding flex before he sinks to his knees. "I dare you to keep your eyes on me while I explore you the way I've been dying to. I dare you to let me memorize every inch of you until I learn how to make you tremble and come undone."

A vision sparks like a fever dream: Malrik, on his knees, looking up at me like he's starved and I'm the only thing that's ever tasted like hope. My hand moves instinctively, tracing his temple, skimming down the cut of his jaw until my thumb finds his mouth. His lips, dusty pink and too soft, part slightly as he leans into the contact. Then he blazes a slow trail up my thigh, turning into my touch like he's asking permission without words.

"It's okay if you're not good at this," I whisper,

brushing damp strands of hair from his forehead. "There's a learning curve."

My thumb lingers on his lips, not quite ready to let go. Not quite ready to trust.

"If it's too much... If anything feels wrong, we can stop. Just say the word."

But I drop my hand anyway because the truth is—I don't *want* to stop.

Not now.

Not when he's looking at me like I'm sacred.

Little does he know, he's exactly where I want him.

20

SINK OR SWIM

She was a dream come true. I still couldn't believe she'd allowed my touch. Her daring impressed me so much that I almost missed the jab about the learning curve. I watched the twist of her lip spread and felt the roll of a challenge light my chest.

She couldn't have known this wasn't about her honesty. This was a reward for *my* patience.

The weight of excitement pulled at my ribs like a stitch drawing together an old wound.

I didn't want to rush. So I dragged my lips across Nadia's fever-warm belly in light, deliberate kisses. I traced long, slow strokes with my tongue, starting at her thighs and gliding up to her hips, teasing both her and myself.

The hunger to taste her gnawed at me. I wanted to devour her. To fill myself with the thrill of her sharp tongue and hot hands. Ever since I'd had her bent over the basement table, it wasn't easy to think about anything else.

I'd told her I'd never been intimate, but that didn't mean I was clueless. This particular closeness had long fascinated me.

It started the night I encountered a passionate couple mid-act in an alley. The woman had leaned against a brick wall, her long leg stretched out across her partner's shoulders, his head buried under her skirt. From that moment, I'd wondered and wanted.

Now I had my chance. But Nadia was as tumultuous as fire and as elusive as smoke. Whenever I thought I understood her, she slipped into some new mask I'd never seen before.

If I didn't get it right the first time, she might never let me do it again.

I needed to be perfect. It's not just to reward her; it's because I couldn't stomach the thought of her running. Not now. Not after everything she'd already taken without asking.

And more than anything, I needed to see her come undone, with her head thrown back and grinding against my face. But not yet.

"Don't look away," I told her.

I needed to read her face and be sure I was doing this right.

If I was honest with myself, that wasn't the only reason. Every time Nadia's gaze landed on me, I felt an exhilarating jolt shoot up my legs.

That intensity only deepened with the knowledge that she would be watching me taste her.

Slowly, I ran the underside of my tongue up the delicate skin of her inner thigh, and she rewarded me with a breathy hitch that tingled across my skin. Her whole body tensed, hips tilting down to guide me higher.

Not so fast, my little thief.

If I knew one thing, it was this: I would explore every inch and every taste.

My hands moved steadily up her legs and hips, then wrapped around her waist almost involuntarily. I lifted one of her legs over my shoulder, pulling her closer to that heat I craved. Her hips flexed toward me, but my hands slid down, cupping and kneading the liberal curve of her ass. My fingers dug in, spreading her pink flesh in a quick flash.

Her silence unnerved me, but I knew I was on the right track when her fingers slid over my scalp and tugged. It was easy to hide my grin in the curve of her thigh as I nuzzled away from where she tried to guide me. *So impatient.*

I opened my mouth wide, stuck out my tongue, and flattened it. This time, I let my treasure guide me. One hand gripped her raised thigh; the other cradled her lower back.

She was my treasure—not just for what I could take, but for what she'd given. This moment, this trust, was a gift I intended to savor. When she began to move against me, lifting and lowering her hips in a silent plea, I pulled back, trailing kisses along her thighs.

"You're teasing me!" she squeaked.

"No. I'm enjoying myself," I said. "This isn't a race, and I plan on taking my time to learn from you."

"Oh, shit," she muttered.

At that, she pressed herself against the shower wall. Water ran in rivulets down her body, tracking her chest and stomach before reaching me. I looked up through the hot spray, watching the flush bloom across her cheeks. Then I saw it: hesitation. Uncertainty.

Was she about to back out?

I couldn't risk it. I pressed forward.

I explored her with my mouth, rolling my tongue along her sides and steadily ignoring the spot she kept urging me toward. I took my time, increasing the pressure of my mouth, grazing her outer labia with my teeth, curling my tongue along the sensitive inner folds. The contrast of textures fascinated me.

"That feels good." She sounded surprised.

I dragged my fingers up and down her inner thigh, slow and steady, closing in. My tongue stiffened into a single, long lick that plunged into her wet heat.

Then I devoured her like I'd been ordered to clean my plate, savoring every moment. Again and again, I licked and teased, each pass edging closer to the hood of her clit, swirling lightly before pulling away while my hands crept higher. Her core began to tighten. Her breath grew ragged. Her hips fought against my hold. Whispered pleas fell from her lips.

Pride bloomed in my chest.

I buried my face between her thighs, tongue swirling and sucking at the bundle of nerves. Her leg locked around my neck. One hand gripped my shoulder, the other slapped against the wall. But it was the strange noise in her throat that stopped me.

"Arrah!"

I pulled back, her scent still clinging to my mouth. Her cheeks turned a deeper pink, her gaze slightly glazed.

"Bad?" I asked.

"Only if you stop," she gasped.

She tugged my ear, dragging me back. I hardened my tongue to a point and flicked it over her clit. With every thrust, she jerked away, overwhelmed. I didn't let her escape. I hooked her other leg over my shoulder. Now, she had nowhere to go.

"Yes, like that," she panted.

I spread her labia and fluttered my tongue along the base of her clit. Her excitement fed mine. I couldn't get enough of the way she writhed and quivered in my grasp.

I just found my new favorite hobby.

The wall behind her shifted at my will, forming to cradle her hips so I could press in harder without risking her comfort. Nadia didn't notice, too lost in sensation. Feminine keens rose above the steady beat of water.

The sight of her hips lifted and breasts beaded with water made me dizzy. I hadn't spent enough time on those, not yet. She caught me staring. Her nostrils flared. She didn't look away.

Very good.

She was breathtaking. But I wanted more. I wanted to see her completely undone.

I stiffened my tongue again, starting with shallow strokes, easing deeper, thrusting in and out until her body strained. I licked my way up again, ignoring her weak whine of protest. My nose parted her folds so my tongue could circle the tiny bud at the center of her pleasure.

Tiny yeses spilled from her lips.

I lifted her by the ass. She spread her legs, toes pointed, head thrown back. Her body arched. Then her heels dug into my back, fists clenched in my hair, guiding me with desperation. My fingers trailed down her legs, memorizing each twitch, every clench.

She was exceptional, like a livewire in my hands, and I was already craving another shock.

Even as she trembled against my mouth, her skin slick and cooling under my hands, I knew I could stay here for hours and still never have enough. I wanted more.

Determined, I pulled her back toward me.

She smacked me lightly on the head, twice. Then, instead of welcoming me, she slipped away.

"No more," she demanded.

Disappointment hit low in my gut. All the things I hadn't done—positions, techniques, tastes—flashed before my eyes like a montage. I tried to follow, but my little mortal pulled back again. I stood there, watching her retreat as the water streamed down my shoulders and chest. She stood before me, flushed, dripping, perfect. But her words held firm.

"Surely that didn't satisfy all your needs," I said. It didn't even come close to satisfying mine.

She looked me over for a long moment, still catching her breath. Then, after one last trembling inhale, she said, "Barely scratched the surface. I told you, it's a learning curve. Besides, you dared me to let you learn how to make me come undone. And you did. The water's getting cold. We're done here."

I stood there as her words sank in. Her voice had turned as cold as the water, effectively shutting me out.

She shifted, slipping a hand between her thighs, not with desire, but detachment. She rinsed me off her skin like I was something to forget. I narrowed my eyes. Did she think she could wash away our connection so easily?

Before I could rise to my feet, she bolted from the shower.

The orgasm left her glowing in the cool light of the bathroom. She didn't glance back; she just grabbed a towel and vanished out the door.

Barely scratched the surface, huh? Then why did it feel like she'd just carved her name into me?

21

LIAR, LIAR, PANTS ON FIRE

Holy shit. Holy shit. Holy shit!

He's a liar.

I storm out of his room, barely resisting the temper tantrum urge to slam his door. If it weren't for all his doors being obnoxiously heavy, I'd give in to the meltdown.

"Fuck, fuck — FUCK, FUCK, fuck — FUCK, FUCK, fuck," I chant, the words falling out of my mouth to the intro beat of *American Woman* by Lenny Kravitz.

I sound like a woman on the edge. Or possibly already over it. I don't care.

Seduction is supposed to be my weapon. So why do I feel like I've just triggered into my own trap?

Frantically, I pat my body dry, breathing in and out like a deranged Lamaze instructor. My skin is flushed and sensitive, which only angers me more. I pointedly avoid the lightning rod of desire pulsing between my legs until I'm decent enough to yank another one of his shirts on.

The brown towel is damp, but I plop my hair with it as I power-walk. I don't have anywhere to go. There isn't any place to hide and decompress, so I pace one big lap of the house. I look up as I pass two towering stone gargoyles flanking the top floor's railing, wings curled like cloaks, eyes blank. Funny... I could've sworn those statues were downstairs.

Shaking my head I continue to pace down and then back.

Why is he so good? How could *I* fall for such a blatant lie? He's supposed to be a unicorn mark, easy to scam and leave. He's turning out to be a lot more than I can handle.

I *am* fucked. That's the kind of tongue-lashing that stays on a girl's mind. For life.

If I *thought* he had skills, I would never play the seductress. Don't go out further than you can swim. Never pick a mark that's craftier than you.

And he *is*. His mouth does tricks I didn't know could be done. I've never had a release rip through me so thoroughly as that one. My legs are still trembling.

As soon as it was over, I knew I needed to dip. I'll go back down to the basement if it means I have space to process what just happened. A complete uno reversal.

I don't want to want his touch. I want it to be good enough to tolerate. Is that too much?

That lying asshole.

And he wants seconds?

At the fresh memory of disappointment, all the parts he's just licked, sucked, and nibbled on clench. I turn the kitchen corner and nearly slam into Malrik—

now dressed in sandy linen pants and a dark blue shirt that hugs every muscle.

Even his thighs. Especially his thighs. *He's going to think I'm a creeper if I don't look up soon.*

"Can we talk?" he asks, shoving a hand in one of his pockets.

"Ugh, yeah." I lift my chin, but my stomach drops.

How can I face him?

How can I not?

"You know, about what just happened." He pulls one hand out of its pocket, then the other like he doesn't know what to do with his hands.

Put them on me... No. Bad. I need control, but my body still tingles from Malrik's mouth. It makes it hard to focus and stay mad at him.

"Yeah, there might have been some miscommunication," I say because I don't know what else to do. I lean against the stairway rail between the kitchen and the living room.

"We don't have to do anything like that again if you don't want to. I'm still unfamiliar with the expectations of Truth or Dare, so if I overstep—"

Oddly enough, I don't like the thought of him shifting the blame on himself. Or at least all on himself.

"You didn't overstep, you lied! When asked to tell the truth, you can't lie or insinuate under falsehoods."

"I never lied. What was my lie?" He steps on the bottom step, and I retreat three stairs higher. With his height, I still had to look up to see his stare.

"You said you've never shared intimacies, *bullshit.* Nobody naturally knows how to do that!"

"You're right."

I tilt my head and level him with an *I told you so* stare.

"But I didn't lie either. The truth is, I've never done that or anything—not even a kiss. But since I've been here, I've witnessed things, seen things in passing, and I might have looked into it a bit." He steps closer, both of his hands at his sides. "So when I finally had my tongue curling around something so beautiful, I couldn't resist exploring all the different feels of you—the silk, the velvet, the cream." Abruptly, he stiffens and steps back to lean against the other rail. "If my enthusiasm has scared you, I'm sorry and understand."

How can a big man like this look so defeated?

"You didn't scare me, I suppose." I try swallowing around my dry mouth twice before saying, "You surprised me."

"How so?" he asks. His brows pull together in a look that's both earnest and contrite.

"I assumed that when you said you lacked experience, it meant all experiences."

"You assumed correctly. Didn't I please you?"

It isn't so much a question as it is an inquiry statement.

"You did."

"And it only scratched the surface of your needs?" He continued.

"That's what I said." Why is it starting to feel like I'm on trial being led by a lawyer?

"So why'd you leave?"

"These things aren't so cut and dry for me. When I

say you surprised me, I mean the pleasure surprises me. I was ready to take pity on your efforts, not..." I don't know how to explain the fear I now have. "What can I say? Good sex is dangerous. It can make sane people do idiotic things."

Like falling in love or stealing from the mafia and framing your family to cover it all up. Because who hasn't committed a little bit of corporate espionage for a lover? I can't help but shiver at the oily memories my past brings up.

But it's a good reminder of what I'm doing this for. It isn't for the treasure or to stay ahead of Darius's blackmail. It's to get rid of Levi once and for all. Then, I can finally live without looking over my shoulder.

The last time I got love and lust confused, I had to fake my death, and the boogeyman's been on my tail since. With each move I make, Levi finds me quicker and quicker. Hell, he might already have eyes looking for me in Boston.

Sooner or later, he'll catch up to me; it'll be me or him. Only losers play by the rules. That means I have to play dirty.

But I can't tell Malrik any of that. He already thinks I'm a terrible person. I can only imagine how he would react if I told him I needed the money to put out a hit on my ex. *Yikes.* Even I would pass on that.

"I'm new and uncomfortable with all of this too, Nadia. But it sounds like you're worried about enjoying yourself. All I can say is I understand. I didn't think tasting you would change anything between us. You're still the thief after my safe, and I'm still the man who kept you in his basement.

But I loved the way you tasted, and I can still feel the hard squeeze of your thighs around my face, and I'm not ashamed to say I want more. However, I need your help getting to whoever's behind this. They're the only ones who know who's truly after my safe. We can be completely hands-off if that's what you want."

"I'm willing to negotiate," I say. Because hands-off is not what I want, as much as I hate to admit it, the big guy's touch was groundbreaking. "I have a saying: No pay, no way. Before I give you the person who gave me this job, you have to open your safe and give me first dibs."

"To get your blackmailer off your back?"

"It's so much more than that, but yes," I agree.

"Tomorrow, we visit your fence, and before we leave, I'll show you my safe."

Yahtzee! "I don't know..." I pause like I'm not squealing with excitement internally.

"And if you can set up a meeting between us, then allow you 'dips.'"

"It's dibs and no way. Darius won't like that I've brought you, but it will soften the blow if I get him what he wants. I'll need access to your safe before I get you your introduction."

"I'm not rewarding you for something you haven't done yet. You might take my treasure and run."

"Don't be ridiculous; I plan on using you to intimidate him into honoring our deal," I think out loud, and

Malrik frowns at me. All I need to know is where this safe is; then, I'll be able to dip in when the coast is clear.

Malrik pulls his lips in what's probably meant to imitate a smile. I smile back, but it falls after a moment.

"Look," I start. "If you think you're going to get a marathon bout of sex before I get my loot, you've got another thing coming. I'm tired, I've had a stressful day, and you haven't made it any easier. Besides, I'm starving."

"We could get pizza?"

"I have a gluten allergy, so it has to be cauliflower crust."

"Is that why you don't like donuts?" he asks, slowly turning toward the bag on the counter.

"Yeah, I have particular dietary restrictions. You kinda kidnapped the worst captive."

"I wouldn't say that." He smirks.

I hate how smug he looks—or more like how good he looks smug. I shoot him a look but can only hold it for a few seconds before turning away. "Let's just get something to eat."

But that only makes his eyes dip to the edge of my shirt. He notices my return stare, and we both look away.

"You can eat whatever you want, but I'm going to need something a little more substantial than dick for dinner."

Malrik's large feet stumble, and he looks at me with a shocked double-take.

Wait. Did I say that out loud?

"So you're saying it's on the menu, just not the main course?"

I freeze. My brain short-circuits trying to figure out how to recover from that.

"I—know—I mean, that's not what I meant—"

He tilts his head, looking so goddamn entertained. "Mmm. Sure sounds like that's what you meant."

Heat rushes up my neck, and I cross my arms like that will make me feel less exposed. "Forget I said anything. You're just hearing what you want to hear."

"I heard exactly what you said, thief."

He steps closer, his size making my breath catch. He doesn't touch me. He doesn't have to. His presence alone is enough to make my skin prickle.

"But fine. We'll eat first." His voice drops, teasing but firm. "Wouldn't want you starving on me."

I swallow hard and turn sharply toward the kitchen, pretending I'm unaffected. I need to focus on food. Not on him. Not on the way he's watching me like he's still hungry.

Just food.

Right?

22

DANGEROUS GAMES IN TIGHT SPACES

Tension crackles between us in the tight steel cage we're trapped in. Space was already limited once Malrik climbed in. His upper body alone filled up the space past the center console. He wasn't spreading either; he was sitting comfortably and relaxed.

The bastard.

It was as if the last fight we shared was already a memory long past.

The big guy drives with one thick wrist on the steering wheel, and the picture of casual control makes me the only one still sulking. I push myself as far away from him as the car allows and watch him pretend not to notice. We sit silently, an Art Bell-style talk radio show playing in the background.

We cuddled last night, tangled in his sheets. It was awkward at first, then too easy. His shoulder is the perfect pillow, and his thick arm is heavy but not claustrophobic. He doesn't even burn like a furnace.

But now, in the tiny space of the car, it feels like there's an ocean between us; the contrast leaves me off-balance. I guess daring him to let me spend some time alone with his safe killed the mood. But I had to try.

When he explored every inch of me, ate me like soup without a spoon, with no thought to himself, and then tucked me tightly into his side, an uncomfortable awareness filled me. He felt good. Now, I need some distance: to think and plot how to keep him. At least long enough to get unfettered access to his safe.

In a way that doesn't leave me looking out a window or checking my phone after I rob him bare.

For most of the trip, I gave him accurate turn-by-turn directions to my house. Keeping me close was his latest condition in what seems to be an endless list of excuses. Everything goes well until I wonder what would happen if I miss a turn.

How would he know? I smother my smile and tell him to get off on the next exit.

It takes one look, and his heavy sigh fills the car as he pulls off the side of the road.

No way.

The seatbelt tightens as I shift away, and my awareness narrows to the two of us. Malrik's chuckle does something to me, something reckless. My skin doesn't flush from fear but excitement.

His hand covers mine, halting my pathetic struggle. The seatbelt clicks free.

"I'm starting to be able to spot your mischief a mile away." He flicks on the hazards, sets the parking brake, and rolls his sleeves.

The thrum of passing vehicles shakes through the car, a jarring reminder that the world hasn't stopped for us.

"What are you doing?"

"I'm going to remind you of the consequences of lying. And if you resist, I'll escalate. You knew the rules. Hell, you helped make them. Now, lay across my lap and take your dues."

"You don't have to do this for every fib."

"Yes, I do." A smirk pulls at his lips as he looks down on me. "Actions have consequences, and I won't let you forget that. But let's be honest, little imp—you knew exactly what you were doing. You wanted to test me. I'm more than happy to repeat the lesson until it sinks in."

His calm control sends a shiver down my spine. His tone should feel like I'm losing. But it doesn't. Our eyes lock in a battle of wills, and after five seconds, I break. I have to exhale to steady myself before slowly crawling across his lap. My cheeks heat, partially from embarrassment, but I'm also excitedly dizzy.

Am I fooling myself into thinking I can manipulate him, enjoy him, and still stay detached? I glance over at him, and even though he sets his jaw in a stiff lock, he can't hide his wild eyes. Is he also struggling for control and desperate to stay grounded?

My movement presses me against the front of his hard form, but I don't stop and look back until my fingers grip the drive's side handle. My head feels full of champagne bubbles, and every muscle in my body is too tight.

His fingers trace my thigh, slow and leisurely,

pushing my trench coat higher. A tremor runs through me as I shift, my legs tensing beneath Malrik's touch. I'm unsure if he curses or prays as I brace for the blows.

The air is cold, but his warm breaths roll across my skin. His hands cup me at my waist and stroke down, bringing a new awareness to my body.

Then sharp swats sting my inner thighs, and I yelp, my body reacting before my brain catches up. By the force of his hits, I spread my legs a little wider.

Heat coils in my belly—until the blaring horn of a passing semi jolts me like a splash of ice water. My head pops up. I've forgotten that we're not alone.

His grip on my hips holds me steady, keeping me from scrambling back. I press my forehead against the driver-side window, torn between resisting and getting caught up in the moment.

"What offends you more, the punishment or the fact that everyone driving by can see?" he asks, sensing my discomfort. Before I have a chance to answer, he lands another solid smack.

The fog starts to spread as I catch my breath. "The only thing that offends me is that you call this a punishment." Thankfully, my voice doesn't wobble. "You think I care if some pedestrians see my ass? I'll take the honks as appreciation."

Only then does he ease up, but his warm breath continues to fan my revealed flesh. The big guy's fingers tumble through my hair and lift my head. My finger drums against the plastic of his car door, determined not to give him what he wants.

Slap. The hit surprises me, and I push against the

door to escape Malrik's hand. My eyes lock with his. A warning darkens his stare, but it's not enough to stop my squirming.

"Don't." His breath tickles my skin, but his hands keep rolling over my clenched muscles.

"Don't what?" I ask, afraid to move.

My breath hitches. A voice in my head whispers a mix of warning and exhilaration: *Oh, you're in trouble now.* But am I? Or am I, like Malrik suggests, exactly where I want to be?

"Don't tempt me." His voice is smooth. But there's a dark edge. Frustration? Or desire? I'm willing to bet he's as hot and bothered as I am. Worse, I hope, since he hasn't had a release. Yet. After all, a man filled with lust is easier to manipulate.

I whimper shamelessly, my hips wiggling, pushing, and groaning when he pulls back.

"You're the one teasing," I remind him, slowly sinking into his touch. "I thought you were supposed to be scary."

His smile lightens the humid air as his fingers trace slow, calculated circles against my skin. "Do you remember your advice to me?"

The realization of what he means makes my breath stutter. I know exactly what advice he's referring to, but admitting it would feel like owning it. I shake my head, but I don't pull away. His hand moves with determination until he palms me, his fingers sliding between my inner and outer lips, tracing a smooth line back and forth over the sensitive skin.

The heat starts to build as he swipes his fingers

between my thighs in that steady metronome. Ever since he told me he wants to learn how to make me tremble and come undone, I've been tipsy with the earnest yearning in his eyes.

"You told me to focus on what I want and go after it. Do you remember?" His finger swirls around, dipping into my channel to the first knuckle, then pulling out.

Breaking me out of my hesitation, his forefinger and thumb press hard, and the pressure steadily builds. Mercilessly, he tugs at the delicate flesh between my folds and my ass cheeks. His dark eyes hold me firmer than his hand, no matter how I shift or twist.

"This isn't what I meant," I squeak. Malrik's one hand cups and strokes, and the other grips my hips until I press against the steering wheel to ease the burden of Malrik's reprimand.

He dedicates his attention to that tender area once more. My pussy clenches in response. Part of me wants to retreat; the other wants to grind onto the hand that's inches away from a pressure that would turn all this pain into pleasure. When I can't take it, I drop my head in a bow, fisting his shirt as I hold on.

"No apologies," he adds.

"No apologies," I repeat.

He lifts my chin with a casual push, forcing me back into his endless stare. How did we get into this predicament? Then I remember: it's me.

"I only want two things: you and honesty."

"You mean my help."

His stare is direct and unflinching, even as I try to spin his meaning. Pulling back, I sit up with my legs curled beneath me—until his eyes dip to my parted legs. The look in his eyes borders on possession. It sets something off inside me. A need. A fear. A flag raised in challenge? I want him, and that scares the hell out of me.

The fact that he wants me scares me even more.

His eyes are onyx stones of greed as he single-handedly unties the belt of my trench. Both his large hands palm my ass cheeks, pulling me close as he squeezes hard. Jerking back into the steering wheel, I cry out as he scoops my breasts out of my coat with an easy tug.

His lips brush my skin, heat trailing in their wake. He parts his mouth, his breath hot against the swell of my breast, before his teeth close around me, abrupt and measured. A sharp sting blooms into pleasure, and I arch instinctively when he groans into me until we're both pressing into each other.

Grinding into him, I imagine myself pulling his head away, but instead, my arms wrap around him, and I hug him close. The wet heat adds to the feeling of being consumed as his teeth clamp and his tongue swirls. All I can do is hold on and try to appease the new ache growing inside me.

"Please, what, *lil mani*?" he asks.

I haven't realized it, but I've been chanting a steady "Please" stream. Once Malrik asks, I know what I want. I want him to take it further and put that growing pipe to use. As soon as I feel it underneath me, it's a pressure I can't forget.

My hands slide between us, and I grip his belt. His eyes are like a weight on me, pressing hard while his fingers slowly swirl in a pitiless tease. When my fingers lower his zipper and my nails graze his skin, his entire body surges forward.

For once, I've surprised him. But he surprises me, too. I don't think I've ever felt a guy so hard for me. He practically vibrates.

"Get ready for me," I instruct.

Abruptly, his hands grip mine and pull them away. "This is a punishment. You don't get what you want when you've been bad."

My head tips back, and I groan. Any other virgin would jump at the chance. Why the hell is he so stubborn?

"It's just one little fib! What does it matter how it starts? That was then, and this is now," I pout.

But under my body's needy demands, the ugly truth of my irritation shifts to worry and spreads. Marlik's self-control might rebalance the scales and leave me without leverage.

Glaring at him, I reach down between us anyway. My hands slide down the shaft that's straining to be free. But before my fingers can do anything more than stroke his silk, his hand grips my wrist tightly.

"Damn you, I said no," he growls as his leg trembles underneath me. "You silly girl. How have you survived this long?"

I wince, trying to jerk away from the bruising clamp, and he immediately loosens his hold; then, after a few seconds, he lets go, drawing in a jerky and uncertain pull of air.

Silence fills the car, except for the angry traffic

zooming past us. Our eyes lock. Or more accurately, my body locks as his gaze penetrates my devious soul.

His hold on my hips tightens, sending a sharp thrill through me. I gasp, but I don't pull away. A part of me craves this. The raw tension between us can only mean he, like me, is on the edge of losing control.

Which is right where I want him. It's just a waiting game to see who can outlast the other.

His voice is low, dangerous. "You will learn not to lie to me." My pulse stutters. It's not from fear but anticipation. "Even if I have to wash your mouth out every time."

Immediately, my mind flashes with images of him spraying my tongue with ropes of his come. I can't help my eyes from darting to his bulge. I don't know if he's fully swelled or just naturally thick, but I hope, by the harsh set of his jaw, I'm about to find out.

Against every survival instinct, I stop fighting his hold and relax my body. The pressure in his hands stops increasing, and I take that as encouragement. Slowly, I lift my fingers to his belt.

Let's see him beat his eight-second record with this.

23

CAUTION: HANDLE WITH CARE

When she gripped my belt, with my hand still around her neck, I nearly exploded. Never before had I been so merciless. I paddled her ass beet red, and still, she pushed back.

I choked her, and she relaxed into me.

This foolish mortal must have had a death wish. She kept pushing, kept inviting danger. And worse, I kept giving in.

For the first time, a threat of self-doubt flickered inside me. What if this little human was more than I could handle?

Then, another familiar hesitation stilled my movements. I'd never done this before. What if I wasn't good at it? What if I didn't like it?

She shifted, sliding her body against me, and every nerve ending flashed with hyperawareness. With an easy flex, I pressed her into her seat, just a shade harder than her grind against me. When her eyes locked with mine, I could have sworn I saw victory in her quick smirk.

Her devious mind challenged me in a way I hadn't realized I needed. It had been so long without the spark of excitement. That was an immortal's greatest curse. When a warrior looks into the endless expanse of time, humor weakens, and passions fade. And when you lose the draw of curiosity, feelings like excitement vanish entirely.

I hadn't been curious in nearly a millennia.

But I was curious now.

What would it feel like, having her mouth on me? I wondered as my fingers cuffed her neck.

I didn't pull her hands away. Funny, I hadn't been thinking of force-feeding my cock down her throat and washing her mouth clean. Until now. That she thought of it sent a jolt of electricity through me.

My hand moved against her throat, fingers resting against her skin, then tightening as those new sensations rained over me.

It happened fast.

Her entire body went rigid. Then she tore away so violently she nearly launched herself into the dashboard.

"Don't—!" The word ripped from her throat, sharp and raw, something between a snarl and a demand.

I froze. Hands up. No sudden movements. I didn't know what I did. I didn't know what to do. So I did nothing.

I'd handled her roughly before. She'd never balked.

But this was different. Her fear wasn't about power. It was instinctual.

She wasn't just startled. Someone or something had ingrained that fear in her, wired it into her subconscious. Her breath came too fast, her muscles coiled tight, her pupils blown wide. But she didn't run.

"All right," I said carefully, keeping my voice smooth. "I won't. Can you tell me what I did?"

Her throat worked, but no words came. She tensed, like she was waiting for something. An argument. A pushback. Maybe even dismissal.

I didn't give it to her.

I didn't press. I didn't ask again. I just waited.

Her pulse still hammered at the base of her throat, but then her fingers twitched, pressing lightly against her stomach. She pulled in a slow breath, then another.

"It was the squeeze," she said, her voice hoarse.

I frowned slightly and lifted my hand, wanting to touch her cheek. Before I made contact, she caught my wrist, stopping me. "I know I've touched your neck before," I said, slowly lowering my hand to the armrest.

"It's not the touch. It's the—" Nadia gestured vaguely, but the words wouldn't come. Whatever thought she chased slammed into her all at once, and she flinched like the weight of it was suffocating.

Her breath hitched. Then she threw a hand between us, shaking it as if to dispel the emotion physically.

What had she endured to have such a guttural response?

I didn't move. I held the space. Let Nadia decide how this played out.

Her fingers curled against her stomach again, feeling the rise and fall of her breath. Slower now. More controlled.

Seconds stretched.

Then, something shifted. The tension didn't disappear, but Nadia carried it differently now. I'd seen a kaleidoscope of emotions dance across her face in seconds; somehow, she held them together. Strength, in a way I never could have imagined.

She rode out emotions that would've crumbled me. And she did it with grace. A kind of control I wouldn't have believed if I hadn't seen it myself, especially from someone so small and fragile.

"Sorry," she muttered, swiping under her eye. Her gaze skittered away from mine. "I think I killed the mood."

A slow smirk tugged at my lips. "Don't apologize." My voice came low and laborious. "I'm glad you told me. Despite how we got here, I don't want to make you feel that way. Ever."

She swallowed hard, blinking too fast. But then, like a switch flipping, her expression sharpened. Humor slid in like armor, casual and practiced.

"Oh, don't worry," she said, arching a brow. "I have plenty more triggers for you to stumble into accidentally."

I huffed a quiet laugh and shook my head but didn't argue. She was taking control: of the conversation, and of what happened next. I wanted her to take that if that's what she needed. And if that meant we moved at her pace, I could do that.

But it did leave me wondering: what exactly had I done?

My attention had been on her, on her mouth. I don't even remember what my hands were doing. Which meant I might do it again.

"Nadia," I said gently, "can you explain what I did?"

She crossed her arms, hugging herself. The sight made my chest ache. I wanted to earn her trust. To be someone she could take comfort in. I didn't want to be anything like the one who had put those shadows in her eyes.

"It was the clamp." She raised her hand between us, cupping it stiffly in a vice-like shape.

"On your neck," I said.

"Underneath my skull."

"Can you show me? On me?"

Hesitantly, she grazed her hand up my spine, over my shoulders, until her fingers circled my neck. Then she clamped down, right where the neck and head met. It wasn't a hard squeeze, but I understood. It didn't take much for that hold to feel controlling. It was meant for domination.

"Of course I've got baggage. Let's be real. Did you really think a thief would come with a warning label?"

So, the mask was back in place.

I tilted my head, studying her. "I think I noticed the warning sign the first time I saw you."

She snorted. "Yeah? What did it say? *Warning: toxic?*"

My smirk deepened, but I paused, weighing my words. Then, "More like *caution: slippery when wet.*"

That earned me a head-thrown-back laugh, a full smile, and bright eyes. My hand shifted slightly, debating whether to reach my delicate mortal again.

But I didn't. Not this time.

I left it up to her. But even as she brushed it off, a darker part of me seethed. I wanted to find whoever had put that fear in her and make them feel it too.

She let the silence stretch.

Then she rolled her eyes and leaned in. "You're lucky you're pretty, Malrik."

"Pretty?" I arched a brow. "That's what we're going with?"

"Oh yeah. Downright adorable."

I was a Stoneborn warrior. A protector of the realms. Battle-scarred, ancient, and now curiously smitten with a thief. But not *adorable*. It was time I remembered that.

Then she leaned forward until we were face to face. Inches apart. I stilled, waiting.

"In fact," she said, her smile so artificial it could've passed for Splenda, "I'd say you're my favorite cuddle bug." She thwacked my nose with her finger to punctuate it and slid across my lap. Her sweet, still-hot ass rested against my swollen, overly sensitive shifter. I closed my eyes. I made no move. Not a single flex.

"And just so we're clear: if you start handling me like I'm made of glass, I will start throwing things."

Her grin was wicked. We locked eyes until she rocked her hips.

My gaze dropped. Then my eyes closed again, fighting to keep still.

"Noted." If my voice came out strangled, it was because I couldn't breathe around the naked press of her against me and still think straight.

That earned me a low, dark chuckle.

She leaned in, and for a moment, I thought she might whisper something or headbutt me. With Nadia, there were no guarantees. Instead, she flung her arms around me.

She let me hold her. For a little while. And it was everything I thought it would be, and more.

"Don't worry, my little thief," I murmured against her ear, voice laced with quiet amusement. "You're not the only one who should come with a warning label."

Her grin turned sharp. Knowing. "Good. I'd hate to be a boring pair."

The little minx had the nerve to smirk as I tucked myself away. That wicked, knowing pull made me wonder if she enjoyed watching me struggle.

I forced my gaze away, choking the steering wheel until my knuckles ached. I needed to focus. I needed to remember why I was here and what I was doing.

"So, eh, what now?" she asked, clapping her hands together and twisting them in her lap.

Why were we here?

Right. I had to find out who put the target on my safe.

"What's the real exit?" I ground out. My voice was rougher than I intended.

"Exit forty-two," she said, sweet and teasing like she hadn't just wrecked me.

I shifted the car into drive, jaw tight.

Focus, Malrik.

The mission. The objective.

Not the woman beside me who, if I wasn't careful, might make me forget exactly what was at stake.

But beside me, Nadia smirked, a challenge and a promise.

If I weren't careful, I wouldn't just lose control.

I'd hand it to her willingly.

24

FLIRTING WITH DISASTER

As he pulls into the driveway of my small bungalow, with its cream siding and brown brick pillars, I can't shake the oddness of bringing him here. We pass the flower bed my neighbor meticulously tends, stopping at the gray half-round mat.

"Hey Katie, I was wondering where you've been." Hank, my hot neighbor and the manager of my subdivision, whom I may or may not tease mercilessly, walks past his shrub and into my yard. He leans against the side of the pillar, comfortable in his usual spot. Hank scans over Malrik, looking past him unfazed. It seems ridiculous, but I feel offended—I don't even know why, which irritates me even more.

Malrik seems to take no offense at being overlooked as he leans against the doorframe, looking as casual as ever. The bigger man watches Hank for a long, unnerving moment, then switches his gaze to me.

Slowly, as his eyes connect with mine, he lifts his hand to his chin and strokes his lip. It is a subtle reminder that has my heart beating over time.

"Oh yeah? Cool." I smile, leaving his unasked question unanswered. Instead of continuing the conversation, I turn to the door. Hank is a decent, if not a bit obtuse, guy. Usually, I would use him as a way to make my escape, but we are past that now.

"Who's the guy, a new buyer?" Hank asks quietly. "If you've sold another house, we should celebrate; I just got a vintage wine collection I'd love to show you." His easy smile brightens his handsome face, making his playful line even better. I make a note to myself to steal those bottles of wine.

"Oh yeah? Anything I'd like?" I play along as Malrik takes his time opening the door.

"Well, I'd have to ask you some pretty personal questions. You know, get inside your head to figure out your tastes." He lifts his hand and ducks it inside my coat, his fingers wrapping around my leg and sliding down the back of my calf. A black boot kicks his arm away—not hard, but with controlled force.

"Don't." Malrik pulls me back, standing and looking down at Hank as if he is ready to bust his face. I gasp, looking between both men.

Hank isn't a small guy; he's probably used to being the biggest presence in any room. I watch as my neighbor's confidence flares. His shoulders stiffen, legs brace apart, and his chest puffs out, like he's ready for a fight.

But his bravado flickers out when Malrik squares against him, silent yet imposing. Malrik stands to his full height, sunlight lighting up his scarred face as he stares down my neighbor. With only a chin drop and a glare, he sends Hank scrambling back.

"Sorry, man."

"Woah. No. Bad!" I scold. "I'm sorry, Hank," I shout after him. "And you!" I grab Malrik's massive arm and pull him in, my eyes still fixed on Hank's retreating form.

"You, don't apologize for me." Then Malrik turned his attention back to Hank. "And you shouldn't be apologizing to me but her."

"You're right." Hank agrees amicably.

Malrik didn't move. I pulled his arm, and it didn't budge. He was locked in place.

"Admitting it isn't the same as actually apologizing. Do it now."

With a look, I turn back to my neighbor. Hank's eyes were wide with shock. I saw the moment his humiliation turned to indignation as soon as his eyes met mine.

"I'm sorry, Katie. I shouldn't have done that." He continued to look contrite, but his eyes held daggers.

I stood there with my mouth open and nodded. What do you say to an apology? Especially one like that. "Thank you. You should go now." I keep my voice neutral and nod towards his house. He leaves but doesn't hustle to get back to his property line.

Great. Now who's going to mow my lawn?

When the door closes, I turn to a man I don't know how to deal with, standing in my living room looking ridiculously big next to my dainty floor lamp.

His focus is already locked on me. I look down at my hand that's still fisting his sleeve and quickly let go. A part of me needs to distance ourselves, while another wants to hold on tighter.

No one has ever defended my honor before. He went all noble, and surprisingly, that shit was kinda sexy. I can't even process how squishy that made me feel.

"That was completely unnecessary." I square off with the mammoth of a man, oddly undaunted.

"You're right. Who does that guy think he is touching you?" He turns, his expression changing from an emotionless mask to something predatory.

"That's not what I was talking about." I take a step back and then hesitate. "And don't you think that's a bit hypocritical?"

"Perhaps, but I wonder how quickly he would have realized you're not wearing anything under that trench coat." He continues, each step pushing me back towards the front door until I feel more daunted. I lick my lips as he nears.

As much as I appreciate his easy calm, I like this side of him just as much. The brief cracks in his armor show the passion and intensity he tries to hide. "And I wonder what he would have wanted then?" Malrik's hand slowly drags up the edge of my coat, just enough to catch a breeze.

I swallow hard around the kink in my neck as he towers over me. He leans forward, lifting an arm over my head while his stare tracks my anxious shift. My heart has started speeding up again. At the rate I'm going, I'm going to have a heart attack.

He surrounds me, and as his eyes dip on my lips, I realize we've never kissed. That stabs me with a spike of regret. A kiss should be my first dare.

After sharing such an intimate moment with him, I find it oddly difficult to play the charming manipulator. What am I doing, thinking of being pressed against this door and kissed breathless? Struggling to lie and cheat? That's not me.

"Let's just get this over with." I clear my throat and look away. There is only so much tension a girl can take. Not that having him in my home is much of a relief.

The reprieve from his stare gives me time to try to see my house through his eyes.

It isn't good.

Not compared to his mansion. Hell, not even compared to his garage. But it is the last bit of security that I have left. Though now that Malrik knows about it, it's ruined.

"It's not what I was expecting," he says, breaking away. "I suppose I pictured you in a high-rise overlooking the city."

"This is one of the first safe houses I stashed away. It's perfect because it's subtle." Now, it is my last.

He looks around my living room, his calm façade in place again, his hand grazing the top of the brown suede corner couch. I feel more exposed now than when stretched across the table. No one comes into my home; I have it that way for a reason.

My style is funky. I realize how much so by the sparkle in Malrik's eyes as he takes in my home. From the cabaret-styled end table that has red, black, and gold dripped beadwork running down three feminine stocking-clad legs to the five-piece set of black-framed expressive eyes that stare across the room above the couch, a rare peek into the truth of me.

It must seem busy and disorderly compared to his spartan tastes.

"And here I thought all you wanted was flashy bobbles."

He picks up a bronze statue of the head of a statesman from the Hellenistic period that is the centerpiece to crawling vines adorning my mantle. The statue is as obviously authentic as the vines are fake.

What can I say? I have a better gold thumb than a green one.

Flicking the switch lights up the living room. It should help ease the new tension between me and the big guy. But with Christmas lights swirling down the curtains, illuminating the pictures hanging across from the couch and woven around my stereo, I give him more to judge.

I inhale hard and fast but slow my exhale to regain my equilibrium. "Yeah, well, it shows how well you know me."

"I do plan on changing that." His sideways stare cuts through me.

He looks so sincere, and it makes my heart clutch. A smile pulls the edge of his lips as he looks away, continuing through the room. I don't know what makes me jumpier: the knowledge that he wants to know more or that what he may find will scare him off.

And not just because he's standing surrounded by all the things I've collected, a houseful of damning evidence I can't seem to part with. What can I say? Stealing gives my bitter heart an ounce of happiness.

But then, why do I feel nothing but dread and shame as he stalks through my home? Maybe because I want him to see me as more than a burglar. Before I can say anything, Malrik starts flipping through some stacks of paperwork.

"Hey! Get out of there!"

I jump between him and my mail, blocking his view.

"What, you don't like a stranger going through your home, rummaging through your belongings?"

"Funny," I say.

"I'm not joking. Get ready," the big guy demands. "Get dressed; you'll show me this shop, Exclusives."

"Listen, I'll take you where you want, but that's where this ends," I say as I lean against my end table.

"That is what we agreed upon, little thief." His voice remains calm and controlled.

I have to decide—protect my interests or keep my pride. "I want to be very clear. You're going to take me to Darius's shop, and then you'll let me go," I demand with a smile as I slip behind my door.

He'll follow me in and forget all about snooping around my house. Grinning to myself, I prop my leg up on the edge of my bed, ready to look sexy.

Nothing.

"Aren't you going to watch my every move?"

But a few seconds turn into a minute, and he is still in my living room, snooping. "I'll allow you some privacy to get dressed," he concedes graciously as if granting me kindness as he blatantly continues his exploration.

Damn. I'd been hoping to distract the man. My lip flares in pain as my teeth nibble a bit too hard. Frowning, I take a deep breath because it doesn't bother me, not at all. I huff and try to reclaim my mask, forcing myself to look as unshakable as Malrik might be.

I set the trap, bait the hook, and step into the fire myself, only to realize he doesn't burn. He flips my expectations on their head, leaving me off balance.

One thing is certain: he has way more self-control than I gave him credit for. Or maybe I have far less control over his desires than I think.

Either way, that's trouble.

"I know I have no right to ask this, but please don't look through my things," I shout. I step out and wrap my silk robe around me. I take a peek from behind the fabric room divider. Instant relief spreads when the big guy is nowhere near my hidey spot. I can relax as long as he is flipping through my obvious loot.

Foregoing my usual underwear for something special, I turn and quickly get dressed. My lace bra presses against my skin, hidden beneath the oversized sweater. It sends a ripple of comfort through me. Yanking a hanger from my hook, I strip the black high-waisted leather pants, trying to sense Malrik through the changing wall.

As I step out, I come face to face with Malrik's intense stare.

"What's this?" Malrik holds the folded square of bleached cardstock between us.

I start to snap at him to leave my things alone, but then I think better of it. "I don't know, I must have stolen it. Are you surprised?" As his hand lowers, my eyes track the letter before I look away.

"This was with a box of mementos. They look important."

"I'm sure they were to whoever I stole them from." I shrug as if the answer is easy, as if I am not lying through my teeth, and I am scared he'll call me on it.

"That's a line no one should cross."

"I would say I don't see the problem with it, but—"

"Now that it's your turn, you're starting to see things a bit differently?"

"Let's just say it's giving me perspective."

"Imagine that, the thief that doesn't recognize courtesy or boundaries until she's asking for it."

"That's the dorkiest thing I've ever heard." I snort a light-hearted laugh as I head back toward the front door.

"I can see how you'd be unfamiliar with terms like honor and integrity, but those don't ever go out of style where I'm from."

Abruptly, he tosses the letter on my coffee table, giving it a curious look before turning for the door.

"Ok, that's the dorkiest thing I've ever heard," I explain as I slip into some sneakers and grab my bug-out purse. It's a nondescript leather bag, but it has everything a girl needs to start over at the drop of a dime.

I have to be ready if Malrik doesn't follow through. I'll have to find my way to escape. It's not like it would be the first time. And if I can pull this off, it won't be my last.

25

COUSINS, CHAOS, AND CLOSE CALLS

We're almost at the shop. We have to get through a tidy alley and cross the street. My best chance at changing my fortune will all be over soon.

My feet feel heavy, and as I drag them through the crumbled pavement, they kick up dirt. I suck in a breath, then let it out in a slow, weary sigh.

"Boy, what have you got, shit for brains?"

The familiar chortle freezes me in my tracks. Ivok. It has to be him. Acid splashes in my gut until I taste it on the back of my tongue.

No. What are the chances that we're both on the same street simultaneously? Unless they're looking for me.

Impossible. I'm just seeing patterns because today's events shook me up. My family hasn't caught up with me. They still think I'm dead. I'm safe.

By now, Malrik is ahead of me, nearly stepping into the street. He doesn't seem concerned about the loud group on the northern corner. That gives me some comfort; after all, Malrik seems like the type of man with a comfortable relationship with danger.

If my feet were heavy before, they are lead now, but I need to know. Is it them? I inch closer to the edge of the alley's brick wall to peek around the corner.

Shit! Ivok, Milo, and Andrei are lounging in a loose semi-circle. They laugh too loudly, their voices thick with smoke and arrogant. My stomach twists as I watch Ivok flick ash from his cigarette, his grin crueler than I remember. Prison will do that.

What the fuck are they doing in Boston!

"Come on, let's take this left over here," I say.

Immediately, I head away from my cousins.

"No, Eternal Exclusives is to the right there, to the right." Malrik stops and points, forcing me to stop with him.

"Put your hand down." I hiss. "What are you trying to do? Draw as much attention to us as possible?"

"What is this?" He looks at me like he's never seen a more puzzling query.

The fool! He might as well have been waving his arms around.

"Would you just calm down?" I'd beg if I thought it would get him to move. I can't afford to catch my cousin's attention. Whatever drew them here, I need to stay away from it.

Malrik follows my eyes and squints at the group for a second. "You're afraid of them. Why?" He leans forward, not quite crowding me but still close enough to ensure I have his full attention. "Do you know how ridiculous it is to be scared of anyone with me by your side?"

"What?" I laugh in four short chuckles before going straight face. "The ego on you!"

I pull back and glare up at him. "I'm well aware," I reply, my voice deep and threatening. That tone rarely gets me what I want. I need him to get me out of this place before my cousins spot me. Moderating my tone, I force a smile, hoping it eases the impact of what I'm about to say. *That you believe...* "You're the bigger threat; you could protect me from them right now. I don't have the luxury of thinking only of the here and now when you're by my side; there are six of them, twelve eyes. I can't have these guys and their friends on my tail. I can't let them see me. So either follow me, or we can part ways here and now." I don't stop but start to veer left. "You know where Darius is now. You don't need me to introduce you."

I get a few steps away when his big hand grabs my arm. I immediately struggle against his hold. At the first pull of my resistance, he lets go, and that leaves a whisper of regret. I dart a glance at my cousin and his cohorts, still lounging. They haven't noticed us. For now.

"What did you do? Did you steal from them too?"

The accusation shouldn't sting, but it does. How can Malrik see the man's nice suit and tastefully expensive adornments and think anything else?

"That hurts, big guy." I lift my hand to my heart and give him my best pout.

"Am I wrong then?"

"Not everything fits into neat little moral boxes, Malrik. Sometimes people have to break the rules to survive," I say.

Malrik studies me, then glances at them. "I don't usually engage with your people, especially when they're organized." He flicks his eyes over me, and I can't read his expression, but it doesn't feel complimentary. "But if they are that big of a threat to your future, I suppose I could incapacitate them for you."

"What? No! I know you're joking, but are you out of your mind?"

Didn't I say there are six of them?

"I'm not. He must have a pleasant mark. Did you love him?"

"Those are my cousins, and they'll put a hit out on me as soon as one of them lays eyes on me. And yes, I did steal from them. I stole from my entire family." This time, I pull away from him, wanting his focus off of me. "Then I did something even worse. And I'd do it again in a heartbeat."

He doesn't know anything about me, not really. By the judgment that furrows his brow, I need to keep it that way. Unfortunately, I might have given him a good spot to dig.

"I guess I'm leaving alone. It's been—"

"We're not doing that, Nadia."

Squaring my feet and pushing my fists into my hips, I show him exactly what I will do. "I don't know what you're doing, but I'm going this way."

"Come here, please," he coaxes. "They can't see us."

Malrik doesn't stop encouraging me to come closer

and closer until we're nearly standing toe to toe. Then, his arms wrap around me. At first, he hovers before touching me, then drops his arms with gradually increasing pressure. I want to resist again, out of principle, but being surrounded by him feels nice.

"Nothing's going to touch you while I'm here. Not now, not ever. You have my word."

I shake my head at his melodrama, ignoring the blush that warms my neck. He takes this honor thing way too seriously.

"You don't understand the kind of enemies I have."

"They're nothing compared to me."

"They're bad, Malrik. It's bad."

"You'll explain it to me later." Then he pulls the trench coat up to obscure most of my face. "For now, stay to my left and walk in step with me. They'll never see you through me."

Tisking, I roll my eyes, but his arm around me keeps me from turning away. I wish I could explain to him. I wish I could say something that clears the suspicion from his stern lips.

"I was just trying to get out of a bad situation," I finally admit.

"Is this why you're so secretive about your past?" Malrik asks.

I pinch the bridge of my nose, this time exaggerating my frustration with a shoulder shrug.

"Keep your secrets for now. I don't understand your fear, but I don't have to. Are you ready to go into your boss's shop?"

"He's not my boss, he's my blackmailer."

"Fine, call him what you will as long as you make the introduction. You want to be rid of me, don't you?" He nods his head towards Darius's shop, stepping aside.

"Of course," I croak as I follow in step.

Ew, why does that feel like a lie?

It must be because I haven't stolen anything valuable yet. I've never left a job unfinished. Treasure unlooted. Because that, by any sane person's standards, is a damn shame.

Yeah. That has to be it.

26

THE DEVIL'S IN THE DETAILS

"He isn't here," I grumbled.

"Someone must have tipped him off," she said, peeking down an aisle of shelves.

How could that have happened? I must have given her a suspiciously pointed look because she swung towards me with a quickfire glare.

"You think I did it?"

"Did you?" I question.

"Wow, you must think I'm pretty impressive—"

"I do," I admitted. After all, my little thief had managed to break into my house and turn my world upside down.

"Oh. Erm, obviously. You don't get to be where I am, from where I've been, without being amazing." My little mortal flipped her hair over her shoulder and shifted from foot to foot.

Was she blushing?

Not comfortable with the compliment, lil mani? Interesting.

"Malrik, you're not exactly built for stealth with all your stomping and big..." Her eyes trailed down my body, and I felt her stare like a torch. "Shoulders," she finally finished. "Besides, Darius probably has cameras all over the place. He probably knew we were here before we even left the parking lot."

"Let's look around and see if we can find anything."

This Darius guy was bad news. Throughout the building, ancient infernal runes carved patterns of protection and something else I couldn't decipher. A stone filled with bad omens settled heavily in my stomach as I noticed a long line of seemingly random scratches outlining a wooden box.

"What did you find?" she asked.

As a mortal, she was surprisingly resilient. Not ten minutes ago, fear had been stamped so deep in her face that her body trembled with the panicked need to flee. Now, she studied herself in a mirror, pressing a dress against her body, inspecting herself from different angles.

I tucked the box behind my back. "Nothing. Just an inventory list."

"Wow. You might be the worst liar I've ever met." Setting the dress on a shelf of unboxed vintage toys, Nadia turned toward me with the focus of a predator.

Energy tingled at my fingertips, quickly turning hot. The banded sigil spilled with infernal heat straight from the churning hellfires. My hand would have melted like plastic if I had been mortal. When she took her first three steps, blisters cut up my arms and shoulder.

Hell, if I'd been human, the shock alone would have killed me.

Fortunately, I wasn't human or mortal. I was Stoneborn, made to endure extreme temperatures. My stone's true form naturally absorbed and evenly distributed heat.

"My people aren't meant for deception. We're made for protection."

"Yeah, yeah, I get it. You're a goodie two-shoes."

"Why would I wear bad footwear? What purpose does that serve?"

"What?" Nadia stopped a few feet away, a hand on her hip, now studying me and the box I was trying to hide. With a casual sidestep, I blocked her line of sight. If she touched it, the heat would burn her.

She didn't stay put for long. She locked her focus on what I was guarding. I'd mistakenly made it more interesting by keeping her away.

Out of nowhere, her delicate wrist flew toward my face, and I cringed, expecting a hit.

"Oh my God, Malrik. I accidentally stabbed you a couple of times. There's no need to flinch like that." Before I could react, she flicked her wrist, snatching the box from my grip with a smug grin.

Breath I didn't even need suffocated me as her hands gripped one of the most protected devices I'd seen in centuries.

Then, something even more terrifying than I'd expected happened.

Her hands didn't melt. They didn't even burn. In fact, in her grasp, the box wasn't even locked. My jaw clenched in an uncontrollable spasm for three beats before I forced myself to swallow the acid creeping up my throat.

"How long have you been working for Darius?" I finally asked after the shock settled.

"Almost two weeks now."

"Two weeks?"

"Yeah, why?" She shrugged, thumbing through the book the box protected, immediately losing interest. She laid it on the counter and sauntered off. Hesitantly, I picked it up.

"I'm just wondering how well you know the guy." More like, just how deep is she into this mess?

"I don't. Not really. Darius is cute, charming, and fun to flirt with, but he gave me this job and lords the evidence he has of me over my head. We're not exactly friends."

Irritation sparked, though I couldn't place where it came from.

"You're working for him and don't know anything about him?" If there was a little snap in my voice, it was because the infernal ledger had Nadia's name written throughout the book. While she'd been flirting with the demon, he'd been keeping tabs. Foolish mortal.

"I mean, I might have found some things, like this shop, but no. I dropped something off, and Darius gave me your file. That's it. He keeps his business to himself, and so do I." Nadia shoved her hands on her hips and shrugged.

"Have you noticed anything off about him?" I pressed.

"Do you mean, has he ever kidnapped me and held me in his basement? Nope, only you."

I pressed my face into a flat stare before something behind me caught her eye. I looked over my shoulder as she breezed past me.

At first, I saw nothing.

Then, as Nadia neared, a glimmer, like leftover Christmas tinsel, scribbled along the face of the door. With each step, a design started to take shape. Like a magnet, she drew closer to the shimmer, and the design grew brighter. Suddenly, my bones became weighted, heavy with apprehension.

"What is it?" she asked.

"It's a door." I didn't bother to explain. She didn't want to know about bloodlocks and demonic hell realms. I might not have known her long. Granted, she was the only exposure I'd had to a human—female or otherwise—but even I couldn't imagine her faring well knowing she'd been working for a demon.

Perhaps she was tied to Darius in a way she hadn't realized. It would explain her resistance to the infernal protections. Hopefully, that's how it went.

"That's blood. Why would this guy have blood on his door? If he's into some weird shit, I'm out."

"You have no idea what you're involved in." I tossed the thick, black, leather-bound ledger onto the counter next to her. It thudded with a weight heavier than itself as if it carried the weight of lost souls it inventoried.

"What does that have to do with me?" She said, waving her hand towards the door.

"It's a ledger, and your name is in here."

"Ooh, oh no!" She chuckled, shaking her head.

I wondered if she'd still be this smug when she realized who she'd been playing with.

"Careful, Nadia." I stepped toward her, hoping to shield her from the weight of the truth. "Some things need to be taken seriously, and others worth fearing."

"Yeah, well, a book isn't one of them." She lifted her chin, her eyes flicking upward, only to stop and flicker back to me. Uncertainty furrowed her brow momentarily before she snorted dismissively, looking away.

"You have no idea what you've gotten yourself into. This Darius guy isn't just some charming shopkeeper blackmailing you. He's making dark deals. You're listed in his transaction ledger."

It took a couple of beats before she lost that absent, wide-eyed, slack-jawed look.

"Okay," she said. "So you think this is some kind of underground extortion network, maybe some snatching."

"You made a deal with a demon. Do you even know the price you paid?"

"No matter how far you go... wait, what?" she mused quietly. She fluffed her hair before she could look at me again, shaking her head.

"Look." I handed her the journal, but Lil Mani's eyes were already tracking the exit. She smiled, but it didn't light her eyes. She shifted to the right, then slowly brought her leg in. Three things registered at once:

Nadia didn't know Darius's true identity.

And she probably believed I'd lost my mind.

She was going to run.

What was I going to do? What was the right thing here? Protect her from the demon or the truth? Which would do more damage? Because knowing that monsters exist is a heavy burden for anyone.

"There are things you don't know. Before you run, look." I opened the book and watched realization lighten her face and darken it. That told me all I needed to know. In the hundred or so lines, Nadia's name appeared in Darius's ledger at least fourteen times. She should be surprised. She didn't even look impressed.

"As long as he's not drawing hearts around my name. Yawn." She studied the book again, this time with more focus. Eventually, she tossed it back onto the counter to her right. "Darius might be a devil, but he's no demon. It's probably just a tally of my debt.

"So you did make a deal with him?"

"No! I mean—yes. Stop trying to confuse me. I didn't make a deal with a demon. Look, I took a job to keep him from leaking the evidence he has against me. It's simple. I didn't trade my soul so I could do more work. Come on, give me some credit. If I were to sell my soul, I'd do it right," she grinned.

My gut twisted. Acid burned up my throat. Fear. For both of us.

She obviously didn't fear for herself, but I feared for her. And myself. Because I'm not ready to know what kind of depths I would go to protect her.

I'd already given her my vow.

My word was an oath.

"This isn't a joke, Nadia. Do you know where humans go when they lose their souls?"

"Hm. Let me guess." She met my gaze with a droll stare, then pouted in mock disappointment. "Come on, big guy. Do you think I'm scared of Hell?"

"You don't need to put on a brave face."

This time, she exhaled so forcefully that her thick lashes fluttered before her eyes inevitably rolled again. "I'm not."

"Enough! Roll your eyes at me again, and I'll ensure they're rolling back for another reason altogether."

At that, her only response was a pouty glare. "You haven't proven anything for me to be scared of, so there's nothing to be brave against."

"If you're ready, I'll prove it. The truth is on the other side of this door."

"Yeah, right. If it could be so easily proven, saints and scholars would be out of a job." She squared her shoulders and rolled her eyes.

That did it.

I darted forward, pinning her between me and the door. A low, dark chuckle escaped my lips. The sound surprised me. Stepping closer, I flattened my hands against the wood behind her, boxing her in.

Her breath hitched, pupils blown wide. And not just from surprise, but something else. Something that made my pulse stutter to match hers. A delicate pink tongue poked from between her destructive mouth and rolled a dark pink sheen across her bottom lip.

I pinched her chin and watched as hesitation and

doubt swam in her eyes. Then I lifted her jaw until she was close enough for me to feel the velvet on her lips. Her breath hitched, and when she looked up, I swore I saw the moment it changed to a challenge.

Fine.

Did she want proof? She'd get it. Let her roll her eyes at the truth.

It could even scare her into good behavior.

She would never understand. She would always be vulnerable to the lie if she remained ignorant.

Hell doesn't exist.

Foolish mortal.

Quickly, I caught her wrist and pressed my thumbnail into her index finger.

If I spilled a little blood now, it might save her later. But even I wasn't foolish enough to lead a mortal through a hell realm.

"Ow! What do you think you're doing?"

She struggled against me, but I lifted our hands and pinched her finger again, spreading her blood into the design. The locking seal broke, and the portal opened.

"I'm going to prove it to you."

"What, are you going to drag me into hell?"

"Do you think I'd let you traipse through the hell realms?" I let out a harsh chuckle. The sound grated on my ears. "That's ridiculous."

Blood was the life force of all things. It could open any portal. Most dimensional beings had more elegant methods for controlling the interdimensional bridge, ways that avoided such barbaric rituals. Demons, however, never had qualms about a bit of bloodletting.

"Then what do you mean?"

"You might not want to know the truth, but I do," I said, finally lowering our hands. "You'll see all you need to without endangering yourself. I'm going, and you're staying here."

27

BETWEEN A ROCK AND A HOT PLACE

"What did you mean I can't go?" I snapped forward from a near-recline, instantly defensive. Who did he think he was, telling me what to do?

"There's a reason your people considered it a one-way trip." He shrugged as if the conversation was already over. Like hell it was.

"This is bullshit."

"You wouldn't like what was on the other side of that door. You might find yourself wishing you'd taken my advice." He warned again.

I forced myself to pause, pretending to consider his warning. But I already made up my mind. No one told me what I could or couldn't do.

"Not likely," I said, tilting my head. "Big talk, big warning, but I'd heard worse. And what's more, I have a problem with that other 'T' word. Trust. That is, I don't trust this isn't a trick."

"A bit ironic, don't you think?"

"You could call me a hypocrite all you wanted, but I'm going."

"No. You aren't." His voice dropped an octave as he shifted, shoulders squaring, feet planted, blocking the handle entirely. He became a wall of resistance between me and the door.

"Wanna bet on it?"

"I don't understand you," he sighed.

"Don't try." I tried to keep my grin to myself, but how his thick brows pulled together told me I'd failed.

"I hope you realize you're risking much more than your life when you step through that door."

"The 'demon door,'" I said with a wink.

His head shook in a hard no. "Because you refused to take this as anything more than a joke, I can't allow it."

"Allow it? Who do you think you're talking to?"

"A thief that knows nothing of the real world."

"I knew plenty. Enough to know that if you didn't play the game, the game plays you."

"Your mind, body, and soul are on the line, and this isn't a game."

"Exactly," I nod my head. "Step aside."

He blocks the door with a swift arm bar.

"I see now. The more I fight, the more determined you become." He relents under the twinkle of mischief that seemed to build every time he tried to protect me. "All right, but you can never leave my side."

"Why?" With a quick pivot, I popped my hip to the side as he settled a hand on my waist.

"Because then you'd step out of my resonance field.

I'll extend it to protect you, but you must stay at my side."

"What would happen if I stepped outside your bubble?" I play along.

"You'd immediately feel the pressure and heat that came from being in the center of the Earth."

"You mean you think this door leads into the core of the planet?"

"Where else do you think Hell would reside?" He looks exacerbated.

"Right, wow. Ok, how much room would I have?"

"Five feet at most. Why?"

My eyes scanned the room.

I did that to give myself time to process.

Oh, how things change. I'm drooling over Malrik's biceps one moment, and now I'm placating to a full-blown delusion. You think you know a person.

It didn't matter; I would step through that door, which probably leads to a hall with a breakroom and office where Darius held himself up. Then, I'd make sure they take care of each other. Maybe then I'll have enough time to crack his safe. Now that I knew where it was, it was only a matter of time.

Why did the thought twist my gut?

"Here." I grabbed a leather leash off the aisle capper and clipped it to his belt loop.

"I wanted to wear a leash?"

"Technically, I'm the one with the handle." I grinned over my shoulder with a devilish wink and an experimental tug.

The stainless-steel snap hooked to his belt

connected to a studded leather leash wrapped like a bracelet around my hand.

"Is this you laying a claim?"

"You got a problem with that?" My chin jerks in the air, ready for an argument.

"If it keeps you from death by internal pressure and prevents you from wandering or getting snagged, then you could handle whatever you want."

I didn't miss the innuendo of his words, but I did ignore it.

28

DIAMONDS AND DEVILS

Nadia reached for the door with that usual air of confidence. I felt my throat tighten under what I knew was coming.

She arched an eyebrow. "You wanted this, remember?"

I forced a nod. "There's only one way to determine how much of a mess you've made." Yet I didn't step aside.

Indecision wasn't something I ever entertained. Until now. If it were just me, I'd risk it. But dragging my mortal into the veil? That was an entirely different matter.

"We need to figure out who has your soul, and for how long," I said aloud, buying time.

"We?" She said as if no one stood with her like this before.

"You think I'm going to let some demon have you?" I lifted her chin, tilting her head back until the long line of her neck was exposed before me.

She smiled up at me, even as her brow furrowed in confusion.

Someone needed to be there when she met the hard truth. I wanted to be that rock beneath her feet. The veil knew she needed it.

I'd help her rebuild from scratch, even if I had to plant the clues myself.

"You're not worried about me, are you?" Her hands pressed gently to my chest. Her lashes fluttered as her fingers curled over the trembling shell of my heart.

I was a fool. Nadia had no idea what she meant to me. She'd take my treasure and leave without a backward thought. Did she really think I would risk losing her?

"Don't be ridiculous. I'm worried about the demon who bought you. They don't know what they've gotten themselves into. Someone has to warn them."

"Well, fine then," she scrunched her nose and gave me that unimpressed look, but beneath it was a smothered smile. "Let's go. We've got a demon to save."

"Exactly." I agreed but stayed rooted in place.

"Well, go on. Lead the way."

"I'm going. It's just that..."

"Why are you suddenly hesitant to step through, Mr. The Truth is on the Other Side?"

How do I explain what she was about to see?

What could I say that would prepare her?

"Nadia, I must tell you something before we go."

"That sounds ominous."

How was I supposed to explain what I didn't fully understand? What no one did. The mortal realm was the only place where beings like me were forced to blend in. Not even the oldest and most powerful could break that law.

Someone or something didn't want Demons, Stoneborns, Celestials, or any other interdimensional creatures walking among mortals, at least not without disguises and shackles to shield fragile mortal minds.

"This isn't my true form. Like Darius, you'll see what I look like once we step through," I said, bracing for her reaction.

"What do you mean 'your true form'?"

"Nadia, I don't want you to be shocked by what you're about to see. It'll be frightening."

Please don't be scared of me.

"Malrik, you've shown me who you really are." Her hand rested gently on my jaw and was gone before I could savor it. "Easy peasy," she grinned. "Can't be worse than some of the apartments I've lived in."

Her flippancy only made it worse. "Don't take this lightly. Mortals weren't meant to cross the realms. The veil is a mask to stop mortals from losing their minds. Besides, humans sure as hell weren't meant to be traipsing through a hell realm."

"Okay, Lovecraft. I'm more of a show-than-tell kinda girl, so put up or shut up."

She talked a big game, but her nerves showed. Fine. If she could fake it, so could I. My stomach felt full of sulfuric pop rocks. It seemed I'd have to worry for both of us.

What if she took one look at me and panicked?

"All right," I agreed.

Then, a disturbing thought chilled me. The cleaners could erase short-term memories, but it was risky. They'd strip Nadia of memories of her terror. She probably wouldn't remember anything about me. But I could live with that. It would be for the best.

Swallowing the bile coating my throat, I said, "I'll go first. Wait ten seconds before following."

She nodded. I knew she understood.

My fingers curled around the warm door handle. As it creaked open, the air shifted. The crisp scent of cleaner and sweat from the shop vanished, replaced by smoke and the stench of burnt eggs.

With a final sigh, I opened the door. A dim red light beckoned beyond. Nadia shifted closer, peeking around my shoulder. It was pointless. She wouldn't see the realm until she stepped through the door.

Her skin looked off against the warm glow. The fluorescent and infernal light clung to her differently. Razor-thin talons stretched toward her, tracing her skin like claws ripping delicate lace.

The illusion could have been a trick of the light or a portent of doom. It didn't matter. It was too late to change my mind. I'd already stepped through the portal.

Two steps in, the sweltering air became oppressive heat, slapping me like a steam-soaked rag. The brimstone vents thickened the ozone with trace metals, distorting my footsteps into muffled echoes.

Unlike some, the heat didn't boil me alive, nor did the pressure crush me flat. Of the three Stoneborn classifications, I was Morphic, born from subterranean pressures, remade in Earth's molten core, and nearly immune to the environment. Still, even I felt uneasy here. Amid the eggs and rot, faint echoes of tormented screams rolled through the cavernous tunnels.

It wasn't sunlight here but the pulsing glow of hellfire. The veil still held its shop shape, but that wouldn't last. Soon, it would peel back reality until nothing of the mortal world remained.

Behind me, Nadia skipped through with a wink and a shit-eating grin. I knew the moment she realized her mistake. Her smile slipped, and the charge faltered.

"You didn't wait." My eyes narrowed, a frown tugging at my chin.

"I got bored." Her voice lost its sharp bravado, now weighted with hesitation.

"There could've been any number of things on the other side."

"Well, it's not what I expected, I'll give you that." Her eyes scanned the area, probably still adjusting to the dim light and crushing heat. Her hands hugged her arms as she slowly spun.

"This isn't hell. This hallway is the veil: a bridge between realms. Soon, the shop will transform into whatever lies below." I turned in a half-circle, trying to gauge our surroundings.

That was the veil's nature: it separated realms into neat layers, only to punch through and let them bleed together. The veil allowed interdimensional travel and realm transition. We depended on it, even though we understood little of its truth.

"Holy molten mountain, Batman!" Nadia gasped. "Malrik, is that you?"

"Yes."

Her breath hitched. I kept my back turned, every muscle tense, bracing for horror, rejection, or revulsion. Not that I'd blame her. If I hadn't scared her with my size before, I was bound to now.

Seconds stretched. My little thief didn't scream. That should've been a relief, but the silence was worse. No whispered prayers, no slap of fainting...just panting? What?

Against my better judgment, I turned back. Nadia's fingers twitched at her side as if wanting to reach out but unsure.

Then she let out a low whistle. "Oh my. How much do you charge for a climb?" It took nearly five beats before I registered her amusement. She wasn't scared or disgusted. She was drooling.

"Wait. Is that a diamond vein?" Her lids dropped, and she bit her lip.

"What are you thinking right now?" My voice dropped deep, cavernous, filled with a yearning I didn't recognize. If her eyes could speak, I'd be dead. Limb by limb, she was running the numbers, little imp

"That's my kind of a happy trail, and I'm thinking I can't wait to lick every jagged inch of you. Especially the shiny parts."

What? My gut clenched like she'd just punched me. Was it my imagination, or was she eyeing me? Not my imagination. Her gaze never left the diamond vein that started at my stomach and trailed down.

When would I learn she was full of surprises?

But it wasn't just her reaction to seeing an interdimensional being for the first time that stunned me. It was what else I saw.

I worried about how she'd react to me, but I never wondered about her. Floating just beneath her skin were black strands. Inky blood clots swam under her flesh.

My chest tightened. Dozens of black streaks stained Nadia's veins. The infernal heat was nothing compared to the ice spreading through my veins. I'd been wrong. So wrong.

Something about her always felt magnetic. I'd chalked it up to stubbornness, her uncanny ability to push back every time the world closed in.

She wasn't caught in a demon pact. It was far worse.

As the veil settled, I realized it wasn't adaptation.

It was recognition.

29

DEMONS, DEALS, AND DADDY ISSUES

"**C**ome on, we need to find Darius," he says, his voice tinged with concern. After seeing Malrik, I almost forgot Darius holds the information he needs.

I still can't get over how huge he is.

I've never seen someone as cut as Malrik like the Hulk had a love child with an Easter Island statue.

Malrik's true form is far from an ancient Grecian statue. His build isn't smooth or buffed; instead, it's layered in rough stone deposits. The rock layers formed thick muscles like plated armor, and underneath, cracks glowed. His entire length was streaked with tiny fissures, no wider than my thumb.

I want to trace those lines to see if the fire beneath his stone skin is as hot as it looks.

After all of Malrik's warnings, I expect him to be terrifying and this place to be, at least, dark and foreboding. Whips and chains forged from hellfire and brimstone? That, at least. But the reality barely stretches my imagination.

We go from low-budget commercial retail buildings with white slat walls for hanging merchandise to more of the same. But slowly, it shifts until we're still in a building—the same one, perhaps. But then, after ten yards, the walls begin to morph.

How is that possible?

Maybe some hell house horror show was attached to Eternal Treasures. I would think this was a prank if it weren't for the blazing heat, low red lights, and steady thrum from all sides.

Soon, the familiar walls end at a heavy, iron-bolted door. With a backhanded touch, as if checking for heat in a fire, Malrik grabs the door by its slide-lock handle. The door groans as it opens, like a resonant scrape caught in a long hall of echoing metal. The corrugated industrial walls give way to sweltering stone.

Thick smoke curls overhead, fed by steam seeping through jagged rock vents and cracks in the ground. Movement spins the steam and breaks the hazy fog. Up ahead, the red sky hovers lazily over the bazaar, churning with sooty clouds and crackling with arcs of lightning that shoot upward instead of down. The air is heavy with smoke and acrid steam, making my hair instantly frizz.

Malrik extends his hand, his fingers brushing my elbow. I hesitate, then rest my palm against his, grounding myself against the relentless groaning hum that fills the air.

"I've changed my mind. I don't think this is a good idea."

"Don't you want to know the truth?" Malrik asks.

"No, not really. I'm okay living with blind optimism."

"It's already too late for that, as you know. Are you ready?"

"Yeah." I shake my head.

I think.

No. Not ready. But it looks like we're about to do it anyway.

"You might be the bravest human I've ever met."

"How many humans have you met?"

"Well, technically, you're the only one I've gotten to know."

"I'm going to pretend you said, 'a whole bunch' instead and assume they are all very important people."

"Nadia. I won't let anything hurt you. Do you trust me?"

"More than anyone in a long time."

Surprisingly, it wasn't a lie.

"Then let's find this demon and get some answers."

It didn't sound like an inside joke when he said it that way. It sounded real. Especially coming from the ten-foot stoneman I'd been cuddling.

The sounds of bartering and bickering led us to an open cavern. In the distance, next to the open market, a glowing river of magma threads the landscape like a fiery vein. The air is oppressive, heavy with the scent of sulfur and scorched earth.

"What is this place?" I ask and immediately regret it. As soon as I open my mouth, metal coats my tongue.

"Welcome to the Demon Bazaar," Malrik says, his voice dry and filled with a hint of danger that sends shivers down my spine.

I can barely process his words and not just because his voice has taken on a deep, resonant timbre. My gaze flicks back to the chaos around me until a sudden flash of silver catches my eye.

Instinctively, I turn toward it, watching as the thread of bright light spirals through the air. The thread floats toward a gnarled, clawed merchant, who grins as the light coils into his grasp. My joints freeze as the merchant feeds the light into his chest, which disappears in a sickening slurp.

"Was that... someone's soul?" I whisper, hoping to hide the trembling of my voice.

"Don't ask questions you don't want answered," Malrik replies grimly. Before I can move, another clawed hand grabs my arm. Grit and grease soil my shirt. I spin to face the asshole who touches me to find a demon with slick, oily skin and too many teeth.

Surrounded by hellish hagglers, none of whom have heard of dental hygiene, I feel a wave of helplessness wash over me. Where has Malrik gone? I pull on the leash three times—quick, desperate tugs. Their words shout at me as another seller, with a thick layer of yellow-green mucus, reaches for my cheek.

"Nope, nope, nope! Maaalriiik!"

"Careful, little mortal, not even that will protect you down here," another creature with beard hair like spiky glass croons, its voice both melodic and predatory. "You could be so much more... if you let me help you." Its eyes shine like a pearl in the moonlight. I step closer, reaching out, suddenly weary of my desperation. They can help me. What pretty eyes...

Something hard yanks my arm, pulling me out of the creature's stare, but more demons circle. Their voices overlap, each offering me something, but the cacophony isn't enough to ease the new ache I have in my heart.

"Your memories traded for strength." One shouts over the rest.

"Your humanity, for immortality," another coos.

"Latent abilities unlocked... for a price." A phlegm-throated haggler hacks.

Images flood my mind: I see myself as a queen, a warrior, a radiant being of power. Each promise is vivid and tantalizing but gone too soon, leaving me with a heavy longing and regret.

"Enough!" A deep-chested shout and a ground-shaking stomp. The force of it was hard enough to throw me off balance and push the crowd back and cut their jeers into silence.

Malrik's voice booms, forcing the crowd to retreat and cutting through the fog in my mind. Finally, I have the space to breathe.

Impressive.

A towering shadow engulfs the more minor bartering demons. Malrik growls low in that penetrating, gravelly way as he draws his sword.

Where did he pull that from?

The threat works. The demons hesitate, their predatory smiles faltering before they fall back.

"Be careful, Nadia. Down here, you're either the servant or the master. Take nothing, not even a compliment."

I swallow hard, and it takes like metal. All around me are all different kinds of beings, and they all look ready to strike. I know something about living with sharks, but this is a hard lesson.

"Do they know you or something?"

"Doubtful, but what's more is now they know you belong to a Stoneborn."

"Belong to?" I scoff, tilting my head to hide the sudden heat in my cheeks. Now, why has that possessive claim sprouted butterflies in my stomach?

I'm not blushing. It's the heat from magma, that's all.

His hand, larger than a textbook, hovers under my chin, just inches away, as if he isn't sure he can touch me with his stone skin. I lower my cheek, resting against the smooth surface of his palm, deciding for him.

I have never felt the weight of someone's stare as intensely as his. Swirling shades of molten amber pin me in place with the intensity of his lingering gaze. His mouth opens, but as our eyes meet in a fleeting, heady jolt, he turns away. "Just keep close."

"Natalia?" The rasp of a voice I never thought I'd hear again turns my blood to ice. My hand snaps out and grabs the smooth stone hand stretched before me. My gaze flicks to Malrik, who goes back and forth as he studies us. Whatever he sees on my face makes him defensive.

Slowly, I turn, unaware that I am breaking away from Malrik's strong protection. I stand frozen in the center of the bazaar, too stubborn to run and afraid to breathe.

A tall, gaunt man stands in a faded suit; aside from his surprise, his eyes are dull and just as faded as his clothes. The short hair he's always kept perfectly combed now lies clumped and singed, sticking out in a mess. The one person I think I'll never see again hoped I never see again, stands before me.

"Daddy?"

"Could that be you?" My father gapes at me with a sneer before his eyes land on Malrik. "With... whatever that is." The sound of stone on stone scraping silences him.

"What did you do to her?" In an unexpected burst of emotion, my father grabs my chin, turning me this way and that way as if studying how much I've changed. "What are you doing here?" His hands grip my arms and grab my shoulders like he can't believe his senses.

"I kinda got caught up in some trouble."

He laughs. It is more like an exhale around a sardonic smile, but it still counts. I made my dad, my always serious father, laugh in Hell.

"You get it, honestly, kid." His hand cups my jaw, his thumb stroking my hair, savoring the touch.

"Dad.... why are you here? How are you here?"

"I get caught up in some trouble, too. I'm a prisoner of my past, paying for my transgressions."

"You mean you can't leave?"

"Not yet, but not forever." He pats my cheek twice. But his reassuring smile slides into a long frown of an abysmal future. "One day, I'll earn my freedom again. Whatever it takes."

My father's grimy hands are tacky against me. I flinch against his touch and look down at the connection. Once, his touch meant protection. Now, all I can remember is the last time he let go. When whatever it took meant selling me off to the boogeyman.

Has Hell changed him that much?

"Whatever it takes," I nod.

"That's my girl. Here, I want you to have this to remember me." My father slides his ring off his soot-streaked hands with a hard tug. I swallow my tears as he brings my hand into his. With a slow roll of his wrist, I watch him pull my hand closer. "I just need to know that you'll take care of things."

His ring. The one he never takes off. It shines as the only thing clean on him. He cherishes this ring. Now he wants to give it to me.

Had he ever given me anything? Other than criticism.

Out of my peripherals, I see Malrik's hands clench to fists as he tilts his head to watch us both intently.

"Nadia, no!" Malrik's shout shakes the cavern. The room shifts and groans in a long, guttural sound like a phantasmal beast bellowing as it charges across the ceiling.

Everyone's eyes dart up, waiting...praying. Stalactites shift, crystal spikes wobble, and waver and everyone holds their breath as a new crack race from one side of the cavern to the other.

No one moves except Malrik, who charges me, looking at me like a Groot linebacker. We aren't even that far apart, but his giant leg-span bridges the gap in a step. His mit of a hand slaps at mine and my father's touch. The ring tosses into the air. Time stills and stretches with silence until I can only hear the groaning from the ceiling above.

"She accepts nothing from you." Malrik steps between me, and I shuffle back.

"That was—"

"It doesn't matter. You take nothing from no one here. Nothing is free in Hell."

In a daze, I watch the silver ring I'd grown up wondering about clatter to the smooth obsidian floor of Hell, spinning noiselessly until a dirty, wrinkly hand swipes out and claims it. My father slides the ring back on his pinkie.

"You should have stayed dead, bitch," he spits. My legs lock in place as if melted to the ground. One question rolls into my head: how could I be so stupid?

I stand shocked. With the weight of everyone's eyes, especially Malrik's, sinking on my shoulders, my stomach drops with lead balls while my skin flushes ice against the firestorm.

Only a loud, sharp hiss behind me turns me back to the vendors. My father scurries to the stall he came from, a sharp wince with each step until he is back behind the counter.

Malrik sizes me up and steps closer. I meet him,

closing the distance. He seems to sense the ground beneath me is split with the fissures of past pain.

I watch my father's retreat, waiting for any connection or conspiratorial apology. Honor amongst thieves and all that. Anything that hints that the streak of kindness was more than just a con.

But he doesn't spare me a second look.

And I can't look away.

Was that even really him? Did I just get my mind fucked? A tidal surge of emotion casts a cloud over me, threatening the fragile control I have.

"Are you okay?" Malrik's mammoth paws cover my back in a hold that should be cold and rough, but it is anything but. I lean into him, grateful I have this mountain of a man to ground me. I need all the extra help I can get.

"If you ever wondered why I don't talk about my past, that's why." A part of it, at least.

Then, a slow clap. Is it a taunt? But from who?

The red light turns every shape into a sinister mask as if the creatures down here needed help. At first, I couldn't see anything further than twenty yards. It is all a shimmering spray of fog that splits and rolls around the busy legs of the demon bazaar's patrons.

But then I notice a stocky form in the back. The figure is so far back all I can see is the dark silhouette of his clapping hands and a beat-up fedora.

Could it be?

Darius.

I know it is him immediately. Somehow, I see it in the cocky swagger and a direct stare that is eerily familiar. He relaxes in his chair, facing the smooth stone platform that acts as a stage or auction. Empty chairs surround him. Further out, a few forms spread out, some even humanoid-looking.

But looks can be deceiving.

30

THE DEMON INSIDE

"How can you be sure it's him?" Malrik, the man who had been both captor and protector, asked with his cavernous voice.

That fedora gave him away. "I just do. Look at him. He knows me."

"He looks like he's waiting." Malrik's deep voice lingered in the open air.

I stepped forward, but the leash at my wrist yanked me back, a sharp reminder. Malrik's pace was slow and deliberate. Three of my steps matched his one.

Each inch forward felt like dragging a mountain. "Can you walk faster?" I tugged on the leash.

Malrik didn't speed up. "He's expecting us. I won't rush into a trap."

I sighed, tightening my grip on the leather. I traced the slick material absently. It grounded me. Steadied me. It was a leash, but here, it felt like a lifeline.

"Traps? Great."

I'd had enough of demons, deals, and family

reunions. To see Darius was to face the truth, of what was crawling under my skin. *No. Don't think about it.* But it was too late. I watched the stain pool at my fingertips, bleeding into my palm, a murky, grim reminder of what's inside me: the darkness that threatened to consume me, the legacy of my father's choices.

Turning away, I closed my eyes, but the image remained. Now I could feel its pressure as it slinked up to my elbow, along my muscles, and between my veins, trailing a slight chill in its wake.

Malrik turned sharp. Whatever he saw on my face caused a frown. "Listen to me, Nadia. You're my fearless and ruthless little thief. That's what I like about you. Are you going to let someone like him throw you off your game? No."

I swallowed, gripping the leash tighter.

"Unless you want every demon and slave here to see what happens when you act against me."

A deep-seated vibration raced up my spine like a purr. Squinting, I looked up at the big guy. His granite lips pulled in a smirk.

"I'd like to see you try," I snapped, but it didn't have my usual bite.

"Perfect, my lil mani."

"Malrik?"

"Yes?"

"What does lil mani mean?"

"Little gem. My little gem."

I tried to laugh, but it came out of a sigh. I was no one's treasure. Hadn't Malrik seen what just happened? Even my father—

Malrik hoisted me up, pressing us chest to chest. My fingers dug into the sharp crystal protrusions along his collarbone—steadying, grounding. He carried me like I was weightless, breakable.

"I can't tell you how much I treasure you."

My heart slammed against my ribs. I wanted to scoff, dismiss it—but the words clung to me, sticky and unwanted. Hope curled up inside my chest like a stubborn ember. *Damn it.*

"You will try though, right?" I bit my lip and looked up at him.

"Will this do? In my very long life, I've only pledged a vow of protection to one person."

"Who?"

"You."

"Me?" I confirmed.

"In the alley, I promised you I wouldn't let anything harm you, and I meant it. No matter what."

"And look where that got you? I've got my cousins sniffing around. We're in Hell, and you've already had to fight off demons and my demented father so that we could talk to another demon who may or may not have stolen my soul."

I shook with a gentle, persistent tremble. Malrik pulled me closer, stroking my shoulder with his thumb. His embrace was cold compared to the furnace we were in, and I took comfort in the cool touch.

"You do have a knack for getting into trouble."

"Malrik, I'm terrified." I pushed my arm between us. The stain danced beneath my skin—tingling.

"That just means you're here for a reason."

"Like my father? Am I destined to end up in Hell?" I asked, my voice trembling with disbelief.

"Your father made his choices, and he'll live with them. You're making yours right here; right now, all you have to do is make sure you keep making the right choices. After meeting him, I'm surprised at how relatively well-adjusted you are. And this," he grabbed my hand, pinching my wrist delicately, he flipped it over to show the black smear that floated like a squid up my forearms, "can be fixed."

"You really think so?" I asked, my doubt evident in my voice.

"I do."

"Okay, I... guess." I smiled, but I didn't feel anything.

"Remember—no matter what," Malrik muttered, setting me down.

It was an excuse when my father said it, but it felt like a vow coming from Malrik's lips.

I wanted to crawl back into his arms. For just a moment, I believed him. Believed in him. My kidnapper, my emotional support rock. Who would have thought?

We end up standing to the left of a humanoid figure in a pinstriped fedora, and to the right of the stage, a grand platform adorned with intricate carvings and flickering torches that cast eerie portents.

The closer we are, the more foolish I feel. This has to be Darius; he has the same ugly pinstripe hat. But his obsidian skin glows like dripping oil, metal shifting like liquid armor.

I try not to stare. Or, I try to stare through the

monster and see down to the man. It was easy with Malrik. Even though his eyes are rubies, how he looks at me hasn't changed. But I only met Darius once.

"Nadia, what a pleasant surprise to see you here and with company." He sounds like the familiar, charming rogue I've come to think of as Darius, except now the smooth voice changes to pop and crackle like a distorted record.

His metal horns curve from his head and shoulders, thick as my fist and tapering into black-chrome points. Like an iron vent, his armored jaw was melded into his cheekbones, concealing his mouth and nose.

"So it is you, Darius?"

"So you recognized me. I'm impressed." The creature turns his head and inspects me. He has eyes of fire and a face plated with metal, and it's impossible to read him.

"You want to talk about surprises? What the Hell did you get me into?" I demand taking a small step forward. Quickly, Malrik pulls me back.

"Only a little breaking and entering. Honestly, Nadia, by most standards, that's child's play. It looks like you failed. I thought you had skills."

"Don't talk to her like that."

Malrik takes a small step forward, just enough to take the lead, but when he stops, his foot stomps with enough force to shake the ground beneath us all.

Gradually, I started to see Darius. It isn't in his flame-flickered eyes that flare for a split second but in the language of his body. He shifts his weight, a casual lean that isn't quite as effortless as before. Malrik takes another step forward, and just like that, Darius's relaxed stance breaks.

He's afraid of Malrik. A demon is scared of my Malrik. Interesting.

Though, I suppose if I were the one to send an innocent mortal into the clutches of an immortal warrior who now has nothing but time to kill on a petty revenge plot, I'd be scared, too.

"Don't get your rocks tumbled, Stoneborn. I meant no harm. She's practically family. Why do you think we got along so well?"

"What do you mean practically family? I barely even know you." I square my stance, finally summoning the courage to face him fully.

"What do you think is floating under your skin? If I had to guess, it's a chaos demon spawn—congratulations."

What? A demon? Inside me?

"You knew?" I choke out.

"No, but there were signs. But who am I to judge? Your path is yours to walk. But who knew you came from a family of degenerates? A trifecta."

"What the hell does that mean?" I snap, and Malrik's hand rests on my shoulders as if he's about to hold me back.

"Of all the places in this city, you end up at my door. A coincidence? No. Your blood was never clean. Do you think you walked into this? No, girl. You were led—but not by me. Someone wanted you to get mixed up in the veil. There's nothing I can do about that."

"You can get this out of me. Now!"

"No, I don't know how to do that. You can't be infected with darkness unless it's already inside you."

What does that mean?

I recoil. "That's a lie." The spawn slips between my ribs, threading through them like tightening a corset. I have to grit my teeth to keep from cursing them all.

Darius tilts his head, ember eyes flickering. "Is it?"

I turn back to Malrik. "You said this was fixable."

"Yes, but I never said it would be easy," Malrik clarifies.

"He's right. I can't get it out of you. The only way is to starve it out. However, I think that's a mistake. You made your choice, and you should live with the consequences; that demon has just as much right to live as you do."

"I didn't ask for this."

"Maybe not in so many words. But come now, think back now and be honest. Was there ever a moment in your life when you knew it was wrong and did it anyway? You called to it with your thoughts and actions."

What if it wasn't me that did those things? What if that nagging itch was the demon encouraging me?

"But I don't want this."

"Well, Nadia, you didn't think those decisions were inconsequential, did you? You chose your path because you wanted your immediate pleasure to be satisfied more than you wanted to be virtuous. We all do. Those actions have consequences that will follow you no matter what you choose."

"I'm going to be like you?"

"Don't be ridiculous. No one can be like me," Darius winks.

"What's going to happen to me?" My sides cramp and ripple as the spawn settles around the base of my spine.

"Eventually, it will grow."

"What happens to me when it reaches maturity?"

"It takes over your body as it feeds on your soul, then it tears you apart like a baby bird breaking its way out of the egg."

Well. That's graphic.

Malrik's voice turns to stone. "You seem pretty comfortable. Don't mess it up by lying."

"I didn't need to lie. That *could* happen." Darius's flames flicker, deepening in hue. "I don't deal in souls; I deal in debts. Besides, I couldn't if I wanted to—someone already claimed her soul."

The air thickens, clawing at my skin. Claimed? My soul was already owned? My ears roar, drowning me in half-finished questions. I reach instinctively for Malrik, and his hand finds mine, steady, real.

No, he's wrong. Impossible. I want to scream at Darius, shake him, make him pull it out of me—but the look in his eyes says he isn't lying.

"Who?" Malrik asks because I can't form words.

"I don't know," Darius admits, leaning back.

The world tilts. No, that isn't possible. That isn't—

"But whoever it is," he continues, "they'd have to be a hell of a lot higher up the chain than little ol' me."

Cold terror licks my spine. Someone out there owns my soul. And I have no idea who or why.

"Because you're just a warden?" Malrik's voice drops, too casual.

I haven't been around Malrik for long. The granite mask of his expression makes him hard to read. But the drop and slow draw hint at his intention. Malrik is back in interrogation mode.

"That's right."

"I've never met a demon that didn't constantly talk themselves up," Malrik notes, now eyeing Darius with greater suspicion.

"That's because I'm not an impressive demon. I'm comfortable enough with myself to own that. And let's be real, no one wants to hear a story where someone skates by." He's still the same easy-going, charming personality, but now he has a visage of some viscerally inspired monster from a horror film.

"How long have you been topside?" Malrik asks, looking the demon up and down.

"Just as long as you. Wait, don't tell me you don't recognize me." Darius finally turns his full attention to Malrik. Tilting his head to the side casts the red light to streak up his horns, swallowing the light as soon as it hits his skin.

At that, Malrik's smooth face tightens into a glare.

"We've met?"

"Not formally." Darius smiles.

"Who wants the amulet?"

"Ah, you're closer than you realize. When you remember who you saw me with, you'll know who sent me now."

Before Malrik can respond, Darius is shaking his head. "So much for stone remembers all."

"I'm tired of playing these games. Answer the question, or you won't have a summer home on realm two; it will be your permanent residence."

"You're so angry at me that you don't even realize I've answered all your questions."

"Why are you helping us?" I ask even though it doesn't feel like much help.

"Yes. Why indeed?"

"Why do you care?" I try again.

"Come on? I don't have to have been born in the mortal realm to love Earth. Why would I willingly invite bigger and worse predators into my feeding ground? So whether through a demonic uprising or alien invasion, I've got a good thing going here, and I'm not gonna let anyone fuck it up."

"Alien invasion? Wait. What?" I say.

"That's awfully heroic of you," Malrik continues, but his eyes flick to me.

"No, it's not. I'm selfish. I'm protecting my interests. Just like you, after all." The fire of Darius's eyes shifts to me. The twin flames are beautiful in a mesmerizing way.

"You think this is a game, Darius? I can send you back to Hell with a whisper, and this time, I'll make sure you're in so deep that you can't come crawling back."

"Hell? You're threatening to send me home? Come on now. What's in store for me if I fail is much worse.

You're wasting my time. I don't need threats, Malrik—I need results. The amulet. Where is it?"

"It's where it always is: safe."

"You're making this harder than it needs to be. Maybe I should take a different approach—start calling in some debts. Nadia's, for example. Haven't you heard she's racked up quite a few? Might be time for her to start paying up."

"You said we would be clean and clear after this." I feel my fists clench and my molars ache. "Where's my amulet? If you don't pay up, I don't do anything for free. I'm a demon, not a saint."

"Leave her out of this."

"No, don't leave me out of this. This is my life we're talking about here."

"You're the one who brought her here." Darius continues with an easy shrug.

I start to see red.

"After you unlocked your ledger and the door. For Nadia. Why?" Malrik demands.

At Malrik's willful involvement in talking around me, I snap. In a moment of pure instinct, I step between Malrik and Darius into the square space between them. I don't face Darius. He's not the one I'm pissed at.

"Let's just say I'm hedging my bets. You better not let me down."

"Speak plainly."

Malrik looks down at me, and for once, I don't try to mask my expression. His eyes locked on mine, and I didn't flinch; I glared deeper. His only answer was to bow his head in a brief incline before pivoting back, opening a space for me.

"She's the key," Darius answers, leaning back.

"The key to what?" Malrik asks.

"The key to the thirteenth realm... and, apparently, to you"

31

EMOTIONAL SUPPORT ROCK

"Are you ready to finish this, lil mani?"

The scent of old comics clung to Darius's topside shop, mixing with the faint metallic tang of Hell's sulfur spray. Nadia hadn't said a word since we left the demon bazaar.

A far-off, lost look had taken over her face. For ten minutes, she'd been whispering a song about "where her demons hide." She was spiraling.

It didn't take a genius to see how her shoulders had drawn in; her usually sharp eyes changed into an unfocused, almost starry fog.

"Nadia," I tried again, softer this time. "Where do you want to go?"

Nothing.

Then—her shoulders realigned, straightening firm like she was about to pull it all together.

Her face crumbled first. A flicker of grief started in her brows and twisted through her body like a wrung-out rag until she collapsed in on herself. My heart broke with every stuttered breath she drew. I wrestled with my indecision.

She curled forward as if trying to hold herself together, and before I even thought about it, I moved.

She didn't resist when I scooped her into my arms; she just held on. I'd never felt as grounded with purpose as when she clung to me. Something in my chest dropped like a heavy plate that finally shifted into place. It knocked around so hard that Nadia's eyes jumped up to mine. Her body was tense and curled against me, but she didn't shift away.

"I'm going to take you back to my place," I whispered as I kissed the side of her head.

Nadia was still lost in whatever inner battle she struggled with. So I lifted her in my arms. She didn't lock up this time. There was no struggle to secure her grip; she just continued to stare ahead.

Please be okay. Please get through this.

But how could she? Blow after blow knocked her back, and she kept coming. For some, it was easier to carry on when there was a war around them, but there was nothing to do in quiet moments. It forced you to process. The quiet demanded attention to the things that your mind has been adamantly avoided.

"Listen, Nadia, I know your thoughts are probably much louder than I am right now, but I just want to let you know how proud I am of you. You pushed through, and I don't know what's stronger than that. That's how I know you're going to get through this. You'll see."

As soon as I set her down in the passenger seat, my arms felt empty and my chest cold. I only then realized how good it felt to have her in my arms. With that came the realization of how dangerous my new need had become, because I wanted more. I wanted to hold her and keep her. To have her for as long as she'd let me.

She didn't stir until long after I'd been on the road.

I glanced over when she finally shifted, blinking at me in groggy confusion. "Welcome back."

Her brow furrowed. "Did you...did you carry me?"

"You needed a minute." Or an hour.

She exhaled sharply, dragging a hand down her face. "God. That's embarrassing."

"It's normal." I kept my eyes on the road. "You handled yourself too well in Hell. I'd be more surprised if this didn't hit you all simultaneously."

She snorted, voice still thick. "So what? You were waiting for me to break?"

"Yes. I'm just surprised it took you so long. You must have some questions."

"Just give me a minute." Nadia tucked her feet under her seat and stared out the window. I watched her in my every spare moment. Her stare didn't seem as lost this time, but it was just as far gone.

After nearly thirty minutes, she finally twisted back to me.

"What are you again?"

"I'm a metamorphic Stoneborn, a race of guardians that stand between your realm, the fourth realm, and the hell realms."

"So wait, does that mean that when you go out, you're fighting demons?"

"Not exactly. Demons aren't the only threat to humanity."

"Not ready for that one. And you can't be killed?"

"I won't die from traditional means or methods."

She was quiet for a second. Then, she sniffed and looked up at me to ask, "Are you still letting me go?"

I glanced at her again, her face partially illuminated by the dashboard glow.

"I'm taking you back to my place, where your car is parked," I said.

"You have my car?"

"How do you think I returned home so fast after you stranded me at the bar?"

She studied me, then exhaled. "Okay. Fine."

"You don't have to leave right away. If you want to stay the night while you wrap your head around everything."

"Like stay close, in case I lose my mind again?"

"I was thinking, in case you have any more questions." Then, after a beat of silence passed, I added, "Not that you can't call me anytime, you know. We don't live that far apart."

She let out a breathy laugh. "Malrik, you want to keep in touch with little ol' demon-infested me? I had no idea you'd stoop so low."

The traffic swooshed past us as I drove along the river. Her eyes held a heavy weight that I felt down to my resonance stone.

I frowned as I looked at her and said, "They say, once you go demon, you never go back."

She jerked her head toward me. "They do not! Do they?"

I let the smirk linger but said nothing.

She groaned, flopping back against the seat. "Ugh, you're the worst."

But the tension had finally eased from her shoulders.

And that? That was a win.

32

SIT AND SPIN

"**S**o that was it then," I said, struggling to keep my voice even. "You did what you said you'd do. You got me to Darius." I handed Nadia her keys back, fighting past the sudden stabbing pain in my arm to release the ring of keys.

"Yeah." Nadia nodded, eyes lost on the horizon. She didn't take the keys dangling from my fingers. Instead, she walked to the hood of her car.

"You can go back to your life now," I said.

"Yeah." The word came flat, lifeless.

"Behaving," I added.

"Mhm."

"Nadia. Look at me." After a few seconds, it didn't seem like my words registered, so I touched her chin.

"Are you okay?" I asked.

"How could you ask that? After going to Hell and seeing my father? He'll always haunt me."

"He's a demon-bound slave, not a ghost. He won't have the mobility for that," I explained.

She cut me with a sharp side-eye, then exhaled wearily.

"I just meant he's the critique in my head, and that doesn't go away; he scarred me so thoroughly I carry him everywhere I go."

I understand now. I'd never had much self-doubt until I lost the tournament. Out of my forty-six brothers, it was the one who beat me whose voice reminded me of my failures.

"You know, I thought I was doing good. Or at least better than what I escaped from, but I see now, I'm more like my father than I care to admit."

At that, I frowned. Nadia showed her vulnerability, and it was raw and exposed. I want to say something and offer reassurance. Instead, I let the silence hold, hoping like a coward that she'd fill it.

Please don't mess this up, Jahziel's voice echoed my silent fear.

She needs to hear your objection, Ezekiel added.

"There are a lot of differences between him and you."

"Not as many as I'd like," she muttered.

The wall was back; her voice was lighter, but forced. "Like right now, I should be worried about myself, what this means, how it will impact my life. But the itch is already on me, and once it starts, it doesn't stop until I scratch. I can't stay here; it's too tempting."

"You mean my safe?" I specified.

She looked at me, drilled me in the eyes, then scanned my body. "Yeah, uh, right. It's only a matter of time before I break into your safe."

"I'll take the risk."

"But what if it gets me to take the amulet?"

"The demon doesn't control you yet; don't give your enemy power it doesn't have and take away the power you do have."

She nodded but didn't look convinced.

"So, what will you do?" I asked.

"A part of me wants to go back home and see what I can find out about who my father's been making deals with. That must be who claimed my soul and slipped me this thing."

At that, I closed the passenger door a bit harder than I meant to, and it slammed.

"But you realize that's a terrible idea because you'd be dealing with your dangerous family and a demon by yourself."

"What do you want from me?" She got up and paced to the other side of the car. "I just found out all this shit exists, and I'm involved in it. Do you think I got all the answers? You think I have *any* answers?" Her hands locked into claws at her sides as she paced.

I watched her wild eyes crash like turbulent seas.

"This was supposed to be my last job. I had a passport packed and ready to go. But what do I know about being a good person?"

"So you're considering starving it out?"

"What else can I do? I have to try, but it doesn't seem feasible." She shook her head and hands as she paced back and forth.

"What do you mean?"

"I've only known how to bend the rules to get what I

want. Stir the pot here to distract from the action over there. I only know how to scam. I don't know how to be good. You know, realistically."

"You can always stay with me. Until you get the hang of it."

"No."

"You're worried you'll lose control and feed the demon spawn."

"Um. I'm calling it Squid."

"Why?"

"Because that's how it looks, and I don't like saying the other 'S'-word — you ain't gotta question it, okay?"

"Your squid—"

"Not my squid, Squid. That's its name."

"You're naming it?" I asked.

"Yes, I'm naming it, okay?"

"Why are you saying okay like that?"

"Because this is a lot, and I'm still struggling to process it all, okay?"

"Okay?" I said, waiting for a beat before continuing, "If you're worried about my methods, if you want, I won't spank you anymore."

That stopped her short. Tilting her head, she looked at me like I'd just dropped my pants.

"First off: no. Spank me more," Nadia winked, "and harder, 'cause I have been a naughty girl," she pushed at my chest, sending a shot of adrenaline through me. I must have damaged the danger center in my brain because when her eyes darkened, my pulse surged with victory. She leaned forward, drawing near to my parted lips.

Her fingers walked up my chest, and something in me clenched at the contact. "But only if you follow through and give me my treat afterward. No more teasing." Her hands dropped until I was gripping the hood as she held me. In what should have been a ruthless grope, she squeezed. Pleasure spiked through my stomach, and I ground into her hand, barely holding back a grunt. "Understand?"

My body tightened, drawing in on itself, instinctually bracing for the storm. Nadia's eyes widened, pupils dilated.

"You're not afraid? Do you still want me after seeing what I am? After knowing my true form?"

"Do I still want to sit and spin now that I know I'm dipping on a diamond disco stick? Uh, yeah! It's the only good thing that's happened to me in that hellscape."

I blinked. That was a lot of words. Half of them made no sense.

"You say these things intentionally to confuse me."

"I'm not denying that, but also," she continued, "because I can't promise to be good unless thoroughly motivated."

"You know I can keep you on track. What more do you need?" I asked, though my focus remained on her hand around me.

"Reward me with your treasure. Give me an hour in your safe, and let me pick any ten things."

"I'll give you ten minutes. You can choose two, and I get to veto."

"Forty minutes, six picks, and you get one veto."

"Thirty, three, and three," I winced around her squeeze.

"Thirty minutes. Five picks. Two vetoes."

I met her stare and let the silence stretch.

Then: "Deal."

She blinked. "Wait. Seriously?"

"Under a couple of conditions." I reached down and wrapped my hand around her fist.

"What's that?"

"You don't get the treasures until I give them to you, and you show me what a spin looks like on a diamond disco stick."

"Deal, I thought you'd never ask." She smirked and threaded her arms over my shoulders.

"Wait. Not in front of the gargoyles."

"Oh yeah, that'd be terrible." She brushed her lips over mine for half a second before pulling back. "Gargoyles are real, and that wasn't a joke?"

"Not a joke. Three sentries cursed to stone for all eternity," I explain.

"What did they do?" She asked.

Tell her no more! Jahziel demanded.

"They got distracted while on duty."

You'd spare us no shame, Hazariah growled.

"And were cursed for all time. Yikes. I say, let the poor bastards watch." Nadia grinned, her graceful hand cupping my jaw.

Bless her as a saint! Jahziel interrupted. *You should cherish this one.*

Damn it. Couldn't they shut up for one moment?

"I'm going to teach you something. Are you ready?"

She stepped closer, watching me as she neared. I stepped back until my boot hit stone steps. Her finger trailed from my ribs to my chest before she pushed down on my shoulder. It was a clear and silent command.

I sat.

Her eyes never left mine, and I swore I saw a promise hinted in their depths. Gods, I wanted this. I wanted her here and now.

She straddled my waist, knees on either side, hands draped around my neck. Her breath ghosted over my lips.

"This is something I've wondered about for too long," she whispered. "I'm going to kiss you."

Heat flared low in my stomach. My mouth opened—

Then she moved. Lips pressing. Her tongue teased mine with a circling swirl. Gods, now I was the one lost.

Slowly, our lips found rhythm as our tongues explored the taste of each other.

Then, my restraint snapped. My arms wrapped around Nadia, one around her waist, the other snaking up her spine until I held her as hard as she held me. There were no demons, curses, or threats with her in her arms: just this kiss, just us. The world's problems fell away.

Then she groaned into my mouth and melted against my chest.

Give this up?

Impossible.

"Malrik?"

"Yes?"

"I... think we stink." She pulled back to sniff my shirt and winced.

I leaned forward and checked. My olfactory senses weren't the best, but I was sure we smelled like rotten eggs and smoke. Tilting my head back, I lowered my hands and somehow avoided grabbing her ass.

It was so hard right now that I couldn't move.

"I think I will stay the night. I should go shower and get cleaned up for dinner."

Nadia smiled as she lifted herself off my lap. I remained sitting, casually stretching a leg and leaning forward until my arm rested across my lap. When she looked at me with that slight smile, I nodded, pretending to be anything other than a man trying not to show off the rager in his pants.

"I think that's an excellent idea. I'll meet you in the kitchen when you're ready," I replied.

"Okay, big guy."

She knows what you're doing. Jahziel laughed at me.

We all know what you're doing, Hazariah grumbled.

33

APRON STRINGS AND OTHER
ATTACHMENTS

After our separate showers, I follow the clatter of metal into the kitchen, where Malrik is at the counter, wearing loose linen pants and a navy apron.

"What's this?" I ask.

"Dinner. Or it will be."

"You cook?"

"I'm doing so now." He states very matter-of-factly.

"How did you order this much food?"

"I have a cell phone, you know."

"I know, but between driving, searching for Darius, and everything else..."

"Google says humans must eat three to six times daily, so you're almost fifteen meals behind."

"So you plan on fixing all of this now?" I scoff.

"Exactly."

"Riiight. Yeah, that's not how that works. If I miss a meal, that doesn't mean I'm eating twice as much the next time I eat. Besides, I eat when hungry, usually several times a day. But I have an allergy to—"

"Gluten. I know. That's why I bought gluten-free and went organic."

He surveys his kitchen like a general recalculating his strategy.

"You did all this for me?" I grin.

"I kept you here, so I'm responsible for your well-being."

"The only thing that would make this better is wine."

Malrik rummages through the bags. "I'm sorry, lil mani. Is that another thing you need for your nour-ishment?"

Again, with an apology. Malrik is making me think it might not be that hard to say.

"Oh yeah, it's vital."

I wrap my fist around the tie of his apron. It's adorable, but now it's in my way. It needs to go.

I'm not happy until we have skin-to-skin contact, my hands skimming his sides. Maybe it's wrong, but I luxuriate in the hard lines of his stomach and chest. I rise onto my toes, pulling him closer, letting my soft-ness conform to his hard body.

He would have won if he had struggled; instead, he let me lead him in. When he can no longer, he plants one hand on my hip while the other rests against a cupboard. That's not good enough.

I drag my cheek against him, exhaling in a huff. He turns into me, arms wrapping around my waist, pulling me in until we fit together seamlessly. Our lips brush, soft, smooth, and hard to pull away from. His hands slide lower, gripping my hips, urging me closer.

Then his fingers thread into my hair, cradling the back of my head as he holds me snugly in a protective curve. His lips move slowly, learning, teasing, tasting. It's not a battle—it's an exploration.

When I finally pull back, I see black spots. I think I've been holding my breath. Chuckling, I wrap my arms around the big guy's neck and knock my forehead against his chest.

"What was that for?"

"A thank you."

"And what would I have gotten with wine?"

"You'll never know," I smirk. "But I can go without it for a few days.

He glances over at me. "Do you still regret targeting me now?"

I hesitate, flashes of our time together running through my mind: the basement, his table, the shower. A smile tugs at my lips. But then the trip to Hell erases whatever warmth has gathered in my chest. "What would happen if I never found out about Squid?"

Malrik's eyes darken. "Your demon... Squid would take you over."

"Then stealing from you saved my life."

He stays silent, returning to the counter.

"How did you get into this mess?" he asks, focused on the pot he stirred.

I meet my gaze in the fridge's reflection. "I needed money. Protection." I sigh. "So I framed my father and fiancé."

Malrik swears under his breath. "Have you always been a glutton for punishment?"

"It's all I know," I say, my body tensing. I can't help but wonder how often Squid influences my actions.

Malrik mutters as he flips the chicken. "It's a dangerous game you play."

I put everything into my safe houses, and Levi burned all but my last one. And with my family so close, it's only a matter of time before that one is gone, too. Soon, I'll have nothing; maybe that's why I persistently clung to this job.

"And what of the games you play?" I snap, back straightening. "Do you think your honor protects you or shackles you?"

His jaw tenses. He narrows his eyes but says nothing, instead tossing vegetables in oil and herbs.

I exhale, scrubbing a hand down my face. Damn it. Is that Squid, or am I just a bitch?

"You know, not all humans are as terrible as me," I mutter, surprising myself. "Some live their entire lives without breaking the law."

He shuts the oven door and then plates the chicken. "You're not terrible. You're a chaos magnet." He smirks. "And I think I like the trouble you bring."

Give it time.

"One thing I don't get is this mortal mask." I frown, turning the conversation to something less intimate. "What or who makes it work?"

"The veil," Malrik answers. "It's why immortals, or most inter-dimensional creatures, hate being here."

"Why?"

"It forces us to blend in with mortals, and some find it unsettling." He studies his hands. "Most find it galling."

"How does it force you to blend?" I repeat.

"No one knows for sure." He glances up from the sauce. "I always assume it's a natural law of the mortal realm. To exist here, we must blend in and be weakened. Our strength, senses, power, even our immunity."

Silence settles between us, broken only by the simmering sauce. Finally, he adds the chicken to the pan and wipes his hands on his apron.

"No one knows why, but it masks our true identities. I suspect it's to protect humans and their fragile minds."

I watch him set a saucepan on the stove and heat oil before adding onions. "Yeah, we're all real fragile." I pluck a sliced jalapeño from his neatly arranged ingredients and pop it into my mouth. "Must sting to be ordered to live here," I say around hard chomps and sharp inhales.

"Yes," he admits. "At first."

"Can you die here?"

"Yes. You've seen how Stoneborn survives wounds, but we die if we don't heal. It's easier to get wounded here without my skin's natural armor."

My brows stretch in disbelief. I'm not sure what's more impossible—that Malrik is practically invincible or that he must focus intently on measuring paprika.

"Immortal, then?"

"I don't think there is such a thing, but my Stoneborn form doesn't age."

"I have to say, you're pretty sexy, all rock-hard and

scraping the ceiling. I might have asked for climbing lessons if it weren't for the never-ending chorus of misery and condemnation."

"Is that so?" His expression turns sharp, eyes searching mine.

No lie here, big guy. Not this time.

I hold his gaze, unflinching, until I've looked my fill. Then I blink up at him, innocent eyes and a smirk.

"Well, I am descended from stone giants, after all." He shrugs as if it's nothing.

"Wait, don't you eat?"

I lean forward to snag some more vegetables, but he nudges me back into my seat with a gentle hand on my shoulder. "No." He adds oil to the pan. "My resonance stone connects me to Earth's core. As long as I remain tied to the Earth and it lives, so do I."

"You don't need food, water, or sleep?"

"I need sleep. But technically, my body sustains itself by the Earth's magnetic field, so I'm susceptible to magnetic field changes."

For someone who doesn't eat, Malrik sure knows how to cook. As the vegetables roast in the oven, water boils on the stove, and the coconut lime sauce starts to simmer, my stomach growls. And it doesn't help that every time he turns his back, that stretch of bare skin above his apron makes my mouth water.

"Field fluctuations? So if the Earth's magnetic field changes, you—?"

"I'd fall apart." He shrugs, unfazed. "But it's never been a problem."

"The more I hear, the more I wonder: are you sure your King didn't send you here to get rid of you?"

Malrik focuses on dropping the zoodles into boiling water.

"My brother is impetuous and cruel," he says. "But I don't think he has the patience to plot a thousand-year revenge scheme."

I snap my head toward him. "Hold up. The King is your brother?"

"Yes." He shrugs, turns off the burners, and strains the zoodles.

"I thought you weren't a prince."

"I said I lost the right to the throne after the tournament." His upper lip stiffens, and his shoulders tense.

Then he pulls the roasted vegetables from the oven. Without a mitt.

"What the hell!" I dart around the island. His palm is raw, but his skin knits itself back together as I watch.

"It's okay. I'm fine." His other hand wrapped around my wrist.

"I see that. Get an oven mitt anyway. Burning yourself just because you can is crazy." Why is my heart pounding?

I shake off the unease, "So... what's special about this amulet?"

"It's not an amulet. It's the Key of Stellos." He frowns. "But I don't know how it got in my safe."

"Well, let's see it."

"Not now, lil mani." He brushes me off and sets a plate on the counter.

"Come on, why not?"

"Because it's time for you to eat."

"Malrik," I whine.

He gives me a long look. "Is this another one of your tricks?"

"No."

"So I shouldn't be suspicious that as soon as I gave you your keys back, you want to see the amulet that cancels your demon debt?"

He places a plate before me—coconut chicken with a lime wedge, roasted vegetables, and zoodles.

I grin, unrepentant. "Malrik, it hurts that you have so little faith in me."

"That's not an answer."

"I'm not going to steal your amulet. I want to see it."

"Eat first."

I roll my eyes, but stop when I remember the last time. Begrudgingly, I pick up the fork and knife and cut my meal.

"Good. Eat up." He turns. "I'll get the amulet. Stay in your seat. Don't snoop."

The locks click behind him. I don't know how he does it, but at Malrik's command, every door in the house seals with a thud.

My grin widens. After everything, Malrik still worries about little old me. I like that.

Before I can get too smug, a shrill screech echoes through the vents.

Wincing, I clap my hands over my ears. "What the hell is that?"

"You can hear him?" Malrik shouts from deep inside his home.

"I'm sure your neighbors can hear that."

"Nadia, meet Ezekiel."

"You have a pet bird?"

Malrik sighs. "One of the gargoyles."

Right on cue, a massive vulture swoops into the room and perches on a stone pillar. It squawks loud enough to rattle the cabinets.

I squeeze my eyes shut, waiting for it to pass. When I open them again, the image of the bird changes to a severe-looking statue.

"What just happened?"

"Ezekiel's been unusually vocal since you arrived."

"Not a fan?"

"I wouldn't say that. He's the one who reminded me you need to stay warm. He insisted that I return to fix my error."

"Aww, thanks, Zeki." I smile at the stone face. "He didn't tell you what I said earlier, did he?"

"No. What did you say?"

"Nothing!" I laugh, too quickly. He doesn't seem to notice.

But the statue's face shifts into disapproval.

"Okay, this might sound silly, but... how is a statue moving?"

"I told you, they're cursed," Malrik says. "Trapped in stone bodies. But when I brought them here, I bound them to my estate. They can move between certain perches, but only within my property lines. When they move, your human mind will see it as whatever makes sense to you; when they settle, they return to their stone form."

"They're trapped here, like that?"

"They have more freedom now than they did when I found them. Now, at least, they can move around and communicate. Don't worry; the laws of the Veil will make humans see what they want. A bird. A shadow. Anything that makes sense. Once they stop moving, the curse takes over again."

I eye Ezekiel. "Why does it feel like he's eyeing me?"

Malrik tilts his head, listening. "He says he was tasked to guard the Key of Stellos and doesn't want it falling into a thief's hands."

"So he stashed it in your safe?"

"I guess." He says it harshly. "You should have told me I had a relic that unlocks the Gates of Stellos. It's the only thing that separates us from them."

"Who's 'them'?" I ask even though I don't think he's talking to me anymore.

"The Dark Mother and her army."

34

TASTES LIKE DISASTER

The tingle of mischief itches my wrist.

Before I can filter the thought, a chunk of veggie launches into the air and splats against Malrik's cheek with a wet flap. He turns in slow motion like a statue breaking from its stone crust. I smile as innocently as I can, fingers still dripping with coconut sauce.

"Nadia," he says, voice low. "Is it still your intention to fight the spawn inside of you?"

"Oh yeah. Squid's got to go," I agree.

I can't help my grin, but I smother the laugh. Malrik watches me with a mix of exasperation and amusement flickering in his expression. When I look into his sparkling eyes, something clicks. He's a good man, and it doesn't make him weak.

Hmm.

My cheeks start to warm the longer I resist my grin. Across from me, Malrik tosses the chunk of broccoli into the trash. When he turns back, a smear of sauce lingers on his cheek. His eyes catch mine, and I bask in that familiar mix of confusion and residual exasperation that's starting to feel like home.

I should feel guilty, or maybe even ashamed for being so childish. I don't. The look on his face makes it all worth it.

"Then why?" he asks. He shouldn't sound so heartbreakingly disappointed. After all, he doesn't think I'll make this easy on him, does he?

"I don't know," I say with a shrug. "I wanted to, so I did. It's as easy as that."

"Have you considered that's the demon's influence?"

"Squid," I correct, "and I have. That's why it was only the one vegetable."

"So, you choose the lesser?"

"I suppose I did."

"Come here," he orders.

Only then do I feel the first twinge of regret. Hopping off my seat, I step closer. My hand holds onto the edge of the countertop, its cold stone gliding smooth as burned ice beneath my palm. Malrik's fingers are even colder when he touches me, but they warm quickly as the pads slide down my cheek and across my jaw, tilting my head back so our eyes can meet.

His strong fingers tunnel through my damp hair as he pulls me into his arms.

"So, what'll it be?" I ask.

"I think you know what to do."

"I guess..." I start thinking about my options. "You want me to clean what I mess up."

Which means pulling from his fixed stare to track the sauce near his lips.

With my cheekiest grin and a shrug, I grab him by the back of the head and pull him down. Malrik bends willingly, without resistance, and I reward him with a long, slow lick up the side of his face.

His padded palms hold my hips in a firm and inescapable grip. Then he lifts me.

"Hey! You can't just go around moving me every way you want!"

Automatically, my ankles hook behind him. His hands shift, scooping under my ass. The cold counter flash-freezes the backs of my thighs to my knees, until his hips follow.

His slim waist pins me as he tugs me close. His dark brown eyes morph into starbursts that melt into amber, and I can't look away. Then, a slow, gliding smile pulls my focus down to his mouth.

He's beautiful in that rugged, jaded way—like someone who's seen the world and prefers solitude. But he wants me. That much is clear now.

Heat blooms between my thighs, spreads across my stomach, and curls around my neck. I flush when I realize neither of us has looked away.

My legs squeeze but it's not to pull him closer, but to pull myself in.

Our past, the punishment I'm likely to receive, doesn't matter. All I want is contact. And the big guy seems to need it, too.

The same hands that scoop me up so easily now trace the sides of my body. It's the kind of touch good girls dream about. A soft reverence, like a princess in a high tower.

But I'm no princess. He must've forgotten.

I earned this punishment, fair and square.

I reach behind me, grab a fistful of my uneaten pasta, and fling it toward his chest.

"Nadia..." he warns.

"I know, I know. Clean it up," I echo, all innocence.

I start with the noodle draped over his shoulder, licking my way up from the bottom. Underneath my mouth, he curses. Around me, he tenses.

He steps forward, less gentle now. "If you want something, you need only ask."

I blink, taken off guard. I expect a payback. Teasing. More spanking or even a flash of anger. But not that.

Pleased looks good on him. And it's aimed at me. Why does that make me feel all... squishy?

My upper lip quivers until I scrunch my nose and turn away. The big guy doesn't let me turn far. It's as if Malik's ready for me to run. His hand cups my jaw, turning me back to face him.

"You think choosing the lesser evil is nothing," he says softly, "but I'm proud of you."

Proud of me? Who says things like that? No one that I've ever known.

I tip my head back, watching him flicker between uncertainty and desire. "Is it enough?" Will it ever be? My voice cracks, and I feel a surge of heat course through my body at the tell.

His eyes search mine, and something shifts. The quick lift of his brow warns me his punishment is yet to come. In one smooth motion, Malrik wraps his arms around me.

"You showed restraint, and it's a start," he says. His hand curls around my neck and cups my cheek again. "And you deserve something for that."

I don't argue. Not when Malrik's mouth meets mine—not in punishment, but in promise. His hands slide around my waist again, rougher this time.

"Guess that means you've earned a reward after all." His hand fists my hair and pulls me back down to the tracks of sauce.

The meal is even better when Malrik's my plate. I grab another handful of food and rub it across his chest. It has to be hot, but he doesn't flinch. His hands flex behind me, massaging my muscles in slow, circular motions, almost absently as I eat my fill of him.

Then, a drop of sauce slides down the waistband of his pants.

I decide to save that one for last.

"Damn it, lil mani; you're not going to spin this torment around on me again."

"What are you going to do?"

"Well, I was going to give us what we both want. But that was before you made a bigger mess."

"But you haven't even let me make amends for that yet."

"Amends?" His brow arches in adorable disbelief.

Instead of answering, I lean in and wrap my arms around him, brushing my lips over his. His acceptance comes with a groan of relief. Abruptly, I end the kiss and slide my shirt over my head.

Malrik shifts as it drops, but I stop his step back with a tug on his waistband.

This time, I don't tease him.

I don't have the patience to torment myself. Instead, I pull him back using my hands and legs.

His strangled gasp, a curse to the gods, settles the matter. With his warm breath fanning my cheek, an inch away from the touch I crave, I finally let go of any reservations.

In desperate need, I wrap my tired arms around his thick neck and lean forward until we're nose to nose. His lips trail along my neck as his hands explore my body. I don't want to wait. I can't.

"Malrik."

"Yes, lil mani?"

"I want you. Right now."

I feel his cheeks pull into another smile. True to his word, Malrik obliges.

My clothes fall away within seconds. Thirty seconds later, his hands roam my body, trailing to the one place I need him to touch. Then, Malrik's lips follow, teasing me into excitement.

Before I can stop him, he drops to his knees. His fingers part me, and his tongue strokes the epicenter of my pleasure. I lift myself, and his hand slides under me so he can palm my ass and pull me closer, teasing that tender flesh with expert care.

With each twirling stroke, he builds me higher and higher until a wash of pleasure floods me. When he pulls back, his mouth, nose, cheeks, and jaw are wet from my desire. Against his leg, his pants bulge, but he doesn't touch himself—hell, he doesn't even acknowledge what has to be a painful distraction.

My foot travels up his hard abs and to his chest. I kick hard enough to send him spilling onto his back. When he rises on his forearms, his pride shifts into hurt.

I slide off the counter and walk the length of his body until I hover over his waist. Then I straddle him. To ease the furrow in his brow, I stretch to place a soft kiss against his forehead, then down his wet cheek. I taste myself on his lips and a new buzzing starts.

"Lift your hips," I say. The big guy complies, and I pull his pants down past his thighs. When I take him in my hand, he flexes. A fine tremble twitches in my lower back as I line him up with my center.

"Nadia, wait."

I want to sink on him, but I stop, hovering just over his swollen head. Underneath me, his leg bounces as if he's struggling for control, just like me.

"What if I don't like it?" he asks.

Then we'll keep trying until you do.

Levi's voice answers from the shadows of my past. The chilling memory should send me running. Before meeting Malrik, it might have.

Cupping his face, I say, "Then I'll stop. It's as easy as that."

"What if—"

"No more what-ifs. I want to show you what it is." I wait for his nod. It's hesitant. His shoulders are tense, but he only grows harder in my hand.

When I sink around him, I silently squeal. I *know*

he's big. My fingers have struggled to wrap around him completely. Once he starts to push through my inner walls, I realize my mistake. The heavy pressure of him impales me.

As I lift myself, not even an inch his bulbous head stretches me again. His hands grip my waist.

"You want me to stop?" I ask.

"Hell no." His fingers wiggle and flex at my hips, squeezing and kneading like he can't get enough of my softness.

"Then patience."

My hands clasp over his, and I draw them both to my breasts. He moans again, this time his hips surging in sync with his clutching palms. The touch borders on pain, a shade harder than pleasure, lingering in that gray area.

A full-body tremble shakes my frame in response, and again, his hips lift, sinking further into my channel. I tip my head back and roll my hips, taking our possession of each other a little further. I want to sink and grind on him, but it's been too long, and the discomfort warns me to take my time.

Again, I lift myself, and again, his hands find my hips. He doesn't stop my movement, but it's more like he holds on for the last of his self-control. My hands fall on his chest as sweat starts to dampen my skin.

"A little bit further," I whisper. My hand reaches between us, but I still have more than a fist left. Frustration spikes within me. "Oh shit."

I already feel so full. Malrik stretches me like a

heavyweight. As much as I want more, I don't know if I can take it.

"Malrik, I don't know if I can do this."

"Then we stop."

"I don't want to stop. I don't know how much more of you I can take."

At that, he sits up. I rock back and slide further down his shaft. My eyes roll back, and my legs start to shake, but before I can sink deeper into the new angle, his hands are already underneath me, supporting my weight.

"Tell me what you want me to do, *lil mani*?"

"I just need... slow. Help me go slow."

My hands settle on his shoulders, and we lift and fall in sync until a new heat builds between us. I don't know who changes the pace, probably me, but the tension that separates us evaporates once the speed picks up. Finally, I sink into his lap.

For a moment, I stay there, breaking our pulsing rhythm. Immediately, Malrik's arms wrap around me, and he pulls me in until my breasts press into his chest. His lips find mine as if he can't bear the stillness between us.

When I roll my hips, his arms tighten. As I start rocking back and forth, he groans, pressing his head into the crook of my shoulder. I never want to leave this kitchen. If I can stay here like this forever, I will. But what I can't do is stay still for another second.

"Fuck me, Malrik. Punish me, reward me. I don't care, don't stop."

That's all the encouragement he needs. At once, his

hands swarm my hips, and between his lifts and thrusts, all I can do is hold onto his shoulders for dear life. I don't know how long we stayed in that kitchen, learning from each other and riding the rhythm of our passions.

"Malrik, please!" I cry. My body shakes uncontrollably. I swear I have no bones left in my legs. That's how gelatinous they feel. Nearly every muscle burns wrenched, and tormented by the waves of pleasure he gives me. Still, he doesn't come.

"Please what, *lil mani*?"

"Come for me. Finish this!"

"Just a little bit longer."

I start to pull away, to crawl away. Malrik's hands stay on my hips, and he follows, never breaking contact or missing a stroke. Dear lord, how does this man have so much stamina?

"Malrik, now!"

At that, he froze.

His thrusts stagger as his body clenches around me. I know the moment he comes, a new warmth fills me, and his release tingles everything it touches inside me. I've been on the verge of orgasm, but when his release fills me—his arms wrapping around me, his mouth pressing to the back of my neck—I find a new kind of release, one that leaves me spinning and spent.

35

ALL ROADS LEAD TO RUIN

Before I left, I tucked her into her bed and ensured Nadia's keys and phone were on the nightstand beside her, along with a glass of water. I let her sleep. If I was lucky, I'd be back before she woke. If Garrett was lucky, he'd be back on patrol tonight.

I made my way through the tunnels easily enough. This time, it wasn't the dark servants I was after. They'd likely moved to a secondary lair. A subway tunnel or an abandoned building.

Finding the location could take time I didn't have. Dark servant safe houses were scattered across the country. I couldn't afford to comb the entire area or second-guess myself.

I certainly didn't have the luxury of wondering what Nadia might be getting herself into.

My fingers flexed around the pommel of my sword. The tension betrayed the real problem, clawing at the back of my mind. Nadia. I shouldn't have been thinking about her. Not about how her eyes flashed with fire when she argued or how her lips softened under mine. But I was. And that kind of distraction could get me killed.

I set my face into a hard mask and pushed the thoughts away. Dealing with dark servants was dangerous enough without being anxious or unfocused. Still, the thought clung to me: would she be there when I returned?

I turned my attention back to the task at hand. Bloodstains and chunks of meat littered the alley. I've never seen a hive this reckless. Even humans would notice.

Dark red smears trailed along the back end of a grimy alley, not even three blocks from a subway exit. The dark servants grew bold enough to send their spawn into the real world to play fetch.

All spawn were filthy things, bursting through the flesh of humans and true immortals alike. Each born in the image of whatever creature their dark priest deemed worthy to mix with the Dark Mother's blood. Their queen. Spawn and servant alike served her.

Everything made sense now that I knew the Dark Mother sought Stellos's key. They were close. She was near.

And the servants and spawn had begun to coalesce, preparing for their hive mother's return. That was why they were growing bold. They believed their time in hiding was almost over.

My eyes adjusted quickly to the darkness as I stepped into a dilapidated shanty about a quarter mile from the pile. The thick smell of rotting intestines clung to the air, but the usual chittering of dark servants was absent. In its place, a rising tide of insect activity buzzed against my resonance field. I scanned the room; everything was layered in dust.

I picked through the remnants of molted corpses, gnawed bones, and half-eaten flesh. Papers and letters lay scattered in a crate, long forgotten. Cobwebs hung from the ceiling like silk nooses. The back corner had collapsed inward, rubble pushed up against the mold-stained walls.

It was all wrong. Too clean. The usual rot felt like someone tried to sweep the filth under the rug. Literally.

It was almost like someone had staged the room, making it presentable for someone.

A draft whistled through the chamber, carrying the scent of rust and old decay. I tracked it to a hidden hatch, opened it, and came to a hard stop.

A body swung, nearly camouflaged against the grimy gray wall. In front of me and chained to the ceiling, a limp, bloodless body hung. The dark servants left the man to swing in a shallow, wreckage-packed room.

They'd drained him. I stepped closer and turned the man's face toward me. Recognition hit like a hammer to the chest. Garrett. A fellow Stoneborn hunter.

In a flash, Garrett lunged within his chains, his

battle reflexes honed over centuries. He had pushed one last time before falling limp again.

His purpled, paper-thin skin tore where metal hooks pierced his shoulders and back.

He wouldn't die from blood loss. As an immortal, even the deep gash from shoulder to hip, the stab wound in his chest, the incisions lining his torso, or the strips of skin peeled from his sides—none of it would kill him.

Few injuries could disrupt a Stoneborn's resonance stone enough to destabilize the very pulse and frequency that held us together. But they'd found a way.

I took the incapacitated warrior under my arm. Just like I had with Nadia in the Hell realms and wrapped my resonance field around him. I stabilized him until he could sustain himself.

It wouldn't last. But it would buy him time.

The sharp, rusted tools in the corner looked designed for extraction and storage. Were the dark servants farming him for parts, perhaps? Another deviation. Another warning.

The dark servants were changing.

I stepped deeper into the room. Near a dirty pot filled with remnants of Garrett's suffering, I found a picture of a woman.

She was walking across a crowded street, smiling as she raised her coffee cup toward the camera. Soft. Pampered. She reminded me faintly of Clarabelle, as all delicate women tended to. But the resemblance didn't hit with its usual pang. My impression of her felt…flat.

Still, the photo unsettled me. The dark servants didn't collect faces. They collected *bodies*, not momentos.

Why her? What did she mean to a warrior like Garrett?

"What did they do to you, brother?"

The more I stared at the photograph, the heavier the unease settled in my gut. If the servants had been watching her and waiting, then this wasn't just a deviation. It was a trap.

I should have made the connection sooner.

Freeing Garrett from his chains was slow work. I try not to do any further damage as I get him down.

"He knows," Garrett surged forward as soon as he was free of his hooks. "They planned it." His body wiggled like a worm as if he were trying to use dead legs, only to realize too late that he couldn't hold himself.

"Who planned it?" I asked as I grabbed him under his arms, catching him.

"Now we're not safe. Not anywhere."

"Who are you talking about?" I ask again, shifting his weight.

"She needs help. I have to get to her. She whispers for me."

"The woman in the picture? Who is she?"

"He knows they planned it all."

"You're not making any sense. There may be more damage than we realize. Rest for now, brother."

"But I have to get to her; she needs me."

"Heal yourself first."

I moved carefully through the building, his weight slung over my shoulder, searching for a back alley. The last thing I needed was a civilian spotting what looked like a corpse slung across my back.

Click.

I froze.

My eyes dropped to my feet, just in time to register the blinking red light. Fire spread like a plume. Heat seared my back.

The blast ripped Garrett from my shoulder. Before I could move, I was airborne. My limbs lifted weightless for a breathless second—then darkness.

I hit something hard. A wall? The ground? I couldn't tell. For a moment, I thought I might be upside down.

Red and blue lights flickered somewhere in the haze. A high-pitched ring drowned out all other sounds. My breath came ragged, cut by pain.

Move. Instinct demanded.

I had to leave before the humans got here. But Garrett was still in the burning building.

I pushed myself upright. Pain lit up every nerve. Blood pattered down the steps. Sirens started to rise over the ringing.

Smoke stung my eyes, bitter and blinding. I stumbled back into the building. The stench of burnt plastic and flesh filled the air. My leg screamed with every step. But I kept going.

Soot caked my skin. Debris crunched beneath my

boots. The explosion reduced the room to scorched wreckage, but Garrett's blackened body still lay inside.

Lifting him again took everything in me. My shoulder relocated with a sickening pop. I gritted my teeth and forced myself forward.

I paused only when my legs nearly gave out. My vision swam. Maybe the blast damaged my retinas. I counted to five before pushing forward again.

Each step was a fresh surge of agony. Fire climbed my spine. My ribs throbbed like they were split open.

When I laid Garrett in the backseat, it wasn't graceful. But I got it done. I collapsed into the driver's seat, tossing a coat beneath me to soak the blood. Sirens echoed behind me.

I gripped the wheel and let out a breath.

Would Nadia be there?

Even now, half-dead and barely holding together, I couldn't keep my thoughts from her. Her mouth, the spark in her eyes, and how she made me feel.

Awake. *Alive.*

But it was a dangerous time to feel.

A quiet part of me, the one I thought had died long ago, wanted her to stay. Even knowing what that might cost. Even suspecting that the servants had used *someone* to lure Garrett into this trap and knowing that, I still want her. Is this what happens when you love a mortal?

"Stay strong, Garrett. You'll be fine." I said though I knew it might be my first lie. Before the explosion, he was salvageable. Now, I didn't know. His wounds weren't healing right. The purple-black veins spread deeper.

What had they done to him?

Gorvoss had sent us into a world that slowly stripped us of our strength while the enemy grew more ruthless. For eternity. Even for a Stoneborn, it was a lonely existence.

Nadia had made me realize how barren my life had become. As if I'd been sleepwalking for centuries, and now I'd woken to hunger.

But all that lay in that path was destruction.

I glanced at Garrett in the mirror. Was *he* the warning? A glimpse of what happened when a warrior let himself *want*?

"Who is she, Garrett?" I muttered. "What did they do to you?"

I *should* send Nadia away. Far away. Even if we weren't already doomed, the timing couldn't have been worse. Mortals didn't survive long in our world—even demon-possessed ones.

Still, it didn't help that she didn't flinch. Not from my stare. Not from what I was. She'd sensed the danger and leaned into it. Her defiance was a fresh wind through my withered soul.

But this was asking too much of her.

Once I pulled from the alley, I unlocked my phone and dialed.

No answer.

That didn't worry me.

Not one bit.

Was it wrong that some of me hoped she'd play nursemaid again?

My vision blurred. I knew I needed to stay focused. But I couldn't stop the thoughts. I couldn't stop imagining Nadia kneeling by my bed, steady hands undressing me.

She was chaotic. Fire.

And I... I was already burned.

36

RAISIN IN THE ROOM

Malrik returned through the back entrance just as I found his safe. *Nothing to see here.* I rush out of the room, shutting the door behind me, trying to be nonchalant.

"So, how was your night?"

"Eventful." He was too distracted to be suspicious. Good.

"I see that. Do you need any help?" I ask casually, but the question puts him on edge. Perhaps it's a matter of pride, or maybe he's just unused to being on the receiving end of help.

Nodding, he turns slowly, and I can sense his nerves. At first, the tension seems out of place until I see the charred monstrosity behind him. The thing was so well broiled that it was practically still smoking.

"What is that?" I ask, wide-eyed. The question feels redundant because I already know what it is: a dead body. What confuses me is why it's in the house.

"This is Garrett. He needs our help."

It has a name? "To bury him, right?" I ask.

I try to keep my tone casual, as if I've buried a dead guy before. No big deal. But even with my family, as fucked up as they are, I've never had to cart around a dead body.

"He's still alive, for now. I'm going to move him to the second guest bedroom. I need you to get rags, bottled water, and the healing stones from my bathroom; I need to see how bad this is."

"Malrik... It isn't good. In fact, it's really bad. That thing is crispy and extra well done."

"That thing is a man, a fellow Stoneborn warrior. Don't underestimate the curse of longevity."

"Wait, there's a chance he can recover from that?"

"Yes, but I need to find what's wrong with him quickly because he won't live long without the aid of my resonance field."

"You're going to try to heal that? Ugh."

"Nadia, sometimes doing the right thing is gross. Now get rags, bottled water, and my healing stones from my bathroom."

I sigh at him and go on my scavenger hunt. I don't want to point out how uncomfortable I am with having a dead body next to my room. Or worse, the living body of whatever that mottled monstrosity is.

I wonder if Malrik has ever been so close to death. I hope not.

Setting the supplies on the nightstand next to Malrik, I lean against the far wall, watching the war chief play nursemaid. So far, I haven't seen any movement from the dead guy, and I wonder if Malrik is wrong about him. Maybe he's seeing what he wants to see.

"How do you know it's not too late?" I ask.

"Every inter-dimensional creature returns to the Earth when we pass on the mortal realm. It's part of the mortal mask we must wear. It keeps us from discovery, even in death." He pours a powder packet into the water bottle and tosses it to me. "Shake it until it thickens," he orders as he cleans some of the man's wounds. Watching the water turn into a mud slurry is easier than looking at the corpse.

Eventually, I pass it back, and Malrik cradles the man's head, spooning some of the sludge into his mouth. His usual steady hands are slow and attentive. It's the first time I've ever seen him hesitate. Whoever Garrett is, he cares for him.

My heart turns over at how gentle he is with the broken body.

I feel like I'm intruding on an intimate moment and wonder if he knows the man well. Slowly, I try to slip out of the room; the tension at seeing Malrik take such care makes my gut clench. Memories resurface at the sight of my mother taking care of Uncle Joey.

After being shot in the stomach, the best my mother could do was shoot him up with morphine and stay with him while he died. My stomach tightens around the dark memory, and I turn quickly, darting out the door to the front of the house, nearly gasping in the brisk outside air.

The fresh air should be cold, but sweat clings to my

back. I grip the railing, inhaling deep lungfuls. A minute passes before I can take a breath that doesn't twinge.

Will the sight of the desiccated body haunt me for the rest of my life? During my time with Malrik, I've seen some incredible things, but the unmoving raisin in the guest bedroom is too far a stretch.

Then Malrik is behind me, his hands firm on my shoulders.

"I need your help, Nadia."

When Malrik starts massaging my tense muscles, my knees nearly buckle. I shake off his dead body, touching his hands. Suddenly, my tongue thickens, and I have to control and conceal my gag.

I've touched a dead body before, but not like this. Not when it still has a chance to move again. My voice comes out colder than I intended. "I'm not touching a dead body."

"I don't understand, you've seen worse. We were just in Hell."

"Nothing in Hell looked like that," I snap. "Even the guy stretched like a human tent still looked human."

"I told you, immortals can shut their bodies down to save themselves."

"Have you ever done that?" I need to hear his denial.

"Yes. We all have."

"You looked like that?"

His skin is raw, puckered, bruised, and stretched taut too thin over jutting bones. Dark veins webbed his neck; his lips were cracked, gray, and charred. I swallow hard. If this is what being immortal looks like, I want no part.

The thought of touching him makes my skin crawl. My fingers twitch, recalling the waxy, swollen skin of Cousin Tim, the way his bloated hand flopped lifelessly in mine. But Malrik is waiting, expecting me to be selfless and good. I clench my jaw.

I shake my head.

Already, he's nodding in acceptance. Damn it!

I wish he weren't so frustratingly understanding. Or that he'd never met my family. I knew it would just stir up trouble and bring up old weaknesses. That's what family is to me: a weakness.

"I understand."

"What do you need my help with?" I ask.

"Keep feeding him while I clean him up to work on the worst."

"Good luck," I agree, my eyebrows and lip lifting contemptuously.

"If it's that intolerable to you, then leave when you're done."

Why does he look so disappointed?

"Are you kicking me out so your friend won't catch you slumming it with a human?" I take the bottle from his hands.

"Don't put words in my mouth."

"Not a denial." I shake my head, running my hand through my hair and shaking it out.

"Why are you angry at me?" Malrik asks incredulously.

I have no idea. The thought of my big guy looking

like that makes me angry. The idea that he keeps going out to save random people makes me want to shake him.

It doesn't register right away that I'm angry because I'm scared for him. When it finally sinks in, I turn back to his friend, hanging my head. I feed the man his slurry.

"I'm not angry at you; I'm just angry."

"At what?"

"The situation, your lifestyle."

"Don't you think that's a bit ironic, coming from you? Some things just are. Destinies are like that. Don't worry; you'll see the difference in Garrett soon."

It wasn't Garrett that I was worried about. My hand lingers on the handle before I go inside. I dread seeing the body again, and I'm not afraid to admit it makes me sick.

I can only hope Malrik is right and his friend made progress by morning. If not, I'm out. Peace. No amount of promises or pretty words from Malrik will keep me here sleeping next to a decomposing corpse.

I hover at the threshold, fingers gripping the door-frame like it's the only thing keeping me from falling back into the past. The walls aren't yellow. The air isn't thick with cigar smoke.

It doesn't matter. This isn't my childhood home, but I know what waits inside. Death. And I can't walk through that door again when every alarm is going off in my head.

Then, my eyes trail back to him.

He's all strong shoulders and steady calm. As if he

felt my eyes on him, he turns back to me, his brow quirks up like a wave of warm water, lapping my nerves into repose. I took another deep breath, and with Malrik's encouragement, I found the strength to step through the door.

37

TRUST ME, I'M NOT A DOCTOR

Blood splatters on the black and white marble floor swirled with grime and trash. Malrik left tools and clothes scattered throughout the once-clean bathroom. I walk in a tight circle, examining him. I raise an eyebrow, leaning over his chest to inspect the damage. Blood mixed with dirt streaks all over his body.

"These look terrible," I complained immediately. "Is your fighting style blindfolded and drunk?" I glance at his skin's rough, loose edges that are puckered and open, feeling sick. I learned early how to stitch up bullet holes and knife wounds, even dog bites, but I've never seen anyone survive an explosion.

"My attention was split," he shrugs casually. "They'll heal."

"Look, the ones from before healed perfectly."

"As I said."

"Well, excuse me for admiring my work," I joke, removing the staples he so carelessly applied. The wounds aren't healing as quickly as last time, and I tell him as much.

"I still have internal damage that takes priority," he explains.

"Do you control where you heal?" I ask as I pull slivers of wood and metal from his back.

"No. My body will shut down to conserve energy and slowly heal if it gets too bad. How do you know how to do this?" he asks again as I poke at a deep gash on his chest.

"I told you—"

"Nadia," he warns.

Are you growing tired of my evasiveness already, big guy? Well, tough.

"I'll tell you if you tell me how you got this awful job."

"Fine, you first," he insists.

"Yeah, right, like I'm going to fall for that."

"I'm not the criminal here," he states factually.

Touché.

I hate talking about myself. Usually, I never share anything about my family or my past. Malrik feels different.

After all, he's already seen and handled most of my family's baggage well enough. And besides, if anyone is safe from the family's 'company,' it's Malrik. I press my lips together, feeling them grow cold with the pressure.

Then I remembered how unattractive pressed lips were and relaxed them into a forced smile.

"I grew up around it. My mom's always been a medic."

"Your mother's a doctor!" he says, impressed.

"I didn't say that. I said she's a medic, for the company. A family business."

"And she taught you this?" he asks skeptically.

"We all learn a lot from our families." I try evading again.

"Your tone drops. Thinking of her makes you sad."

"You don't know me."

The words come out sharper than I intend, an old defense mechanism I've perfected over the years: social workers, cops, priests, and do-gooders with kind eyes and empty promises. I said the same thing to all of them, but this time feels different. Maybe because, deep down, I want Malrik to know me.

"I had to leave my mom behind. I blew up our entire family, her entire life, in my escape and left her to pick up the pieces alone.

"Not as well as I'd like." He watches me momentarily before continuing. "Hunting has been my entire life's work since I became Rorurik. After the Dark Mother breached our defenses, each realm offered up its best hunters to combat the rising tide of dark spawn.

"Our leaders sent us topside to the fourth realm to protect humans. And that's where we've been ever since, fighting off the dark servant threat. We are the only thing that stands between the monsters and humans because they don't just kill," Malrik says, his voice tight. "They change you. Hollow you out and let something else grow where you used to be. And when that thing finally crawls free and when you come apart, they use what's left."

"How?"

"You don't want to know."

I angle him with a glare. He doesn't resist for long before he shakes his head once.

"Bio-metallic resin and skin grafting."

"Okay. I see your point."

"They never really die. It's a never-ending cycle unless we can cut off the head of the snake. If not, the dark servants who breed and resurrect the spawn will continue creating their monstrosities."

Instead of responding, I accepted the two stones he handed me, taking my time to spread them along his chest. I'm not sure if I'm stalling to avoid more questions or just enjoying the excuse to touch him. I've never really been impressed by a man's chest. In fact, I'm more of a material girl, but the expanse of his pecs is awe-inspiring.

Especially knowing what his body *really* looks like.

He remains stiff under my gentle pressure, waiting for me to make a move. Instead, I lift my hands and gently trace a wound down his bicep. He barely makes a sound.

As my fingers graze the red welt on his shoulder, they skim past almost-healed scabs on the back of his arms. Looking closer, I see the raw flesh of his scalp as it heals back together. His healing abilities are remarkable.

What would happen if I bottled his blood and sold it to a pharmaceutical company? I could make billions.

My thoughts of money end abruptly when I see his back in the mirror. Two-inch-wide sections of burns so deep they're nearly as charred as the corpse, I mean, Garrett. The rest of his back looks like it's been thrown into a grinder. He has small flakes of metal, wood, and what appears to be bone or rock embedded in his skin. At least fifty shards scatter the expanse of his back.

"Holy shit, Malrik. Don't you know how to duck?"

"I haven't found an effective way of avoiding a bomb yet," he snaps. Sheesh, sensitive much?

"So, getting caught in a bomb is a regular day at work?"

"No. Yes, sometimes. Are you going to help or keep criticizing me, lil mani?"

"I'm going to do both," I say softly, reaching for the tweezers and the towel, unsure how to handle the damage. I grab the wastebasket, hesitating. "You should lie down. It'll be easier on both of us."

I see the muscles in his neck and shoulders tense with his unease, and I'm not ashamed to say it affects me. Oddly enough, my heart aches, and though it's a foreign feeling, I know it's for him and his pain. Not good.

38

BEDSIDE MANNERS AND BAD IDEAS

"Get on the bed and lie face up," my mortal ordered.

I stood, once more, towering over her. I looked down at her, squinting, not in a glare, but in a measured study. She tilted her head back, watching me just as intently, perhaps expecting me to show some resistance. I didn't.

Instead, I walked to the bed. It was the perfect fit for someone my size. When I lay to the side, there was barely enough room for her to sit beside me.

"You should have your doctor on hand if you're going to get hurt this often," she muttered.

"If you have something better to do with your time, little thief, then by all means—" I began, pushing myself up.

She squeaked in an entirely undignified sound. With nowhere else to push me down, she swung a leg over my waist and slid on top of me, halting me mid-motion. A deep sound rumbled in my chest, but I swallowed the curse and sank back onto the bed.

"Nadia," I groaned as she settled atop me.

"Yes, Malrik?" she asked, all faux innocence.

"Move your right knee back."

Her face flushed when she realized the groan had come from pain. I heard her curse herself as she scrambled to get off. My arm moved of its own accord, barring her movement until she settled back in place.

"I'm sorry; I didn't mean to hurt you further," she said. And it sounded sincere, disarmingly so. It's almost like she cared. About me? Or about something beyond the treasure?

She could have left. And now she was being kind. Was it pessimistic to think she was up to something?

"Malrik?"

"Yes, Nadia?"

"Why do you do this to yourself?"

"It's my job. I am a Rorurick," I replied, the words familiar, well-worn.

"If you were no longer Rerurick, what would you do with your time?"

"The position cannot be absconded. Only through death is there escape." The truth landed heavily between us, just as it always did.

"Well, that's an awful retirement package," she muttered. "How long do Reruricks usually live?"

"Rorurick," I corrected, my voice growing slow with the onset of sleep. "Like row-rawr-rick. And not indefinitely."

She rubbed the magnet along my back with careful, clinical precision. It's nothing like the slow, painstaking strokes we'd once shared. I kept quiet, head turned to the side, arms folded beneath me, each breath slow and deep.

"I have a job for you," I said, finally working up the courage.

"If you need me to steal something, I'm trying to put that life behind me."

"It's not that. I, uh... need a date for a party I've been summoned to."

"A date?"

"Yes. A friend's five-hundredth birthday."

"The big five-oh-oh?"

"Some immortals tend to celebrate milestones like that."

"So, you want to take me out on a date or need an excuse to babysit me?"

"Let's not use the term 'babysit' again. Ever. I need a distraction. I haven't mingled with my kind—or any kind—in what seems like eons. But I know when word gets out that I brought you, a beautiful, free-spirited mortal, it'll stir enough gossip to keep the tongues occupied. Whoever went after Garrett might be there, and with you by my side, they won't suspect a thing. And really, who better than you to create a little shock and awe?"

It wasn't a lie. I couldn't tell Nadia she would encounter multiple Kings and Queens, my so-called friends and fractured family. There wasn't enough time to explain the history we shared. I'd be asking her to walk in blind. And yet, with her at my side, the prospect didn't feel as draining.

She pulled back as she weighed the offer. She wouldn't back down. Nadia never did. "Okay. But it'll cost you," she said with a steady smirk and a resolute stare.

"Doesn't it always?"

"What's that supposed to mean?" she asked. It's not accusatory, but curious.

"Only that with you, everything seems to come with a price."

"Not like this," she warned. "This one is gonna hurt."

"What do you want?"

"Something that you now can't deny me." She tugged my ear with a mischievous grin, a small chuckle escaping her lips.

When she finished with my back, she stepped away. Regret pinched the edges of her expression. I watched silently as she washed her hands in the bathroom, carefully putting everything away. Almost as if she were stalling.

"You can always sleep here," I said, my voice low, "if you'd prefer more distance between you and Garrett." I opened a hand toward her, inviting, not demanding.

She hesitated, biting her lower lip as she glanced at the door.

Just when I thought she would leave, she turned and crawled into bed beside me. The narrow mattress all but guaranteed closeness. She pressed herself to my side, legs draped over my thigh, one hand curled over my chest.

A man could get used to this.

As we lay there, pressed together, I imagined her stretched out in my bed, wearing nothing but my shirt, curled against me. That image brought rare, unfamiliar peace and lulled me into sleep.

For the first time in centuries, I dreamt not of tracking monsters but following laughter.

39

SAND, STONE, AND SURRENDER

A crisp breeze had lifted the saline-heavy ocean spray, flooding the car with the scent of midnight jasmine. Above, the stars glittered across the nearly moonless sky while a westbound wind skimmed the ocean, chilling the air. Outside, birds whorled in unusual midnight patterns while nocturnal creatures kept to their dark corners.

But it was my little thief I couldn't look away from.

She'd gazed at the navy-dark sea, transfixed by the neon-tipped waves crashing against the shore.

Despite needing to watch the road, I kept glancing her way. A quiet sorrow had settled across her face in the flicker of passing headlights.

"The ocean's beautiful tonight," I finally said.

"It is." Nadia turned her head, refusing to look away from the horizon.

"Do you want to walk the beach?"

"What about the party?" She asked.

"It'll wait."

"Well... my shoes aren't exactly sand-friendly."

Each protest had slowed my speed. But her gaze never left the shoreline. Less than a mile from our destination, I'd pulled over.

"What are you doing?"

"Showing you the ocean."

"But...my shoes, my dress!"

Instead of answering, I stepped out and opened her door. Crouching beside her, I caught the battle in her eyes; her curiosity was wrestling with suspicion.

"What?" she asked.

"Give me your feet."

"Why?"

"Because those ridiculous shoes are coming off. We're going for a walk."

"But my dress might get sand on it," she'd whined, even as she lifted one leg.

"So be it. You want to see the ocean, don't you?"

I didn't need her answer. Nadia's eyes consistently tracked what she longed for, never letting it disappear. She'd swung both legs into my lap with a put-upon sigh as if I were being utterly unreasonable.

I'd lifted her foot to my lap and undid her heels. Her ankle felt so slight beneath my calloused hands. Gently, I'd lifted the edge of her lace dress that hinted at everything beneath. I knew her shape intimately and not just her body, but how she transformed desire into resistance, fear into fire-forged steel. If I'd closed my eyes, I could still taste her skin, still remember the ache of wanting what felt forbidden.

I'd never cared for moonlit strolls, but the whole

world had looked different with Nadia tucked against my side. Her arm around my waist grounded me in a way I hadn't expected. At the water's edge, I'd let her set the pace.

She wandered to where the tide licked the sand. We'd stood in silence for what felt like hours. I hated it. I wanted to know what soured her lips into that stubborn pout. But the more I'd reached for the words, the more they scattered.

"I told myself I'd never come back. I didn't think I'd ever see the ocean again."

"Because of your family?"

"Because I burned every bridge to get away from them."

Her stare tightened my gut, and I'd had to brace against it like a punch.

"This is the first time I've walked a beach in eons," I murmured after another long pause.

"Why? The beach is breathtaking."

"It's the sand. It's what sand represents. Ground-down remnants of stone."

"Are you afraid of the water?"

"No. Not afraid, but respectful. Most third-realm beings like me don't mesh well with the creatures of the fifth."

"The fifth realm?"

"The oceanic realm. For most of my life, I've had few equals. But water is persistent. It wears even the strongest down."

"Stone survives pressure, heat, and weight, but even it succumbs to the ocean," she said quietly.

I nodded. "Grain by grain, water reshapes what once stood whole. I've faced oceans before, but none like you."

She hadn't been a crashing tide. She was the slow seep: unyielding, relentless, unapologetic. I'd thought I was unbreakable.

"I can't believe you're afraid of something," she teased.

"I'm afraid of plenty of things. Like the dark servants breaking their patterns. I'm afraid I won't be able to stop what they have planned. Or that I'll hurt or scare you away. That—"

"Careful, Malrik. You almost sound like you want to keep me." Her fingers trailed up my chest. "Almost like... you like me."

I did.

"Whatever gave you any idea to the contrary, lil mani?" I asked, wrapping my hand around hers. I kissed each knuckle, unable to resist.

Somehow, we moved closer. I didn't know if she'd stepped in or I had, but we were suddenly toe to toe.

"I..." She blinked up at me, surprised by the question. "Don't you?"

"Since you walked into the bar, I've wanted you," I said easily.

"It's the shoes. Red bottoms are hard to ignore."

Not likely, lil mani. "I didn't even see the shoes. It was you. When our eyes met, I felt your spark, or maybe the cut of your tongue captivated me."

I kissed her then. She didn't pull away.

Instead, her lips curved into a smile just before her

tongue traced the seam of my mouth. I'd opened to her, and she took over: bold, sure, surrendering and leading at once. Who would want to deprive themselves of this?

"You say the sweetest things," she murmured.

"Only the truth."

"Truth or dare?"

"Dare."

"I dare you to make love to me. Here. Now."

Love?

I didn't hesitate. I stripped down, starting on myself before reaching for the zipper at Nadia's back. I'd zipped her in earlier, but now my hands felt too clumsy, too eager. Still, I'd found the metal pull. The dress slid off, puddling at her feet.

Her scent filled my lungs as my hands roamed my lil mani's bare skin. She was softness wrapped in sass, fire dressed as elegance. I kissed the hollow of her collarbone, the gentle slope of her throat, the swell of her chest.

Desire pushed my kisses into something more urgent. I'd nipped, and Nadia's hand shot to my head, not to push me away, but to draw me closer. She arched into me, breathless, her surrender turning gravity inside out.

Something inside me broke—or fused. I didn't know. I only knew I needed my lil mani.

I cradled her body, kissing her again. My hand slipped between her thighs: already warm, already moving, already anxious for my touch. I laid her down on a grassy patch and followed, my body aching with hunger.

She stretched beneath me becoming mischief and magic incarnate. I started with her toes, trailing kisses up her legs, her hips, her ribs.

"Don't tease, Malrik. Please."

"I'm not teasing, en mani. I'm holding back."

"You won't break me. Take me," Nadia begged, her voice shaking.

Now I understood why mortals chased desire so recklessly. Once passion sank its teeth in, nothing else mattered.

I shook my head as she pulled her touch away.I wanted her hands on me until her palms started trailing her own body. Those small fingers scooped up her breasts and squeezed, her thumb tracing the indent of my teeth. My cock throbbed at that image, at the vacant stare.

Then, she wrapped her hand around my wrist and brought my hand to her lips. She fisted my hand but freed my index finger. In one smooth motion, she'd leaned forward, and her pink tongue curled around it.

Holy hell.

With slick strokes, she'd licked at my finger the same way she'd teased my cock. As if the thing could feel each motion, the hardened shaft nearly vibrated with need.

I pulled my hand from her grip and leaned down. The kiss we shared as I entered her wasn't wild or frenzied but slow and thorough. She'd asked me to make love to her, and that's precisely what I'd intended to do.

It had taken all my willpower, but I'd built a steady rhythm to work completely inside her. I didn't stop the slow, shallow thrusts until she was slapping at my back and squirming beneath me. When I was fully inside, I paused. I'd thought I was going to explode.

She shifted under me, rocking her hips, and it took everything I had not to lose control. I'd wanted to grab her hips and pound into her. I wanted to be so deep inside her that I disappeared. So that I could find my way out again, a changed man. And by her mewling, she'd craved it, too. But she'd asked, and I would give her what she needed.

Because I needed it, too.

When I'd regained control of myself, I began to move, deepening my thrusts and building a rhythm that would carry us both into ecstasy. My hand found the little bud of pleasure at her core, and I pressed against it with my fingers. With each motion, I rubbed slowly and deliberately until her whimpers turned to moans, then to throaty pleas.

Her legs slid up the sides of mine and wrapped around my hips. The angle shifted, and I felt myself sink even deeper inside her. It was like the final piece of a puzzle locking into place. Her head tipped back, and her hips twisted as if to feel every way I filled her.

Warmth bloomed in my chest as I looked down at Nadia. Her skin was flushed and slick with our shared sweat, stretched out and drawing me in. I found myself trapped in her eyes as luminous in the starlight. Immediately, like a landslide, I knew.

I was in love.

I'd fallen in love with a mortal thief. And in that moment, I couldn't think of a single reason to care.

"Do you give yourself to me?"

"Yes, Malrik, yes!"

That was all the encouragement I needed. My hips picked up speed as her legs cinched tighter around me. The long, slow drag became a hard, steady drive. Our lips met again in a kiss, and I swallowed the sounds of her pleasure as my own threatened to unravel me.

Higher and higher, I'd pushed us past her first orgasm, even as it tried to pull me into the fire of her passion. And still, she held on, chasing more, and she pulled me with her.

It was everything. Yet somehow, it wasn't enough.

Nadia did this.

She filled my life with contradictions, a beautiful, confusing paradox.

I wanted to keep this feeling forever.

When the pressure in me rose too high to contain, my mind blanked. I was sure no one had ever felt tension like this, like a balloon on the verge of bursting. With nothing but sensation and my lil mani's coaxing sounds, I surrendered, lost in the overwhelming grip of her release.

Then I thrust once more. Her back arched, and another tremor fisted my cock in spasming waves. My mouth dropped to her bare skin as I spilled into her, giving her everything I had.

Spent, I rested my forehead against her chest, not bothering to control the twitching muscles that refused to still. I was content here. Beneath me, she panted, catching her breath. Then, instead of pushing me away, she nuzzled into the crook of my neck and sighed.

"Do we have to go to the party? I'd be okay just staying here and making love on the beach all night."

"Never has an order been so tempting to beak."

"It's hard to imagine anyone ordering you around."

"I don't see why. You order me around all the time."

Nadia threw an arm at me, and I caught it. In an easy move, I spin her into my hold. Her grin with the starry night and the ocean backdrop would stay imprinted on my mind forever.

I've never been this happy.

40

TONGUE TIED & TIE TUGGED

As we take the white marble steps, the nude slip rains a chill down my thigh that only real silk can. Behind us, the short train of my black lace floor-length evening gown trails. With a modest plunging neckline and an eyebrow-raising backless drop, I feel deceptively seductive.

I can't keep my eyes or hands off of Malrik. He looks stunning in his three-piece navy blue suit with a tie he's already tugged loose. I have to admit, even if only to myself, that he could be wearing a burlap sack and still look sexy.

Stumbling, my foot skids, but in his big arms, I'm secure.

"Are you ok, lil mani?"

"Yes, I was just thinking about it." I bite my lip and look back at the car driving off with the valet, debating how to explain the direction of my thoughts.

"If you keep smiling like that, you'll see it again, but we'll have a crowd this time."

"If you keep holding me like this, I might just let you."

His lips pull in a smile, but it's reserved compared to before.

"Remember the plan," he says, but I think it's to remind himself.

The plan was in jeopardy the moment he stepped into that suit. And the tongue-lashing he gave me at the beach doesn't help. My thighs still feel weak.

I shiver as my core body temperature rises faster than my skin can follow. Soon, I'll have a blush to mark my all-too-telling thoughts, which will contrast nicely with the dress. Before I step out of the protection of Malrik's arms, his nose drags along my cheekbone.

Suddenly, I become hyper-aware of the audience we're attracting. The people behind us, those already in the building, hell, even the valet, have stopped to watch. Smiling, I follow his subtle guidance until our lips brush back and forth before I cave and lift on my tip-toes to increase the pressure.

His lips over mine are firm as he controls the kiss. With his arm wrapped around me, holding me tight to his chest, I sink into the connection. Smooth demands guide me until his tongue strokes mine into surrender.

For the moment, I forget we're in public, that we have a growing audience, and that this kiss is a setup. I do the one thing you're never supposed to do: forget why we're here. I fall back to reality when Malrik's big hands surround me. He pulls back first, with glassy eyes that look too intense for a party.

Remember the plan. Get the tongues wagging and find someone who knows more about soul deals. As in, who the fuck claimed mine?

I swallow my final lungful of crisp night air and straighten the crumpled jacket. "Don't worry, big guy, I'll give them hell in a good way." I chuckle and step back. His arm drags for a moment between us before he settles at my side again, my hand in his, as his other hand rests gently on the small of my back like a brand.

Shortly after Malrik leads me into the towering mansion, he grows distant. Next to me, Malrik slowly stiffens, easing back into the emotionless warrior he was when I first met him. Across the long stretch of the white and grey marble ballroom, Malrik nods to the men and women all around.

We ignore the wide-eyed looks and hushed whispers as we pass, but we share a discrete look each time. It's working. I can't help but watch the crowd in fascination. It's like watching The Real Housewives of Immortals—extravagant luxury and the bare minimum of genuine emotion.

The people here are all controlled in a manner I've recently grown reaccustomed to; I thought it was just a Malrik quirk, but apparently, most of the presumable immortals here share the trait. They murmur, rarely smile and have entire conversations without laughter. After a few hundred years, jokes and humor, in general, must lose their impact.

The sad thought makes me frown. I wonder if Malrik even realizes he lives without joy—they all do.

Almost an hour into the night, whatever Malrik is searching for seems to frustrate him with its absence.

Instead, I push off the door frame with a sexy stretch and twist and walk up to him, my hands skimming lightly up his stomach and chest to straighten out his tie. I focus on my task, not letting my eyes wander to the lips I want to bite. When I finish, I step back and walk toward the bar, where a charming, most definitely human man is preparing a drink.

I can feel Malrik's eyes on me now, and I don't stop the sensual roll of my hips or the subtle over-the-shoulder pouty face. It has absolutely no effect since he's too busy staring at a beautiful raven-haired woman built like a short Playboy bunny. Her hair, fluffy as cotton, falls straight down her middle back with a curl at the bottom. She wears a shell-pink flare dress that's sophisticated and youthful at the same time.

Though I came to this party with a secret hidden agenda, I hadn't expected the same of Malrik. I'm left thinking about his invitation here. He didn't ask me out. He asked me to be a distraction, his cover. I shouldn't be hurt, but I am.

"What will you have, Miss?" my bartender asks. He looks in his early twenties, his black hair styled in that typical hipster fashion, and his fitted uniform emphasizes his slender build.

I planned to order something super classy, but now it's a wasted effort as it seems another woman holds my date's attention. "Victory Cocktail, heavy on the absinthe."

"My kind of drink." A tall blonde with her hair piled in an artful top knot stares down at me.

She probably has a lot of practice doing that since she has to be at least six feet tall. Her amethyst gown has a long slit up the side of her leg. The woman is stunning with a moon-shaped face and penetrating brown eyes, a sight to behold, especially with genuine gemstones stitched underneath the bust of her dress, emphasizing her small waist.

I focused on the bartender, ignoring the itch that spread over my skin at her bodice's first glimmer.

"Then, bartender, make it two." I grin and refuse to let my eyes stray lower than her chin.

My fingers twitch once, then twice before I scrape at the edge of a non-existent hangnail.

"Yes, ma'am."

"I'm Sopria."

"Nadia." I know my voice is low and dry, without its usual humor. It's not a pretty or seductive sound, just pouty.

"To future victories, both little and large."

"Cheers to that." I lift my drink, and we clink glasses.

"What's an offer you can't refuse?" She asks.

There's only one thing I want right now, and he's focused on someone who might as well be a fairy princess for all I know.

"A clean convertible loaded with gold bricks, diamonds, and pearls, a glove box full of deeds and bonds with a trunk full of money, preferably in hundreds?"

"Oh yes, Nadia, my kind of gal."

Doubtful. Especially not since I have to concentrate on not staring at Sopria. That dress. Those jewels. She's a walking temptation.

I wonder what it would be like to pin her to the bartop and strip her of her dress? Then run. Because those jewels aren't just beautiful—they're a trap. And I'm far too tempted.

No. I'm being good. I'm not giving in to my inner demon.

"Well, shit, Nadia, you didn't think you could keep the attention of the Slasher, did you?" I jerk back, snapping into reality. While I've been fantasizing, I've been staring at Malrik.

I only have the original file reference for connecting the dot from Slasher to Malrik. It takes a mere second to realize that this woman has insulted me. I could pretend to be affronted, but I suddenly don't have the energy to put in the effort.

I don't have any information. I don't have that beautiful dress. And I don't have Malrik by my side.

"I don't know what you're talking about." I feign ignorance as I take my glass and sip the sweet, sharp drink.

"Don't play the fool; you're better than that."

"I suppose you're right." I sigh. I'm too good to be playing the fool, even for Malrik. Once more, I glance at him. He's made his way toward the woman who holds his attention. "Who is she?" I swallow my ego to ask.

"Clarabelle, his ex. From forever ago. Also, his Queen. And if I remember my third realm lore correctly, she's his brother's wife."

Even though I've figured they have history by the longing looks, the easy declaration of their history sends a surprising punch to my kidneys.

"Don't look so put off. It was all for love. The love of power."

"Is that how you've acquired your power?"

"What makes you think I have any power?" She grins.

I look around pointedly. People quicken their steps to hurry past. Very few people look our way. None make eye contact.

"Yeah, I can't imagine what gave me that impression." I shrug.

"Scaring these guys has become a point of pride my sisters and I share. We can't let our image slip."

"How could anything slip with a dress like that?"

"That's not the image, I mean." Sopria's lips pull in a smirk. "That's just a consequence. Because no matter what we do to have, hold, and sustain power, it's all a strategy in a game with the same ending."

"Well, you know what they say about playing fair," I add.

Power doesn't always look like Malrik with his brooding stares and tragic exes. Sometimes, it wears amethyst and smiles with teeth. Or is a thief with sticky fingers and trust issues.

"Exactly. It's always better to be feared and respected than adored and blessed." She doesn't say more about the matter; she just stares across the room. I follow the trail of her focus. A few women chat on the patio while another larger group circles something out of sight.

"I never say never to having it all," I smirk into my glass as I take another sip.

"Now you're starting to sound like one of my sisters. Come now, Nadia; no need to pout. Let me make some introductions."

I must be watching Malrik again. Oops.

As we step past the dance floor, the final peal of a piano ends. In tandem, the dancers stop, and after a few seconds, the low thrum of a violin starts in five choppy notes before smoothing into an upbeat number, and like a music box, they all start dancing again.

The itch to pilfer shot up my elbow, and unlike with Sopria's gem-encrusted bodice, I didn't resist. I remember the big guy's words well, but "trust no one" now seems to apply to him. With a decisive snort, I walk along the line of dancers, and slip behind Malrik and his group.

I lift my hand to Malrik's wide shoulders, rubbing his back and drawing his attention to me for a moment. It's a casual touch, but around here, even a small move was telling. With a smile and a conspiratorial wink I slip past.

And just like that, the thick square of paper, pressed into my palm.

I wind my way through the soft-spoken men and women. Broad shoulders, long legs, delicate wrists covered with expensive jewels. It's all a blur as I follow Sopria outside.

The smell of midnight jasmine and earthy pine warms the air as we near the patio.

I shouldn't feel so betrayed, because I don't like him. I'm using him. That's the whole point. But the letter burned my hand and turned my stomach. Until suddenly a gloomy part of me, crouched in a dark corner of my mind, whispers: *What if he's been using you all along?*

41

______

MOONLIGHT, MORTALS, AND MISTAKES

Ten women swarmed Nadia when she took her first step onto the patio. I hadn't been able to do anything to warn her. A single hard look from one of the women was all it took to send Magnus, a celestial guardian, and his date scurrying back inside.

The celestial glared at them as he passed but wisely said nothing. No one challenged the Sisters of Selene. Of course, they would take an interest in her: my mortal.

They came in every form: a petite brunette, a tall and powerful Atlantian, a goth girl in black leather straps and pigtails. Every one of them powerful, every one of them dangerous. The Sisters of Selene were lethal, and they circled Nadia like a prize.

Together, they stood outside, bare skin lit by the moonless sky, radiant and unbothered. They lounged comfortably among the rest of us: immortals, warriors, nobles. They were speaking with her now, likely exchanging names.

I should have been glad Nadia was making connections. I was, in a way. But why the Sisters?

"Are you even listening to me, Malriksan?"

"Of course, my Queen," I responded automatically. It was a lie. One that came far too easily. Nadia was rubbing off on me.

"There you are, and you brought a nice little surprise, too." Gorvoss grinned as he wrapped an arm around his wife. For the first time, the sight didn't make my skin crawl. I felt only relief as he pulled her closer to him and away from me.

"Here I am, at your request," I said, though we both knew it hadn't been a request. It was an order.

"Is that a jest? We say we're worried about humanity softening your edge, so you bring a mortal date?" My brother's glare made his feelings plain. Bringing a mortal, even as a date, was a misstep.

The plan was working.

"Malriksan, this is no place for a human. How could you?"

"Someone else brought her into this world; I'm simply enjoying her company. Isn't that why you sent me on this vacation?"

"I meant you should mingle with immortals across dimensions," he said, throwing up a hand.

"What does it matter to you? My love life is of no concern to you."

"Love life? Oh, whispering steppes," Clarabell muttered, turning away.

"All I meant was that she's mine. She's who I want." My gaze found Nadia without effort. She was speaking to Cathrine, and by the tight lines of her body, it wasn't going well. Should I step in?

"Yours. A human?" Clarabell's question barely reached above a whisper.

I moved to leave. It was a breach of protocol to do so before being dismissed, but my feet decided for me when the women around Nadia suddenly recoiled.

"I heard she dragged you through the infernal realm like a lovestruck cow!" Gorvoss's accusation cut the air. Not the words themselves, but the venom behind them made me stop.

"The infernal realm. Really, Malriksan?" Clarabell's voice trembled with disbelief.

"It was the only way to keep her close and safe. And what does it matter what demons gossip about?"

"The Stoneborn have a reputation to maintain. We can't appear weak."

"If anyone thinks I'm weak, I'll show them how wrong they are. I've nothing to prove to demons or tail-wagging infernals. And if the Trials ban were lifted and you led the charge, you wouldn't need to worry about appearances, either—only how much pressure to apply."

I was even surprised by the edge in my voice. It hadn't been a calculated challenge, but it was one nonetheless. Since failing the Trials, I'd resigned to duty, never questioning my path. But now, with Nadia's defiance still echoing in me, I wanted something different.

Change. It felt good, unfamiliar but good. For someone like Nadia, change came as naturally as breathing. For me, it had been a lifetime out of reach.

"I heard you kidnapped your human. Is it true?" Gorvoss asked, clearly savoring the unraveling.

"It was a punishment after she tried stealing from me."

"Oh, you're worse off than we thought." Clarabell wrung her hands, twisting her gown between pale fingers.

"Enough, both of you. I'll spend my time with whoever I choose." The judgment, the veiled disgust—it scraped against something raw.

"She tried to steal from you?" Gorvoss's gaze shifted to Nadia, calculating, as though seeing her for the first time. Not good.

"She didn't get far."

"Farther than most, apparently," he muttered.

"What could you possibly own that's worth confronting a Stoneborn?" Clarabell wondered aloud, her voice light and lilting but irritating nonetheless.

"What indeed," Gorvoss said, eyeing me with an unsettling calculation. "Well, if she came with ill intent, I call it justice. Do what you will with her."

"Now that I have your permission," I said flatly. They didn't know what to make of the sarcasm.

"As for your treasure," Gorvoss went on, "you can store it in my vault. Not the people's funds, of course, but the royal one."

"How generous. But I think I'll keep my belongings where they are. Excuse me."

"Malriksan, please," Clarabell said, her cerulean eyes searching mine. I'd long stopped trying to decipher the messages buried there. "Take care. You've always stayed the course. It's what we all depend on."

"I won't answer to either of you in this. If I want to be with Nadia, I will."

"We just don't want this to become a loyalty problem, do we, wife?"

"Exactly. You've always been so strong, but I hardly recognize you anymore. You've changed." Clarabell's fingers clamped around my wrist in a tight grip, not by force, but out of fear.

"I mean... a human, brother. Really?"

Gorvoss's eyes flicked past me. I didn't need to look to know where they'd landed. The curve of his lip told me. Nadia. And from the flicker of awareness on her face, I knew she noticed, too.

I saw it in real time, the effect she had on men like us.

Her expression darkened, her eyes narrowing into a glare before one brow lifted. She rolled her eyes and turned her nose up in perfect disdain.

Amusement sparked somewhere in my chest. But Gorvoss and I had always been different kinds of men. Where I saw her fire as freedom, he saw it as a challenge. His gaze turned heavy with intent.

And then, his eyes dropped to Clarabell's hold on me.

"Enough of this," he said, low but firm. He pried Clarabell's hand from my wrist, her fingers resisting before finally releasing.

A slow heat bloomed across my back. I scanned the crowd, already guessing the source. Nadia.

"We'll talk later," Clarabell said, her gaze lingering too long.

The only courteous response I could give was a nod and to step away.

I thought Nadia might come to my side, but when I turned, she was already at the bar, chatting with a cloaked figure. Too familiar. His hand was on her arm.

My fists clenched before I forced them open. This was what I wanted, wasn't it? Her distracting presence. Somehow, that made me feel like more of a fool.

Then I noticed something else. I wasn't the only one watching my little thief. She'd stolen everyone's attention.

Gorvoss's eyes were locked on her, on *my* mortal, with a look I couldn't read. His fingers clenched around Clarabell's wrist as he guided her away, but his attention never wavered.

I didn't like it. Any of it.

Not Gorvoss's sudden interest.

Not the stranger touching her like they were long acquainted.

And especially not that I couldn't place him. His posture was all wrong, and his energy was distorted. Something about how he moved, how his shoulders hunched, was unnatural.

Like a fool, I'd asked Nadia to make an impression. She had. And now I couldn't look away.

42

TO LOVE AND LOSE

"**D**on't do it," a hunched figure croaks beside me.

A guttural growl startles me out of my jealousy. I turn sharply, only now noticing the cloaked figure beside me.

When I turn, his hunched form tucks deeper into his coat. I meet his gaze, holding it until he flinches. His body curls even tighter, and then—recognition clicks.

"Garrett?"

"So you recognize me?"

He takes a slow, measured breath, his voice heavy with something I can't quite place—pain, perhaps?

"Barely. But now that you've healed, you almost look human."

"I didn't before?"

"Hell no, you were disgusting looking. If it weren't for Malrik, I would've only touched you to bury you." I pull back and feel my face scrunch at the memory.

"Gee, thanks."

"Sorry," I say. "You might not be the first dead body I've seen, but thanks to someone I know, you are the first one I've had to touch."

"If it weren't for Malrik, I don't know where I'd be. I owe him everything."

"Join the club," I glance at my date.

He's in a small group, listening intently to the smaller man who speaks with his hands. As if he feels my eyes, Malrik looks up and smiles. It's one of those slow-building smiles that makes you hold your breath, the kind that stops your heart.

Butterflies stir in my stomach. I step forward but then catch myself. Malrik's gaze meets mine, amusement flickering in his eyes.

I look away abruptly, warmth spreading through me. Is it more than attraction? Or the creeping realization that I care more than I should?

Ugh, girl, pull yourself together.

Garret's gaze catches mine. "He's a fine man, you know? Maybe too honorable for his own damn good," he sighs.

"Too good, you say?" I mutter.

"Malrik was the first one exiled. He's been alone the longest. And he still honors the old ways, even after everything. That's the kind of man he is." Garret trails off, shaking his head. "And all he wants, what we want, is someone who sees the sacrifices he makes. Someone who will miss him when he's gone. But his loyalty..."

Everything in my stomach curdles. "Would Malrik still want her even after she left him?"

I watch how she clings to Malrik's arm. It's not just

nostalgia. Something lingers between them. Something left some things unresolved.

"He's Stoneborn; we never stop once we set our minds on something. That, you can count on."

"Yeah, I think I've heard as much."

Malrik hasn't pulled away. Something in his rigid stance, like a deer trapped in headlights, makes my heart twist uncomfortably. My date's calm acceptance of another woman's touch cracks something I've long kept safe, something I hadn't realized was vulnerable: my heart.

I watch the two of them intently. Because of that focus, I see Malrik's ex pull out a white square and slip it into Malrik's jacket pocket.

What could she want? Is that a love letter? A note for a secret rendezvous?

Garret chuckles, low and bitter. The sound snaps me out of my doubt. He leans back, his expression unreadable. "He's not like the rest of us. Some men fight for themselves. Others fight for a code, for something bigger. Malrik, he's all honor and tradition, even when it breaks him."

I swallow, the weight of his words sinking in. Great. That's what I'm afraid of.

I blink rapidly to cool my heating eyes, and before I decide how to respond, I turn my face away.

"But better him than them." Garret nods to Sopria, who speaks easily with the older woman, Catherine. "Promise me you'll be careful with that lot," he murmurs. "The sisterhood... they don't play fair, they don't do rules. Never have." Garrett starts to lift his arm as if to show me proof of how dangerous the sisters are, but instead of pulling his coat back, he slowly sets his arm back down.

I arch an eyebrow. "I take it you would know?"

He leans back, wincing slightly as he adjusts his posture. "You learn a few things when you've been around as long as us." Garret's expression darkens, the moment of quiet reflection passing. "But the sisterhood, they don't just take from you, they take from you. Memories, skills, pieces of your soul."

"Soul-sellers, you say?" That's just what I've been looking for.

"Yes, the worst kind. Ruthless. Greedy. The sisters of Selene will step on anyone to get what they want."

"You're not warning me off. You're drawing me in."

Garret shakes his head. "I'm scared for you should you get caught up in their drama. They are loyal to each other in the worst ways. Cross one, and you cross them all."

I smile and consider his words. That doesn't sound half bad. "If you knew me better, you'd realize I thrive on chaos."

Garret shoots me a surprised look that raises an eyebrow. Ruthless and greedy? That sounds perfect, except that I only play solo.

"I don't think Malrik will like it," the old warrior adds subtly.

If I give him a droll stare, he deserves it. "I don't do groups, but I like a woman who knows what she wants, especially when they're not afraid to take it. I can respect that."

Except when she wants my Stoneborn.

Garret frowns. "They'd eat you alive."

"Maybe," I murmur, "but I bet it'd be fun." My eyes travel back to Malrik. His back is turned to me, sending a prick of irritation spiking through me. "In my experience, you can't trust someone to do what's right, but you can trust them to do what serves them best."

Garret's body language softens, but he doesn't press.

"You remind me of my... well, my mortal mate. Can you do me a favor?"

Trepidation starts to creep in at the word favor.

I shake my head, already ready to deny him. "I'm not the most reliable—"

Garrett doesn't wait for my agreement; he clasps his hand in mine.

That's when I see it. A sliver of skin peeks between Garrett's coat and glove, showing a dark, polished, almost insect-like shell. It is as if bone and muscle have been replaced entirely with something else.

My fingers twitch before my brain catches up. I try to yank back, but his grip holds. Not tight. Not desperate. Just unyielding.

My breath catches, but my mind refuses to stop spinning. I can't think of anything sarcastic to say for the first time in a long time. Instead, a cold, primal part of me screams to pull away, because whatever Garret is now, it isn't human or Stoneborn anymore.

"Garret... what the hell is that?"

Before I can react, he presses a crumpled letter into my palm before pulling his hand back. But my focus isn't on the letter. It's on his arm, the darkened, inhuman surface as if his skin were replaced with polished chitin.

He sinks deeper into his cloak in a jerky shift, more shade than form. He doesn't feel like Malrik, with that soft skin over rock-hard muscles. No, Garrett's hold feels like a shell, textured with grit.

"It's the reason I can't tell her myself. I don't have much time left, but this letter has to reach her. You can find her at In Absentia, give her my letter. Please."

The thick paper feels like a brick in my hand. The weight of responsibility. It sounds like a deathbed wish, and I automatically want to shove the paper back to Garrett, but I can't bring myself to touch him again.

His words hang in the air as I finally lift my eyes to his shadow-covered face. I stare into the outline where I know his head must be, but no light catches. I try to look where I think his eyes are, resolutely not looking down at his hand again.

I didn't even want to look at what he gave me. The letter was thick and velvety, nothing like modern paper, and its thick wax seal pressed like a brand into my palm. My pulse spiked, and a heavy heat crept up my neck.

"Why does this sound so ominous? I thought Stoneborn were immortals; you can give it to her once you heal." I set the letter on the bartop beside us. Our eyes connect for a silent minute. He waits, giving me time to understand.

"Sometimes immortality is more of a curse." His other hand wraps around mine, pushing the letter back into my fist. His touch almost feels normal this time, making my alarm ring louder.

"Wait—" My pulse roars in my ears, drowning out the music, the chatter, everything but the unyielding grip of his fingers. "Let me get Malrik." I turn, but Garret's grip tightens.

He doesn't let go, and I don't try to pull away. The man's grip is stiff, pleading. It's a resignation. A finality that settles over my skin like a cold splash. I don't want to hear what he's about to say next.

I don't want to be here. I've taken a dying man's last request before, but this feels different. He isn't asking for peace or forgiveness.

He's asking for hope, something I'm incapable of handing out. And still, I stay. Garrett's voice is rasping but steady.

"Nadia, I know you did more than enough for me already. And I'm grateful. But I've got one last favor."

I exhale, already suspicious. "I don't like where this is going."

"Take care of him."

At that, I blink.

"That's vague. Are we talking about your dog? Please let it be your dog." He gives a weak chuckle.

"Malrik."

"Ugh. Knew it. That's not a favor. That's a setup."

"I see how he looks at you. Don't let fear keep you from something real."

"It's a phase," I say flatly. "Malrik's having a mortal moment."

Garrett smiles faintly. "He only knows how to protect people. But someone needs to protect him."

"Garrett." I cross my arms. "You want me to be a life-jacket for a nine-foot mountain with abandonment issues?"

He doesn't flinch.

"No. He's stone, Nadia. He sinks. He holds everything down, never lets go, even when it drowns him. You don't need to keep him afloat. You're the lighthouse. You show him there's still a way home. Even when he's too far under to believe it."

I open my mouth, but he cuts me off.

"For people like us? You're fresh air after years underground. You make life feel possible again. Even, no, especially for someone like him."

I groan.

"I didn't realize Stoneborn had such a penchant for poetry. Say one more metaphor, and I'm walking." He rasps a low laugh. "You want realism? Fine. Malrik did everything our people asked of him.

"He followed every rule. Malrik fought every battle. And still, they left him behind. Clarabell walked. His family turned their backs. His people disavowed him.

"He did everything right, and he was still disposable." His voice cracks, then steadies again. "You get what that can do to someone, don't you?"

I do, but I don't answer. I glance across the room, searching for Malrik. He stands at the edge of the dance floor, too stiff to be comfortable. His features, carved to withstand time, become even more unshakable, immovable and forever eternal.

But Garrett is right. Stone sinks. And Malrik is sinking.

I can see it now. The quiet drowning of someone who refuses to reach out for help. Just quietly going under. The way people do when no one's ever come for them.

I know that posture, the not fitting in, the waiting to be needed, the pretending not to care. I know it because I've lived it.

"I thought you just said he was still in love with his ex?"

"I said he honors the old ways. Once he gives a vow, he'll keep it. He was willing to pledge everything to Clarabell, but that wasn't good enough for her. I hope it can be good enough for you."

We both look back to Malrik, watching him, reading the distance in his posture, the steady calm that never seems to waver. But then he looks up.

Just for a second.

Like he's felt me thinking about him.

The dance floor opens up as if clearing the way for him. It feels like an invitation. Couples in muted tones sway effortlessly, their movements like rippling silk. Each step is studied, graceful, and too perfect.

The dancers between us move like they were born knowing the steps both elegant and effortless. They've known these steps and each other for longer than I've been alive. How could I possibly catch up?

"I guess I—" But Garrett is gone just like that. No goodbye. Not waiting to see if I agree. Like the other night, we checked on him and found only the quiet he left behind.

A black cloud falls over me before I can feel like a fool for talking to myself. Then, the temperature drops.

A figure too tall, too thin, steps into my space. Not Garrett. Something worse. A man I vaguely recognize steps up to me, his expression sharp as a blade.

"She's always adored your precious soldier. So predictable. So noble."

"Excuse me?"

The man has long inkjet hair that he pulled back and dark blue eyes that shine with unbridled hysteria.

"We need to talk. Now," the man hisses.

I recognize the man from earlier. He was the one who ripped his woman off Malrik. This must be his brother. His presence is like a cold spray of saltwater on the face, abrupt and with a sharp sting that burns anything unprotected. He nods toward the shadows, expecting me to follow.

Around me, quiet conversations mingle with the gentle clink of glasses and heels. No one seems to notice either of us. I try to lick my lips, but my mouth has gone so dry that they can't breach the seam.

A cold weight settles in my chest. I don't need to turn to know Malrik is still across the room, unaware. And this man? He isn't asking. He's demanding.

This could get messy.

I step into the light instead, leaning against a pillar. "We'll talk here."

With only a tick of disapproval, he positions himself opposite me, keeping himself in the darkened corner.

He has a tailored suit, expensive shoes, and a faint smell of ozone that lingers around him.

"You're playing a dangerous game; be sure to make yourself useful."

"I don't know who you think you are—"

"Is it true?" He interrupted. "Are you the thief that Darius hired?" the man demands.

"And who are you?" I demand.

"I'm the one who got you the job that you failed."

"It was you? You're the buyer?"

Though tall, he has thick joints and muscles, without the bulk that Malrik and even Garrett probably had before his torture. For someone who works with demons, he looks average.

"Yes, and I should boil you alive for incompetence."

"Careful, no one likes a petty King." I shift away, not liking his leer. "Why?" I ask

"Because that amulet that key is dangerous. One of the most powerful items in existence is locked in a safe in Boston."

"No, why didn't you ask your brother for the amulet?"

"Ask him?" He looks genuinely confused as if the thought had never crossed his mind. "Don't be ridiculous. I'm his brother; I don't want what he gives me; I want what I can take. And I'll happily take from Malriksan twice in one night."

Yikes. Malrik and I have more in common than I thought.

"Oh, I thought my family was bad," I smile.

"Maybe you're right, little mortal. I might enjoy it

too much," he grins, his finger trailing down my arm. Warning bells shriek, but before I could jerk back, he grabs my arm and drags me into the shadows with him. Now, I cherish my wife. I'll give her whatever she wants, but there are some thrills a girl can only give once."

"If this is your version of flirting, you should have spent more of your eternal life on the practice."

"Careful, you don't joke your way out of a deal." He steps even closer until his shadow hovers over me like a death shroud.

"What could you give me that I can't take myself?"

"You mean aside from Malriksan's safe? I have a key that will disrupt his safe's camouflage. If what Darius says about you is true, you shouldn't have any more problems." He passes me something metallic and smooth.

"A snail fork?"

"It's a tuning fork. Strike it inside a room to find what's hidden."

I close my fist around the tuning fork. The weight of Garrett's plea, the warning about trusting no one, and Malrik's unreadable expression across the room all tangled in my chest like wires sparking beneath my ribs.

"What makes you think I won't just go to Malrik and tell him what you told me?"

But a small, dark part of me wonders how far I can get before Malrik finds me.

"Because you know as well as I do that he loves her. That he'll never stop loving her. She thinks she can keep Malriksan in line with duty and old memories. But it's not him she wants.

"It never was. So name your price—wealth, status, limited immortality, or maybe you want me to clear any debts you have? Tell me, has Malriksan offered to pay off your debts, or did he give you a lecture about duty and integrity?" The man laughs, and it is as emotionless as you'd imagine an immortal king with a heart made of stone. "We'll trade tonight at eleven in the Old North Church."

"I haven't agreed to anything."

"You already took the job. And if you want to know who's claimed your soul, you'll be at the church with the key in hand."

43

BETWEEN THE LINE OF DUTY AND DESIRE

My granite heart squeezed, and not for the first time, I felt the sting of jealousy. There she was. My little thief was so close yet so far away, drawing smiles and laughter from men and women I've only ever known to be apathetic, like me. Suddenly, I didn't want to share.

"I'm not done talking to you!" Clarabell's tone shifted from sorrowful lament to sharp demand.

I hadn't realized I'd started moving, needing to close the distance between Nadia and me. Rolling my eyes, I inhaled deeply and turned back to my Queen.

"My apologies." My bow was short and quick, but my gaze struggled to stay on the woman in front of me when the one I wanted was behind me, surrounded by Veilkin, who could eat my mortal alive. Literally.

The unease churning in my gut was what I deserved for risking Nadia's life like this. I should have known I wouldn't be the only one enthralled by her unpredictability. I wanted her to be a distraction, but I didn't want her to distract me.

How foolish I've been.

"What about this mortal has such a hold on you? It couldn't be her looks—she's average, at best."

Was that jealousy? From an immortal Queen to a mortal thief? "She's—" The words stalled, caught between a truth I barely understood and a lie that would improve this conversation. "I don't know. But when I'm with her, I—" My throat tightened. I wasn't ready to say it. So instead, I said, "Feel." A pitiful word that could never encompass the whirlwind of what being with Nadia was like, but it would have to be enough.

"There are immortals who are capricious and passionate—"

"Surely you didn't come to talk to me about Nadia, a poor, lowly mortal thief?"

Clarabell's eyes flicked past me, lingering momentarily with a slight smirk that faded too quickly to place. "No, of course not. I'm just worried about you, that's all."

"Your lowly mortal thief needs to talk to you."

Nadia stepped up beside me, shoulders stiff. She didn't look at me; she locked her focus on Clarabell. A new unease slithered down my spine.

Clarabell glared, an unusual amount of bite in her voice. "We're talking right now. You'll have to wait."

Nadia didn't flinch. Her voice popped with honeyed steel. "Yeah, see... I skipped obedience training. And I sure as hell don't care what you think you need to say to my date. Step aside."

Clarabell didn't move. Her voice dropped, low and laced with deeper meaning. "Maybe you should reschedule that appointment. Learn something about respect. Loyalty. The purest form of love. The hardest, too. You'll understand when you're older."

Nadia's smirk didn't falter. "Cute lecture. But I don't do leashes, collars, or commands. I'd rather bite than heel."

Clarabell's eyes narrowed. "Yes, I must remember that your age accounts for most of your arrogance."

Nadia tilted her head. "And I'll be comfortable knowing you'll always be older than me."

Clarabell's smile turned glacial. "You won't look it for long."

Nadia swept her gaze down Clarabell's outfit. "Mm. And with all your years, decades, millennia, you still thought that dress was a good idea? Now that's arrogance. Yikes."

Clarabell leaned in. Though Nadia was shorter, she didn't budge. Both women locked eyes, unmoving. The air between them crackled with something just short of violence.

I couldn't take it anymore. I stepped forward.

Clarabell broke the stare first, drawing back with syrup-sweet grace and a smile that didn't touch her eyes.

"Well, Nadia, it's been delightful. We'll have to keep in touch."

Nadia didn't wait. She stepped between us, linked

her arm through mine, and pulled me away without a backward glance.

I could have stopped her. I should have scolded her for her rudeness. Instead, I followed, giving Clarabell a shrug.

"What was that, lil mani?"

"Girlie things. I found out who the buyer is."

"Who?"

"Her husband. He still wants me to steal it."

"That's impossible."

But was it?

"I know a drowning man when I see one." Nadia grinned slowly, but it held a dangerous cut. Then she pulled out a tuning fork.

My body locked as the shiny metal spears dragged my darkest fears into the light. There was no way.

"What did he say?" I probed.

"That the key was dangerous and you wouldn't be able to keep it safe—"

A crash in the main ballroom cut her off. The conversation died in an instant. The cloaked figure Nadia spoke to stood in a circle of shattered crystal. With a shuffle and a stumble, the man removed his hood.

Garrett.

But not.

A blackened layer of what looked like a beetle's exoskeleton had transformed his arm into pinchers, his back into a hardened shell. The purple bruises I'd attributed to his torture had spread. In just a few days, Garrett had gone from a noble warrior to a grotesque mutation. He'd become a creature born of the very corruption he'd spent his life battling.

I should have seen it. Garrett slipping away, changing. I should have known he wasn't the same. But I was too caught up. Too distracted.

"I can't get her voice out of my head!" he screamed, his claw and remaining hand pounding against his temples. "But you will not take what's left of me. I will not help you destroy our world!"

Then Garrett turned to Nadia, my Nadia, who stepped toward him despite his monstrous transformation.

"Tell Sandayah I loved her with my last breath."

I seized her arm before she could take another step, pulling her back to my side. A sickening sense of inevitability churned in my gut.

Garrett closed his eyes, tilting his mottled face toward the chandelier. A smile spread across his lips as though he heard celestials calling to him. Then, swiftly, he struck a match against his thigh.

Blue flames rolled like thunder clouds over a plain until they covered Garrett in an angry, crackling inferno. The fire swallowed him in a gulp before anyone could move.

Celestial fire. One of the few forces capable of destroying an immortal.

He collapsed to his knees within seconds. A blood-curdling scream split the stunned silence. The chitinous plates overtaking his body wavered before they dripped like oil, evaporating into the air.

"Malrik, you have to help him!" Nadia fought against my grip.

I looked down at her, then back at Garrett.

My feet remained fixed like an anchor sinking into the dark ocean floor. "There's nothing we can do, young one."

The flames climbed higher, their talons reaching the ceiling, shattering crystal in a deadly cascade. As the shards rained down, I realized, this was how it would end for all of us. Clinging desperately to what little honor remained as corruption devoured us, with only the name of a lost love on our lips.

The fire seeped under the plates of his true form, burrowing deep. Then, with a deafening crack, the stone shattered. Nadia flinched into me, turning away. Her body trembled against mine. I watched his stone core split from the inside out, releasing a cloud of white smoke and the acrid stench of sulfur and mud. His screams faded long before he collapsed—not as a warrior, but as a sacrifice.

"You must stop him. You must... stop... Go—"

A scream tore through his final words. Clarabell wailed—a sound of raw grief that pierced the air. "Garrett, no!"

Then he collapsed, his body crumbling into a pile of rocks, a real death for a Stoneborn. Silence gripped the room momentarily, the guests' panicked retreat halting as the boulder fell. In my arms, Nadia quivered, burying her face in my shirt.

I held her tighter, offering what little comfort I could.

44

THE LETTER AND THE LIE

From the corner of my eye, I saw Clarabell race forward, arms outstretched as though she could halt the destruction. Her next howl layered itself over the chaos of the crowd. Then she turned toward us, her face a mask of fury frozen in bitter horror.

In three steps, she closed the distance between us. Her long, tapered finger rose in accusation. As she neared, a lethal chill smoothed her features. "You did this," she breathed, her voice as sharp as a blade. Her expression didn't waver—it cut. Nadia flinched as if struck.

"What are you talking about?" Nadia turned and pulled away from me.

"Be careful of how you speak to my date," I warn my Queen.

"I waited, but you never came." A mournful melody rang, tinged with regret.

"My Queen?" I asked.

"Do you still resent me so much that you would dismiss your Queen's plea?"

"I don't know what you're talking about. And I don't resent you." It was true. I'd never resented her, but I'd never understood her either. "If this was about our conversation earlier, telling you to stay out of my personal life was not a violation of my duties in any way, shape, or form."

"Check your pocket."

I did as she asked. There was nothing.

"Someone must have seen me slip my note to you. Someone who didn't want us to meet."

"Your husband, perhaps?"

"More likely your date."

"Nadia wouldn't do that." But even as I said the words, I knew it was a lie. She absolutely would. But why?

Drawn like magnets at her mention, my eyes sought her out. Her gaze was already on me, a caress of attention that felt like a stroke from a silk-gloved hand. I summoned all my self-control and dragged my focus back to my Queen.

"I didn't believe him, but Gorvoss was right. Being topside for so long has changed you."

"Yes," I agreed, bringing my attention back to Clarabell.

The only difference between us was that I no longer saw that as an insult. The thought of going back to my topside home didn't seem like a punishment anymore. It felt like a relief. At least, now it did.

"She didn't have to do much, did she? Just keep your

attention on her. Distract you long enough. And now Garrett is dead."

"You can't blame me for that," Nadia sputtered.

"Malrik." Her voice faltered as she looked up at me, eyes wide with sorrow. "I tried to warn you. I reached out because I knew something was wrong. But you never came. I don't blame her for taking the note; I understand wanting something so badly that you can't let it slip away." She paused, her gaze lingering on me. "But I can't help but think, at what cost?"

I looked at Nadia, and I felt it again. That pull. But wasn't that the problem? Nadia drew me in, and I allowed myself to fall. I'd let my judgment blur. And Garrett paid the price.

I shook my head, but the weight in my gut only deepened as Nadia stepped away, turning to face Clarabell.

Nadia stiffened, squaring her shoulders. The two women locked eyes briefly before Nadia jerked her chin up. "I don't know what you're talking about."

She was lying. I knew it instantly by her pressed lips and rigid shoulders.

"Is it true, Nadia?" My voice dropped. "Did you take a letter from me?"

"Of course she did, and now Garrett's dead. Oh, Malriksan, if only you'd seen the note. If only you'd met me, and maybe all of this could've been avoided."

"Clarabell, I'm sorry. I didn't know. I'm sure Nadia didn't mean to—"

"I don't want to hear it. Do you really think she stumbled into this by accident? This was her plan all along. Gorvoss sent her here to get to your safe. She just needed your attention to distract you. That's what this has always been about, hasn't it?" Her voice turned brittle, and she quickly looked away, shielding us from the full force of her grief.

Nadia's jaw tightened, but she said nothing.

"And you want proof?" Clarabell sneered. "Search her."

I hesitated. Nadia's eyes widened, just slightly, but it was enough.

"I'm sorry," I muttered, stepping closer to my mortal. "But I have to know."

Nadia didn't stop me as I reached for her arm. When my fingers brushed the edge of her dress, something small and metallic slipped free, falling to the ground with a sharp ping.

We all looked down.

A tuning fork.

My stomach dropped. Recognition thundered through me.

It was a tuning fork with a resonance frequency meant to uncover a hidden vault. A tool made specifically for theft.

Clarabell took a shuddering breath before spinning back around. "And there's your proof," she said coldly. "Still want to defend her?"

Nadia didn't deny it. Her eyes dropped to the floor, lashes low, face unreadable.

"Malrik, I—" Nadia started, her head bowed. She looked up at me through thick lashes, unable to meet my gaze fully.

"Don't. What were you thinking?"

"It's not what you think." Her voice cracked as her hand lifted to her forehead, pinching the bridge of her nose.

"I understand the tuning fork, but why did you take the note?"

For a moment, it seemed like the truth was right there, perched on the tip of her tongue. I waited, but all I saw was defiance in the tilt of her chin. We were always on opposite sides.

"Because." Her voice hitched, and she swallowed. "I had to," she whispered, but wouldn't meet my eyes. Her nails dug into her palms, turning her knuckles white.

"You just couldn't help yourself, could you?" Even I heard the change in my tone—guarded, distant.

"Nope, I guess not." She shrugged, lips pressed tight, her arms folded across her chest.

My grip loosened before I even realized it. Then Nadia was gone, and my arms were empty once more. I should have said something—anything. But the words stuck, and all I could do was step back. One step. Then another.

"You'll never change," I muttered. But it wasn't just frustration. It was the truth. A vision I couldn't unsee. A door that had never been mine to open. I stared at the rubble. Garrett's unformed body still steaming and felt something inside me break.

"I could have told you as much." If her lip quivered, she pressed it out with a glare.

"Do you hate me so much that you'd let my people die?" I asked.

"No!"

"Then are you so selfish you'd let the world burn just to make a few bucks?"

"That's not how it was."

"Then why did you steal the letter?" My hands gripped her shoulders, forcing her to face me.

"Because! I had to know what it said. Okay? I was scared."

Gradually, I let her go. My hands dropped, retreating, defeated.

"I just needed to know," she continued. My heart clenched, an unfamiliar heat rising in my eyes. When I looked at her, it was as if I'd never seen her before.

"Needed to know what?"

Silence stretched between us, and I couldn't help but wonder if she was taking her time thinking up a lie.

"If she wanted you back. But I couldn't read it, and then everyone swarmed me, and I couldn't slip it back into your pocket. I'm sorry, Malrik."

"Sorry, don't bring back my friend."

"You're not going to go to her, are you?"

"Someone needs to clean this mess up. Might as well be me."

"But what about what I told you? Her husband was the buyer. Garrett was about to tell us who it was when she screamed over him."

"Take my car. I'll find another way home. Just go."

It was the hardest thing I'd ever done—turning away from her. It felt like shutting out the sun, like cutting off a limb.

Nadia reached out, her fingers stretching between

us, but she hesitated. Her hand dropped to her side. "Fine. If you don't care, I don't see why I should. Here."

She slapped a crisp white letter onto the stone railing beside her. With one final look, she shook her head and walked away. And I knew, I'd never be the same.

Unfolding the note, I immediately recognized Clarabell's penmanship. No wonder Nadia couldn't read it; Clarabell had written it in our native language.

My Dearest Malrik,

I pray this letter finds you swiftly and safely, though my heart trembles at the thought of it falling into the wrong hands. Forgive my boldness in writing to you after all these years. I have no one else to trust. In times past, it was always you who could be relied upon for guidance, and now, in this most delicate matter, I turn to you once more.

I am in desperate need of your counsel. Dark forces gather, and though I hesitate to burden you, I have no choice. You have always been a light in the shadow of uncertainty, and now, I fear my strength alone will not suffice.

Please, I beg you to meet me at our most intimate place, you know it well. I trust you understand the gravity of my request. I cannot say more in writing, but the forces gathering are no longer just outside our borders. They may already walk among us. There is much at stake, and the hour grows late.

If your heart still holds a place for the bond we once shared, I ask that you come without delay.

With all hope,

Clarabell

She had been trying to warn me, after all. Hanging my head, I let the remorse settle over me like a shroud of resignation.

I'd always believed duty and desire could live in the same man. But maybe I was wrong. Maybe all I was now was the fool who let both slip through his fingers.

If I'd seen Clarabell's warning, I might have stopped this. I could have saved Garrett. But I never saw it. I never knew it because of Nadia.

"You're too beautiful to look so upset." A smooth voice whispers, sending a warm breath across my overheated neck.

There is nothing I want to do more than race home and hide. I feel my stomach drop, and my head shakes before I can stop it. I'd crawl under a rock if it wouldn't remind me of Malrik.

The bastard.

I turn, and the owner of that refined voice stands there: tall, impossibly graceful, and with the unmistakable aura of charisma that seems to shimmer off his skin. His light eyes sparkle as he smiles, extending his hand.

"I'm Draven. Do you care to dance?" the handsome man asks, his voice like wine-drenched velvet. Who would want to dance after what just happened? I pause to meet his light brown eyes, almost as gold as his hair. I forced a smile, and I tried to keep it up.

"I don't know." I sigh. I was just on my way out when he stopped me. "I'm not really in the mood."

He winks, and I can't help but grin a little at his audacity. "Oh, don't be like that; it's not a party unless something overly dramatic happens. Besides, you look like you could use a little break from reality." He locks eyes with me, and something about his bold, magnetic gaze tugs me forward. "Just one dance," he promises, his hand still hovering between us. "I won't bite... unless you ask."

I feel a lopsided grin pull my lips, and I roll my eyes before he thinks I find him charming. I'm striding forward before I can think better of it. An icy chill curls through my ribs. It's a feeling I've come to recognize. Squid.

"I said, I don't feel like dancing," I say, stopping. I backtrack back to my spot as a new unease rallies my determination. I don't know how any of them can go back to pretending someone hasn't just killed themselves.

"I love a woman who knows how to keep me waiting."

I ignore everyone's looks as the Casanova continues undaunted. He is all effortless charm, his movements as fluid as the sway of the dancers. When my eyes lock with Draven's, I want to feel my world tilt. It doesn't.

"What's your name?" he asks.

"Nadia," I reply.

"I haven't seen you around before. We don't get many new faces."

"Oh, I came with Malrik."

Even though it doesn't look like I'll be leaving with him.

Draven's charm falters for a moment; his movements stop, and the amber liquid spills over the rim of his glass. I quickly shift, lifting my foot just in time to avoid the splash.

"You're Malrik, the Slasher's, human?" He recovers quickly, but I catch the hint of respect or fear.

"No... it's complicated."

"Malrik isn't exactly a complicated man," Draven says with a raised brow.

"Funny how you think you know someone," I dodge the question. "But does it matter who I come with?"

"As long as you leave with me, I suppose not," he quips, flirtatious.

I throw my head back and laugh hard. What a terrible line. For someone so old, he should've had plenty of time to come up with something better than that. I tell him so, and he flushes a deep red in embarrassment.

I can feel his focus wavering as he tries to regain his composure, probably thinking of a way to exit gracefully. Shaking my head, I catch a few curious glances from the crowd but return my attention to Draven.

I bump into his arm, drawing his attention back to me. "Do you have a map?" I ask with a sly smile. "Because I'm getting lost in your eyes."

Draven's grin widens in surprise, his golden eyes gleaming with amusement as he looks down at me.

"If being sexy were a crime, you'd be guilty as charged," he shoots back, his voice smooth.

"Careful," I warn with a grin. "I'm fighting the urge to make you the happiest man on earth tonight."

"What's there to fight?" Draven leans in closer. "We should get out of here. I'm sure the other women are about to ask you to leave for making them look bad."

I shake my head, but for a brief moment, I consider going with him, just walking out arm in arm, having an unforgettable night. But when I glance over at Malrik.

His gaze pins me in place, raw and unreadable, and for a second, it's like he's asking a question he doesn't know how to say aloud. One that I wouldn't know how to answer.

He continues watching me as a small group gathers around Garrett's body, removing him one piece at a time.

I shiver under his stare.

"How about you get us something to drink instead?" I suggest, pulling my gaze from Malrik and back to Draven.

"Of course," Casanova agrees. He stands between the chairs when I sit down, his hip lightly brushing against my thigh. One of his hands rests on the back of my chair while the other lies casually beside mine.

Looking down at our proximity, I can't help but wish it was Malrik touching me instead.

Sighing, I turn my attention to the bartender.

"Another Victory, ma'am?" he asks with a wink.

"Yes, but don't call me 'ma'am.' I'm not nearly as old as the rest of these women," I joke.

"What can I get for you, sir?" the bartender asks.

"How about a woman who's not out to seduce every

man in this damn place?" Malrik's voice cuts through the moment like a blade, filled with a heat I hadn't expected. He's angry—furious, even.

I can't help but gloat a little inside, maybe things aren't going too well with the ex. Too bad. But if Malrik thinks he can spend the night ignoring me and then take his foul mood out on me, he's about to be very surprised.

"Is Clarabelle still everything you want and more?" I turn to Malrik, leaning against the bartop table, my forearms pressed against the top as I try to look casual.

"Is that jealousy, Nadia?" he asks, his dark tone taunting.

But as I catch Malrik's eye, something ugly twists in my chest.

"Jealous? Of what? Clarabelle?" I scoff. "Even I wouldn't aspire to be that self-centered."

I expect him to snap back, to defend her with a fierce denial, maybe even threaten me for speaking ill of his Queen. But instead, there's silence. And for a split second, I swear I see him agree.

"Maybe I should go?" Draven looks between the two of us but doesn't move.

"No," I say.

At the same time, Malrik turns to him and says louder, "You think?" The tone must be enough to get the other man in gear. With a formal bow to Malrik and an uncomfortable nod to me, he tactfully withdraws.

"You two have... unresolved friction. I'll be at the bar, trying not to get zapped."

"Rude," I mutter.

"No, what's rude is watching your date oogling another."

At that, I laugh harder than before. The irony. The hypocritical idiot.

"Am I still your date after you told to fuck off?"

"Don't put words in my mouth. And apparently, I can't trust you to get home by yourself. Are you ready to go, Nadia, or must I continue to watch you flirt your way around the room?" he asks, his voice suddenly tense.

"Is that an actual option? Because if it is, I pick option B, Bob."

"I don't have the patience for your sarcasm right now."

"Wow, it must be worse than I thought." He leads me out of the building, his hand pressed tightly against the small of my back.

We follow the stone walkway that curves through the front yard, and Malrik hurries me toward his car.

"Slow down! You might be in a rush, but it's my ankle you'll break," I snap, trying to rein in my temper. But I know he can see the anger in my eyes as I stumble forward. I can feel myself heat with my turbulent emotions.

Anger, jealousy, and a pang of sadness I never expected swirl in my gut, filling my head with uncomfortable discord. I don't know how to feel everything immediately, so I focus on my anger.

Watching him fawn over his genteel, soft-spoken ex makes me sick, not just with disgust, though there's plenty of that, but with fury. How dare he! Taking me to that party, knowing she would be there, then ignoring me? Does he think, for one second, that he wouldn't ignite a firestorm?

I force myself to calm down. The defensiveness feels foreign. But the thought of Malrik and Clarabell twisting together like vines in the dark? It makes my stomach knot.

Still, that doesn't mean I'm jealous. Right? That's for people who care. For people who fall.

I don't do that. I'm not that dumb.

46

RUBBLE AND REDEMPTION

After we spend the entire drive in silence, I calm my anger and summon the nerve to ask what has been burning in my gut. It's easier now that we are parked.

"Why did you even bring me if you are too embarrassed to introduce me to anyone?"

"Is that what you think? Because everyone knew you belonged to me, even that satyr."

A satyr? Is that what Draven was?

"Isn't that what you wanted? Bring the pathetic human that everyone can laugh at so they aren't focusing on you. I'm surprised you'd let me roam around with all these dangerous immortals."

"I know you can handle yourself, even if you are a fragile human. Besides, you never left my sight, not even when introducing yourself to the Sisters of Selene on the patio."

There is no way I would let him manipulate me. He hasn't changed in the last two thousand years. I can't stand it anymore. It's too sad, not for me, but for him. He deserves better than Clarabelle.

I'm not sure if I am that "better," but at least I see Malrik for who he really is.

"Nadia. I'm not embarrassed by you. But you're a mortal, and I don't know what that means for us."

"It means I'll get old while you stay the same. I'll be dead, and you'll still be longing for your ex."

"You're the one who's slinking around every unattached immortal. Maybe you should leave if anyone will do!"

"You want me to go? Fine. I bet you'd love that, won't you? You get to push everyone away because the only thing you care about is the hunt and your damn treasure!" I snap, slamming his car door behind me. I stomp with my heels in an angry march toward the front door.

"At least I know my role! On the other hand, you have been nothing but chaos since the day you arrived. Are you staying, are you going, what's going to go missing when you leave? Why don't you make up your mind already about what you want." His long legs eat the distance, and he cuts the stairs in half.

"I know what I want, and I know what I don't need, and that's your holier-than-thou moral compass." My legs wobble like stretched rubber bands to keep up with him in my heels.

"At least I have something," he snaps.

You could have me, you fool! If only.

"Yeah, well, let your honor keep you warm."

"Gold's no better bed company," he says.

"Don't I know it? You'd rather die alone in this cold

fortress than admit you need someone." I envelop the front room and living room in a grand gesture. "Fine. Enjoy your hunt, Malrik, because that's the only thing you'll ever have to look forward to."

"Don't act concerned now. The only reason you're here is because of the treasure. Don't pretend it's anything else."

"Maybe you're right. Being bad is all I know."

"Then don't worry about sparing me a cent. Take it all if that's what you really want. If that's what's important to you."

Heat fills my eyes, and I want to screech. I have no words, only my ragged breath and the hammer of my heart.

"You're a fool, Malrik. I didn't stay for the treasure."

"And yet you keep running. What am I supposed to believe?"

Then, a creaking sound from upstairs. A shadow moves. We share a look, Malrik's face tightening into an unreadable mask. His eyes turn into a sheet of stone. The only movement comes as his head shifts left and right as if he is searching.

When he pulls back, his eyes return to normal. He immediately reaches for me. A different kind of anxiety tightens his body as he turns and starts rushing me towards the front door.

"Someone's here. Get back in the car and go!"

After his first step, the ceiling light shakes, crystal rattling. Around us, the scraping hollers turn to screaming in a three-beat squall, so loud that I clamp my hands over my ears, and my eardrums still ring.

An alarm, ancient, unnatural, rips through the house. The gargoyles.

"They're going after your safe. Go! You have to protect the amulet. It's too valuable."

"I'm protecting the only thing that matters." He says as he presses me tighter into his body.

I don't get to respond. A deep, ominous crack echoes from the kitchen into the living room, loud enough to drown my thoughts. At the moment, I want to argue against the somber set of his face, but before I can open my mouth, a bright light bursts overhead, and Malrik's eyes widening in fear is the last thing I see before I squeeze my eyes shut and instinctively brace.

Hairline cracks in the drywall streak down the walls. Subconsciously, I press into Malrik, and reflexively, he positions himself around me. We were fighting. We just broke up, but I don't doubt he'll keep me safe.

Then, a loud blast shakes the ground. The single burst of a heat wave overwhelms everything. The force of the surge lifts me off my feet. Malrik doesn't budge; he draws himself around me even tighter. My thoughts vanish under its impact.

Then comes the explosion.

A wave of heat and pressure compresses my skin. Before the collision, a vacuum of air and silence pulls my dress and singes my hair. Then, around us, the world falls apart.

I don't know how much time has passed when I open my eyes again. Stone surrounds me in a near-perfect circle. The room we are in has collapsed. I'm alone, somehow curled into the fetal position.

A rustle of feathers behind me gradually shifts into the grinding of stone. I flinch instinctively, and when I look up, all three statues—Smiles on my right, Grumpy on my left, and Zeki behind me—surround me. I lean back, resting against their wings while I compose myself, oddly comforted by their presence.

What happened?

Where did Malrik go?

My vision tilts on its axis as I try to understand what just happened. Chunks of debris continue to slam around me, but the gargoyles stand in protection. In the distance, there is a loud creak, then a ground-shaking slam. Behind me, another wall falls. Smoke and fine dust spin like a tornado into the room. It coats my tongue and throat, and with my first full breath, I choke on it.

Where's Malrik?

The long, smooth slats of stone move as soon as I shift my weight.

Three sets of wings pull apart so that I can stand.

Zeki moves first, the quiet grinding of his steps directed up. Following his lead, my stomach drops at what I see: a giant hole in the second and third floors, like someone used a massive stick of dynamite on a tiny door.

Then, I remember Garrett's crumbled form. A pile of rubble. That's all that's left when a Stoneborn dies.

Had Malrik ordered them to protect me, leaving himself vulnerable?

No. He wouldn't do that. But immediately, I knew that was a lie. Yes, he absolutely would. But why?

Where is Malrik?

"Malrik!" I shout.

Silence. Just the sharp, endless ringing in my ears. Wincing, I rub my itchy cheek on my shoulder, and it smears with red. I yell Malrik's name again, but I still can't hear over the ringing. I shout again, louder. I yell until my voice breaks and my knees collapse in the ruins, which might be my lover's remains.

Tears fall freely. I sniff, trying to hold a sob back, but it rips out anyway.

My stomach churns, and I scramble with weak knees away to throw up the night's victories. Sickness shakes my body, and I wrap my arms around myself, squeezing my eyes closed. Salty tears sting the cuts on my cheek as they drip down my chin. When I open them, Malrik will be standing in the distance. He'll be fine.

But when my lids lift, they burn from the acrid heat. I squint through the pain, searching the wreckage. His home is gone.

From the exposed beams, shattered windows, and charred stone, the front half of Malrik's home has burst open. The blast destroyed the entryway and cut an opening that exposed the second floor. I search for anything salvageable, there's nothing. Only the ruins of his home.

The invite to the party is just a ruse to get him out of the house. And we fell for it, damn it! Where is he? Where is Malrik?

Fresh tears continue streaming down my cheeks and chin, but I can't blame the air this time. My lips tremble, and I shift to tighten my face, but a hiccup forms in my diaphragm, and the jerk upends all my control.

I can feel my body shake, but it's not real. Each staggered breath and the thick weight of soot on my once pristine dress, now in tatters, isn't real.

I sit down on a broken chaise, choking on the screams I can barely keep control of.

What do I do now? Run? It's what I'm good at.

No.

Not this time.

They messed with the wrong thief.

47

FROM BAD TO WORSE IN STILETTOS

I might not know how to fix this, but I have a name.

Darius.

He set me up on this job. I didn't deliver, so he handled it himself.

It has to be him. Because if it isn't, I have no idea.

Each step crunches and pops beneath my heels. My stilettos wobble across the debris as I climb the stairs. I would hold the railing, but it's hanging upside down, dangling by a single board. I use the wall instead. The soot greases my palms, just one more layer of grime.

The destruction barely fazes me. Even as I step over a toilet in the hallway, my mind struggles to register the damage.

Get to the safe. That's all that matters.

Gold gleams in the small fires that still flicker throughout the house. The sparkle leads to more gold than I've ever seen. Coins, vases, framed pictures, scrolls, treasure chests—all untouched by the explosion.

None of it matters.

Where is it? Where is that damned amulet? I spot an empty pedestal. Could it be—?

No. My head turns fuzzy, and for three heart-pounding seconds, I pitch forward, overwhelmed with vertigo. I rub my eyes with shaking hands.

Has someone else taken it? Whoever broke in? What am I going to do now?

No one has ever depended on me, let alone with the world.

Frantically, I search. I knock over treasure chests and find plenty of necklaces and pendants, but not the ugly lump of crystal I needed.

This can't be happening. There is so much loot, and yet I feel so heavy.

It's not here.

Whoever broke in got what they wanted. And left with a bang.

It is gone.

And so is Malrik.

I slump down in exhaustion and pull my phone from my clutch. It looks oddly pristine in my dirty hands, surrounded by rubble. Within a minute, it's ringing. I lean against the safe I've spent the last week chasing, rolling a fist-sized raw ruby in my hand. It reminds me of Malrik. His eyes are calm, comforting, and sturdy. Silly, maybe, but it makes me feel grounded.

"Hello?" Darius's smooth, deep voice rolls like a late-night DJ.

"You low-down, dirty son of a bitch. Did you just set me up, blackmailed me into this job, and then left me for dead?"

"Laura?"

"Nadia! How many...never mind. Listen, you demonic mother—"

"Hey! Don't bring my matriarch into this," he warns. "How did you get this number?"

"Google. Did you steal the amulet and try to blow me up?"

"Of course. You don't think I'd leave it to you after you flopped, right?" He laughs. I can hear traffic zooming past him. "I'm a little surprised you survived. But I'm impressed. It must be the demon in you. Way to go, sis."

"I'm not—" I stop myself. I take a deep breath. My fist clenches the ruby, and my breath steadies me enough to continue without screaming.

All that control almost shatters the moment he opens his smug mouth.

"I know you're still working through accepting your inner demon," he says, "but don't be ridiculous. Do you think this is personal? It's not like I want the Dark Mother to return. Taking your lover was just a plus. Simple math."

Relief surges, quickly followed by dread.

I press my fingers over my eyes and squeeze. The pain keeps me focused.

"But how?" My voice cracks, fear lacing every word. "Why Malrik?"

I grip the ruby tighter. My chest aches like something with talons has latched onto my heart. Heat surges from my palm to my sternum. It burns, but only for a moment. Then calm spreads through me, like ice water on a hot day.

I can breathe again.

Like distant thunder, a low rumble echoes through my chest in the following silence.

He doesn't answer. He murmurs, almost to himself, "You don't always have to fight your inner demons. Sometimes..." He pauses, intentionally dramatic. "Sometimes you surrender to them."

"I'm not going to surrender and be like you," I hiss.

"Whoa. I'm an entirely different breed of demon, and I find your assumption of my upbringing offensive. You act like being a demon is a bad thing, Nadia. But haven't you ever wondered what it would feel like to stop fighting?"

I tilt my head and stare into the wreckage of Malrik's bedroom. His words worm into my mind and twist my gut. I look around at all the gold.

It would be easy to slip back into the old me. The one who only looks out for herself. Take the money and run, a part of me whispers.

Squid, the demonic spawn under my skin, rumbles in agreement.

The words echo long after I hang up.

Surrender.

My fingers lift an ancient gold coin to my face. It shimmers, but nothing is smooth or conforming. It must be worth a fortune. What Darius has got me into makes my family's illegal businesses look like a lemonade stand.

I step back from my phone. The weight of the revelation presses down on me. My mind races.

No.

Surrendering isn't an option.

Because the question I have now is, am I already too late? Will I find Malrik like Garrett—twisted, mottled, no longer himself?

My throat works overtime to swallow the bile, rising in disgust. I can't let that happen. But what can I do?

Nothing.

The word hits like a blow.

I have no answer.

My mind spins.

I massage my aching throat with the cold tips of my fingers. The chill helps settle some of the fear.

But maybe...

Maybe it isn't surrender I need. It's leverage.

I might not be an ancient immortal warrior, but I still have some mischief left in me.

With shaking hands, I dial the one person I'd been thoroughly warned against.

"What do you want?" The firm feminine voice ordered in an abrupt greeting.

"This is Nadia, we meet at the—"

"I remember you, Nadia. What do you want?" Sopria said again.

"You seemed," I start, unsure how to ask for help. "This might be rude, but I need some backup."

"What do you want, Nadia?" This time, it's Kathrine's voice on the line.

"I need help."

"With what?"

"Malrik's been taken, and I plan on getting him back."

"What makes you think we can do anything about that? And don't you think another Stoneborn would be better suited?"

Which brings me to a new awkwardness. Do I explain that the Stoneborn King might be in on it, or is that too much?

"Well, you're the only Vielkin I shared contact info with. And everyone at the party is scared of you, so..."

"Do you have a plan to track him?"

"I think I know where they're going."

"How?" She continued like a hammer.

Ugh, here goes nothing. "Gorvoss cornered me and insisted I steal something from Malrik. He gave me the address for the drop."

"No wonder you don't want to tell the Stoneborns."

"Can you help? Because the only other person I can turn to is a demon." I lie. Anxiety fills my head with bubbles. Or maybe I'm concussed from the explosion.

"Demons on your contact list? Well, aren't you a surprising mortal?"

"You have no idea."

"Do yourself and your lover a favor, and don't call your demon. He could just as easily be working for Gorvoss."

Oh, how right she is.

"When's the drop?" Something sharp snapped on the other side of the phone, and immediately, there was rustling in the background. Activity.

"I have until ten. It's a quarter till eight now," I answer.

"Do you have what he wants?"

"No. He gave me a—" I started to explain.

"Get whatever it is and get ready." Kathrine cut me off.

"But this is the piece that will—"

"Plague, ancient evil, or another hippy nymph summoning Care Bears. I don't care what it is this time."

"He's trying to open a portal for the Dark Mother."

In the background, I hear, "Ugh, her again," said someone who sounded like they smoked fragile egos for breakfast.

"Whatever," another says in the background. "I still think the Care Bear thing was worth a shot," I can hear the grin through the line.

"The Dark Mother isn't a joke," says another, more serious voice.

"She's right. We don't have much time. If you want your boyfriend to live, steal what you must, and we'll handle it later."

"What do I do after that?" I ask.

"Change out of your dress and hang tight. We're coming to pick you up."

"All right, I'm at—" But it's too late. The line has already gone dead.

Hold on, Malrik. I'm coming. I'm bringing the cavalry.

48

FURY, FLIGHT, AND FEMME FATALES

The gargoyles stand ready. They must want to help. Poor things.

But it didn't change the fact that they let Darius take Malrik.

"Why didn't you stop them? You should have saved him! Isn't that what you're supposed to do?"

All three gargoyles bowed their heads.

Zeki reaches out and points a wing at me with movements that echo the slow grind of stone scraping on stone. I have a bad feeling about what that means.

As soon as I settle, I hear a deep, angry voice.

"It can't be helped."

I jerk forward, scanning the area. "Who's there? What can't be helped?"

Scooting forward, my jeans scrape against the rough stone until I can kick off the gate. I lower myself and creep to the corner, peeking around the edge of the porch.

Nothing. Not even footprints.

Behind me, more rustling—scraping stone. When I turn, a gargoyle is on my heels. My hand touches its chest as I step back to regain my balance.

"Can you hear me? Don't let go."

I yank my hand back and step away—straight into another statue.

"Stop pulling away—"

"What the fuck! Stop doing that!" I yelp, scrambling back and putting space between me and the moving stone.

They don't listen. The shuffle of wings and grinding stones grow louder as shadows fall over me. Ducking, I cover my head and crouch. When I peek up, they form a stone wall around me, their wings trapping me in the center.

"Think she can hear us?"

"If she keeps running away, I will drop purposely on her foot."

"Give her time. Remember, this is new to her."

"Why can I hear you?" I ask, wide-eyed.

"See! I told you she can hear us."

"No one appreciates an 'I told you so'-er."

"Will someone answer me? You're up, Smiles."

"What does she mean by Smiles?"

"You, Jahziel. You're always grinning when she's around."

I am starting to distinguish between their voices. It's mostly the two bickering.

"Okay, if Smiles is Jahz, who are you, Grumpy?"

"Grumpy? I've never had a harlot insult me in such a way!"

"Harlot? Never mind, I don't have time for this. Get out of my way. You won't stop me from saving Malrik."

"What does the mortal think she can do to help Malriksan?" Grumpy says.

"You have to let me go. I already have help on the way. Just let me through."

"There's no way Malriksan would want her anywhere near the Dark Servants. We must keep her here."

"Keep me where? In a crime scene? It's only a matter of time before the cops show up. I need to do this. I can't let him believe I only want him for his gold."

"I'm not going to let him end up like Garrett. He won't spend his last moments wondering if I ever cared about him. Please. He has to know. I have to show him. So get out of my way!"

"Nadia," a new voice rumbles, the deep bass intensifying the pressure in my chest. "What did you do?"

"I didn't do anything, yet. But I will take a sledgehammer to your pal's wings if you don't back the fuck up."

It's a tight squeeze. No matter which way I turn, the stone jabs into me. Still, I manage to twist and face Grumpy. Before I can follow through with my threat, squealing tires send gravel flying as a black SUV barrels toward us. Stone scrapes against stone, shifting into wings. Grumpy gets in a few good flaps that smack me on the way up as they all take off into the air.

"Yeah, that's right! You better run! I would fuck you up! Today is not the day!" I scream, stomping like a child on the verge of a meltdown. I want to cry. To scream until my throat is raw. But oddly, yelling at the warriors eases some of my anxiety.

They form a triangle in the sky, circling once and twice before diving toward the oncoming vehicle. They are going to destroy the cavalry before it even arrives.

A cold lump drops in my stomach. I stumble forward a few steps, knowing it's too late to stop them. "No! Don't!" I cry, arms over my head, fingers tangling in my hair. I can't bear to look.

But the sound of impact never comes. No crunch of stone hitting metal. No shattering glass or screeching tires.

When I look up, all three gargoyles have pulled up just feet from a collision, flying parallel to the ground before rising again into the dark skies. The SUV probably never realized how close they come to being wrecked.

The vehicle pulls up before me, and the door swings open. About nine women peek from inside the vehicle, all staring at me.

Before I can step forward, the woman behind the driver leans to gape at the building—or, more accurately, at its destruction.

"Holy shit, girl. Were you in there when it exploded?" The woman in the red gown has swapped it for leggings and a cropped top, now strapped with knee and elbow pads.

"Of course, she was inside. Look at her face," Julee says, clearly offended by the question.

What's wrong with my face?

"Keesha, JuLee. Chill," Sopria scolds, but the others only grin as she leans over the armrest.

As I climb in, the women in the back row chat animatedly. One girl with pigtails sits on another's lap, her legs stretched across two other women. She waves at me as the woman beneath her sighs and checks her watch.

"Hi, I'm Baby." I immediately understood the nickname. She doesn't look like she is a day over sixteen.

"Are you sure you should be here for something like this?" I ask.

"Oh, we always take Baby to fights," says the goth girl casually.

"You're sure about that?" I ask, still skeptical.

"Oh yeah. Trust," Keesha grins.

"So, Nadia, where are we going?" Katherine calls from the front.

"The Old North Church."

A round of groans follows as the car accelerates with the same wild energy it arrived with. I slap the seatbelt into place and ignore the chuckles from the backseat.

"The bad guys always go underground," Keesha mutters.

"Every time," Julee agrees, picking at her A-line tunic.

"They have zero respect for the garb," another woman adds from the back.

Overhead, three vultures, the gargoyles, shriek angrily as they circle the SUV, keeping pace.

"Did you get it?" Katherine asks, glancing back from the passenger seat.

"No. It was already gone."

The women exchange a look. I don't ask. I've brought them into this; whatever strings or agendas come with their help, I'll take the consequences.

Which means I have no leverage.

I have nothing to negotiate Malrik's life with.

Nothing to stop the Dark Mother's invasion.

We lose. Earth loses.

Because of me.

Surrender. The thought came unbidden.

Like hell.

"That's going to make getting you close to Malrik a challenge. Any thoughts?"

Surrender and live.

A chill lined the inside of my stomach. This wasn't an itch to steal or a tingle that beckoned a little mischief.

"No. But I've got a question." The goth girl, whose name I still haven't caught, smiles and points out the window. "Why are we being chased by three pissed-off gargoyles?"

"Don't worry. They work with Malrik. They must have felt bad for what happened to Malrik. I did lay into them a bit."

"You...talk to them?"

"Only if I'm touching them." I pretend not to notice the skeptical looks exchanged around me. Whatever judgments they have about the gargoyles, I don't want to know. "They are the guardians of the key."

"Well, that's three more warriors. Good. We'll need them." Kathrine broke the stretch of silence.

"Good," I echo. "Then we go in. And we don't stop until we have Malrik. So... what's the plan?"

Surrender and survive.

"Is this a gargoyle?"

"Who are you talking to?" Baby blurts, beating everyone else to the punch.

You know.

I suppose I did.

"Squid?"

"What's a squid?" One of the women asked.

"It's a mollusk with eight arms and two tentacles known for their jet propulsion."

A round of groans filled the vehicle. I barely noticed. The conversation about me happening around me was a thousand miles away compared to the one happening in my mind right now.

Suppose I hadn't known about Squid. If I'd remained ignorant to the fact that there are gargoyles and satyrs, let alone stoneborn, and whatever these women were, I might have thought I'd lost my mind.

I still think that maybe I've taken one too many falls. That this can't be real. I'm not talking to my inner demon as I make my way to my lover's rescue.

Surrender to me.

"I won't do it."

Inevitable.

"You don't know how stubborn I can be."

Survive.

"I'll figure out a way that doesn't resort to that."

Surrender and survive.

"Resort to what?"

"Surrender."

"Obviously."

"No, I mean. I think that's the plan."

"Wait—what do you mean, 'that's the plan'?" someone asks, but Katherine spins her tablet around before I can answer and taps the screen.

"Here's what I'm thinking," she says.

49

NADIA'S LAST PLAY

The demon had strapped me down to a gurney. Pain radiated through every joint as the pressure seemed to try to fracture me. I struggled against it, trying desperately to hold on, but a dark fear clouded my usual focus. I'd been captured by a frequency device that held me in place and tried to rip me apart.

Hundreds of spawn huddled into an unusually communal mass as they waited for their Queen. The hive grew louder as the gateway continued to open as if they wanted to greet their mistress with welcome songs.

The dark servants seemed the most agitated. They glared at each other suspiciously, shifting and pacing the perimeter. Each tattered-robed figure watched intently for movement behind the growing portal.

My time was nearly up. It is surprising that it would end so abruptly after such a long life. And that only now I fully understood my arrogant ways. Or the depths of my foolishness.

"I really couldn't have planned it better myself. And to think, I was worried the mortal would hinder my plans. Not only did she manage to distract you from your hunting, you gave up your guards to protect her—leaving yourself ripe for the taking!"

My brother gloated.

My King.

"There's a flaw in your logic."

"And what's that?"

"She will never give up that amulet—not for me and not free."

"Well, luckily, I already have the amulet. But she'll come anyway because I have what she wants most. It must be insufferable to know that I can provide what your woman needs before you even realize she needs it. Again."

It was at that moment I knew—my brother hated me. For what, I didn't know. Neither could I fathom how it had taken me this long to see it when Nadia could spot it right away. I should have listened to her. I should have trusted her instincts.

Crack!

Boom.

A swirling cloud of miasma swept the air. Gorvoss turned sharply toward the noise. He signaled to his dark servants, then slinked into the dark. The chittering from the spawn slowly quieted.

In the distance, the sounds of a fierce battle rage. They were too far back. There was no way they would get here in time.

Hissing and popping echoed from the portal. Each

sharp snap of irritation makes Gorvoss twitch. His eyes never seemed to be able to stray too long from the dark mass behind the portal.

"Someone's figured you out already?" I taunt regardless if it was too late for me. "Are you afraid yet, brother?" I ask.

Already, I could see the Dark Mother's metal-plated torso swaying back and forth impatiently.

"Are you?" he snapped. "You see, it doesn't matter what tries to stop me. It's almost time now. The Dark Mother's arrival is inevitable, as is your death. You feel it, don't you? The infection crawls through your veins. She'll take you like she took Garrett and twist your body until there's nothing left but a shell. Then she'll lay her eggs inside, and they'll eat their way out, piece by immortal piece. And that will be the closest thing to a family you'll ever have. You can thank me now."

"BABY SMAAAASH!" A shriek yells from deeper into the tunnels.

I felt the difference in a snap.

His army buzzed with movement and aggression. But then I heard nothing—just the crunch of bone under steel and the soft hiss of flesh torn apart. A plunging silence followed. Unnatural.

Gorvoss shrank back.

His shoulders hunched as he stepped away from the shield-sized hole that now pulsed with the same darkness leaking from his skin. He felt it, too, whatever it was.

With every ounce of strength, I turned my head toward him.

"So, you came after all?" Gorvoss sneered, voice soaked in false calm. "Well, you're too late. I already have the amulet."

An outline shifted behind him. It was just a flicker in the peripheral gloom. His smug smile twitched toward it, but the shape vanished before his eyes could land.

"I'm not here for you," Nadia's clear and cutting voice said. "I'm here for him."

Nadia. Damn it. What was that foolish mortal thinking?

As soon as I saw her, a shudder chills my body. There Nadia stood with a swarm of spawn behind her, but she didn't look shaken. She looked resolute. Her usual confidence was gone, and something dark had taken its place.

Squid.

No. Please tell me she didn't surrender to the demon to save me. I wouldn't be able to forgive myself.

Commotion surged again—but not like before. Too clean. Too timed. There was a scuffle there. A snap of bones. Growls that died mid-breath. Tension coiled and snapped in a pattern only a soldier would notice.

"Oh, it's too late for that, too," Gorvoss laughed. "He saved Garrett. So now, he'll take the man's place."

"It'll never work," Nadia said, stepping closer, too casual, like she was bargaining for a discount, not her life. "Everyone knows what you did. He's stronger than anything you could try to twist him into."

And somehow—she believed that. I felt it. And it held me steady like a rope in a storm.

"No one knows a thing. And by the time the Dark Mother is done with them, they won't be around to ask." Gorvoss said. "Besides, Malrik's strength will make him the perfect offering for my Dark Mother. Once the Dark Mother uses him up, I'll turn him into a failure— a traitor. Our people will scorn him. He'll have nothing. Not even the memory of his honor."

"I won't let you do that."

"Let me?" He chuckled. "I've been playing this game for a thousand years. You think someone as insignificant as you can stop me?"

"Bigger men, then you have counted me out too."

"Why choose loyalty now? It will just get you killed. Do you think Malrik cares for you? Were you actually imagining a future with him? You're just a tool. A distraction."

Another flicker. A silhouette darted low between the shadows, but closer this time.

Gorvoss's eyes narrowed.

"You're a monster," Nadia said, her voice cracking and bringing his attention back to her. She covered her mouth like she hadn't meant to say it.

Behind her eyes, something shifted. Like embers fighting to start a wildfire, her fury cracked just beneath the surface.

Gorvoss seized on it. Stepped forward, hulking and smug. "You have no idea. Oh! Don't pout. What does it matter to you? This ends now, whether you help me or not. But you can choose how much you lose. Forsake him or forfeit your life, and don't worry about his. It's already claimed."

Nadia tilted her head. That sly, crooked smile bloomed again. The one she wore when holding the ace no one saw coming.

"You know," she said lightly, "you might be the first villain in history to lose to a girl in pigtails, a cursed gargoyle, and a lowly mortal thief." She sealed it with a wink.

Behind him—a soft click of stone sliding across the debris.

Gorvoss stiffened.

He turned to the gurney I was strapped to. But he didn't see me. He looked around frantically, his attention switching from one disbelief to the next.

The altar was empty.

I was gone.

"How was that possible?" Gorvoss muttered.

The portal began to dim.

Hazariah, a wraith-like shadow slipped back into the darkness, unseen but unmistakable.

Gorvoss turned back to Nadia, face contorted with rage.

"Come now," Nadia said, tone bright and flippant, "don't pout."

Gorvoss didn't move.

Not because he didn't want to, but because he couldn't. Ezekiel stood behind him like a bloody grim reaper, one clawed hand resting around his throat, not quite touching, but close enough to promise a death that wouldn't be slow.

Gorvoss's gaze flicked to the altar again as if it might

miraculously restore what was lost. But I was gone. Nadia and the gargoyles ruined the ritual.

"Pissant!" screeched from the portal.

"No," he breathed. "That's not possible," he whispered. "The mortal shouldn't be able to—" But she did. "This can't be. I couldn't have failed her."

"Oh, but you did," Nadia taunted.

A snarl twisted across his face, part fury and part disbelief.

"You think this means anything?" he spat at Nadia, his voice ragged, unraveling. "You've delayed the inevitable. You—"

But Ezekiel didn't let him finish.

Metal swooshed through the air, and rock clanked in resistance and then crumbled.

Gorvoss's body collapsed to the ground while his head rolled some distance away.

With the help of Jahziel, I stood. Nadia looked over at me. I'd never been so completely humbled. And to think I had thought she was an ordinary mortal. We shared a moment of relief. It was finally over.

"Malrik, there's so much I want to tell you. I've—"

Nadia was still smiling at me when a flash of silver —then the Dark Mother's tail impaled Nadia mid-sentence

"Nadia, no!"

Her arms stretched from the force of the pull. All I saw was the fear stamped on her face. I lunged forward and caught her, pulling her into my arms before the portal collapsed.

My voice cracked as I held her, "You're going to be

fine," I tried to convince myself of that as much as I tried to convince her.

She lifted a hand to my face, touching the tears I didn't know were there. Her eyes watered as she stared up at me, a smile of wonder that abruptly turned into a wet cough.

"You did it. You stopped the Dark Mother. You saved humanity," I croaked.

"Didn't do it for them." She smiled weakly, her lips colored with blood.

Her hand raised and then fell back down. I grabbed it and brought it to my heart, then my lips. I kissed her knuckles slick with blood, and I couldn't think about the question: What was I going to do without her?

"Don't leave me," I begged.

But my lil mani didn't respond.

No sarcastic bite. No sharp look. No wicked dare.

No more light and no more hope.

I threw my head back and roared my anguish.

The force of it cracked the ceiling, shook the walls —but I didn't care.

Blood pooled beneath us, her warmth sinking into the fabric of my clothes like a fading heartbeat until she was nearly the same color as the shale she lay on.

She hadn't just chipped away at the stone I was carved from.

She'd reshaped it.

What was once hollow now beats with something fierce—and fragile—because of her.

My kind was never meant to feel.

But I do.

Because of her.

She made a home in the hollow place I never dared to explore.

And now that she's there, I'd turn the world to rubble before I let anyone take her from me.

I wouldn't let her go.

Not to Hell. Not like this.

She'd accepted her demon to fight off the Dark Mother and her servants.

And then she gave her life to save mine.

Why? Why would she do that?

This was why mortals were never supposed to get involved.

I never should have—

Even now, with her breaths growing fainter by the second, I couldn't wish to have never known her. I only knew one thing with certainty: I'll rip Hell apart to bring her back.

50

A HEART ON DISPLAY

"Give her more time," JuLee says hesitantly outside the door. "Her demon may have spared her life, but it's not speeding her healing."

"I won't wait any longer." His voice boomed.

Heavy footsteps ascend the stairs. Malrik. My heart begins to squeeze and rattle, still tender.

I'm not ready to face him—not yet. Too many wounds still bleed and most of them invisible. My vulnerability is a raw, palpable thing.

I turn toward the window, pretending to study the garden while steadying my breath. My body tenses as Malrik's footsteps near.

Outside, two vultures squawk, bickering, while Zeki remains an immovable sentry outside my window.

Bound to me. Somehow.

They were no longer prisoners of Malrik's estate—but not free. Nothing made sense anymore.

Memories of Malrik's capture by the necro-tech monstrosities, the tears in his eyes as I faded, cling to me like blight. After everything we put each other through, he wept for me, my granite-hearted protector.

I can't make sense of my feelings, let alone his. The emotional turmoil is overwhelming, a storm raging within me.

He nears. My body tenses, and I feel the ache of my wounds respond to the shift. Can I face him now? The emotional weight is thick, hanging like a heavy fog.

The door creaks open, but I don't move. Instead, I sit very still, continuing to stare out the window.

For a moment, neither of us speaks. The air is thick with unspoken friction, a tension that crackles like static electricity. Malrik stands just inside the doorway, and I know the instant he sees me. His breath catches. I don't have to look to feel his eyes on me.

"Nadia."

Malrik's deep voice fills the small room, reverberating through me from the roots of my hair to my tingling toes. Despite myself, my heart lurches at the sound of him.

I must still look as wrecked as I feel. The image of me, pale and weak in bed, flashes in my mind. Immediately, I sat up straighter. Where the hell's a mirror when you need one?

The movement pulls my still-healing wound, and the tight twinge starts at skin level but then deepens into a throbbing pain. When was the last time I touched my hair?

He steps in close, arms hovering as if unsure I'd let him help. That hesitation bolsters my confidence. Maybe I'm not the only one feeling out of place.

"Why are you here?" I croak. "They told you not to come," I add, my voice low but thankfully not weak. I might feel fragile as if one wrong move would shatter me, but I'd be damned if I let him see me without my spine.

"I couldn't stay away."

"How do you disregard everyone else so easily?" I challenge.

He shrugs, eyes steady. "Finding and protecting what I care about most... it's what I do best."

The words catch on something inside me. We aren't from the same world. We never could be. And yet—

"I have nothing that belongs to you," I say.

"You stole something. I checked my safe."

I stiffen. "I didn't have time to take anything. I had to get to Gorvoss before he hurt you."

"But you still took something."

A pause stretches between us. "Yes," I admit, barely above a whisper.

His sigh is soft—but not with relief. It holds a weight I hadn't expected like he'd hoped for more and gotten less.

"It's important, Nadia. Just tell me who you sold it to."

"I can't."

"I'll pay whatever it takes. I need it back."

"Why?" My voice cracks.

He meets my gaze, raw and unwavering.

"Because you stole my heart."

I freeze. My heart slams against my ribs. Slowly, I turn to face him, eyes stinging.

"All I've ever done is steal. But maybe I found something worth keeping."

He blinks like he hadn't expected that. "You think my heart is worth keeping?"

I almost laugh—how can he not know? "I don't think I've ever wanted anything more."

A pause. Malrik's jaw flexes. "That's just because I'm one of the only Veilkin you've met."

"No. It's because no one compares to you. Not one. And I don't need to meet the rest to know that."

"You really mean that?" His gaze flicks to my chest, to the healing wound. "Even after what I let happen to you?" he asks, his voice barely holding together.

I don't flinch. "Ask me again if I regret stealing from you."

Tears pool in my eyes, and for the first time in longer than I can remember, I'm not scared to cry. Not in front of him. A man so honorable he'd sacrifice his life, wealth, and duty for a defective mortal's flimsy life.

"I thought you crashing into my life was a disaster," he says softly. "But you, chaotic, reckless you—remind me that life isn't just survival or duty. That it can still be beautiful."

A nervous laugh slips out before I can stop it. "Good. Because you stole my heart, too."

His breath hitches. The tension shifts, charged and intimate.

I nod behind him. After a hard look where he pins me with his stare, he turns to the shelf, always within sight of my bed. The jagged stone, perhaps a crystal from his home world, sits on full display, where I can see it always.

"You kept it." Malrik's hand grazes his chest, his fingers curling around it as if holding a fragile artifact. "Why didn't you sell it? It would be worth a fortune."

"I guess I didn't have the heart to."

The truth is its value is that it reminds me of him, which is worth more than any amount of gold.

He looks at me, torn between wanting to dispute my claim and wanting to leave, but he can't do either.

"Do you know what this is?"

"A crystal...from your home?" I reply.

"Close. Why did you take it?"

"It felt... right. Like it calms something inside me."

So, I made a decision. And for once, I didn't choose the money.

"Just take it."

"No. Some things, once taken, can never be reclaimed. That is my heart. Not metaphorically. Not symbolically. That crystal? It is me."

Malrik's gaze lingers on the crystal for a moment longer, his fingers twitching at his side as if torn between speaking and holding back. I follow his eyes but say nothing. So many questions hang unspoken between us.

"Why do you keep looking at it? Is there something I should know?" I ask, my voice low, unsure if I want to hear the answer.

Malrik exhales slowly, the breath rattling through him. "That's... complicated." His voice trails off, but something in the silence lingers, a sliver of a truth he isn't yet ready to share. "It's not something for tonight. Just rest." His tone is gentle but tense, a subtle crack that betrays the depth of his emotions.

His eyes flicker back to the stone again, almost as if he is considering whether to explain more. But he holds back, pulling his focus back to me instead.

"So..." I pause, humiliation draining me of strength. "So when you said I stole your heart, you mean I..."

It wasn't a declaration of love. Oh god. Did I just say I love him? Why am I like this?

"A long time ago, I chiseled a piece of my heart away for greater protection. I bound three gargoyles to it so that they could have some sense of freedom and self, and then I tucked it away in my safe."

It isn't a declaration of love. I did just confess my love to him when he's only here to pick up his things? Oh no! This can't be happening.

"Oh. I—I had no idea. You never mentioned your heart was detachable," I say, immediately feeling even more lame.

"Just take it and go—I'm sorry I stole it."

"No." He pulls back as if I'd just slapped him.

"No? Malrik," I say, my voice faltering as I try to keep the vulnerability at bay. Should I take it back? "Like you said, we can't. We're not compatible."

"I was wrong."

"You mean nothing to me." I shake my head and turn away.

His finger hooks under my chin and turns me back to him. "That's your first lie. And that," his voice drops as he points to the crystal, his heart, on display, "proves it."

A thrill shoots through me, and I know he feels it by the tension in his shoulders, too.

"It's not a lie," I insist. "I was manipulating you from the start."

"I know. I let you, and I'm not sorry. I needed to know you," Malrik interrupts, his voice cracking. "You asked why I'm here? The truth is, I'm here because I can't stomach the thought of going back to the life I had before you. I thought I lost you, Nadia. When she—"

He stops, his hand going to his lips.

"When she stabbed you, I thought it was over. I couldn't breathe. I couldn't think, not about duty or honor, only about everything I should have said and everything I am willing to do to get you back."

I shake my head, unable to respond. He sits on the edge of my bed, his weight dipping the mattress, pulling me toward him. I glance at him. The pain in his eyes is almost unbearable.

"I know I failed you," he says, frustrated. "I thought... you could never be more than a distraction. It would be enough to keep you to myself for a little while. But maybe I was protecting myself from the truth."

"What truth?" I demand.

There is a long silence before he finally speaks.

"That I am falling in love with you. A mortal. A woman who would be lucky to age into death. The heart I've guarded for so long now belongs to someone so reckless she would sacrifice herself for the world. Someone foolish enough to see the worst parts of me and accept them without flinching."

"But I..."

Malrik leans closer, the air thick with years of loneliness, unspoken pain, and the fear of love—both his and mine. He gently lifts my chin to meet his gaze.

"I don't want to lose you again, Nadia."

My breath stutters around the pain in my chest, but I don't pull away.

"And how am I supposed to believe that? It's not like you'll suddenly trust me."

In response, he sets a ring of keys on the bed between us.

"What's this?" I ask, confused.

"The first is a key to my house, ruined as it is. The second is to my safe. The third is figuratively, the key to my kingdom."

My eyes stare down at his keys. It is more than just metal. They are symbols—his trust, commitment, and responsibility for what lies ahead.

I can't quite process it or grasp how these tiny, cold objects hold the weight of so much expectation.

I blink as the weight of his words sinks in. I have heard rumors, whispers of Malrik being declared the new King of the Stoneborn people.

"You... trust me with that?" I whisper, disbelief tinging my voice.

He nods, eyes filled with raw sincerity.

"I love you, Nadia. I have since you stole my keys

and set me up to get jumped. I'm done being the man the world expects me to be. I only want to be the man you deserve—if you'll have me."

I lean into him, the comfort of his arms a temporary escape from the chaos of my emotions.

But even as the world seems still, a gnawing fear pulls at the back of my mind. The demon is still inside me, waiting. It watches me from within, patient, calculating, and waiting for me to get too comfortable. We had an agreement, Squid and I, and I would have to uphold my word because something much worse might happen if I didn't.

Love is powerful but won't protect us from what is coming.

He places something else beside me: a velvet box.

Before I can react, he kneels beside the bed.

My heart pounds as I open it: a marquise diamond. Gleaming. Impossible.

"Please say yes."

My heart pounds in my chest, each beat an echo of long-established doubts. I want to say yes, to trust him and myself entirely, but fear holds me back. It is too much. I don't know if I can— I cut myself off, my fingers brushing the edge of the ring, the cool metal a stark contrast to my fevered skin.

"No."

His face crumples.

I reach for the ring.

"Not like this," I add, slipping it onto my finger. "The next time you ask, I'd better be in a beautiful dress, looking glamorous."

His gradual smile warms the room. I feel my face heat but hold his gaze, refusing to shy away from the moment.

"You're alive," he says softly. "I don't think I've ever seen you more beautiful."

"Look, this won't work if we're both liars—"

But before I can finish, his lips are on mine. Smiling, I wrap my arms around him, pulling him down beside me, kissing until we are both breathless.

I pull back just slightly, my eyes searching his. I don't know if we're ready for this or what's coming. But as his hand brushes against mine, I feel something solid, something unbreakable. And I know we are in this together, no matter what.

"You're not saying yes just because you want to be Queen, are you?" he teases.

"What?" Queen? Is that on the table? "Can't a girl want it all?" I whisper with a grin.

Malrik's breath is warm against my skin as he murmurs, "As long as you take me as the man who loves you, the man who would upheave the immortal world for you."

At that moment, I knew. I am not afraid anymore—tears well in my eyes, a different kind of happiness flooding my heart.

"You don't have to disrupt the world," I whisper. "Just keep looking at me like that."

He pulls me into his arms, and I cling to him as tightly as possible. For the first time in a long time, I am not afraid to be soft—not with him. I still have doubts, but in his embrace, I know I am strong enough to fight —for him, me, and us.

"Don't go," I murmur.

"I'm not going anywhere," he whispers into my hair, his breath warm against my skin. "Not ever again. No matter where trouble finds us."

EPILOGUE

I grip the steering wheel, my heart hammering as I wonder if trying to outrun Malrik in my Nissan is the best decision. I have a good lead, but I can't shake the image of his sleek black car closing the distance behind me. I spend more time checking my rearview than the road ahead, praying I won't crash.

Despite risking the new Stoneborn king's wrath, there is an undeniable thrill in being pursued by a man as dangerous as Malrik. My smile turns to a grin, then a chuckle bubbles up, followed by a throaty laugh. The thrill of stealing from an immortal king, of sneaking away and getting away. It is a temptation I couldn't resist.

Yet, a nagging doubt creeps in. How did I manage to escape so easily? He could catch me instantly, set up roadblocks, or even buckle the road beneath me. But here I am, speeding away, his ominous presence still lingering. It sends a shiver down my spine, but I shake it off, floor the gas pedal, and crank up the stereo to drown out my racing thoughts.

I see his obsidian gaze—hot, commanding- whenever I close my eyes. I swallow. My skin heats, my heart races. Desire contracts in my stomach then drops lower.

I jerk the wheel just in time to avoid two gargoyle statues soaring toward me. My heart clutches in my chest, panic surging. Gripping the wheel tightly, I slam on the brakes, coming to a skidding halt.

"Shit," I mutter, my pulse still racing as I scan the area.

The road is clear.

No gargoyles.

Did I imagine it? A slow drip of relief washes over me, easing my thundering pulse.

I step out, my hand instinctively reaching for the dagger in my purse. The low grinding of stones breaks the silence. On the rooftops surrounding me, three gargoyles perch, watching and waiting. Great.

I turn to look behind me, but there is no escaping this now. I return to my car, trapped between a row of self-storage units and an abandoned auto shop.

"What do we have here, a thief disguised as a lady?" Malrik's voice vibrates in my chest like a low growl.

"Maybe I'm a lady disguised as a thief," I reply, trying to stay composed.

"Give me what you stole, and the punishment won't be too uncomfortable." His voice is low, but there is a dangerous edge I can't ignore.

I grin, stepping forward. "You must not have seen what I did to your car."

His eyes narrow. "What did you do to my car, Nadia?"

"I keyed it. And that's not even the worst of it."

"What else?"

"I racked up your credit cards."

"Which one?"

I laugh, tipping my head back. "All of them."

He raises an eyebrow. "Anything else?"

"I promoted Darius to Director of Finance."

He frowns. "You promoted a demon within the Stoneborn ranks?"

"I might've pushed through some much-needed legislation while at it."

"You've been busy while I've been gone." He steps closer, his eyes darker now, his expression unreadable.

"Idle hands and all that." I shrug, glancing over my shoulder but not backing away. "You never should left me on my own for so long."

"Is that all?"

"For the most part."

"You've fed your inner demon well. Is she pleased?"

"She is."

"Are you ready for your punishment, wife?"

It should terrify me—how easy it is to hear him say 'wife.' But I've already risked my life for him. Risking my heart seems like the next logical crime.

"Yes, husband."

The words are barely out of my mouth before he's on me, his hands finding my hips and pulling me close. His chest presses against mine, and I lose myself in the feel of him. It doesn't matter that my world has expanded beyond belief. With him, I feel normal.

Because stealing from him and watching him chase me down? That's just our love language. I couldn't think of anything better.

I whisper, "What are you waiting for? Fortune favors the bold," and press my lips to his. He responds instantly, his arms enveloping me, pulling me tight against him. My feet leave the ground as he lifts me, and for a moment, all I can feel is the weight of his heart against mine.

We may not be perfect. A mortal thief and an immortal king? Impossible. But I will keep his heart locked away—because it takes a thief to know how to protect what's truly valuable. No demon, ex, or spawn can touch my immortal's heart.

ABOUT THE AUTHOR

H.L. Hines is an Ohio native who weaves complex tales of strength and survival into all her novels. Her writing immerses readers in an intricate blend of dark, female-led fantasy, romance, and political intrigue, merging the forces of magic and science with high-stakes power plays in richly crafted fantasy worlds. With a focus on deep character development and dominant themes of rebellion, loyalty, and redemption, Hines explores the delicate balance between personal and political stakes in realms where magic and passion collide.

She enjoys learning anything and has a penchant for the dark, and unexplored. When she's not crafting fantastical realms in her novels or creating adventures for her D&D group, Hines finds solace in nature, drawing inspiration from the wild to fuel her story-telling.

You can find her on Amazon, Barnes and Noble, as well as on her website hlhinesauthor.com

ALSO BY H.L. HINES

Seasons of Treason

Winter's Kiss

Vernal Tempest

Summer Reign

The Forever Fall (Pre-order only)

Savage Shadows

Will of the Wild

Way of the Wild